Blue
Plate Special

FRANCES NORRIS

Blue
Plate Special

A Novel of Love, Loss, and Food

St. Martin's Press
New York

Note to Reader

This novel is a work of fiction. All the characters, places, and events portrayed in this book either are products of the author's imagination or are used fictitiously.

www.stmartins.com

Design by Kathryn Parise

ISBN 0-312-32232-1
EAN 978-0312-32232-8

First Edition: January 2005

10 9 8 7 6 5 4 3 2 1

For my parents, Jane and Jim Norris,
whose love continues to bless my life.

And in loving memory of my sister Libby
and brother-in-law Glenn Bogitsh—
dear friends who still live in my heart.

Acknowledgments ♛

My love and thanks to remarkable friends and family who saw me through—especially Ellen and Alan Ehrlich, Zsa Zsa Gershick, Marika Morgan, my sister Susie, and my brother Jim. Most of all, I thank Caitlin Flanagan, a gifted writer and dear friend who advised and supported me at every turn, always made me laugh, and dreamed up a great title.

I owe the greatest debt of gratitude to my mentor, Elinor Lipman, who shepherded this book from start to finish. Throughout the years, her editorial insight and generous encouragement were invaluable to me. I am also deeply grateful for Jane Rosenman's inspired editing and her willingness to take a chance. Thanks as well to the diligent efforts of Nichole Argyres at St. Martin's and to the wit and wisdom of Jay Mandel, a very literary agent.

I have been through some terrible things in my life, some of which actually happened.

— MARK TWAIN

Blue
Plate Special

1 ❦

The Return

I have lived away from this small Kentucky town for ten years. Occasionally, postcard images of it returned to me, usually in response to something particularly ugly in L.A. My mind had a way of caramelizing these scenes, making the Ohio River pristine, the dogwood trees forever blossoming, and the downtown bustling with shoppers who called "Good morning!" to one another. But now, as I drive down Central Avenue, the main drag of my idealized home, I realize what lies I've told.

The downtown has become a naked, neglected place. Technically, everything is in the same location—Weaver's Department Store, French's Pharmacy, the First National Bank, Hal's Donut Shop—but the people are gone. It's three o'clock on a Friday, and I count only four souls strolling past the tattered brick buildings. Going-out-of-business signs hang inside the display windows of the town's two main retail establishments: Chantilly's and the Debonair Men's Shop. If the giants of commerce are falling along Central Avenue, the rest of the shopkeepers are sure to follow suit.

I didn't really see the decay when I was here three months ago for the funeral. I confined myself to the cemetery and funeral home on the outskirts of town and couldn't look beyond those places. Of course, Constance, my stepsister, doesn't find anything wrong with her environs. I should have realized what the reality was when she bragged, "We have the lowest cost of living in the entire state!"

And now I'm back in town because Constance begged me to attend this family reunion of hers even though I am the only one left in my patch of the domestic quilt. In her best sorority-sister plea, she said, "Oh, come on, Julia. It'll be fu-u-un!" She always has been one to turn words like "fun" and "sweet" into multisyllabic orgasms, as if the added emphasis could enable me to see things her way.

The truth about my return is that I have business to take care of and would rather see the places of my true family instead of my stepfamily—the boat dock where my father taught me to skip rocks, the woods that my mother painted and that I wandered through and photographed, and most of all, the house that despite all the changes over the years still holds the memories of our life together. I imagine the reunion is Constance's attempt to put a positive spin on our recent tragedy, a party to make us not feel like the orphans we both are. It struck me as perverse. All the same, I couldn't refuse her. Death forges strange alliances. And I didn't think I had the strength to swim upstream, to forget obligation and create a tiff by telling Constance that a reunion might be more enjoyable when we're not racked with grief. So I let the current take me.

Three months ago, in late December, her mother and my father were killed in a plane crash. They were in an American Eagle twelve-seater that slammed into a North Carolina mountainside fifteen seconds after taking off. "Like a bomb going off," I remember someone saying, "with those tanks full of gas." The black box revealed nothing. There were no signs of equipment failure from the puzzle of wreckage on the ground. The only thing anyone could conclude was possible pilot error, and he was dead. There was no one to blame, really, and if there had been Constance probably would have hunted them down and sued them by now. I'm not the suing type. I prefer polite, silent scorn to any kind of direct confrontation.

The only comfort I found during the days after it happened was in the word "instantaneous," which I must have heard twenty times in North Carolina as we waited for the dental records to confirm their deaths. "They never knew what hit them," said a fleshy, teary-eyed representative from the airline whom I tried not to hate. "They didn't suffer," he said, and I chose to believe him, but I pulled my hand away from his sweaty grasp as quickly as I could and retreated from the hospitality suite to my room at the Ramada, compliments of the airline. I couldn't talk to anyone. I did nothing but watch movies, order room service, and wait.

Naturally, I feel the loss much more for my father than I do for my stepmother although Edna wasn't a bad person—just more of a breezy acquaintance than a mother. I never knew what to call her. She had always been "Mrs. Davis" prior to the marriage. Afterward I didn't feel comfortable enough to address her as Edna, and certainly not as Mom. So I continued to call her Mrs. Davis. She and I talked mostly about food styling, my professional penance at *Mangia!*, a not-yet-profitable, adamantly upscale gourmet magazine in L.A. During their marriage, I only came home a few times. So often they were traveling, or I was traveling, or we were just too busy in our new, separate lives.

I am still trying to accept it all, not just my father's death but the fact that the world insists on continuing without him and without my mother. It was ten years ago that she died of cancer, yet it seems to be happening all over again. I catch myself in small, familiar tasks—straightening my apartment, balancing my checkbook, even just pushing in a desk drawer—and I feel callous and guilty for doing so. Furious that the world demands that I carry on.

At the funeral, I heard people mutter the same desperate, heart-felt reassurances—that Edna and Dad were lucky to have had several good years together; that they were lucky to have died together because they did love each other so much. Lately, I have found it difficult to understand two things: 1) how people can talk of luck in regard to senseless death; and 2) how my father could have married a woman capable of producing someone as different from me as Constance.

Constance thrives when she is in control, and her bossy side did come in handy after the crash since I was unable to decide on anything, except what to eat. She arranged all the logistics—the flight back to Kentucky, the funeral service, the burial. All I did was show up and say thank you to the people who claimed to know my father and me, but I recognized only a few of them. Still, I pretended to know them all and responded in kind: "He was a good man." Thank you. "I'm so sorry for your loss." Thank you. "He's with Jesus now." Thank you (but I can't imagine they'd have a lot to talk about since he rarely went to church). I took a 7:00 A.M. flight back to L.A. the day after the funeral, calling Constance from the airport TraveLodge to say good-bye and, naturally, to say thank you. Yet with her, the words felt more genuine, and I suppose that showing up for the reunion is the least I can do to repay her for taking care of the grim details.

I stare at street signs now and other buildings as if readjusting my eyes to a darker light, trying to decipher the ghostlike images of the past. It's perplexing and a bit depressing—how a place once familiar can become unknown.

Somehow, I remember the way to Martin Hill and, after downshifting the economy rental to third, start the climb to Constance's house. Suddenly, my heart beats faster, and I am overcome with an unsettling mix of nausea and dread, the sensation you feel when they lock you into one of those death-defying thrill rides at an amusement park. You don't even know what lured you there—a TV ad, the desire to say you survived. And it's only after they pull down the bars that you see the signs imploring you to remove earrings and eyeglasses, to keep your limbs inside at all times. The signs say, Do Not Ride If You're Pregnant or Suffer from Heart, Neck, or Back Trouble—because this isn't just a ride: it's a nightmare.

I dread the terrifying plunges and treacherous curves—the strangers in my life posing as family. But there's no way to escape now. The only thing I can do is breathe deeply, hope for a better kind of luck, and try to keep from falling off the tracks.

2 ✿

The Code of Hospitality

Among other idiosyncrasies, Constance is excessively color coordinated. I am reminded of this bizarre fact as I drive up to her white Colonial with turquoise shutters and park next to her white T-Bird with turquoise trim. Both she and her husband, Ed, own these monstrosities, but I consider Constance the keeper of the keys. Ed has always seemed like an accessory in Constance's life, a housebroken former good-old-boy who still secretly pines for his wild Lynard Skynard nights. He always has a slightly cowed, uncomfortable look when he's with Constance, straining the seams of the tailored suits she buys him. Ed and Constance inherited the town's lumber store when his father retired, and he spends most of his time either there or at the country club playing poker.

Constance sashays down her front steps to greet me. Along the sloping yard, there is not a hedge untrimmed, neither a rock nor plant out of place. Landscaping like an Etch-a-Sketch.

"Woo-hoo!" Constance calls.

The well-sized pleats of her fuchsia jumper attempt to hide her girth, which she blames on her pregnancies that resulted in Clay, now eight, and Candy, age five. Colorful, odd-shaped designs dot her ensemble, but I don't look closely enough to distinguish them. I have been told that I have a very expressive face, and that when I don't like something, it registers immediately even though I would never admit it openly. So I gaze up at the silver beech tree and try to avoid eye contact, only to notice Clay poised halfway up with binoculars trained on me.

"You're finally here!" Constance says and hugs me like a thirteen-year-old—pressing her cheek to mine and patting my shoulders vigorously.

"Yes. I can't stay very long, though. . . ."

"Now, Julia Ann, I won't hear about you staying any less than a week, at least a week—or two!" Before I can protest the invitation or the unprecedented use of my middle name, she says, "Oh, let me take your bags." She withers under the weight of them and asks, "What on earth are you carrying?"

"Some photography equipment."

"Oh, that's right. You're into the artsy stuff. Well, I'll have to assume it's worth the effort."

Constance is forty, only seven years older than I am, but manages to tease me as though I am a perpetual teenager and she is the wise matron. When we first met, her favorite nickname for me was "the Yankee traitor" because I went to "one of those fancy prep schools in Connecticut" for my junior and senior years. It was irrelevant that I hated it, that my existence there, after coming from such a small backwater town, was isolating and strange. And even though I moved farther south for college, to a small liberal arts school in D.C., my status as a turncoat was inescapable. To Constance, a graduate of the University of Kentucky, my absence from state education implied that I thought I was better and smarter than everyone else schooled there. However, Constance's code of hospitality forbids her from directly saying this or anything disagreeable.

I suppose I am not without my own code. I vowed, before I made the journey, that I would employ chivalrous charity in dealing with Constance. I would rise above our differences, her condescending and petty instincts, my resentments. I would at least smile as she prattled on about her ancestry, ignore the way she bosses Ed, marvel at the garish silk draperies in the living room, praise her beaten biscuits served with a leathery salt meat known as Kentucky old ham. Basically, I would lie. So, on our way up to the house, I compliment Constance on her jumper and its unusual designs.

"Well, thank you. Can you guess what they are?"

I can't.

"They are amoebas! I bought it at the science museum in Cincinnati. Isn't that clever?"

Clever isn't the word that comes to mind, but I say yes.

She leads me up to the guest room—a spacious loft over the garage. The hotel had vacancies, but I knew Constance would be offended if I didn't accept her invitation.

"Take some time to freshen up. Then I want to take you all on a tour of the house," she says regally, full of throaty, Confederate affect.

"Sure," I reply, even though I have seen the house before. Even though there is only one of me standing before her.

"The only thing we might not take too close a look at is the kitchen," she says. "It's a mess! Aunt Lucy Davis was making her barbecue in there today and Eugenia, you remember my cousin Eugenia? She's rather large and messy so it made things even more . . . unwieldy! Anyway, they were cooking the barbecue and then my grandmother, Nana, was cooking a peach cobbler. So I wouldn't want you to even go near the place until I get a chance to undo the damage! Anyway, I'll let you freshen up, and then we'll go on the grand tour."

Constance disappears down the steps before I can respond. It's a good thing she hurried away because the words now pounding in my mind are virtually irrepressible: Who are these people, and what the hell am I doing here? Aunt Lucy Davis? Nana? And why should I remember her large, messy cousin Eugenia when I've never even met her before? It was a mistake coming here. I should have arranged to meet with the lawyer some other time.

I try to calm myself and remember that in some ways I didn't have a choice. I was summoned by estate business and my indebtedness to her for organizing the funeral. Besides, who would want to miss the bicentennial magic? Constance planned the reunion for this particular weekend because the Davis clan allegedly first landed on the Kentucky side of the Ohio River 200 years ago to Saturday's date. She is her family's self-appointed historian and lets the free world know that only they—meaning no other Davises in town—are direct descendants of Henry Clay Davis, who is a "northern descendant" of Jefferson Davis. I've always doubted her claim, especially since her mother never talked about it. To make matters worse, somehow Constance wangled her way into the DAR and now more than ever considers herself a torchbearer of southern aristocracy.

My family wasn't big enough to have either lineage or reunions, given that I come from a distinguished line of state-hopping, one-child couples. My father was from Virginia by way of Oklahoma. My mother grew up in California and then met my father at UVA. I don't even have what Constance calls "a blood connection" to the state—all the more reason to wonder what I am doing here, far away from what everyone in this house calls "crazy L.A."

"You seen any of them gangbangers much?" Ed asked me after the funeral. We were eating from small plates on our laps and there were strangers milling about. We didn't call it a wake, but that's what it was.

"Those, Ed. Any of those gangbangers," Constance said.

"Well, did ya?" Ed asked me.

I shrugged my shoulders, and replied, "Now and then," like we shop at the same supermarket. It was a lie, but I was tired and jet-lagged and didn't have the patience to explain that not all of the city was ruled by East L.A. and South Central gangs. There were many different types of gangs—the legal gang, the entertainment gang, the real estate gang, the plastic surgery gang. But it was more than I cared to discuss. So I let them sit there in silence and wonder if I had any tattoos, if I packed a piece.

The truth, of course, is that my life couldn't be farther away from the gangs—but that doesn't exactly make it fulfilling. I came to L.A. after my mother died, and my family cocoon suddenly un-raveled. It didn't matter that her cancer had dragged on throughout my college years, supposedly giving us time to prepare. Her death still came as an impossible shock.

Toward the end, before she lost consciousness, she and I would sit on her bed and play hearts or blackjack—something sim-ple. And she would smile more when I won than when she did. We talked about the game, or the weather, or the squirrels outside her window and how busy they were in the early fall. Sometimes, on her more lucid days, she asked about my job prospects, and I chat-ted about fictional leads in New York and Washington for photog-raphy work. And neither of us could talk about the inevitable. It was understood that she would keep trying to get well, that we would focus on the positive. After she died, I still heard the echo of her words—that she would fight it, that she would be okay.

I boarded a plane for L.A. on a gray, freezing day in January, four months after her funeral and a half hour after my father told me his plans to marry Edna. I was furious enough about the relationship—marriage was unthinkable. It was too soon, yet no waiting period would have been long enough. I had no choice but to run after he found such quick comfort in a woman he barely knew. And when I discovered he didn't want me to go, the journey became irresistible.

I arrived by airport shuttle at my college roommate's apartment in Hollywood, having received a tour of scorched oil fields, suburban streets lined with palm trees and prison-barred homes, and the tacky, vainglorious billboards along Sunset Strip. Hollywood shimmered in an unreal light, as though poised on the surface of the sun, and the sky seemed made of chrome. Without a doubt, it was the ugliest place I had ever seen.

But when my roommate took me on a walk in Palisades Park, my senses were revived. We walked along the cliff overlooking the ocean. It was sunny and warm, and the ocean churned with the Santa Ana winds. I loved the fury of the winds and how they held a chaotic promise of things new and unpredictable. But what I liked most was the feeling that I was on the farthest point of my small universe. It felt right to be perched on a cliff at land's end. I could cast away everything—all the anger, confusion, sadness. I could start over.

I tried to get work as a photographer, sending out résumés and attending classes at the L.A. Photography Institute where I met my closest friend, Claire. She's the most well-adjusted thirty-three-year-old I know—gainfully employed, involved in community service, polite to telemarketers, and happily living with her husband, Jay, in a Spanish-styled bungalow in the Hollywood Hills. I try to ignore how much I want her life to be my own, denying my feverish longing for love and children until it gains the upper hand, rendering me anxious, sullen, and mired in hopelessness.

The only relief comes from whirling around the carousel of men I've dated over the years, the reasons why they didn't work out, and realizing those stallions have been put out to pasture for good reason. I have no regrets—just fears. I don't dwell on them when I talk with Claire, though. I simply say her married life, its relative health and normalcy, always gives me hope, and she doesn't forewarn me of the obvious work it takes. She just says she married a good man, which I find more instructive than anything.

I had hopes of getting hired by a magazine (preferably travel) through my work at the institute, but no art director was interested. Through a series of disastrous interviews, I learned that my portraits were bland and uninspired. My candids lacked real spontaneity. And, according to one particularly haughty director, my overall photographic palate was "at best pedestrian, at worst beggarly."

What was there to do but become head majorette in a parade of temping jobs? For six years I answered phones at offices, became an expert at international faxing, and tried freelancing on the side—mostly doing head shots of wanna-be actors or time-lapsed, pseudo-artistic images of L.A. to impress glossy magazines. But nothing worked out.

Claire went on to become a fashion photographer for *Ménage à Trois* and *Paparazzi,* both of which folded. She now photographs and directs shoots for *Mangia!* and helped me get my job—first as an assistant stylist, which turned into head stylist when the woman left and the magazine decided to save money by not replacing her. Claire tells me to keep photographing things on my own, that I have the talent, that the asshole art directors didn't know what they're talking about.

I'd like to believe her. I'd like to think of myself as more of a photographer than a food stylist, but the camera doesn't lie. I look at my portfolio of *Mangia!* work, resplendent with glistening fruit cobblers, fanciful pastas, and stolid roasted meats. There are no surprises, no Walker Evans nuances that elevate objects beyond the realm of the practical. I set up the food, the magazine photographers shoot it, the public eats it.

Claire and I have a running joke about our banal line of work. After Sally waxes poetic about some frilly dish, like seared ahi tuna medallions with a fennel–passion-fruit remoulade, and how I need to design and "plate" the entrée carefully to achieve its unique, artistic potential, Claire pops her head into my cubicle and calls, "One blue plate special."

"One blue plate special coming up," I reply.

The big name food magazines pride themselves on photographing food in its true form, exactly as it should appear when cooked at home. We at *Mangia!* don't. We use every whacky trick in the book to make food both appealing and artistic, even if it does render the grub inedible.

Before my father died, I did get some work published in a real estate journal called *Location! Location! Location!* I actually had hoped my boss, Sally, would give me a chance when there was a staff opening for a regular photographer. But she only humored me, smiling as she turned the pages of my portfolio and uttered specious intonations of delight normally reserved for a five-year-old's finger paintings. I wasn't able to photograph anything for a while after that.

She wound up giving the job to an unwashed phenomenon named Richard Stone who was a hot ticket around L.A. magazines, known for his portraits that were simple, almost candid black-and-whites, free of the more popular, überstyled sepia tones. He worked for *California* and *L.A. Style* before they folded along with others during the recession in the late '80s and early '90s. Like Lazarus, *Mangia!* rose up impossibly among the dead—miraculous in its ability to attract editors, writers, and photographers who were far too talented for its kitschy, ad-driven pages.

Losing out to Richard Stone might have been easier if he were personable. People call him by his last name because he never speaks to anyone. Stone just lopes around the darkroom, stares at his pictures, and runs his hands through his long, graying, oily hair. Claire said his ex-wife, some Hollywood yum-yum, broke his heart and that's why he's so quiet. I don't see how a sexy actress could fall for him.

I went back to work ten days after my father was killed, thinking the activity and familiar routine would do me good. But my perceptions of the job had changed. I began to think of how infinite a photograph is, how it can preserve an image in time forever without the threat of destruction. Whether that moment—the "eternal moment" as one college professor of mine called it—was founded in the name of art or commercialism didn't matter. It was the concept of permanence that captivated my mind.

Consequently, perfection became the single most important yet unattainable pursuit in my food arrangements. Nothing suited me. On one shoot, I spent hours rearranging a plate of quiche, fiddling with the garnish of orange slices, carrot curls, and cilantro until my fingers cramped and the freelance photographer, who was trying to be patient, stormed out of the studio. Stone took over and told me it was okay, but it wasn't. It was useless. Nothing looked profound enough for eternity.

Before coming out here to the reunion, I wanted to leave the job for good and try freelancing again. I spent two weeks hustling, following up on leads, sending my portfolio to every publication in town—newspapers, trade magazines, entertainment rags. But Claire begged me not to quit, to consider my options, even though she knows as well as I do that it's a dead-end job. She advised that I put down the flamethrower and step away from the bridge until I had a plan and an income, and until I knew what I wanted—which might take forever. Maybe I just wasn't ready to be back, she said. Maybe I could ask for some time off without pay, some family leave. This made sense to me since I had become an official orphan. My family certainly had left.

When I asked Sally about taking time off to deal with my father's affairs, she agreed to one week without pay. "Of course you need time off. I understand about these things, and you've been through quite a lot," Sally said from across her desk. "But just make sure it's only a week. I mean, I just don't want you or anyone else to make a habit of it."

I wanted to tell her that incomprehensible sadness and rage were not habitual, and that there were more important things in life than the "Summer Sensation" picnic issue, but I refrained. I simply nodded and left, secretly glad that I wouldn't be pouring motor oil over Crisco scoops to fabricate the perfect sundae, let alone searing semiraw burgers with Sally's cast-off curling iron. Her office motto: "Why buy it new when we can make do?"

And now I am here, reclining on a four-poster bed that probably once cradled the body of someone's prominent forefather. The rest of the decor is equally antiquated—frilly lace curtains, old brass floor lamps, gilded portraits of tight-lipped nineteenth-century men and women, an antique mahogany rocking chair, and dead flower arrangements hung upside down on the walls. Hidden sachets of lavender and rose make the orderly room even more cloying and unnatural, as if the whole space has been embalmed.

I have pulled the curtains aside and gaze out the window. In late March, the trees in Kentucky are just beginning to show their pale green buds, but I can look through them and find the familiar silhouette against the fading sky: the home where I grew up. It's on the hill above Constance's house, part of a residential enclave with houses built along winding slopes.

I couldn't bring myself to go near it when I was home for the funeral. I wasn't ready. I knew I would walk in the foyer and see my mother's Victorian bellpull hanging on the wall and remember her needlepointing it, the slow spread of colors as she worked on it in her living room chair. It seemed that she needlepointed in the evenings for most of my childhood and in the threads of floral pillows and bellpulls and cushion covers I could always find my more placid childhood moments: days of playing in the woods with my neighborhood friends, my father reading *The Wind in the Willows* to me before bedtime, resting by the warmth of the fire with my cat, Wiz, as the rhythm of the day slowed into night. We were comfortable being the three of us until I went away and until her illness changed everything.

I remember arriving home after graduating from high school, still stinging over the fact that she hadn't been able to make the trip. I was just eighteen and immortal in my Jordache jeans and new identity as the next Ansel Adams—unable to understand how serious the cancer was. I could comprehend things much better after seeing her struggle through to remission that summer. But she would have another bout with it a year later, and then it would spread from her colon to her lung. The doctors radiated and removed the tumors as best they could, but there was always another fight until she could no longer win.

And I remember a subsequent moment of entry into the house—two years after her death, Christmas Eve. I was standing in the foyer, yelling at my father because Edna had taken down the bellpull.

"It's her house too, now," he said. "She has a right to decorate it the way she wants."

"She doesn't have a right to decorate it in a way that's disrespectful to Mom. What's next? Is she going to take down her paintings, too?"

"You watch yourself, young lady."

"That's not an answer!"

Edna came in from the kitchen just then, bearing a tray of mini-quiches.

"Who's hungry?" she asked.

My father took one, sighed deeply, and popped it in his mouth. I ran upstairs, shut my door, and didn't come down until dinner was ready. We didn't discuss it again that night. But the next day Edna hung the bellpull back up without a word of explanation.

With each visit, I wanted to reclaim every memory I could of my mother in that house, and now that our life together is gone completely, I feel more desperate than ever to find traces of her and my father there. I look beyond the hill and survey the town, wondering if there is any place or person salvageable from my past, something that can give me not just comfort but some sense of belonging. Tomorrow I will go exploring. I will break free from the yoke of lawyers and Constance in search of some better reason for being here.

At dusk, I awaken out of an unintentional nap to find Clay and Candy sitting on the carpet several feet from my bed. I rub my eyes before I can focus completely on them. At first I think maybe it's a dream, but after a moment I see that they are definitely here, working quietly on coloring books. I'm not exactly sure if they're here of their own will or whether Constance sent them on a reconnaissance mission.

I sit up in bed and notice a light in the corner of the room and someone sitting in the rocking chair. At first I think it's Constance until I look more closely. I see the deep lines in her brow and cheeks, and her ever-youthful hair—still dark brunette and coifed into a small bouffant swirl. She wears a white sweatshirt with "Foxy" emblazoned on the front in sequined letters, which makes me smile. That she is here seems like the lucky break I've been needing.

"Trudy," I say as I get up. "What a great surprise."

Trudy cleaned house for my mother and evolved into something of a caregiver for her when she became too ill to cook or garden or even leave the house. She puts the beads she's stringing down and stands up to wrap me in a hug, a solid one—not like the jittery thing Constance doled out. I return it full measure, remembering the way her arms once hauled the grocery bags in, helped me change my mother's bed. When my father wasn't there to do it, she could actually lift my mother and carry her down the stairs. Trudy's arms are still strong, and I can hardly believe that it wasn't just yesterday but a decade ago that both my mother and I leaned on them.

"How's my sweet girl?" she says. "I hope I didn't wake you."

"Not at all. It's so good to see you."

"I tried calling you a couple months ago, but your number was disconnected."

"I know. I've moved around a lot in L.A., and the phone company doesn't leave the forwarding number for very long. I'm sorry we didn't get a chance to talk."

"Well, I'm here now. Ed told me you was coming, so I figured I'd sneak up here and see you—and keep an eye on the kids. I bet that's something you don't wake up to very often."

"What?"

"Them two." She points to the two pairs of legs that now stick out from underneath the bed.

I laugh and say, "That's for sure."

I search my memory, rifling through some of the funeral faces that appeared in front of me three months ago. I feel like I must have seen Trudy then but can't recall it. I remember seeing her at the bank during Christmas a few years ago when I was home. Had it been that long?

"I can't remember when I last saw you," I say.

"I seen you at the funeral, sweetheart. Just for a minute and then me and Harlan had to leave because, well, you know."

"No. I mean, I don't know. Who's Harlan?"

"My husband. Ed's daddy. You mean you didn't know we got married?"

"Oh my God. I didn't even know you were . . . uh . . ."

"Dating? Come on, now. Sixty-seven-year-olds need love, too," Trudy laughs.

"I can't believe my father didn't tell me, or that Constance didn't."

"Well, I'm not surprised that she didn't tell you."

"Why?"

Trudy holds her finger up and then points to the kids, and I nod and mouth "Later" to her. She looks at me over her bifocals and smiles warmly.

"Yes ma'am," she says. "Harlan decided to make an honest woman out of me last year, and I am now known as Trudy Fletcher."

"She's our Mamaw," Candy says. She gets up and puts on Trudy's thick-heeled pumps and starts to clomp around in them. "Look at me! I'm Mamaw!"

"Now, Candy, gimme them shoes. You're gonna fall right smack on your head," Trudy says. Candy smiles and hands them over just as Clay crawls out from under the bed and holds up a Bart Simpson doll.

"Look at me," he says, "I'm Candy." He prances around and Candy yells at him to give it back.

"No, it's mine," he says, "you've had it all day. It's my turn to play with it," which incites another tirade. Trudy quickly intervenes.

"Now, y'all better settle this, or I'll do like King Solomon and cut that doll baby into two, give each of you half. Then what'll you do?"

They think about this for a moment, and then Clay yells, "I want the head!"

"No, I want the head!" says Candy.

Trudy and I burst out laughing. She tilts her head back, revealing a mouth full of gold and silver fillings. A memory returns to me, a nasty remark Constance made about a year after my mother died, about Trudy being from Byron Hollow and how people from there were "hicks living like pigs." I wanted to tell Constance just exactly how porcine she herself was, but my father anticipated my rage and hustled me into the kitchen to help him fix another round of drinks.

Trudy holds out her hands for the doll, and Clay gives it to her.

"Now is it really your turn to play with this doll?" she asks Clay.

"Well, not really. Not till tomorrow."

"All right. So Candy, why don't ya'll put him up for now and run and get me them dinosaur pictures you drew for school," Trudy says. "I'm fixing to leave, and I want to see them before I go."

"Okay! Hey, we can show you some rocks we found too!" she says.

"Great! Now, y'all run along."

The children scurry out of the room. Trudy sits down again and starts to put away her beads, still smiling and shaking her head.

"So much for the Bible."

"Well, at least you tried."

"Oh my. Clay and Candy tickle me so—I just love seeing them, but I can't very often. Constance doesn't much like me, which is why I didn't stay very long at the funeral by the way or come to the house." She looks at the beads in her hand, fingering them delicately. "Me and Harlan was so awful sorry," she says as she looks at me. "Your Daddy was such a good man."

I have heard so many condolences in the past three months. In spite of kind intentions, not many are comforting. They are awkward and effusive when the person either has no conception of loss or is terribly afraid of it. The least comforting type of sympathy is bitter shared experience. A woman who used to work as a receptionist at the magazine lost her son in a plane crash and her mother to suicide. She never said she was sorry about my father. She just cornered me one day at the copy machine and recounted her own grim tale. I said nothing, except that I was sorry, and waited for her to wind down and leave me alone.

Generally speaking, my response to sympathetic chatter is surprisingly adept. My words are gracious and controlled, devoid of any real emotion. Often the person comments on how strong I am. I can fool the best of them.

But with Trudy it's different. She knew his goodness well, and I am moved by the simple truth of her words and the way she looks right into my eyes when she says them. Her condolences seem to capture more than his death, and I vaguely wonder if she knew about the way he and I had become increasingly estranged during his marriage to Edna. It seems petty to bring it up now, so I say, "He was a good man. And I guess he and Edna were close."

"I reckon. But he sure did love your mama."

My tears, which I vowed to leave in L.A., well up. I will them back as I walk over to the window. Trudy follows me and touches me on the shoulder.

"I'm sorry if I said too much," she says.

"No, I just haven't remembered them together for a long time. It's good to remember them being together."

"That don't mean it's easy," she says as she wraps an arm around me. Oddly enough, I would like just to stand for a while and lean again on this kind woman, but some habits are hard to break and after about two seconds, I retreat to my safe havens—diversion and avoidance.

"Then there's this silly reunion," I say as I pull away and sit down on the window seat.

"Is that what brought you home?"

"That and the estate business."

"Is it your high school reunion?"

"No. The family reunion. She didn't tell you about it?"

"Shoot. She don't consider me family."

"I'm sorry," I say.

"No reason to be. I wouldn't want to spend five minutes with them people. They ain't all of them bad. But I know what her and her sisters think of me. I try to be nice to her cause I know she's sad over losing her mama, but Lord, it's like trying to cozy up to a polecat."

Suddenly, Constance enters the room without knocking. She looks at Trudy and then over at me and back to Trudy, startled and flustered.

"Good heavens, Trudy. I wasn't expecting to see you." Constance says with a brittle, false cheerfulness.

Trudy waits before responding. Her face is steely as she walks back to the chair and carefully places her beads into her basket.

"I came to see the children," she says.

"Well, I don't recall—"

Trudy cuts Constance off as her eyes find Clay and Candy peeping from behind the door.

"I see two bed bugs that fell out of the mattress. Y'all come here and show me them pictures."

They quickly oblige, pointing out the various kinds of creatures they drew. They couldn't find the rocks.

"Now, this here is a Tyrannosaurus rex," Clay says.

"Oh my, he's fierce," Trudy says.

"Clay, we don't say 'this here is.' We simply say, 'this is,'" Constance says.

"Okay. Hey, Trudy, can we come see you at the farm?"

"Yeah! I want to see the cows!" Candy says.

Constance stiffens at this remark.

"Well, you'll have to take that up with your mama," Trudy says.

Clay starts to ask if they can, but Constance cuts the question off with a very terse, "We'll see."

"Now, ya'll give me a big hug," Trudy says.

They wrap Trudy in a joint embrace. She laughs and gives each a peck on the cheek. I find myself smiling. Constance, however, frowns even more sternly than before.

"Y'all go and wash your hands," Constance says. "Dinner's almost ready."

The two race out of the room, calling good-bye to Trudy. She stands up to leave, but Constance resumes her inquiry.

"Ed didn't say anything about your being here."

Trudy checks the contents of her basket and says, "Well, Constance, I admit it was a spur-of-the-moment visit. I was in town visiting Ed at the store, and he didn't think it would be so awful bad for me to visit the children and see Julia."

"How long have you been here?"

"Only about an hour. I come up the back stairs and they led me up here."

"You *came* up the back stairs so that you could disturb my company," Constance says with a bright smile, flashing me a horrid, conspiring wink that compels me to rise to Trudy's defense.

"She didn't disturb me. In fact, Trudy probably helped to keep the kids quiet while I slept."

I didn't mean to criticize Constance's children, but the damage was done—as if my defense of Trudy weren't betrayal enough. Constance stares coldly at me and strides over to the bed and starts fluffing up the pillows and straightening the spread.

"What I mean is nobody caused me to wake up. And after I did wake up, we were having a very nice conversation—"

"Well, I'm glad," Constance says, retreating to the polite lie. She finishes pounding the pillows into uniform submission, and without looking up says, "But Trudy, you know it confuses them to see you."

"No, I do not know that. When I am here, I do not see confusion in their faces."

"Well, of course not," Constance snaps. "Not when you're here, but after you leave it's a different story."

I can't believe what Constance is saying and don't want to hear the rest. I have enough to worry about. This is too much.

"I think I'd better wash my face," I say, quickly rising from the bed.

"You don't need to leave. Constance and me been over this a hundred times and we don't need to go over it again. It's always the same," Trudy says as she stands up and heads for the door. She reaches out her hand to me, and I take it. "Good to see you, honey. Will you give me a call before you leave?"

"Sure thing," I say, wishing I could thank her for the kind words but not wanting to let Constance in on it.

Constance stands motionless and silent as Trudy walks down the stairs. It's only after she hears the back door shut that she expels a long breath and then, forgetting my role of accomplice, lets her anger spill out.

"That awful old woman. She has made my life a living hell."

I say nothing and head toward the bathroom. Constance follows me.

"I know she can seem all sweet and nice, but she is very manipulative and demanding. What did she say to you?"

"Nothing really," I say as I turn on the faucet and splash my face with water. I thought the inherent privacy of bathroom activity would make her leave. I was wrong.

"Well, she must have said something if you all had a conversation."

I dry my face with one of the hand towels by the sink.

"We only talked for a few minutes. I had no idea that she and Ed's father married. I didn't even know they were an item."

"Some item. His crazy father met her at some arts and crafts fair. I try to make sure people know she's only a step-relative, not a true member of the family."

It takes Constance only a moment before she realizes her gaffe. It makes no difference to me. I know I don't belong with her in Kentucky any more than she does with me in Los Angeles. But she tries to save face as she follows me back into the bedroom.

"Now, it's not that way with you," she says. "You are family, of course. Of course! But with Trudy, well, obviously, it's impossible."

It is the "obviously" that makes me break the don't-argue-with-your-hostess rule. I move to the window and look out at the fading sky, now barely able to discern the shadow of my former home.

"Why is it impossible?" I say, facing her again. "The children love her. And she was nothing less than a saint in helping take care of my mother."

Constance looks at me with a mixture of surprise and betrayal. I recognize the expression from years ago when she discovered I didn't know that the University of Kentucky basketball team had won the national championship. How could anyone not know? she asked.

"Well, Julia. My goodness. I mean, I don't doubt that she was a help to your mother, but . . . well, I thought you would understand."

"Understand what?"

She takes a deep breath as she looks up at the ceiling and clasps her hands in front of her, one over the other, like she's getting ready to sing a hymn.

"It's not that I am a snob," she says in a half whisper. "But some people are just too common, if you know what I'm saying."

"Well, I don't really."

"Julia, it's as plain as day. That woman is trying to better herself by marrying Harlan. She knows what she's doing. I don't think Harlan has a clue. Anyway, it won't work. She'll always be what she is."

"You mean she's poor, and you think she married Harlan for his money."

"No. She has the money, selling her wood carvings and jewelry, which everybody says is folk art, but I think it's junk. Trudy's got everybody fooled."

"Then how is she trying to better herself?" I get up from the chair and move to my suitcase, pretending to search for something so that I don't have to look at her when she says it.

"Because she's from Byron Hollow, Julia. My goodness. You know about people from there. They're so backward. . . ."

She might have planned to say one of the local hyperboles—so backward that they marry their cousins, they still have feuds, they think a seven-course meal is a six-pack and a package of pork rinds. But she opts for a more realistic generalization.

"They don't even bother sending their children to college."

"Don't a lot of the farmers need their kids to help them in the fields?"

"Some do, but most just don't care about education. Clearly, Trudy doesn't care about it. Just listen to the way she talks."

"I like the way she talks. Besides, there are other kinds of education, and not using proper grammar doesn't make a person evil."

She doesn't respond. After a few seconds, I turn around to face her. I expect her to be at least a little contrite—maybe averting her eyes to the floor. But she stares at me head-on, as rigid and unyielding as a bird dog. She wipes her hands on her apron and speaks in the soft, halting tones of a soap opera martyr.

"If you want to taunt me you can. But there is more to it than just grammar."

"Constance, I'm not trying to taunt you. I just think Trudy's a good person."

She says nothing and continues to stare at me. Finally, I propose what's been on my mind ever since I arrived.

"Maybe I should stay at the hotel. I mean, we both might be more comfortable."

Constance walks over to the window seat and eases herself down on it. The room seems more airless than before and the light is nearly gone, but neither of us moves to open a window or turn on a lamp. I watch Constance's silhouette, unsure of what she'll do next, and notice that her shoulders are shaking. I think she might be laughing until she sucks up a sob so surprising and helpless that it makes my heart flutter into sharp, tight beats.

"I don't know. I don't know," she says in between breaths.

"It seems like everything's falling apart. The family's falling apart. I thought if we could have this reunion, it would pull things together. And now you don't even want to stay here. I just . . . I don't know." I can see she's trying to control the sorrow, anger, confusion—whatever it is that is making her cry. She opens her mouth but can't find any other words.

"Constance, I'm sorry. I didn't realize you felt this way," I say and move beside her, but she scoots away when I do, making sure she's not within my grasp.

"I know. I suppose I didn't either. You know, it's getting late. I better go see about supper," she says.

"I didn't mean to make you feel like things are falling apart. They aren't. I only mentioned the hotel because I thought we both might be more comfortable. I mean, I don't want to get in the way here." The language of polite avoidance—translation: we're too different to live under the same roof.

"Oh, you aren't in the way at all, Julia," Constance says, standing up and quickly wiping away her tears. "Now, I want you to stay. I really do. I'd feel awful if you stayed at that old hotel." Her voice quivers slightly, yet I can tell she's forcing the bright melody of happy hostess back into it. I take a deep breath and try to unearth the real issue, hoping to resolve something between us.

"Of course I'll stay. But listen, about Trudy, I think people sometimes—"

"Water under the bridge," she says even more merrily. "We'll just talk about other things. Are you hungry? I imagine we'll have dinner around seven."

"Constance, that's a lot of water we're talking about," I reply, still angling for some truthfulness between us.

"Don't be silly! People have their differences and they live with them," she says lightly as she walks toward the door. "I'm just glad you're here, and I want you to stay here. Now, if you need anything before dinner, you just let me know."

She doesn't wait for a response and I don't have one to give anyway. I hear her footsteps down the back hallway and then, after a few seconds, jump at the sound of *Eine kleine Nachtmusik* blaring from the stereo in the hallway. The music fills the house, pushing away all else, and I feel like I have compromised perhaps too quickly, letting reality slip away on account of her tears.

Perhaps her crying has nothing to do with our argument or the embarrassment of my offering to stay at the hotel. Maybe it has to do with her mother being dead and the feeling of being overwhelmed by the sudden loss and the helpless longing and the tedious chore of settling the estate. Hadn't I been sobbing only a few days before when I went looking for the lawyer's letter in my desk and found this year's Christmas card from my father. "When are we going to say Merry Christmas in person?" he wrote. "Next year I hope." I stared at his familiar scrawl as if willing more of it to appear—the lines between the lines that could somehow assuage the horrible guilt I felt.

We each have our private pain. Until now, it hadn't occurred to me that the reunion could be more about easing her grief (and mine) than touting her lineage. So, I will let her be during the four days I am here, searching for the similarities instead of the differences between us. I will go along with the smiles and the return to politeness—and I will not speak of Trudy again.

3 ❦

Mourning in America

At age thirty-three, I no longer have the spontaneity or impulsive desperation it takes to move to a strange, faraway place after a weekend visit. But things were different when I was younger. I didn't give going to boarding school in Massachusetts a moment's hesitation. It seemed like the right and romantic thing to do at the time, to leave the disappointments of sophomore year behind me, to head east in worldly style.

The summer I turned fifteen, I would have never dreamed of leaving. Armed with a learner's permit, I was the official chauffeur to any of my friends who had a car and wanted to avoid drinking and driving. Finally we were old enough to slather on makeup and drive the bridge across the Ohio to the discos that played Madonna, the Police, and still the occasional Donna Summer torch song. During the day, I took a photography class at the college, and sometimes my parents and I would have lunch together when my mother came to pick me up. I would help her with dinner and would sit for her some evenings because she was tired of landscapes and wanted to get back to portraits. Too often I was fidgety, much more content to cruise the Bluegrass Diner and drink beer at the lake with my friends—a fact which now amazes me. What I wouldn't give to sit still and look into her pale blue eyes, to spend hours watching her make delicate strokes across the canvas.

What sophomore year brought was drama, drugs, and a failed crusade for Jesus. Trouble began when I broke up with a boyfriend who had become born-again in the fall. He was a popular school senator, good-looking, athletic, and everyone thought I was crazy to give him the heave-ho. I tried to explain what agnostic meant, that my father said honest doubt is better than half the creed, but most kids who believed just shook their heads and said, "I'll pray for you." I became even more alienated from his friends after I questioned their absolute belief that I would go to hell if I didn't get right with God. Even worse were the fights I had with my best friend who, on the other end of the spectrum, just said yes to a lot of booze and pot. Suddenly, I was in a no-man's-land between the party hounds and Bible thumpers, and I didn't like it. And when another friend left school in order to avoid being paddled for cutting class—corporal punishment still being legal in the early 1980s—I realized that my mother and father were right: the time had come to broaden my horizons.

My father viewed it as a strictly educational move, a way to get into a good college. That was my sole mission, he said, because it was costing a lot of money. My mother whispered to me later not to worry about the money, to study hard but to make friends. "You know your father," she said. "He treats everybody like a plebe when he's upset. I think he really doesn't want to let you go—though he'd never admit it."

I wound up studying perhaps too much, trying to catch up to where my classmates were, landing in the uncomfortable role of odd southern recluse—the shy Kentucky kid who liked photography, nearly failed math, and had never even heard of Wallabees, Brooks Brothers, or cocaine. I became close with a couple of midwestern girls who were also junior transplants and equally out of place. The three of us worked on the school newspaper together, played only intramural sports, and lived to graduate.

From the time I went away, it seemed like I couldn't really get a foothold anywhere. In college, it wasn't homesickness that pulled me away as much as it was Mom—worrying about her illness, wondering how long I would have with her, which made any time away seem like a waste. I had even wanted to take my senior year off to be with her, but my parents urged me to get my degree even though my father groused that fine arts was not nearly as useful a major as computer science.

Not surprisingly, when I decided to move to L.A. after my mother died, it was the ocean and palm trees, not economic opportunity, that beckoned. Dad didn't hear the sirens' call.

"You need a job. You can't just up and leave," he said, stabbing at a piece of bacon. We always sat at the counter of the Bluegrass Diner—never at a booth. His standard routine was to eat the same meal every morning—bran flakes, two pieces of bacon, toast, and prune juice. It was the same meal he ate in the marines, then before going to work at the state recruiting office, and—for twenty years—before going off to teach history at the community college. My father understood schedules and routines. Going to some far-flung place like L.A. without so much as a duty roster was inconceivable to him.

"I'll find work when I get there," I said.

"What will you live on until then?"

"I'm going to sell Mom's stock."

"She wouldn't want you to do that."

I glared at his profile and replied, "She wouldn't want you to do certain things either."

Death made me bold. I never challenged him when my mother was alive, but things had changed. I watched the muscles in his jaw furiously work the piece of bacon. My heart was pounding. If we had been home he might have exploded. I had seen him lose his temper enough times over far lesser transgressions of mine. But the public place made him check his anger. He stared straight ahead and didn't say anything else. I pressed him further when I tried the honest approach and said, "I'm upset about Edna," but he still shut me out with his standard defense, "We'll talk about it later."

We never did. He just gave me the money—hush money, I called it. And I was angry enough in that first year to take it without apology or thanks. I became self-supporting once I got a steady job, and we never talked about Edna again. You could say we were disciples of the water-under-the-bridge philosophy.

Constance and I are equally adept.

I was up this morning before her and crept out of the house to get some coffee and a little exercise. It's 8:00 A.M. and I'm walking around the town park, wishing I could see my father for just a moment, thinking about all the words unsaid between us. If I had tried harder to tell him what I felt, he might have put down his fork and listened since Mom was no longer there to be his apologist. If I had refused to leave the diner that morning, staged an emotional sit-in, maybe he would have explained his own feelings in return, and I wouldn't have wasted so much time being angry with him. I would have seen him over Christmas; I wouldn't have left him wondering whether or not I still wanted to be his daughter.

Suddenly, I am pulled away from my thoughts as a pudgy, balding man starts waving hello. He's jogging toward me, and I don't know him. He's up in my face before I can recall his name, saying, "Hey, Jules!"

I draw a blank and he says, "Don't you remember me? It's Bobby . . . Powell."

"Bobby! Oh my gosh. I didn't even recognize you."

"Well, it's been a long time. And I guess I've changed a bit," he says, slightly embarrassed as he sucks in his gut and smoothes the few strands of hair on top of his head.

It was a profound understatement, and I begin to hear the parliamentarians who live in my head and plague me when I feel fearful or confused. I imagine them variously arrayed in their black robes and Bond Street suits—civilized yet vicious. Usually their wrath is turned on me or others close to me, full of judgment that is always destructive and self-defeating. Today is no exception. *You were in love with him? He looks like my old nanny! He looks like mine, too! Quite right! Hear, hear!*

When I knew him eleven years ago, Bobby Powell had a full head of hair and the body of Michelangelo's David. He was a kindred outsider, an only child who went to boarding school for a couple of years and then off to college in Connecticut. He was the only one I knew of my peers who had ventured beyond the state for college. He was hooked on lacrosse, bluegrass music, and something he called emotional honesty. He prided himself on his ability to feel and recognize his emotions—good and bad—and hated it when people said jocks were insensitive morons.

More than anything, it was the emotional honesty that brought us together back then. It was Bobby whom I called when things got awful at home, when my mother was beginning to die. Bobby was dependable, but what I loved most about him was that he knew how to cry. His father was dead and his mother, an alcoholic, spent most of her time with a wealthy boyfriend in central Kentucky. I had never really seen Bobby or any man cry until one Friday night after he had gotten off the phone with his mother, who was drunk and cursing him for ever being born. All Bobby kept saying was, "I gotta go. I gotta go." When he hung up the phone, Bobby sat down next to me and simply began to weep. He mourned in a way that I envied.

So I would show up at his house, and he'd turn off the television and make me a whiskey sour even though he didn't drink. He'd put on Emmylou Harris's latest record, and I'd listen to her sad, sweet melodies, and sometimes I would cry because I couldn't cry at home. It wasn't allowed. It would upset everyone. Both my mother and father laid down that rule. After I had a good cry or after we finished playing backgammon or when we simply ran out of things to talk about, Bobby and I would always leave the world behind by finding each other—usually in the bedroom or den.

"You still living in Los Angeles?" he asks.

"Yes."

"Wow, that's something. You're the only one I know who lives way out there. You ever see any movie stars?"

"Not really. I mean, you sometimes catch a glimpse of someone who looks like a movie star—maybe—but so many people out there try to look like movie stars. Anyway, you catch a glimpse, but then they're gone before you can figure it out."

Bobby nods vigorously. "Guess they hide away," he says. I look at my watch and then over my shoulder purposefully, like I have an appointment with the swing set. There is so much I'd like to say to him, but too much time has passed. I don't know where to begin.

"I was so sorry to hear about your daddy."

"Thanks," I say. If we were still in college—or maybe if I had stayed put—I imagine he would have stopped his jog indefinitely upon seeing my eyes tear up and would have gathered me in his arms, telling me to let it out. But he doesn't. I look down at the ground and try to keep my sadness at bay. A few more seconds hang in the air.

"How long you in town for?" he asks.

"Only a few days," I say. "You know, dealing with the estate."

"Well, if you want to let off some steam, you can come on over to the YMCA. I'm manager over there now."

"Sure," I say absently, trying not to look at his protruding, anti-YMCA stomach and stunned by the fact that he isn't just visiting but actually lives here. I look at his ringless left hand and wonder what his offer means, so I ask, "Are you still living out on Charleston Road?"

"Yes indeed." He takes a deep breath and says, "Mom remarried and moved to Lexington. She gave me the house when I got married. Maybe you can drop by and meet my wife and kids or something."

The news shouldn't surprise me, but I can't help but feel a flutter of shock, perhaps laced with a little regret. I know I should congratulate him and ask who and how many kids and boys or girls and what ages and all of that sociable prattle. But the offer to meet his progeny and the missus, to walk through rooms where he and I used to laugh and cry and make love, is enough to land us both into an abyss of awkward silence. I could say some pleasant lie—sure, great, love to—but Constance has drained by reserve. All I can utter is a vague, "Yeah."

We avoid each others' eyes at all costs. Finally he says, "Well, it was real nice seeing you. Take care of yourself."

"Yeah, you too."

I watch him jiggle away and marvel at what a stranger he is to me now. Too much life has happened, and too much death.

As I start my climb toward the house, I am preoccupied by the questions that I hoped to avoid for a while but that always find me with the news of friends getting married and having children: Where is the on-ramp to the freeway of love? How long do two people stumble around together before they find each other, before they have enough of dinners and movies and polite strolls through public places?

I had a lot of relationships before and after Bobby, but none of them lasted very long. My friends in college called me the Whitman Sampler. I was determined to leave my boyfriends before they left me, so I never got too close to anyone except for Bobby, and then Matthew, a theology student I met in L.A. about six years ago. He had plans to go to graduate school and become ordained, and I now wonder if being with him was nothing more than my indirect, misguided way of finally trying to get right with God. Maybe I was drawn to him because he seemed more gentle and prone to reflection than other men I knew or because my great-grandfather had been a minister, and I was looking for some connection with my past. Whatever the reason, it wasn't compelling enough to keep us together.

When he left for his year-long missionary internship in Nepal, we promised to write and stay together—that is, until he converted to orthodox Buddhism. I didn't really understand what a transformation it was until I picked him up at LAX. It was shocking to see him stride through the terminal in a flowing orange robe, his head shaved, his ear pierced—he was hardly the Lutheran I once loved. I soon discovered that his devotion had rendered him so serenely mute that I felt I was talking in a different language.

He didn't relate to any of my work experiences, could no longer console any residual difficulties I faced over my mother's death. He looked omniscient, like he'd heard it all before, and it drove me crazy. Amazingly, he still retained his Western libido, but I made some lame excuse about having to get up early the next morning. So I pretended to sleep while we lay next to each other without touching. And when I did finally drift off in the early morning hours, I was soon awakened by his chanting, to my ears a sound oddly akin to Porky Pig's stutter. That confirmed it. We were through.

Since then, I've continued exploring the curious world of post-collegiate dating, but nothing's come from my excursions. The names and faces elude me and only the bizarre antics linger—the blind date whose juvenile humor inspired him to arrive at my doorstep with a sack over his head; the bankruptcy attorney who took me to Musso & Frank's for dinner and stuck me with the check; the accountant who loved karaoke. What do you do when you aren't styling food, Julia?—Grieve, I often thought, but would give the inquiring man a socially correct answer—biking, hiking, movies, books. I would stop there, however, never talking about photography or asking him about his dreams and passions—always keeping him at a safe distance.

I enter the house through the garage and walk up the back steps to avoid the commotion in the kitchen, exhausted from my stroll down memory lane. It's nine o'clock and I hear what must be the aunts and cousins swirling around each other—stirring things, chopping, blending. I'm halfway up the stairs when I hear a "Woo-hoo" behind me, softer and a bit more tentative than Constance's. I turn around to find a shriveled old woman wearing an orange-and-cream polyester pants suit and sporting a short, softly curled silver perm. Her eyes bulge behind her thick, cat's-eye glasses and she says, "You must be Julia. Well, aren't you up early! I'm Nana, Constance's grandmother."

"Nice to meet you. Constance was telling me about how busy you've been in the—"

"Kitchen? Oh yes! You don't know the half of it. Come down and have some coffee," she says as she reaches up toward my arm with her bony fingers. "We been cooking all sorts of things, and course the reunion is tomorrow, and we haven't even started mak-ing the cold salads. Come on down and have some coffee."

She takes a quick step up and clutches my arm, partly to keep from falling.

"Well, that's very nice of you, but I've already—"

"Had some? Well have another cup. I make wonderful coffee. Come on down. Come on down."

Clearly, this is one of her good days. I remember what Ed told me after dinner last night, how hard Nana had taken Edna's death. "You know, it's just not the natural order," he said. "Nana keeps saying, 'I was supposed to die before she did. I was supposed to die.'" Just the thought of her words makes any pain I feel seem mild. So I smile as she tugs at my arm, tell her I'd love some more coffee, and follow her down the stairs.

Nana introduces me to Aunt Lucy and her daughter, Eugenia. Constance had briefed me about Eugenia, but I am hardly prepared for the untamed folds of flesh that hide under her red-and-white muumuu. She sits precariously on an old metal-legged stool, the kind that doubles as step ladder when you lift the seat, and I wonder how anyone could allow such a hazard. She eyes me suspiciously, without getting up.

I imagined Eugenia would have a somewhat corpulent voice—gravelly, deep throated—but it's high-pitched and squeaky, almost childlike.

"You're from Los Angeles," she says.

"Yes. It's, uh, pretty warm there this time of—"

"I know what it's like," she says a bit too quickly to be kind. "I don't see how you live there at all. Even if the weather is good."

I had been forewarned by Constance not to ask about Eugenia's experiences with the city. It seems that after graduating from UK in 1975, a thin, beautiful, and talented Eugenia went to Hollywood in hopes of breaking into acting. But within two months she was back in Kentucky. She refused to say what happened. It was rumored that she met a producer who did something awful to her. "Not rape, but *something* awful," Constance told me. To this day, no one—except maybe her mother—knows what that awful thing was. Once she was home, Eugenia became introverted and began to overeat. She never left the town again and now manages a fabric shop and still lives with her mother. Constance told me that Eugenia becomes enraged when anyone tries to pry into her dark L.A. secrets even though she views herself as worldly for having them.

Nana hands me a cup of coffee, breaking the awkward silence. I taste it and compliment her on the flavor.

"French roast," she says.

"Oh, it's wonderful."

"Are you surprised that we have fancy coffee all the way down here?" Eugenia asks.

"Not at all. In fact, the magazine I work for did a story on coffee consumption in American, and Kentucky was one of the leading states."

"*Mangia!* magazine," Eugenia says with a slow, twangy Italian accent. "Where did they get that name anyway?"

The answer is attempted by Aunt Lucy, whose fashion sense

appeals to me more than anyone's. She wears a black turtleneck and long jean skirt and has her hair knotted into a stylish-looking bun. "It means 'eat' in Italian."

"Oh, well, thank you for the news bulletin, Mother. I know what it means. I'm just wondering where they got it," Eugenia says.

Oh, sweet Jesus. This woman-child is going to drive me mad. Her mother just shakes her head and continues stirring the contents of a ceramic bowl.

"I think our original publisher was Italian," I reply. "I can't remember his name. But I'm pretty sure that he was born in Italy or spent a lot of time there as an adult. Anyway, his time there greatly influenced his view of food."

I go on about the publisher's roots even though every word is a lie. I have no idea where the name came from. I don't feel bad about lying to Eugenia. I consider it self-defense. I want to appease her curiosity so that she doesn't launch into another inane orbit around the magazine. If she finds even its name objectionable, there's no telling how ridiculous the task of food styling will seem.

"Personally, I think all those gourmet magazines are overrated," Eugenia says.

"All right, Eugenia. I think we've heard enough of your opinions this morning," her mother says. "I need you to run down to the store and get some more sugar."

"You don't need any more sugar. You've got a whole bowlful right there," Eugenia says.

"Eugenia, please don't argue. I need the sugar because I haven't even measured the amount for the Transparent Tarts yet."

"All right," Eugenia says as she hoists herself off the stool and lumbers silently out of the room.

Her mother wipes her hands on a kitchen towel and extends her hand toward me.

"I'm Constance's aunt Lucy. Please excuse Eugenia. She hasn't been feeling well lately."

"Oh, it's okay. No problem," I say.

"Isn't she just like her mama," Aunt Lucy says as she still holds my hand between her two. "Nana, don't you think so?"

Nana comes over and takes off her glasses to look closely at my face.

"I reckon so," she says. "But she's got her daddy's eyes and mouth."

"No, I mean in her manner. Isn't she just like her? I used to be nurse at St. Joseph's, and I got to know her pretty well before she passed," Aunt Lucy says.

Before I or Nana can comment, Constance interrupts the conversation.

"Julia, I imagine you'll want to shower after your exercise. Do you know where the extra towels are?"

"No, but that's okay. I doubt I'll need extra towels."

Aunt Lucy and Nana laugh, somehow charmed by what I've said.

"Isn't she swe-e-et!" Aunt Lucy says, and I smile back at her as she pats my hand.

"Well, I'll show you where they are just the same," Constance says. I say good-bye to the others and follow Constance up the stairs. She doesn't speak until the door to the back stairway is closed and we're in the alcove that leads up to the loft.

"I wanted to rescue you before they became morbid," she says. "I love them, but they always want to conjure up dead people in the living."

"I didn't really find it morbid," I say. "I mean, not many people have told me that I resemble Mom and Dad, at least not in a long time. Nobody in L.A. knew them."

"Well, they can get a little carried away," Constance says. "Now, if you need anything, just holler."

"Okay. Thanks," I say as I climb the stairs, somewhat resentful that Constance hauled me away from Aunt Lucy and Nana. It felt good to have some kind of connection to them and to my past.

Lately I've wished I knew someone in L.A. who was from my town, just so that I could exist in someplace other than my current sprawling environs.

Above all, I want to hear more about the presence of my parents in me. I know it's their better sides that I'm now showing—kindness and graciousness. When I was in L.A. after my father's funeral, I could feel nothing but their lesser natures. I became restless when waiting in lines, irritated by slow shopkeepers and bad drivers, constantly furious over small inconveniences—lightbulbs breaking, packages that were impossible to open. I wore myself out with rage over insignificant things.

I look in the mirror at eyes that seem more tired than wise. A mouth that rarely smiles. If I were in L.A. at my apartment, I might take the portraits of my mother and father from my desk and set them up by this mirror, trying to find vestiges of them in me. I remember what the photographs look like but still want to see their faces. I didn't bring any pictures with me. I figured I should stop carrying them around, that I should move on, yet I wish I had them now.

You never imagine that the casual snapshot, which on another day you would have thrown away, could become a crystal ball into the past. You sit and stare at the face, the expression, the scene around her, and try to relive that moment. You try to reconstruct the conversation, his reaction to being photographed, and why you took the picture to begin with. Every time I look at an old spontaneous shot, I can't help but take that journey. It has that kind of power over me. Surely, in this archival room, there exists a photo of at least my father.

I find a photo album on the top tier of the bookcase—thick, leather-bound, and old. The album contains mostly 1950s snapshots of Davis family relatives whom I don't know. There are portraits of Constance from her high school and college days. I imagine they were taken in the 1970s but have the style of the 1940s. In each one, Constance's face is posed to the left or right and is bathed in a soft, flawless studio glow. She could pass for a B movie actress, perhaps one of the teenage extras who gets devoured in *The Blob*. There are more snapshots from college—a cluster of girls wearing T-shirts with Greek letters, laughing, screaming, and surrounding Constance, who sits on a stool and has curlers the size of bowling pins in her hair. "Before" is the caption below it. The "After" picture captures Constance in a white strapless antebellum formal dress, hair piled in a curled coif, corsage on her wrist. The mystery date, perhaps Ed, slumps behind her, out of focus. She met Ed in college, but there is only one photo of him here. He's wearing a denim leisure suit, smoking a cigarette, and leaning on the hood of a black Corvette. The caption reads, "Ed and Miss Molly."

At last I find pictures of Edna, but there are none with her and my father. Instead, I find snapshots of her with her first husband, Jack Davis, who appears dapper and alert—always dressed in double-breasted pinstripe suits. Constance told me that aside from being an only son, the heir apparent of the Davis name, he was a "noted ophthalmologist." She failed to tell me another important detail: he was a hopeless drunk. That's mainly what he was noted for, according to my father. His examinations and fittings were often flawed because his own vision was either blurred or double. His binges led him to Las Vegas once or twice a year. He traveled first class, stayed in high-roller suites, and slowly crumbled into debt. He died of cirrhosis of the liver, in hock to Uncle Sam and acquaintances for about $200,000.

Dad didn't know whether Jack was physically abusive to Edna. He had witnessed their "scenes" in public before, once with Jack drunk and audibly cursing Edna at a party. Still, it wasn't his place to pry, he said. He figured Edna would reveal what she was comfortable telling. Constance ignores her father's dark side altogether, atoning for, if not erasing, his social sins by way of the DAR.

I replace the album and then look out the window toward my parents' house. Why am I staying here and not there? It's all very legal and complicated and springs from my father's largesse. His will stipulated that in the event of his death, Edna could continue to live in the house if she chose, or profits from the sale of the house and its contents would be split 70–30 between me and Edna, or, as it turns out, Constance. I'm sure his decision had to do with Ray's debts, which Edna was still paying off, and the fact that she had no savings or inheritance of her own. Perhaps he wasn't sure whether Constance would be able to take care of her.

To ensure fairness, the contents of the house are to be "parceled under legal supervision," which means we can't go near the house until an appraiser makes a list of the belongings inside. Constance and I will then "buy" items from the estate with the price of each item deducted from our respective shares. I imagine we'll probably wind up buying things that belong to each of our families. The legal business is more of a formality than anything.

Someone else might have pitched a fit over splitting the profits. But I don't want to battle over money. Right now, all I really care about is seeing his and my mothers' things. And the thought of having to wait as long as six months before everything can be appraised makes me search for alternatives. I still have my old key to the house. I don't want to take anything. I just want to look at the books, his old writing desk and dictionary stand, her paintings, without some official of death looking over my shoulder and watching me cry. Surely Constance must feel the same way. I won't ask her with all the relatives in the kitchen. There's no doubt that Eugenia wouldn't understand. She would probably accuse me of being a lawless L.A. freak. And I'm not sure whether Constance will call me humane or morbid. It will probably take me the whole day to get up the courage to ask. So I'll wait until the time is right, after everybody has left.

After showering, I get ready to go into town, packing my camera into my oversized black leather bag. I pack it against a pouch that has money, clean underwear, a T-shirt, toiletries, and granola bars. I always keep the pouch in my bag in case of earthquakes or other emergencies. In case I need to make a quick escape from someone or something.

I offer my help to Aunt Lucy and Nana in the kitchen and am

thankful when they decline. However, they do say they would be honored if I would arrange the food on the table tomorrow. I guess Constance filled them in on my illustrious career.

"You know, you never think about food styling when you see those fancy magazines. But somebody's got to do it," Aunt Lucy says.

"Yeah. It's kind of like putting makeup on movie stars," I say.

"Exactly! Only you're prettying up the food," Aunt Lucy says.

"That sure is a strange thing to do," Nana says.

"Nana!" Constance says.

"I don't mean it's bad. But, well, it's just kind of strange. You don't think of it as an occupation."

"Nana, you are insulting my guest," Constance says with mock indignation.

"No, she's absolutely right," I say. "It *is* odd, and I don't really think of it as a serious career—at least not for me."

"See there. What I said was perfectly fitting," Nana replies. She pats my hand and says to me, "You know I wouldn't insult you, honey. You're too sweet to insult."

"Well, if you don't see it as a career then why are you doing it?" Constance asks.

"Now, that's a rude question," Nana says.

Constance sighs and rolls her eyes at Nana.

"It is not, you old bug."

"Don't call me an old bug!"

"It's just my pet name for you, Nana."

"Well, I don't like it," she says moodily, resuming her duty of snapping string beans into a pot.

"I'm trying to break into photography. You've got to start somewhere. Actually, I thought I might go out and take some pictures today."

"Pictures of what?" Constance asks.

"I don't know. Whatever looks good," I tell her as I pull out my camera and aim a shot of Nana at the stove.

"Oh Lord, don't do that." She laughs and flops her apron over her head. I wait and she slowly lowers it, and I snap the shot while she giggles at me. That will be a good one.

"Since I won't be helping out until tomorrow morning, I figured I would wander around a bit," I say to Constance.

"Oh, there's lots to see. We got a brand-new mall out on Route 38, and there's the new fountain in the park, and of course the old Hayland mansion on Fourteenth Street now has the town archive and museum on the first floor," she says. "Any of those things would make a fine picture."

"Sure," I say, not intending to take any of her suggestions.

"Of course, it's kind of strange to see anyone wandering around town with a camera. I'm sure people are going to ask what you're up to."

"I'll be discreet," I reply with a laugh, but Constance doesn't return it. Something doesn't sit right with her. She knits her brow and looks out the kitchen window. I wish I could just walk away and not worry about her. But I am bound by the code.

"Are you sure I can't help with anything?" I ask.

"Well, I did have an errand that I thought you could do," Constance says. "Didn't you say something about the cemetery last night?"

Bloody hell! shout the parliamentarians. *Why didn't you leave when you had the chance? Quite right!*

"Yes, I said I didn't want to go there," I say firmly even though she knows that's what I said last night because she looked surprised when I told her.

"Well, it might be good for you to go."

"In what way?" I ask, cleaning my lens filter nonchalantly, trying to keep a civil tone in my voice.

"To have time to reflect on things."

"I've had more than enough time to reflect."

"Well, it won't take very long," Constance says. "Some of the family graves need these markers." She shows me two black wrought-iron circles attached to stakes. The markers say, Revolutionary War

Soldier 1775–1783; Recognized by the Floyd County, KY, chapter of the DAR.

"Why do you need this done today?" Aunt Lucy asks.

"Because of all the family that's coming. Some of them might want to go out to the cemetery, and I want these to be there. For many people, having a relative in the Revolutionary War is a great honor," Constance says much too stridently for any of us to disagree.

The whole idea seems ridiculous to me. Family reunions ought to be about visiting with the living. Let the glorious dead have their own party.

Sensing my discomfort, Aunt Lucy tries to rescue me. "Well, I'll take them out there if Julia doesn't want to."

"No, I need you here to help with the cooking," Constance says.

"Then I can send Eugenia out to do it," Aunt Lucy says.

"Eugenia doesn't even think our ancestors are legitimate. But they are, and I don't want to hear her try to tell me otherwise."

Constance is beginning to unravel as her eyes slowly fill up. Nana looks confused by it all, slumped over and staring deeply into her pot of beans. Nobody knows what to say, so I decide to make the sacrifice in the name of peace.

"Look, I'll go out and put up the markers. It seems like everything would be easier if I do it."

"Are you sure you don't mind?" Aunt Lucy asks.

"No, it's fine. No big deal."

Nana and Aunt Lucy exchange a glance because they know I'm lying. Constance is as unaware as ever.

"Well, I would appreciate it," she says, slightly martyred. The tears, however, are long gone. "I've been meaning to do this for a long time and just never got around to it."

She probably put it off because Rosemount Cemetery is not a fun place to visit for the living or the dead. It's on the outskirts of town, on a hilly incline that looks out over the town's steel mill— one of many industries placed at a "safe" distance from the town although the nighttime pollution from the mill makes the town streets sparkle with flecks of steel dust. The cemetery has dozens of huge oak trees, dogwoods, and lush rows of azaleas, yet it hardly evokes the peace and beauty of wilderness. Even though the mill, along with other factories in the town, has cut its operations in half, the machinery still constantly whirs, clangs, and hisses in an industrial tempest. Whistles and buzzers announce various starting and stopping times throughout the day.

The cemetery planners were probably wise to choose the steel mill location. At least it doesn't smell bad. The tannery and cobalt mill are still dreadful, and the oil refinery clouds the air with its endless smoke. I had ignored these details over the years, opting instead for the standard Kentucky image of pristine rolling hills. Behold the truth of Appalachia.

I pass the ornate wrought-iron gates and drive the steep climb to the headstones. Nothing about the place seems familiar. My father's burial occurred at the end of December, when the entire world seemed frozen and dead brown. He was to be buried next to my mother, and Edna was to go alongside Jack. So we held the graveside service on neutral ground, with the caskets on tables next to each other and away from open plots—I preferred it that way.

The service was held under a small tent to shield us from the chill and wind. The sun was brilliant that day but, like most winter suns, lent more decorative glimmer than warmth. The wind was fierce, and I wondered if it could be some kind of spiritual force generated by the two souls who weren't ready to be taken. I remembered what my father himself had told me during my mother's burial when I burst into tears with the reality of her body in a box in the ground: she's not here, he said. She's someplace else—in heaven. But she's not here.

"I don't believe in heaven," I said, still cemented in my agnostic phase.

"Then she's someplace else. Someplace beautiful or desirable to her. Her spirit isn't here."

Like my father, I've now come to believe the spirits of the dead don't linger at cemeteries if they visit or remain on earth at all. And if they do travel to places that are beautiful or desirable to them, then my father is probably gliding through the Library of Congress, and my mother is wandering the halls of the National Gallery. They met in Washington and always talked of going back there to live. And if they are not there, then they are somewhere else—but not at the Rosemount Cemetery.

Constance wrote directions to her family plot. The old stones are easy to spot by their rough-hewn texture and ornate inscriptions. I don't know what happened to the art of stone carving, not to mention the epitaph. Any decent inscription could hardly fit on the modern, utilitarian stump of polished granite.

William Thornhill Davis is the first revolutionary step-relative I come upon. The slab of stone, weathered white by time, makes the black, cursive writing easier to read:

Captain William Thornhill Davis
Age 60—Died 1806
All you that read with little care
Who walk away and leave me here
Should not forget that you must die
And face damnation
Or Heaven on high

If the captain's last name doesn't prove his relation to Constance then his attitude does—what a martyr. I place the marker and flag to the right of the stone. I had strict instructions from Constance. I find the next grave, shadowed by a towering, rectangular pillar. The pillar has urns and palm fronds carved on the sides that lead up to two gates that open to an image of the Almighty that looks like a huge sun. I deliver the goods and then read the epitaph, which is a little more friendly than the first:

> *This Monumental Stone is erected in the*
> *Memory of Maj. William Robert Hall*
> *Who died in July 1825 aged 67.*
> *He was a firm believer in the Doctrines of the Blessed Nation;*
> *Affectionate to his friends; benevolent to the needy;*
> *And his death remains greatly lamented*

My service to Constance's dead is complete, but I walk among more nineteenth-century graves, reading the inscriptions, amused by their odd mix of intimacy and pomp. Among those who died back then were: an amiable consort, a pleasant neighbor, an honest man, a respectable merchant, and an apostle of faith and freedom. I take out my camera and focus on a few of the more memorable sayings and epitaphs. I take a picture of my favorite, a small, humble stone in memory of a twenty-seven-year-old woman that reads:

> *So fades the lovely blooming flower*
> *Frail smiling solace of an hour*
> *So soon our transient comforts fly*
> *And pleasures only bloom to die.*

Almost everything does seem fleeting, and it's a wonder why I look for anything to last. Even if a person's life lasts, his memory often doesn't. I think of the one visit I took with my mother to a nursing home, not long before my grandmother mercifully died, and remember the sea of white heads in the living room. Most of their bodies were slumped in wheelchairs, and they were lined up in front of a game show broadcast on an enormous TV console in the center of the room. Although the sound was loud, no one reacted. They just stared blankly at the bright colors flickering across the screen.

At least my parents were spared the horror of growing old and losing their minds and senses. And my father, I know, did not suffer. He never even saw it coming. These are the things I hold on to.

My parents are buried just over the hill from where I stand. I could easily walk over and hold a brief vigil over their graves, seeking some kind of communion, but the gesture is pointless. Their spirits come and go as they please, and I know they are not here. They find me elsewhere—in a picture, diner, art gallery, or library—in any unsuspecting place or moment that somehow beckons the memory of them. And today, when Nana and Lucy marveled at the resemblance, that's when they found me again.

4 ♛

Tourist Attractions

In high school, before my mother got sick, my photographic palate was pleasing to the eye, inspired by Ansel Adams's many paeans to nature. I could lose myself in the tulips in Mrs. Edelman's garden or in the sunset over the hills above the Ohio River. I could turn the trees of winter into ice candy.

But I gave up the beautiful for the bizarre when she started chemotherapy, telling myself that the conflicted and disturbing moments in life were the more real and meaningful. During college, as she continued to relapse, I abandoned the misty Allegheny Mountains (along with sororities, fraternities, and the ubiquitous kegger) for depressing street scenes in nearby Washington. I tried one on-campus project, exposing a fraternity's *Deliverance*-inspired hazing ritual of hog-tying pledges in their underwear and then making them drink until they "puked like a pig," but the brothers chased me off. I forgot about photographing the dark side of Greek life but still found my fringe element of poets, painters, and musicians to run with. In the company of a like-minded friend or boyfriend, I always tried to capture the more incongruous, troubling, and real-life city moments—a homeless man passed out on the steps of the Lincoln Memorial while a Japanese tour group photographed him, an antiabortion protest turned violent, overflowing trash cans underneath a blossoming row of dogwoods during a city workers' strike.

It didn't matter if it was someone else's trouble I was photographing. Weren't we a nation of voyeurs anyway, never averting our eyes from a good blood-letting? I continued my exploration of urban malaise in Los Angeles, easy pickings since people can become so readily unhinged about being cut off on the freeway, shushed in the movie theater, and questioned by the cashier in the 10-items-or-less checkout line. There's always a scene to be shot.

I've specialized in Hollywood Boulevard—the Walk of Fame—or what my friend Claire calls the End of the World. I live a few blocks north of the Walk, in a run-down building just below the Hollywood Hills. I have taken pictures of a hooker fighting a cop while being handcuffed, an insane man screaming at an Elvis replica outside of the Wax Museum, a crying child on a leash trying to escape from his mother as she videotapes celebrity footprints outside of Mann's Chinese Theater.

I admit that when I clicked the shutter, I was just as detached as people who gawk at twisted cars on the freeway. I got the shots, calmly moved on, and felt for at least a moment that things could be worse. In the past decade, I photographed everyone's misery except my own, refusing to take a picture of any part of my former home or the cemetery or anything else that might remind me of my parents' deaths.

The truth is that I'm tired of focusing on unrest. And maybe it's the search for harmony and lighter moments that now leads me to the park where I played as a child. The Spring Fling Festival is going on, so I walk past the playground and veer left, toward the open spaces and the sounds of children screaming and laughing over the rumble of the Tilt-A-Whirl. There's also a "rocket ride" that swings back and forth until it whirls into a series of gravity-defying loops.

I hear applause and a country fiddle tune coming from the park's band shell. The noon sun is warm and it feels more like a day in early June—hopeful, with the whole summer stretched out like a canvas waiting to be painted on.

I continue through the surprisingly flush crowds toward the panels and tables in the distance that display arts and crafts by local artists. I stand among the handcrafted quilts and wood sculptures, inspecting the curved wing of a small hand-carved bird when my eye catches a brightly colored array of wooden jewelry in the next booth. I walk around the side panel and find her sitting in a lawn chair.

"Hey, Trudy."

"Well, hey, Julia. How you doing?"

"Pretty well," I say. I could leave it there but since Constance isn't around to disapprove, why not tell the whole story? "Considering I just got back from Rosemount."

"Oh," Trudy says as she folds her newspaper and places it under her lawn chair. "You were visiting your mama and daddy's graves?"

"No. I was on an errand for Constance."

"Good Lord. What kind of errand was that?"

"I had to mark a couple graves with DAR plaques for the reunion."

"I swear. She'd pull them dead people right out of the ground and set them at the table if she could."

I laugh at this and Trudy does too.

"Well, how did you wind up at the park?" she asks. "Are you on another errand?"

"No. Constance told me about the festival. Plus, I like the park. I used to play here in grade school," I say, lost in the memory of running up the hill, past the Indian Mounds, to the swings and merry-go-round and kick-ball games. It was always such a safe haven from the airless classrooms and their paddle-happy teachers who terrified me into good-girl submission. I've heard physical abuse is no longer used as a "teaching aid" in the local schools—whether the change came from enlightenment or litigation it's hard to say.

"Here," Trudy says as she unfolds a lawn chair. "Why don't you set a spell?"

"I don't want to pull you away from your customers."

"Honey, around here you have to have a Tilt-A-Whirl to get anyone's attention."

I settle into the chair as she gets up from hers to pick up a necklace that has fallen from the panel. She inspects the necklace and hangs it tenderly, turning the wooden animals so they're facing each other. She sits down and smiles at me. Finally, I tell her what I wanted to the other day.

"I really appreciate what you said about Dad."

"Well, it's only the truth. You know, after your mama passed, I seen him at the college when I talked about my art one time to a class, and he made a point of saying hello to me and thanking me again for all I done when she was alive, which wasn't that much. Anyway, I could tell he didn't care what Constance and Edna thought, and it meant the world to me."

"Was Edna mean to you, too?"

"No, but she didn't exactly have me over for tea neither. Edna always spoke nice to me, but you know. She liked to put on airs, though not as bad as Constance. And she was awful jittery. I reckon I brought that out."

"I don't know. Her first husband was an alcoholic who bullied her. My father thought it scarred her for good."

"I never knew that about him," Trudy says.

"I'm sure Constance wouldn't want people to know."

"Yes ma'am, specially me."

I don't say anything, trying not to reenter the ring of Constance-bashing. After all, I have to live with her even if it's only for a short time. So we sit in silence and listen to the blue jays squawking over something in a nearby tree. After a few moments, Trudy changes the subject.

"So how long you here for?"

"Just a few days. I suppose I'll leave after we meet with the lawyer on Monday. But I thought I would go to the house first. Technically, we're not supposed to enter it before an appraiser does, but I need to look around and just, you know, see their things again. Of course, I'm going to check with Constance first."

Trudy nods and then looks down at her table of carvings in progress. She picks up what looks like a partially formed penguin, sets it down again, and says, "Are you sure you want to bring her into it?"

"I think I have to. Just to keep things fair."

"I don't know," Trudy says faintly, shaking her head.

"What do you mean?"

"Well . . ." She stops herself, trying to find the words, and says, "I just don't want to see you get hurt."

"The most Constance can do is say no. And if she does, then I'll have to settle for seeing it with the appraiser around. I don't think it'll hurt to ask."

"You're probably right. I'm just a worrywart," Trudy says as she gets up from her chair. Some would-be customers stroll by, and Trudy says hello to them, but they keep walking. She waves a dismissive hand at them and sits down again. She eyes me for a moment and writes something down on a piece of paper.

She hands the paper to me and says, "But if you do have any kind of trouble, you call me. Or just come to the farm—anytime day or night. Either me or Harlan is always there."

"That's very kind."

"Honey, I'm not just being kind. I'm being practical. I seen how mean she can be. But I've said enough. I don't want to borry trouble. Harlan always says I'm doing that. Still, you call or come by anytime."

"Okay."

"You promise?"

"I promise," I say calmly, although the seriousness of her tone gives me a flutter of anxiety. Then again, it could be that Trudy's just been burned by her too many times.

Trudy sits back in her chair, still looking at me. I smile a bit self-consciously as her expression softens and turns sly. "Now, how about a necklace?" she says. "Oh, honey, I got one that would make you spark them L.A. boys."

"I bet you say that to all your customers."

"Course I do." Trudy digs in a box behind the panels. She holds up a necklace made of cylinders of cherrywood and white ivory beads dotted with bright hues of gold, black, and forest green. On the end is an oval scrimshaw pendant—a perfect, delicate engraving of a rose.

"It's beautiful. But I'm sure it's more than I can afford," I say.

"Well, why don't you take it anyway."

"I can't do that. I wouldn't feel right."

"I want you to have it," Trudy says as she drapes the necklace over my head. "Beautiful. It even matches your hair."

"I never thought anything could match it," I say, running my fingers through the short, straight lines of a bizarre color created by an overzealous L.A. stylist—"electric sunrise": spawned from henna, bleached red, and my own humble shade of brown.

"Thanks, Trudy."

"You're welcome. Just don't wear it in the shower," she says. "It'll wash that paint clean out."

I'm walking toward the steel-and-glass structure of my grade school, past the swings and slides, past the echoes of children playing. I wave good-bye to her again, making sure the phone number and address are in my pocket, grateful that I can still count on her. I pass between the Indian mounds and touch the pendant that rests not far from my heart, as if it were a talisman, and hope that my fortune is changing—moving away from misery and closer toward peace, maybe even belonging, as I wander through the past and present.

This year I became hooked on college basketball even though I had never watched more than twenty minutes of a game when my father tuned in. I scheduled my weekends around the games of March Madness as they lead to this weekend's Final Four, mapping the fervent progress of not only Kentucky but also of North Carolina and Duke. I suppose I watched it because I found the spectacle—the manic cheers, bold colors, and jaunty bands—strangely comforting. The sights and sounds of basketball seemed to pull me back into small-town America, cradling me in the myopic simplicity of rooting for a team. Everything else fell away for those few hours. And I remembered there were people in the world whose lives were free from grief, people who in the name of youth, sport, or alumni nostalgia were trained on only one thing: victory.

I am glad to have basketball somewhere in my brain when I walk into the kitchen and find Ed sitting at the table in the breakfast nook, slumped over a tuna sandwich and diet Coke.

"Hi there," he says. "Want some lunch?"

"Oh, no thanks," I say with a quick glance to him as I walk through the kitchen and toward the back stairs. Although I've been implored by Constance to make myself at home, I still feel like an intruder when I interrupt any ritual.

"You sure? You need to eat. And there's plenty to go around."

It's almost one o'clock, and I haven't eaten anything all day except a piece of toast. It's unlike me to forget to eat, given my profession, and I chalk it up to being preoccupied.

"Well, okay," I say as I put my bag down and head toward the refrigerator. "I am pretty hungry. Would you like another sandwich?"

"Naw, I better not. Constance has been after me about my weight. These days, three is my limit."

Ed would probably love my job. You can eat whatever we don't mutilate or spray with water or oil when the shoot is done. Of course, I never do. The thought of putting food in my mouth after I've been poking and prodding it sickens me.

Constance's refrigerator is so laden with casserole dishes, platters, and salad bowls that I have to look for a moment before I can spot the sandwiches tucked away in the back of the bottom shelf. I grab one and try to continue the small talk.

"Well, it's not easy to cut back."

"You're telling me," Ed says, frowning at his last half sandwich.

I sit down at the table, eat a couple bites, and detect sweet pickles in the tuna. I hate sweet pickles. Ed and I munch our food quietly and look at our plates. I know the silence makes him nervous because of the thin film of sweat on his upper lip that wasn't there when I sat down. So I start in.

"Too bad about Kentucky not being in the Final Four."

"Shoo-wee. I'll say. Thought for sure they'd make it—lost about fifty dollars on that deciding game. Course, you didn't hear that. If Constance found out I gambled on basketball, she'd tar and feather me."

"I won't tell."

Ed smiles at me.

"How about you?" he asks. "I bet you could find some serious gamblers in Los Angeles. Did you drop any money on the games?"

I had to smile. Did old Ed really think I was a high roller? That I'd place a few C-notes on Duke by a ten-point spread?

"I'm trying to quit," I say, which makes him laugh. "I don't know that much about basketball. I never really watched it until the play-offs this March."

"Seriously."

"I'm afraid so."

"Well, you missed some pretty great Kentucky teams."

Ed was off, unwittingly talking over my head about Rupp's Runts and the real mastery of the four-corner freeze offense and pressing defense when the Wildcats dominated college basketball in the early 1970s. He talks about why they lost to Duke this year, and I listen and nod my head, trying when I can to offer benign observations about the number of fouls called against Kentucky, Duke's aggressive offense, and the likelihood that the Blue Devils will win the title this year. Mostly, I echo what Ed says, but the conversation still delights him.

"Well, Julia, I hope you keep watching the game. You have a good eye for it."

"Maybe I will."

"Course you will," he says as he gets up and stretches. "If you're from Kentucky you can't escape it. It's in your blood."

He turns to place his dishes in the sink. I like that he's somewhat beyond Constance's reach. She dresses him in a respectable navy suit, but he still bets on basketball. She gives him tips about not picking his teeth at the table and made him quit smoking, but he still has a supply of toothpicks in this shirt pocket and a canister of snuff in his back pants pocket. I see the outline of it, and I imagine he'll take a dip from it when he's back in the office.

"Back to the salt mines," he says with toothpick-edged smile. "I'll be seeing you later."

"Okay. Thanks for the sandwich."

"Anytime. And you be sure to eat anything else in that refrigerator—even if it is for the reunion. Nobody's going to miss a few bites of something, least that's what I always say."

"Thanks, Ed."

For the first time, the offer to make myself at home feels genuine although I wouldn't dare raid any of the reunion food. It would be my luck to have Constance walk in just as I was sneaking a bite of her vegetarian delight salad—about the only thing that isn't cooked in bacon grease or slathered with mayonnaise. So I don't even open the refrigerator again. I rinse my dishes and load them into the dishwasher.

I wipe the kitchen table with a rag and notice the morning mail tucked away in the corner. I know I'm doing more than making myself at home. I know I'd be better off eating the vegetarian delight rather than snooping around Constance's mail. But I can't resist.

They are mostly bills: the phone company, Visa, Jenny Craig. I find an envelope from the Concerned Women of America, addressed to Constance Davis, Chairwoman, Floyd County Chapter. On the back of the envelope are statistics about the number of abortion clinics nationwide, the number of school districts that offer sex education, and the number of gay advocacy groups in America. Underneath, it reads, "Antifamily, anti-Christian, and antilife coalitions threaten our way of life. Now the CWA must fight for what is morally right! Let's lower these numbers and raise America's pride!"

My mother's liberal political views always balanced my father's more conservative leanings. But Edna was a different story—she was far right and had voted Republican her whole life, she said, "because all the men in her life did." When I asked her what her own preference was, she just smiled and said she didn't really have one, but that she guessed it would be Republican on account of school prayer. She believed in it wholeheartedly.

Mostly, I ignored Edna's mindless, passive politics. But the fact that Constance is a leader of the rabid right, not just a follower, alarms me. Is she one of the crazies who throw blood at women on their way into abortion clinics? Despite her genteel pretensions, I can picture Constance screaming and standing rigid in her A-line skirt, circa 1957 Little Rock, her teeth bared and tearing at hateful words. Maybe Trudy is right. Maybe I should back off from my plans to visit the house. Maybe I should meet with the lawyer and leave.

Then I find the envelope. It is the only one of the bunch that has been opened by Constance, and I am startled to recognize the stationery of Ronald Jeffries, Esq., my father's lawyer. I stare at it, start to pull the letter out, but then I think better of it. I know it's the wrong thing to do. I put the envelope back where I found it, at the bottom of the stack, and wipe down a few more counters. I sweep the crumbs off Ed's chair. I open the refrigerator again, stare into it, and shut the door. It's no use.

I rationalize that it's a test: if it's important information, she'll tell me and I can trust her about the house. I further justify my actions by imagining that the very same letter is probably waiting for me in L.A. since I know Mr. Jeffries is very efficient and thorough. Because I have never even contemplated reading someone else's mail until now, I do so with the care and precision of a CIA agent. I pull my shirtsleeves over my hands to keep from making a smudge or print. I note the angle at which the letter was left in the envelope. Just for good measure, I run to the window to make sure Constance's car is nowhere in sight. Then I pull it out and read.

The letter says that Mr. Jeffries will not be able to meet with us on Monday due to a court obligation and that the settling of the estate, i.e. the attendant paperwork and appraisals, has taken longer than he anticipated. Also, he has discovered additional assets in the form of stock owned jointly by my father and stepmother. The stock will be split evenly between the heirs, but both Constance and I must sign an enclosed form to verify ownership. He asks Constance to obtain my signature and proposes a date this summer when we can sign all the remaining documents.

Of course she'll tell me that the meeting is off, but will she tell about the rest of the letter? I place the letter back in the envelope, still knowing it wasn't right but not entirely sure that it wasn't necessary.

A minute later I hear the car pull into the garage. I pick up the rag and am swiping the counter with innocent abandon when Constance opens the door and calls, "Woo-hoo!"

"Hi, Constance."

"Oh, Julia! I am so glad you're back!"

I go to the door and relieve her of a grocery bag full of 7Up and Hawaiian Punch.

"I realized at the last minute that we had forgotten the drinks!" she says as she hobbles into the kitchen and dumps the other bag on the counter. "I have another case of pop in the car."

"I'll get it."

"Oh no! We'll let big strong Ed get that when he comes home from work. Well, how was the cemetery?"

"Oh, fine."

"Did you find the graves?"

"Yes. And I stuck the markers and flags to the right of the head-stones."

"Wonderful. Pretty impressive, don't you think?"

"They are. I think stone carving has really become a lost art."

"I mean about the people. It's impressive that the Davises have been on this land for so long, isn't it?" Constance says.

"Oh yes. That's impressive, too."

We hang suspended in another awkward moment.

"I thought maybe we could fix a few platters today," she says as she heads toward the cupboard in the hall where she keeps the trays. "Just so we don't get backed up tomorrow. Maybe the meat and cheese trays. I thought you could help if you don't mind me bossing you around a little."

How on earth do I respond to such a statement? Oh, please, do boss me around. I'm so lost without the lash of your whip. I remain silent, looking at the pile of mail with the hope that she'll follow my gaze and remember. It doesn't work.

"Okay! Why don't you start by leafing through the lettuce bin — no pun intended! I know I put some mint in there yesterday."

I rummage through at least ten firmly knotted plastic bags before discovering that there is no mint in the lettuce bin. Constance pokes her head in the fridge and says, "That's odd. I could have sworn . . . oh, here it is! It's on the condiment shelf."

Constance gets out the platter of lamb, roast beef, and ham. In my infinite wisdom, I lay the mint under and along the edges of the lamb, so that the herbs can flavor it, and put some fresh rosemary outlining the beef and ham just to balance things out. For a garnish, I cut carrots into curls and make roses out of radishes.

"That looks beautiful!" she says. "You really are good at this."

"Thanks. Of course, being good at arranging meat and cutting vegetables is a dubious distinction for a fine arts major."

"Well, it is!" Constance says genuinely, proving that either she wasn't listening or the word "dubious" isn't often used in bodice-ripping romance novels or unauthorized biographies of movie stars. I don't know how long I can sustain the chatter and contemplate saying something like, "Boy, I'd rather be manicuring vegetables than signing legal documents."

"I can't believe everybody's going to be here tomorrow," she says. "It'll be a busy day, but I think we're ready. And then on Monday we have . . . oh, my goodness. I didn't tell you yet."

At last! She tells me everything, showing me the letter. I pretend to listen and read, but can only think of how relieved and grateful I am that Constance passed the test—although I feel somewhat ashamed that I doubted her. I make a silent vow never to be dishonest with her or anyone again. She may have differences with Trudy and me, but at least she can respect the wishes of the dead.

"I am so sorry because I know it's an inconvenience for you to come all the way back down here," she says.

"It's okay. Maybe Mr. Jeffries and I can work out some arrangement so that we can do everything by mail. I don't know. We'll work it out."

"Absolutely. And you know, it's better this way because everything, except for these papers, will be signed all at once," Constance says. "It'll probably take them until the end of summer to get everything together."

After we finish cutting and arranging, we sit down to sign the documents. Constance takes out a Mont Blanc fountain pen from her purse, dabs its nib with a Kleenex, and smiles at me.

"I just love fountain pens. Ed gave me this one for my birthday last month. He couldn't believe how much it cost, but I told him it was the only thing I wanted. I figured if I was going to be signing all these papers, I might as well do it with style."

I watch the dance of hand and pen as she makes her capital letters swirl and tower above the illegible scrawl of the rest of her name. It's a celebrity signature, as stylish and grand as they come.

I take my turn and then say, "Well, I guess that's it."

"For now. They'll be a lot more papers to sign before we can settle the estate."

"Right," I say, thinking I had better ask now while we're on the topic. "I had a question about the estate. Well, it's not at all about the estate, really. In fact, it has nothing to do with it."

Constance gives me an exaggerated look of confusion, scratching her head and making a goofy sitcom face. I get to the point.

"I'd like to go inside the house before the appraiser does."

Her expression is neither disapproving nor enthusiastic. As far as I can tell, it's somewhere between curious and amused. Her eyebrows, plucked and honed to tadpole shapes, raise a bit and she blinks her eyes once.

"I don't want to touch anything or move anything. All I want to do is just look at the place without a stranger standing over my shoulder," I say.

"Well, you're going to have to touch a few things," Constance says with a coy smile. "You're going to have to touch the doorknob to get in."

"No, I mean . . . you know what I mean. I don't want to take anything from the house. I just want to look at it before it begins to change, before people start tagging things and talking about what they're worth. I just want to take the time to remember. I know it's technically illegal, but would you mind if I went in?"

Constance looks at me as she licks the envelope and then averts her eyes as she seals it. She pauses a moment and then faces me squarely, putting a hand on my shoulder.

"Of course I wouldn't mind. And I didn't mean to make light of it. The fact is it doesn't matter whether going in the house is legal or not. What matters is that you do what you need to while you're here."

"I'm so glad you feel that way," I say.

"Of course I do. In fact, I'd like to go too if you wouldn't mind."

She has as much right as I do to see the house. After all, her mother's things are there, too. So I say, "That would be fine. I just don't want strangers around."

"I agree. It's a very personal time, and I think it will be a very healing time."

I look at her and smile, nodding my head. Once again, her eyes begin to well with sudden, mysterious tears. I know better than to try to find their origins with condolences or tender inquiries — and after what I did with the letter, I don't exactly feel worthy of her trust. So I simply touch the arm that now encircles my shoulders, as if to say, whatever it is, I understand. She looks away, pats me on the back, and then walks to the sink where she turns on the faucet full blast and rinses out the rag from the table.

She faces me, cheery again, and says, "Well. We have a big day tomorrow. I've got to get the vacuum going now that the food is done."

"I think it will be a great reunion," I say, still riding the wave of charity.

"I hope so," she says as she hefts the monstrous machine out of the closet.

"Let me know if I can help with anything else," I say as I head up the stairs.

"All righty."

The words follow me up the stairs and linger in my mind, carefree and warm, like sunlight that slips miraculously through dark, stormy clouds.

5 ♛

The Final Four

8:00 A.M. on Saturday morning and the first thing I hear is a thudding sound outside my window. I part the curtains and see Constance in the driveway, surrounded by patio furniture cushions on the ground. Raising a tennis racquet over her head with both hands, she swats the dust out of the fat, flowered shapes. I watch as she spins herself in a slow circle, like some crazed mechanical doll escaped from its place in a German clock tower. With each hit, she knits her eyebrows and clenches her jaw—like she's trying to kill the cushions instead of clean them. It's overcast and I wonder if she's venting her anger about having a sunless sky on her special day.

I promised her I would be downstairs by 9:00 to help the food brigade. I shower and throw on a drop-waisted T-shirt dress—long-sleeved with a jewel neck. It's the dressiest thing I brought.

I had intended to wear it to the lawyer's office. The color is jade and goes perfectly with my new necklace.

After I make my bed and put away my suitcase in the closet, I walk down the front staircase and am stunned by the antiseptic grandeur of living and dining rooms—cleanliness that almost upstages godliness, an immaculate reception. The French provincial tables shine under their coat of lemon-scented wax. The rose carpet still holds its wide, vacuumed ribbons of welcome. And everywhere, in centerpieces and bud vases, are arrangements of orchids, gardenias, lilies, snapdragons, and pink roses. Constance must have been up at 4:00 A.M. to create such a presentation.

I walk into the swirl of kitchen activity, which momentarily stops with my arrival.

"Don't you look pretty!" Aunt Lucy says.

"She looks like an angel!" Nana says.

Constance stops chopping tomatoes to look at me. "That is a fabulous color on you! Not everybody can wear that color. I know I can't."

Even Eugenia pokes her head from behind the morning paper to say, "Great dress." I'm not used to such attention and am embarrassed by it, but maybe slightly pleased. It's been a long time since I was complimented on how I looked in a dress. I smile but avert my eyes from them, feeling a bit breathless and nervous as they admire me.

"And look at that necklace," Nana says as she moves toward me. "That's a pretty thing." She fingers the necklace and takes her glasses off to inspect the beads. "I reckon it's handmade."

"Yes, it is," I say.

"Where did you get it?" Constance asks as she starts chopping again.

"A friend of mine gave it to me."

Aunt Lucy winks at me. "A friend? What kind—male or female?"

"Now, don't you pry, Lucy," Nana warns.

"Female," I say. "A very kind woman."

Constance hands me a full-length apron and says, "You need to put this on so you don't mess up those pretty things."

"Thanks," I say as I tie on the apron, eager to focus the attention elsewhere. "Constance, the house looks beautiful."

"Well, thank you!" she sings, drawing the "thank you" out from high to low pitch.

"Okay, Constance. Eugenia and I are going home to change and then we'll be back to heat up the barbecue," Aunt Lucy says.

"All right. But try to be back no later than eleven o'clock. I told everybody to get here around eleven-thirty and that lunch would be at twelve-thirty."

We say our good-byes to them, and I turn to Constance.

"So how can I help?"

Constance debriefs me. When the time comes, I will help her supervise the order of how the foods are placed on the table. I think she figures food styling also gives me knowledge of catering, but I don't protest. I keep playing along, trying to remain supportive.

"I'm ready to layer the Mexican nacho dip," Constance says. "My main dilemma is what to do about these olives that my cousin Henry from Mt. Olive gave me this Christmas. I want to use them but don't know how."

"I didn't know they made olives in Mt. Olive," I say.

"They don't. It's a biblical name. But he likes to give olives as gifts anyway."

"Oh."

"The problem is that they're stuffed with garlic," Constance says and makes a grotesque face, as if the olives were stuffed with meal worms.

"They're actually considered a delicacy. I mean, if you like garlic," I say.

"Well, that's just it. Henry's a garlic lover, but nobody else is. I know I'm not."

I decide against informing Constance that I adore garlic-stuffed olives.

"I think the olives just need something else besides garlic, you know? I was thinking cream cheese might be good, but I don't know how you could serve it," she says.

"If you have something like a frosting bag, you could soften the cream cheese and squeeze it on or around the olives," I say.

"Ooo, sounds yummy," Nana says.

Constance nods her head and stares for a moment above her, like she's choreographing some intricate dance and is trying to work in my suggestion.

"Yes. That will work. If you can find something to squeeze with. Yes. Great."

She turns back to her Mexican dip preparations and I set about my task. The best I can find is a gravy syringe. I zap the cream cheese in the microwave and take my project into the dining room to begin work. Constance pops in after five minutes.

"How's it going?"

"Fine, I think. Care to sample one?"

"Oh, I would if it weren't for that garlic," she says with another facial contortion. "I thought you might be able to do something with these pimentos. I don't know what, but I thought they might add a little extra taste and color."

She hands me the jar, and I tell her it's a perfect touch. The very thing these olives needed along with garlic and cream cheese.

"Well, I'll leave you to it," she says.

I give it my best effort. Since they're large and heavy enough to lean on each other and stand upright, I make four clusters of olives and place them at the corners of the tray. In the center, I place the remaining olives, outlined by a swirling cream cheese and pimento design so that people have the option to dip. On the sides I place red-leaf lettuce for decoration, along with a few cream cheese sconces, just enough for a little flair.

The process takes me about a half hour. I carry the tray into the kitchen and set it on the breakfast table, next to Nana. She looks up from the pie she's slicing and gasps.

"What a beautiful creation! We should take a picture of that. Constance! Come here and bring the camera."

Constance rushes in, ripping the disposable camera out of its package, and says, "Is someone here already?"

"No. I want you to take a picture of what Julia made. Look at it. Isn't it stylish?"

"Yes," Constance says. She puts down the camera. "It's, well, it's quite unique."

"I hope I didn't overdo it," I say.

"Oh no! I think it will add . . ." She pauses, searching, and then lights upon an idea. "I think it will add some history to the proceedings."

"Do what?" Nana says.

I'm just as puzzled as Nana, but I let her do the talking.

"I see history in this," Constance says.

"How do you mean?" Nana asks.

"Because, well, you all might think I'm a bit eccentric, but it looks like a battlefield to me."

"Constance! That's hardly a thing to say!" Nana cries.

"It's a compliment, Nana. Look here."

Constance quickly explains about how the olive clusters could be forts, and the cream cheese and the pimientos in the center represent the swirl of fighting.

At this point, I think Constance is more than eccentric. I think she's chugging around the loony bend on the DAR express.

"Fine," Nana says. "Whatever. I still think it's a lovely tray of olives. Nothing more than that."

"Oh, Nana the naysayer! I bet Julia can see it. Can't you see it, Julia?"

"I'm not sure. I mean, what battle are you talking about?"

"It doesn't have to be that specific," Constance says. "It could take place anytime in history. We could say it's during the Revolutionary War or the Civil War."

"You might need some miniature burning oil wells if you want to make it the Gulf War," Nana says as she takes her apron off and walks to the door.

"How amusing. Are you gonna go on the *Tonight Show*?" Constance asks her.

"Never know when I'm gonna go," Nana says as she walks out the door.

"Well, good-bye, then, you old bug," Constance says.

She waves good-bye in the air without turning around and says, "Don't call me that." She takes one step at a time as she makes her way down the side steps. I watch her from the window and smile.

"That Nana," Constance mutters as she positions her Mexican dip in the cramped refrigerator.

"She's a character," I say lightly.

Constance replies with nothing but "Mmmm," a dead-end sound that says, Don't get me started. She closes the door carefully and resumes her cause. "So, would you mind if I put little American flags in your olive forts?"

"That would be great," I say because I know better than to disagree with Constance today. With her, I must choose battles wisely—historical and otherwise. On this day, Constance seems more like a New York cabby than a perennial debutante. The cabby turns down a one-way street, but you don't stop him because he's underpaid, frustrated, and maybe doesn't have much to live for. Nobody's going to tell him how to drive. So you pray that the traffic yields for you, that people will understand, and that the road is a short one.

"Ed, I'm not going to let you hide down here, watching those basketball games. You're the host. You need to be upstairs to greet everybody," Constance says as she follows him up the basement stairs. I'm in front of the hall linen closet, fetching the linen tablecloth with the eyelet lace.

"All right. But I'm going to pop back down after lunch," he says.

"No. You cannot."

"Constance, some people might want to watch the game," Ed says. "Don't you think it would be rude if they wanted to watch and you said no?"

"I doubt that anybody will make such a request," she says.

It sounds like things might turn ugly, so I make my presence known.

"Found it!" I say, holding it up to Constance. "Do you want me to iron it before I put it on the table?"

"I ironed it yesterday. You can lay it out as is."

I walk into the dining room, but the swinging door is open and I can still hear the fight.

"Look, it's the Final Four. It's *the* competition of the season. I know people will want to watch," Ed says.

"No, they won't. Kentucky's not even in it."

"Fine. But if they ask, I'm not going to say, 'Constance says no.' If people want to watch the game, I'm going to invite them to it."

"Okay, Ed. But you better not bring it up in conversation."

"But—"

"In all fairness, you let them bring it up. I don't want it spoiling my reunion. So we'll leave it up to the guests. Don't you say a word."

Constance goes out the kitchen door that leads to the garden. I look out the kitchen window and see her clipping a few jonquils for yet another arrangement. Ed stares into the open refrigerator.

"Hell, she's got enough food in here for ten reunions," he says.

I drop my voice to a whisper. "Do you have any bets going on the games?"

He looks at me and then back to the food, nodding his head dejectedly. "North Carolina by five. About one hundred bucks. But last I looked they were trailing Kansas by twelve in the fourth quarter."

"Maybe they'll make a comeback."

"Lord, they better. I've got some money on the second game this afternoon, too. Not that watching will make them play any better. But I want to be able to talk about it, be in on the action," Ed says.

"Well, maybe someone at the party will want to watch."

"I hope so," Ed says and starts up the stairs when Constance returns with the flowers.

"Don't wander off, Ed. We might need you to haul some things around."

"That's me, honey. Your sweet beast of burden."

"Go on, silly," she says to Ed and then smiles at me.

Constance and I set up the food around the table. She decides where things go. And when she asks me, "Don't you think that's right?" I reply, "Absolutely." Everything is ready—the drinks are chilled, Aunt Lucy's stirring the barbecue, the casseroles are being heated. The house scent alternates between cooking smells, lemon wax, and White Shoulders perfume. It's a picture of taut, preparty perfection, and Constance shuffles at the starting gate. Flushed with excitement, she glances out the window, checks on the food, and smoothes the creases of her white apron and royal blue silk dress. At one point, she looks at me and says, "It's so thrilling!"

So it is something of a false start for Constance when the first guest to arrive is her cousin Henry from Mt. Olive. Pudgy and graying, he appears older than Constance, somewhere in his forties, yet is dressed in collegiate style: wrinkled khakis and a thin yellow button-down that reveals the bold blue lettering of his undershirt: Go Wildcats! She introduces him to me and then shows him what we did with his olives. Constance tells him about it being a culinary representation of a Revolutionary War battle, but all he can do is pick up an olive, inspect it, and say, "Huh." He doesn't even eat it.

"Won't you try one?" Constance asks.

"No, thank you. I'll wait. Say, do you mind if I watch the ball game?"

Constance has the smile of a marionette frozen on her face as she says, "Fine." She looks down at the olives and then at me, still smiling. "Julia can show you where the TV is. I'll be busy in the kitchen," she says and vanishes through the swinging door.

I can't help but feel sorry for Constance. That the Final Four would be turned on was inevitable, but I thought people at least would have waited until after lunch.

I walk Henry to the TV room, and he says, "I drove down here with one of them little TVs on my dashboard. I pert near wrecked cause I was watching so close." He thanks me, declines a drink, and zeros in on the game with the remote control, oblivious to all else.

Back in the kitchen, Nana has returned and consoles Constance as she breaks the shells of two dozen hard-boiled eggs. It was decided at the last minute that we needed some deviled eggs.

"It won't spoil everything. There's something like a two-hour break between the games anyway, so we can all visit during lunch," she says.

"That's right. And not everybody will watch the games," Aunt Lucy says.

"I know I won't," Eugenia adds.

They wait for Constance's response as she continues breaking eggs in stoic silence. When she places the last slimy oval in the bowl, she rinses her hands and then sighs dramatically.

"Sometimes I don't even know why I try," she says. Nana hands her a towel and she wipes her hands. "It's not that I hate basketball. I am very proud of basketball. But this is my day—my family's day. Can't they just tape it?"

"You would think," Aunt Lucy says.

"Well, with the play-offs, everybody wants to see the game as it happens. Nobody wants to be left out," Nana says.

Constance isn't listening. She has her head buried in the refrigerator and is searching for mayonnaise. "Don't tell me we're out," she says. "I can't believe we're out." She looks in the cupboard and comes up empty. "Damn."

"I'll go to the store and get some," I say. "I'll be back in a flash."

It's about eleven-twenty when I spring myself from the house. When I return at eleven-fifty, four cars are in the driveway and the festivities have begun. I walk into the kitchen just as an unfamiliar man's voice says, "Don't you know what a shroud is?"

The old man must be about a hundred years old. He has the manner and appearance of a snowy egret—very fine white hair, a thin, angular face, eyes that are twitchy and serious. He leans on his cane in the kitchen but still towers over Clay and Candy, whose stunned faces reveal a mix of confusion and abject terror.

"They lay you out on a cold marble slab, and then they put a shroud over you," the old man says as he continues to stare intensely at the pair.

"Hi, there. I'm Julia Daniel," I say as I walk into the room. He sticks out a claw, all bone and knuckles, and I shake it. His grip is surprisingly strong.

"Jefferson Harris from Lexington," he says. "I was just telling these younguns what a shroud is. I'm gonna have somebody make me a shroud before I die, so's I can be laid out proper."

"That's a good idea," I say and then turn to Clay and Candy. "Can you guys run out and tell your mom I'm back?" They dart away without saying a word.

He eyes me suspiciously. "You know what a shroud is, don't you?"

"Yes, like in the Odyssey, when Penelope weaves a shroud for Laertes."

He doesn't make the connection and asks, "Where are you from?"

"Los Angeles."

"Los Angeles? What in the world are you doing here?"

Constance comes in and says, "Uncle Jefferson! This is my stepsister, Julia Daniel."

"Oh," he says, a bit subdued. "Well, I'm going back to watch the basketball game."

After he hobbles away, Constance explains that her great uncle is ninety-eight years old and a bit eccentric. I would call him senile but opt for a less confrontational remark.

"I got the mayonnaise."

"Oh, that's great. While I fix the eggs you can pass the Mexican nacho dip," Constance says.

Aside from Ed, Uncle Jefferson, and Henry, everyone is out on the porch. Aunt Lucy hovers around them, bearing a silver tray with glasses of red punch and white wine. I circulate among the strangers with the dip, explaining its contents as I go. I see a woman wearing a lavender-and-gold silk sarong with a matching silk blouse—by far the most exotic attire. She bears a striking resemblance to Aunt Lucy, and I figure she must be Constance's aunt Jessica from Lexington. She was the one who married well—a millionaire owner of a local video store chain who got his start in the fertilizer business. I offer her some dip.

"Why, thank you. What's in it?" she says in the same breath.

"Guacamole, sour cream, refried beans, black olives, and tomatoes."

"Sounds delicious." She takes a chip, scoops up a healthy dollop, and bites it daintily. She then stares at me under her knitted eyebrows as if to say, how good, how sinfully good. She eats the rest in one bite and holds up her index finger as she finishes chewing to keep me from leaving.

"I can't resist. This is wonderful," she says as she scoops another chip into the bowl.

It's a bit awkward, standing there watching her chew, so I take a breath and say, "I'm Julia Daniel—Constance's stepsister."

She holds up her finger again.

"Nice to meet you. I'm Constance's aunt Jessica. My, that is good. Cheryl, did you try some of this?"

Jessica reaches past me to grab the arm of a teenage girl who looks as out of place as I feel. She has spiked platinum hair and wears cutoffs, a black spaghetti-strap tank and matching blouse, purple Converse sneakers with no socks, and a nose ring. I expect Jessica to introduce Cheryl, but Jessica's expression hardens when she sees her.

"Take off that nose ring this minute," Jessica whispers fiercely to Cheryl.

"Mom, it's who I am." She sneers as she fingers it and looks at the dip.

"Not for today. Now, we have been over this before. You will take it off right now." Jessica still has a grip on Cheryl's arm. Cheryl rolls her eyes and scoffs audibly. But she relents and tugs the ring from her nose.

"There. Are you happy? Am I socially acceptable now?"

"It's a start," Jessica says.

Cheryl pulls her arm away and takes her turn with the dip, cramming a laden chip into her mouth.

Jessica watches her chew and then asks, "Isn't that good?"

"It's all right," Cheryl says with a shrug.

Jessica sighs and looks at me. "Teenagers," she says.

Suddenly, Cheryl covers her head with her arms as if she's in an air raid. "Mom, I hate it when you say that. It's like I'm not a person. It's like I'm this category."

"Don't say 'like,'" Jessica says, which prompts another guttural sound of disgust from Cheryl. "Have another chip."

"I don't want another," Cheryl says.

"Have you met Constance's stepsister?"

"No."

"Then let me introduce you," Jessica says and then proceeds with the lesson.

"Hi," Cheryl says as she looks over my shoulder. "Oh, there's Jenny. Oh my God. Uncle Jefferson is trying to talk to her. I better save her. See you later."

Jessica shakes her head and munches another chip as she watches Cheryl run off.

"All the drugs and MTV and what-not in society," Jessica says. "You send them away to the East for boarding school, and they still come back looking trashy and swearing and saying everything 'sucks.' Only without the southern accent. I couldn't get over how quick Cheryl turned Yankee. Her accent was gone after the first semester. For Christmas, as a joke, I gave her this book called *How to Talk Southern*. Course she didn't think it was funny."

"I know how that goes. I went to boarding school too," I say.

"Oh, really. Where?"

"Stilton Academy in Massachusetts."

"Milton?"

"No, Stilton."

"Never heard of that one," Jessica says.

"It was small."

"Uh-huh. We sent Cheryl to Andover." Like her daughter, Jessica eyes the crowd beyond my shoulder. I've gotten that kind of response many times from the set that measures existential worth by educational pedigree. Not that I really care that Stilton is a name better associated with a blue-veined cheese than a well-heeled school. In truth, aging cheese sort of captures the gestalt of the place since most of the faculty had been there for over twenty years and prided themselves on their aversion to change. But I don't tell her any of this, nor do I hold her hostage with small talk. I simply say it was nice to meet her and excuse myself to the kitchen.

After my encounter with Jessica, I don't bother introducing myself to anyone else. I just let them think I'm the caterer as I pass around different trays of food. Things are easier that way. If people ask, I'll tell them who I am. But I don't see the point of trying to chat with people I will never see again, people who are cousins of cousins who probably never even knew that Edna remarried.

By twelve-thirty, everyone has gotten a plate of food and sits either in wrought-iron chairs on the terrace or on blankets on the lawn. There must be about forty people all together. Constance doesn't sit down to eat, but she has been intercepting food all day in the kitchen. I saw her wolfing down a barbecue sandwich when I was helping Nana refill the various casserole and vegetable dishes. On the terrace she eats not a crumb, opting to flutter about "her people" and make sure they've got enough to eat. She chats gaily, smiles insatiably, and strikes cheerful poses—arms akimbo, her head tilted back by peals of laughter.

But I can tell that a few people talk beyond the surface of things, giving embraces and sad-eyed expressions, no doubt offering condolences about her mother's death. Perhaps that's what enabled

Constance to do something I hadn't expected her to do. Before dessert, while everyone was still digesting or, like Ed, still grazing, Constance went to the center of the terrace and called for everyone's attention.

"Heaven knows I don't want to stop y'all from eating—there's tons of food left—but I just wanted to say how wonderful it is to have my family here today. I so appreciate you all coming here for this special day. But I know the reunion wouldn't be complete if I didn't ask you to raise your glasses to two people we still miss and love so much: Edna Davis and Sam Daniel. I believe they're here with us, and I know having you all here—and having Julia here, all the way from crazy L.A.!—I know that's what brings them back to me. So here's to Edna and Sam—and to all of you."

Constance sips from her punch, and everyone follows her lead. Nana dabs her eyes, and I feel myself start to follow suit. Who knew that Constance would actually acknowledge her grief so openly? And even though I'm not related to any of these people, I feel for a moment that I am. Someone, maybe Ed, starts applauding and yells out, "Here's to you, Constance." And everyone cheers. Constance takes a dainty half curtsy, and I watch her laugh and wipe away—at last—a few tears.

But the moment of gracious recognition soon fades. Constance asks me to "load a few dishes in the washer," and I spend about a half hour plowing through the piles. I go to the bathroom upstairs and am walking down the hall when I hear voices underneath a window. I watch as they all pose for a picture. I hear Nana's faint voice saying, "Where's Julia?" But the timer is set and they huddle close together for the shutter's snap. They say cheese. Uncle Jefferson says whiskey.

I'm still up to my elbows in soap when Nana finds me in the kitchen.

"Where were you for the picture?" she asks.

"In here."

"Well, shoot. You should have been in it."

"It's okay. I like taking pictures more than I like being in them," I say lightly. Never mind, I think. Constance probably just got caught up in the moment.

She walks in just then, and Nana turns an angry eye toward her.

"Constance, why has Julia been doing most of the work in the kitchen?"

"She hasn't been doing most of the work."

"We're all out there getting our picture made, and she's stuck back here washing dishes."

"Nana, I don't have time for this," Constance says as she hauls more coffee cups from the cupboard.

"I don't mind helping out," I say.

"See? Julia likes being in the kitchen, and why shouldn't she? Food is her specialty," she says with a little smile toward me.

"She should be meeting people," Nana says angrily. But Constance swings out of the kitchen door without saying a word.

"I swear. I don't care how nice her speech was. Sometimes that girl shocks me," Nana says, shaking her head as she shuttles plates of pie to the dining room table.

It's two o'clock and people have gathered in smaller groups to digest. A few families lie on the blankets. Constance and her aunts are on the terrace. The children are playing horseshoes in the side yard, and most of the men are clustered around the television set for the game between Duke and Indiana. Uncle Jefferson is upstairs resting, having overexerted himself by trying to lift a fallen branch that was obstructing the patch of yard set aside for the children's games. Despite shouts of warning from Constance, Nana, and others, Uncle Jefferson flashed his dentured, impish grin and defied mortality and reason by tugging on the branch until he lost his footing and fell backward. The younger men rushed to help him up. He said he was fine, but then quietly excused himself for a nap. Nana had also stretched out, exhausted from her food preparation.

By four-thirty, everyone who is leaving has left. There have been waves of contingents piling into their cars, taking last-minute pictures, promising to write. I asked Constance why people weren't staying longer, and she said one-day reunions were all anyone had time for, including herself. I think one day is probably all people can stand before they run out of things to say to each other. After his nap, Uncle Jefferson was his usual spirited self. When Nana dabbed her eyes after kissing him good-bye, he said, "Don't go crying over me, girl. I ain't dead yet." Then he elaborated again on the specifications for his shroud.

Constance's aunt Jessica and her bilious daughter have decided to stay overnight. Not that I was in on the conversation. I found out when Cheryl began to wail about why she didn't want to stay, that she had a date tonight, that it wasn't fair. Jessica assured her that she could use Constance's phone to call her "beau." All Cheryl said before slamming the door of the other guest room was, "This stupid reunion sucks!"

I'm in my room reading the April edition of *Mangia!* that I was amazed to find in the supermarket. I didn't know our circulation reached this far and asked the manager about it. He told me that one of his customers kept requesting the magazine.

"A tall, thin man? Late sixties?"

That was the one, he said, though he couldn't remember his name. I thought about telling him my father's name but was too preoccupied with the revelation. I never imagined Dad to be the secret admirer type and was moved to think that he would pester the manager into stocking the publication. Whenever we talked about my career, it was clear that he thought there were more important things to life than food.

"If you want to take pictures, why not get out of the studio. Work for *Time* or *Newsweek* or a news service like Reuters or UPI. You could see the world."

"I don't want to see the world, at least not like that. Do you know how grueling those jobs are? You have to be willing to go anywhere at a moment's notice."

"Sounds like the military."

"It *is* like the military."

"That's not all bad."

"For you, but not for me."

He paused a moment, looking away from me and smiling.

"I know you'd rather follow your muse. That was your mother's way, too." His no-nonsense gaze wasn't gone for long. "But I just don't want you to get lost doing it. I want you to find your way and make your mark. And you have to ask yourself, can I really do that by fiddling with food?"

I joked, "A pastry chef swirled my initials on top of a coconut soufflé in our feature on tropical desserts. Does that count?"

"Very funny," he said. But neither of us laughed.

Back then I didn't say it, but I wondered why he was so concerned about my venturing into the world to make that elusive mark. So that I could provide a return on the educational investment? So that I could be both financially secure and socially impressive? So that something would be left of me when it was my turn to die? My mother's artwork made its way into galleries in Kentucky, Cincinnati, and Washington, D.C. But that didn't protect her from being forgotten too quickly by him after she died. Maybe he just felt more compelled to push me since he was the only parent left to do it. But those kinds of conversations always managed to push me away instead of forward.

I start to thumb through the pages and the memory of February's work returns. I never know when a certain shoot will appear, except if it has a holiday theme. As usual, the magazine gives a religious nod to April and this year the cover article is entitled: "Luscious Lambs and Beautiful Briskets—Making the Most of Your Holiday Table." Aside from the lamb's rosemary glaze that didn't have enough sheen, the shoot was easy since there were fewer props on account of the platters and because I knew the process so well. It's the same routine for turkeys, chickens, and other roasted meats: blowtorch the carcass so the meat doesn't pull away from the bone, paint it with a mixture of bitters, motor oil, barbecue sauce, or whatever else is needed to give it just the right appetizing tone and shimmer—pretty straightforward and trouble-free.

But nobody knows the drama behind more frilly dishes. I glance over photos of "Pastas from Around the World" and remember a fussy chef and the great debates over Italy's lemon shrimp and basil linguini—how much oil to use on the noodles so that they were maneuverable yet not overly greasy and whether to use dollops of actual goat cheese or the more heat-friendly Crisco. Morocco's couscous infuriated the editor with a delay resulting from the chef's inability to find any cardamom seeds for the spice mixture. "Who the hell cares?" Sally said. "We're just photographing it, not serving it to the Moroccan ambassador." The worst, however, was the Nova Scotia angel hair, which I had to reset seven times on account of a tomato puree (laced with ketchup) that refused to keep its star shape after being injected into the tarragon cream sauce on the salmon. A sweaty spread on holiday havarti required four applications of spray deodorant to slow down the cheese's demise under the lights. The sidebar on bacon-wrapped delicacies was a greasy, nauseating mess.

The thought of such tedium reminds me of something I wasn't able to tell my father before he died: that he was right. *Mangia!* isn't a place for me to make my mark; it's a place to make, at best, very little money. That became clear when Sally passed me over for the photography job.

Right before I came to Kentucky, quitting was all I could think about, and Claire had a hard time talking me down off the ledge.

"The way we define the world by food is so ridiculous. It's indulgent to the point of being grotesque," I said as we were bent over the lighting table, peering at pictures of a meringue/shaving cream nightmare called Chocolate Mousse Seduction, a prop-heavy shoot that I styled with opera glasses, Don Giovanni sheet music age-stained with coffee, a gold-rimmed faux china teacup with a swirling, ornate handle—all set against a backdrop of lush red velvet. I would have preferred a simpler design—a satin ribbon, a candle, elegant red roses. But Sally wanted the shot to convey a lifestyle of opulence, grandeur, and conspicuous, seductive consumption.

"You're taking yourself far too seriously," Claire said as she looked at me through the loupes of magnifying glasses that rendered her bug-eyed. When I didn't laugh, she let them drop into her hands and followed me into the food preparation studio. "Food offers escape from the world, which everybody needs at one time or another. And the advantage of working here is that food is always in style. It's always acceptable as a conversation topic. It has glamour. It's safe."

"I'm tired of being safe," I said as I pulled squares of key lime Jell-O and a bowl of lemon-raspberry curd out of the refrigerator.

"What do you want to do? Be a war correspondent?" she said.

"You know that's not what I want," I said, a bit stung because I had talked to her about my problems with my father and his military worldview. I stopped talking and concentrated on the task of building a Jell-O pyramid. Sally wanted childhood whimsy for this one.

"I know," Claire said. "But right now I think you're better off staying put. You need people around you to support you, people who know you and love you."

"The way Sally loves me?"

"You know I'm not talking about her," Claire said.

"The problem is I can't stop thinking about my father and what he said about the job. It *is* a waste of time. I feel that way more than ever. Maybe leaving would be a way of honoring him and what he wanted for me."

"Sorry, but I don't think he'd be very honored by your collecting unemployment," Claire said.

"I'd get another job."

"Are you sure about that? This isn't New York. Sometimes you have to look for months to get a staff position, and freelancing is totally unstable. I know you've been sending your portfolio out to places and hustling to find something else, but I really don't think you should leave until another job comes through."

I stopped construction, wiped my hands on a dish towel, and sighed.

"You're right. I know you're right. But then I think about this shoot coming up on cool summer drinks—spending hours on end talking about backgrounds, and props, and where's the sun in this shot, and you need more corn syrup on the glass to create condensation. It's just not what I've been trained to do. Sometimes I think I would be better off freelancing or even taking stills for a production company. At least I would be working with the living."

Claire dug her hand into a bowl of Jell-O squares, lifted a pile to my face, and said gravely, "Julia, you can't tell me this isn't alive. Look at it. It sways. It undulates. It breathes, Julia!"

I laughed and finally stopped arguing with her, content in that moment to follow Claire into the escape hatch of silliness and ignore my professional angst. But whenever I leaf through the latest issue and relive all the bizarre gastronomic manipulations and tribulations, the dread finds me again.

So it's a welcome diversion when Constance knocks and enters my room simultaneously, still wired from the festivities. She tells me how much she appreciates my help, and that everyone was so complimentary of me. I start to remind her that I didn't meet many people but decide to hold my tongue.

"So you were pleased with the way things went?" I ask her.

"It was better than I ever imagined! I think everyone was so impressed with the house and the food of course. Some folks hadn't even seen the house until today and couldn't get over how elegant it is. And all the adults got caught up with each other, and the children played well together. Even the timing for the basketball game was perfect. Oh, and I told people to stop by the graves on their way out of town, but I don't know whether they will."

"You never know. They might get inspired."

"That's right! You never know," she says as though she's won an argument. She adjusts the books in the case, from where I had pulled out the photo album, and then continues her evaluation of the day. "The only slight disturbance was Uncle Jefferson's fall, but that was to be expected. He always does something foolish when he's around people, trying to show off how strong he is for his age."

"It's funny. He does that but then talks about his shroud," I say.

Constance seems suddenly exasperated by my remark and says, "Oh, don't remind me. I think he scared Clay and Candy half to death talking about that."

I laugh, but Constance remains silent. She walks over to the window and looks out. "You can see the house from here pretty well," she says.

"Yes, you can."

"Well, why don't we go over there?"

I'm surprised by the abrupt suggestion, thinking Constance would be tired out by the party, but I would just as soon go now rather than wait until tomorrow. I might even be able to get a flight back to L.A. tomorrow although right now the idea sounds as tenable to me as cardamom seeds did to Sally. Still, being back amid the city's activity might do me good. Maybe I can spend the rest of my leave looking even more intently for a job that I wouldn't want to quit.

"Okay," I say as I put down the magazine and pick up my camera bag. "I thought I would take some pictures of it as a keepsake."

"By all means," Constance says as she walks down the stairs. "Whatever you need to do, now's the time to do it."

It's dusk and the dark house stands out against the amber and pink tones of sky. It's my favorite kind of dusk, with a few dramatic streaks of cloud that reflect the light and somehow maintain their shape and position for hours. I walked under a similar sky one time when I returned from college in the spring of my senior year, after we found out the cancer had returned and spread to her bones. My mother always turned on most of the lights at dusk because she thought a well-lit house looked so cheerful and inviting from the street. When I saw that the lights were off, I knew she could no longer get out of bed. I knew she would die sooner rather than later.

I fit my key into the lock, and Constance and I enter through the kitchen door at the side of the house. I flick on the light, and we stare at the room in silence. A house seems suspended in midmotion when its occupants die suddenly and unexpectedly. Edna and my father had no idea that the breakfast dishes collecting dust in the drying rack would become a monument to their daily routine.

We wander through the dining room and into the hallway. The only sounds are our creaking footsteps on the wood, the clicking of lamps as Constance turns them on, and the rustle of my camera bag against my hip. I feel as though I couldn't even lift the camera, let alone take a shot. I see familiar hallway things: the lamp she painted, the bellpull, pictures of my father in uniform. I didn't expect to be overcome with such emotion. I thought enough time had passed, but there is not enough time in the world to keep me from feeling—what? Not nostalgia, but a disturbing tangle of panic and fear and sadness. They swirl around me like the particles of dust that awaken with our movements through the house. They are everywhere, and I breathe them in deeply enough to make my eyes burn.

My heart beats faster and I tell myself not to cry, to hold out and then sob later into my pillow. Constance asks me if I want to sit down for a moment, but I say no because I am too focused on what is upstairs. I need to see more. When I enter my father's dressing area and see his shirt hanging on the chair, I sink to the floor and break down completely.

"Oh dear," Constance says, walking quickly up the stairs. "Don't cry. It's all right."

I feel her arm around my shoulders. I try to apologize in between the sobs, saying that I didn't know I would react this way. Constance seems at a loss for words, and we crouch like that in the doorway for I don't know how long.

Finally, I contain myself and say, "I shouldn't have come here. This is all wrong. It's too much."

"You can go. You don't have to stay."

But I don't really respond to her because I can't stop my thoughts from spilling out.

"You know, it's different when someone dies in a house, like when my mother died. The house kind of took on death, just like Dad and I did. We sat in the house and grieved for her while she was dying. I knew exactly where I was in the house when certain things happened, good and bad. I was somehow comforted because the picture was complete. But this house has no death in it now. It's still a place where people live. The dishes, this shirt. I mean, their life in the house isn't dead."

I probably could go on, propelled by the haunting, insistent images, but Constance takes control.

"You're just worn out," she says.

"No," I say as I search her face for some glimmer of recognition. Has she understood a word of what I've said? "I'm not tired. I'm just upset by all of this." I lift my arms to indicate the house, the reality of their deaths, the world in general. "I'm trying to make sense of it all."

"I don't think this is a good time—"

"Is there ever? I mean, what should I do? Wait until they invent a fifth season for grief and then come back?"

Constance bristles a bit with my tone, and her words come back firm. "No. I think, as you yourself said, that you are upset. If you want to look at his things, you might feel better if you came back in the morning."

I wait a while before I speak, feeling uncertain about everything. "I don't know if I can face the house today or tomorrow." I find a tissue in my bag, wipe my eyes, and try to collect myself. "I'm sorry. I know you're right. I should come back later when it's not such a shock. Maybe the next time I'm back in town."

"I think it'd be easier. I hate to see you so upset, Julia. Why don't you let me take you home."

I raise myself slowly and am just about to say all right when I hear the most inconceivable and startling sound, a sound that some-one else might call a ghost, but which I know to be trouble: the doorbell.

"Holy shit," I say and with teenage reflex cut the hallway light and drop to the floor again. "We're not even supposed to be here. Oh my God, I bet it's the police."

I expect Constance to follow my lead, but she smiles in an odd, detached way, and says, "Don't be silly." To my amazement, she turns the light back on and descends the stairs in eerie calm, like some kind of neo-Stepford wife. I hear the latch click and the famil-iar squeak of the front door being opened. When I recognize the distinctive voices, I understand why Constance is so cool and know exactly what kind of trouble has arrived.

Lucy and Jessica have brought their purses, which tells me that they aren't just casually passing by. They are here on business and clutch their handbags to their sides, tentative, perhaps, given that I now stand on the staircase in full view of them and say not a word of welcome. The three of them stand in the foyer as Constance re-counts that we were just looking through the house and that I was somewhat overcome. An awkward silence follows until Jessica makes the first move.

"Well, Julia, we thought it might be best if we came by and helped you sort through things," she says as she places her purse on the chest of drawers.

"I'm not sorting through things. I'm not even touching things," I say.

Jessica turns to Lucy who tries a gentler approach. "We know that, honey. What Jessica means is that you might want to consider going through and, well, collecting a few things before the lawyers come. You know, to avoid some of the taxes. And since all the immediate heirs are here together, we thought this might be the right time."

"Yes," Jessica says. "Now is the time." I watch her hand trail over the chest of drawers as she inspects the wood. She looks at the bell-pull that hangs above the chest.

"Pretty pattern," she says to no one in particular. I remain silent. But when she reaches up to finger the material and examine the stitch, I strike.

"That belonged to my mother, and you have no business examining it or the bureau!"

Jessica expels a little huff of surprise. She looks to Lucy for support, but Lucy only looks sternly at her and shakes her head. Jessica backs off and they fall silent again. I glare in disbelief at Constance, who rubs her forehead and stares at the carpet.

"I know it's upsetting," Lucy says, "but we just thought it was best to do it this way."

"Maybe you did. But good intentions don't matter," I say. "I mean, the plan is still there: 'Let's go in and start grabbing!' I told you, Constance. I told you what it meant to me to come here. I told you I don't want to take anything, and I don't want any strangers around."

"They are not strangers," she says.

"They are to me. And you might as well be one too. How could you do this to me? How could you?"

Constance says nothing.

"I mean, aside from being greedy—"

"It is not greedy. It is practical," Jessica says.

"The hell it is! It's completely immoral, not to mention unlawful!"

"Oh, come on," Jessica says. "Do you really think the law's on our side? Once things become part of the estate, you're looking at tax that's just going to eat away the value of everything."

"The law divides things fairly. That's why it's there," I say, but Jessica only gives me a dismissive wave of her hand, like I'm some kind of pesky insect.

"Come on, Jessica. We better go back home," Lucy says, trying to keep things from getting worse.

"What do you mean? I've come all the way from Lexington—"

"Jessica, shut up and get your purse," Lucy says. "This is not working out, and we're leaving now."

The two exit the way they came in. Constance and I are left standing there. Her arms are crossed, and she finally lifts her eyes to meet mine.

"We had every intention of being fair," she says.

"Sure you did."

"Julia, I am only looking out for your best interests."

"You lied to me about everything."

"I did not lie to you. Lucy and Jessica are not strangers."

I can no longer look at her. Instead, my eyes travel over to the living room that no one has entered yet. The reflection of the foyer light in the mirror over the fireplace sheds a glow over my mother's creations, paintings and needlepointed pillows, and a small square of light on my father's dictionary stand and its opened book. These were the things that they loved. In an instant, both of them travel back to me and put their arms around me.

"And if you're worried about the things in the living room, we're not talking about them," Constance says. "All we're talking about is the good stuff in the attic."

"The good stuff," I say as I walk to the base of the stairs and a picture of the attic comes to mind. I see the dusty tattered box with the smooth wooden toys that were my father's and became mine when I was a child. I see my mother's paintings, ones she thought weren't good enough for any place but the attic, and I remember that through them she did in fact leave her mark. My father couldn't part with them after she died because they filled his mind with memories. He knew exactly what was going on in their lives when she was painting each one. "I'll never let go of the things that hold so much of her," he once said.

And I know exactly what Lucy, Constance, and Jessica would see. They would find most of it in the far corner of the attic, amid the jungle of boxes shrouded in heavy plastic. They would sort through the silver trays that have "D" engraved on them and claim them for Davis, not Daniel. They would grasp the crystal goblets and hold them up to the dim, naked lightbulb, flicking the glass with their fingers to see if it sings.

I look back at Constance. She averts her eyes from mine, for a moment seeming to acknowledge what she's done.

"I had no choice. They were pressuring me about it."

"Everybody always has a choice, Constance."

She doesn't retreat for long. "Well, I don't think giving everything to the government is right!"

I stand my ground and say, "I want no part of this."

"You need to be here."

"I don't need to be here. And I am not going to take any silver or crystal or china from the estate. Neither are you."

"Don't tell me what I can't do. Last thing I need is your damn permission."

She starts up the stairs, so I'm forced to play the trump card.

"I have an inventory of the attic's 'good stuff,' Constance."

It's a bold-faced lie. But it stops her anyway.

"You do not."

"I do," I say calmly. "Dad had it drawn up after Mom died. He gave a copy to Mr. Jeffries for safekeeping. You do what you want, but let me tell you: If one thing is missing from that list, you and your sisters are the ones who'll be subpoenaed."

Constance stands rigid. I can't tell whether she's buying it or not. So I add, "I'm sure the local paper would get a kick out of that story."

That does it. I can see her bottom lip quiver slightly.

"You cannot do this! You are already part of this and you have no case!" Constance screams. "I'll tell the lawyer it was your idea to come here because it was!"

"I don't care what you tell the lawyer. If he's got half a brain, he'll know what the truth is."

She sways a little, as though she might fall down. She puts her hand on the banister to steady herself and slowly walks down. I expect her to call me a thief or a whore or any other random insult as she passes by. But she says nothing, holding her head high in righteous indignation as she walks past me and out the front door.

I look at the living room one last time before turning out the lamps. I leave the porch light on, remembering its timer, and shut the door firmly, making sure it's locked. Constance stands on the edge of the porch. I start to walk past her but she grabs my arm, tightly enough to hurt. I wrest my arm from her and turn back to face her. She takes a step backward, the way a boxer might position himself before throwing a punch.

"If you leave, I will never speak to you again," she says. "You will cease to be a part of this family!"

I walk halfway down the steps before turning back to look one last time at her hulking shadow that fills the doorway. I say the only words that come to mind after hearing her threat. I say them loudly and clearly, just as any truth should be told.

"I never was part of your family, Constance."

She has no reply, and I wouldn't wait for it anyway. I am halfway down the hill and free from her and the house, both blazing in the darkness with a harsh, new light.

6 ♛

Narrow Escapes

"You're in your bathrobe. I hope I didn't wake you, but I had to get away."

"That's okay," Trudy says. "I was up anyway." She bends down to pick up a cat at her feet and looks at me on the way up so that her eyes meet mine. "I'm glad you came here."

I nod my head absently and look away from her, out at the dark fields. The ripe, early spring smell of mud hangs in the air. Shadows from porch-lit trees dance around me. The air seems cool and pure up on the ridge, a welcome contrast from the staleness of my former home.

"I need to tell you what happened," I say.

Trudy opens the door wider. I walk through the threshold and she says more softly and earnestly than before, "Whatever it is, I'm glad you came here."

The house fits her well—friendly and communal, with the kitchen, dining room, and sitting room combined into one open area. The walls are decorated minimally, with black-and-white photographs of farm scenes, a reproduction by Andrew Wyeth, and two multicolored wood carvings. We sit at the butcher block dining table, next to the maroon, wood-burning stove. I drink a cup of coffee and tell her what happened. She seems concerned but not surprised by anything I tell her. She's seen it all before.

"It's not that the stuff matters so much. But it does have some meaning and it's the principle of the thing. I felt I had to stop Constance from taking anything—so I lied about the inventory."

Trudy leans forward and puts her hand over mine.

"You done the right thing."

"But what do I do about the lawyer? Should I tell him what's gone on? I mean, am I going to get in trouble for lying?"

"I don't know, honey. But regardless, you got to call him about Constance. She'll get in the house and rifle plumb through everything if nobody's around to stop her. She will now."

"I don't even feel like dealing with this. I feel like flying back to L.A. and forgetting everything."

"Well, I reckon you could," Trudy says. "You could leave and just wait until you hear from Mr. Jeffries. But you wouldn't feel much better. In fact, you would feel worse knowing that a tornado's blowing through your mama and daddy's house."

"I hate her for what she's doing."

Trudy gets up from the table and returns to refill our coffee cups.

"If she lives her life hurting other people, it's a gonna come back around to hurt her. You mark my words."

"You have an awful lot of faith in divine justice."

"All I know is what I seen."

You can't exactly argue with that logic. I smile and take a sip of coffee.

"I know it sounds funny, but I think there's a good side to what happened."

"It does sound funny," I say.

Trudy runs her palms over the smooth surface of the table. They stop just short of mine. "Well, y'all weren't that close before, right?"

"Right."

"So death didn't change things. That's clarity. You know how different you are. You know you can't trust her."

"I thought I could. I thought she felt the same way I did. But to her, going through their things is like shopping at a flea market. There's nothing sacred about it."

"I reckon she locked up what she feels a while ago. She don't know what but to hide things. And that's an awful way to live," Trudy says.

I think back to Constance on the first day of my visit, sitting in the window seat. I remember her inexplicable tears and how they quickly retreated under her tyranny of cheerfulness.

"I know I should pity her, but I don't feel that charitable right now," I say.

Trudy nods her head. "Charity takes time."

We sit silently for a few moments in the dim circle of light that surrounds the table. She gets up and puts another log in the wood stove, and I think about how safe it feels to be here. I had spent the night before in her farmhouse, which her great-grandfather bought and worked on until the day he died, she said. It was before she married Harlan, when my mother and father had to travel to Columbus to consult with more doctors. Trudy took my mind off the trouble back then, enlisting me to help her make fried chicken for dinner and then hot spiced cider to ward off the spring chill identical to the one tonight. I had been as grateful then for her company as I am now.

She leads me to my room upstairs. Harlan has been asleep the whole time in their first-floor bedroom. Trudy tells me that he could sleep through anything. She tells me to sleep as late as I want, and I thank her again. I put on a T-shirt that she lends me and, before climbing into bed, check for crickets or other crawling things that I tend to be slightly phobic about, given the roach-infested status of my apartment in L.A.

I stare at the ceiling and listen to the sounds of the country. I think about the things I used to listen to as I fell asleep in L.A. and how different they are from the ones I hear now. The wind whistling in my windowpanes, instead of through twenty trees. The click and scuffle of shoes on the pavement, different from the tapping of bugs on the window. Car horns honking, not bullfrogs croaking. I remembered the country as being quieter but am strangely comforted by all that I hear. At least the world seems alive again, unlike how it was in the hermetically sealed loft in Constance's house. At least I have a place to rest for a day or two—a place where I have no history or future, only the present.

In the morning, I meet Harlan. There's no resemblance to Ed, except in his easy-going manner and very blue eyes. He is thin and has a thick head of white hair. He's maybe about seventy and could pass for a typical farmer in his khaki work pants and flannel shirt—except for a rather stylish thin mustache that makes him look more refined than your average eastern Kentucky plow pusher. He didn't always farm. Constance made sure I knew that. He had owned and operated the town lumber store for years, but when he met Trudy after his wife died a few years ago, he "went country" as Constance says. It seems to suit him well.

He stands and shakes my hand when Trudy introduces us and says, "Glad to know you." He makes no mention of Ed or Constance as we sit at the dining room table and eat an obscenely huge breakfast of sausage, eggs, grits, and biscuits. Instead, he tells me about the farm and how they raise a little bit of everything: tobacco, dairy cattle, beef cattle. He was up this morning at five o'clock to milk the cows.

"But the dairy cows are Trudy's specialty," he says. "She's a true innovator."

"No." Trudy laughs as she pats Harlan's hand. "I don't know about that."

"Well, they been producing more than before on account a your idea," he says.

"What was your idea?" I ask.

Trudy smiles shyly and explains. "We didn't really know what we was doing with the cows and at first they was having trouble producing. I figured they might loosen up a bit if we pampered them a little. So I rigged up a brushing machine that rolls over their hides real nice and slow as they're being milked. At first they was a-scared of it, but now I reckon it relaxes them and kindy comforts them while those big, cold tubes pull the milk out of them. I can't imagine how uncomfortable that would be for a human. I reckon cows feel some discomfort, too."

"It's a decidedly feminine solution," Harlan says and we all laugh. "It's hardly traditional to sympathize with a cow, to understand what it wants and needs. But she did and it worked. So I followed her lead, and I been learning about growing cucumbers and other vegetables since the writing is on the wall for tobacco, what with people talking about suing the companies and all. The European market is still strong, but it's a different story here; the lobbyists at home can't hold things together forever."

"So you're an innovator, too," I say.

"Well, the local farmers wouldn't say so; they think we're nuts. Most haven't given up on tobacco yet, and I can't say I blame them. It's more lucrative than growing vegetables, cheaper too. Still, we don't mind if they laugh at our bell peppers. We're used to it," Harlan says and smiles at Trudy, who returns it. It's the kind of knowing, wordless exchange that you see between couples that has layers of conversation behind it, conspiracy, and undeniable love. I had seen it many times between my parents, and seeing it again always makes me yearn for that kind of love of my own. I had glimmers of it with one or two boyfriends but nothing so mature and enduring—sort of like the musical difference between the Bee Gees's "How Deep Is Your Love?" and Rimsky-Korsakov's *Sheherezade*.

Despite my longing, which I've learned to batten down, I am

comfortable listening to the gentle rhythms of their talk. It's a different world on this ridge. They have no cares about what the farm people think of them, no desire to be well received. They live simply, acting on the impulses of their hearts.

After breakfast, I call Mr. Jeffries and find out that I can meet with him on Tuesday morning. I ask the secretary to inform him that Constance and I will have separate meetings with him from now on. She asks if there is a problem. I tell her yes, but that it's something I need to speak with Mr. Jeffries about privately.

Figuring that some kind of activity will do me good, I offered to help Trudy in her studio even though I don't know the first thing about wood carving.

"You don't need to know. I'll just explain things as we go along," she said as she handed me a pair of paint-spattered overalls and an old flannel shirt. "Put these old things on and meet me in the studio."

I roll up the legs and sleeves of the outfit, looking like a reject from a *Hee Haw* audition. The left clip of the overalls keeps coming undone. I am snapping it for the fourth time when I walk out the kitchen door and nearly run head-on into an enormous black cow. It stands about ten feet away from me, eyeing me with its head turned. I look beyond the cow to its brown-and-white compatriots still standing behind the torn fence. There are about six of them and they look like some kind of bovine delegation, waiting for the black one to negotiate for the herd.

The black cow pulls a plug of grass from the yard and chews languidly. It seems harmless enough. But when I start toward Trudy's studio, the cow snorts and takes a step closer to me.

"Go on, cow," I say, but the creature doesn't flinch. My knowledge of farm animals is not enviable. I know about geese and how to wave your arms at them to keep them from attacking. But I do not know how to shoo a cow.

I start to pick up a stick when I hear Harlan's voice behind the screen door.

"Don't move, Julia."

"It's okay. It's just a cow."

"It's a bull," Harlan says.

"Oh my God."

"Don't move. He saw you reach for that stick and he's watching you real close. You don't want to make him charge you."

"Oh my God. Harlan, are you sure? It doesn't even have horns. Are you sure it's a bull?"

"He's a young one. The horns haven't come in yet."

"Well, that clinches it. I'm in trouble."

"Listen, when I say 'now' I want you to walk quickly backward into the house. Don't run—that'll make him charge for sure. I'll have the door open, and I'll help you up the steps. You just keep moving, okay?"

"Okay," I say, determined not to die at the hoofs of a bull. My heart pounds and my legs are taut. I begin to sweat as the bull continues to stare at me for what feels like a half hour though it's only been minutes. Suddenly, I hear the scrape and crush of car tires on the gravel road that leads to the house. The bull hears it too and turns his head toward the noise.

"Now!" Harlan screams, and I start backpedaling with my eye on the bull. Harlan scoops me up the steps with surprising strength just as the bull realizes his prey has escaped. The screen door slams and the bull trots up and buts the metal base with his hornless head anyway, as if to give me a warning or maybe just to complete the dance.

"Are you all right?" Harlan asks. His arms are still around me, and I feel faint enough to need the support.

"I think so. I'm a little dizzy."

Harlan leads me to a chair.

"Just take deep breaths," he says. "Good thing J.T. came with his truck. He lives next door. I reckon Trudy called him from the studio phone."

"Thank God."

"You didn't hurt anything did you?"

"No, I'm fine. Just a little humbled."

Harlan smiles and says, "Bulls have that effect on people. I'll be right back."

He walks outside and I hear the voices of three or four men, whistling and yelling as they drive the truck into the yard and herd the bull back behind the fence. I don't look out the window, partly because I'm not sure my legs are ready to walk over to it. I stare blankly at the wood stove, still in awe of how close I came to calamity.

I hear the screen door open. Trudy walks in and asks if I'm okay.

"I think you and Harlan saved my life," I say.

"I don't know that you would a been kilt. You might've had a few busted bones," Trudy says.

"What a terrifying animal."

"I'm so sorry he got loose. Would you like something? A glass of water or a cup of tea—something to calm you?"

"Water would be fine."

Trudy returns with a glassful and I sip it. She sits across from me and watches me as I continue to sit in dazed silence.

"Are you sure you're all right?"

"Yeah. It's just funny. I think I know so much sometimes. I even doubted Harlan when he told me it was a bull. I honestly thought it was nothing but a harmless cow."

"Shoot. Anybody'd make that mistake if they didn't live on a farm," Trudy says.

The parliamentarians burble their collective dissent: *Not just anybody! It takes a true imbecile! Hear, hear!*

"I've made more than a few mistakes lately. I should have listened to you in the park. You tried to tell me not to go to the house. If I hadn't gone, I wouldn't even be here right now."

"Listen, you had to go. You had to see it. Plus you saved that house from being tore up by Constance."

"I guess you're right. But lately it seems like there's always a bull around whose horns haven't come in yet, you know? I mean, everything looks fine, harmless, and then suddenly I'm getting charged. You can't go by the way things look. I should know that from food styling, but I always forget."

"Well, what's true for bulls or food ain't always true for people," Trudy says.

"It was true with Constance. It was even true with Dad. I just assumed that he'd live into his eighties or nineties even though Mom got sick so young. He was healthy, active, never ill. And then suddenly he's gone, and all I can think about is how he and I could have gotten along better if I hadn't been such a jerk."

"'Could have' is a dangerous phrase. You both did the best you could."

"I'm not so sure," I say. Trudy waits until I look at her for a response.

"Honey, that kind of thinking is a one-way ticket to hell on earth. You couldn't stop what you was feeling about the marriage and Edna and Constance any more than he could. That's just the way it was. And remember, you're still standing. The bulls ain't knocked you down yet."

"No, not yet."

We sit for a while and then Trudy tells me she has to get back to work and asks if I'm still interested in helping her. Why not? I'm dressed for the occasion. With a smile, she offers to go out first—a little bull reconnaissance. I follow as we make our way through the muddy yard, carefully placing my feet in the treads of her boots.

On Tuesday morning at 10:55 A.M., I meet Mr. Jeffries and waste no time getting to the point.

"I'd like you to begin assessing the house tomorrow if possible."

He's in his fifties and has the classic look of a distinguished southern lawyer—graying temples, bifocals, navy suspenders under his demure charcoal suit. Having only met him once before, I don't know whose side he'll believe.

"Well, now, that's not much notice. I have to get in touch with our appraiser and he's in Cincinnati," he says.

"I realize it's inconvenient, but it's very important that it begins now."

Mr. Jeffries looks at me for a moment over his bifocals. He gets up and strolls over to the small coffeepot by the window.

"Would you like a cup?" he asks as he pours.

"No, thank you."

He sits down again in the leather swivel chair behind his desk. He takes a sip of his coffee, sits up a little straighter, and asks the question that's been hanging in the air.

"Why is it so urgent?"

"Because Constance wants to steal things from the house."

I do not fidget after I say it. I look directly into his eyes, as if daring him to doubt me. Go ahead, question me. I'll tell you every sordid detail that comes to mind.

He holds my gaze for a moment then looks down at his desk. The clock on the wall strikes the hour. After the last bell rings, he finally speaks.

"Well, between you and me, I'm not surprised."

I didn't expect pay dirt, but I'll take it and run—at last, an objective witness, perhaps the most important person in all of this, who sees Constance for the wicked stepsister she is. I feel like thanking him for making me feel less alone and overwhelmed, but not before encouraging him to unburden himself—to recount all the salacious evidence that tipped him off. However, I control myself, sit quietly, and wait for him to continue.

"Now, understand, that's off the record."

"Yes, of course."

"But I've known her for a long time. My wife has too," he says, shaking his head.

I take a deep breath and try to sound more concerned than derisive, "So she's stolen things before?"

"Well, nothing that's easy to prove. My wife works at the historical preservation museum, which Constance manages, and she has doubts about how things are run." He hesitates for a moment. "Specifically, how contributions are accounted for."

"I see."

"But again, all of this is confidential."

"I understand, and I won't say anything. But I'm relieved that I don't have to fight you."

"Not me," he says. "But Constance is going to be another matter."

"I don't want to sue her. I just want her to keep away from the house."

"It's a reasonable request, but the problem is she might deny having been there at all. Or at least, she won't admit to wanting to take anything." He gets out a legal pad and pen from his desk drawer. "First of all, how did you find out about her being in the house?"

"Well, it's kind of complicated. I know it may sound strange, but we were both at the house two nights ago."

He puts his pen down. "Both of you? How could that be?"

I explain the whole story. He listens patiently, withholding judgment, yet I am compelled to justify my actions.

"I had to see the house one more time before it became so depersonalized, before everything was appraised and tagged and turned into nothing but money."

He sits back in his chair and chews on one of the temples of his bifocals. He rubs his forehead, puts his glasses on, and sighs deeply.

"I don't blame you for wanting to see the house in a more personal way. But, it does make you something of an accomplice. In other words, you couldn't sue her even if you wanted to."

"I don't want to. I just want her to stay away."

"But I can't come out and say that to her. Constance is going to use your presence against you, especially since it was your idea in the first place. So I've got to treat the whole thing objectively and without blame. Otherwise, she just might turn around and try to sue you. She's proud enough to do something like that, you know."

We sit in silence for a few moments, and I begin to feel foolish—the plaintiff without a case.

"I'm sorry about this," I say. "I had no idea things would get out of hand."

"It's all right. They aren't out of hand yet. What we'll need to work on is some kind of agreement between you. In fact, why don't you come back around one o'clock. Maybe we can all sit down and start to settle things."

I thank him and take my leave, walking down the quiet, tree-lined street to a nearby restaurant, The Lion's Den. It's a dimly lit place, and I sit in the darkest corner, trying to gather my courage, out of sight from any other old acquaintances who might pop up. I consider ordering a Bloody Mary before my lunch but think better of it. Having alcohol on my breath would cast me as even more of a reprobate in Constance's warped mind.

I return to Mr. Jeffries's office at the appointed hour. The secretary tells me to go right in. My heart pounds, and I wonder if she's here, if she'll yell at me again, if she'll even acknowledge my presence. I pause before opening the door, telling myself that I'm not the one at fault.

Mr. Jeffries leans on the front of his desk, his arms crossed in front of him. Constance sits silently in an adjacent chair, dressed in high style. She wears a tailored, vaguely funereal gray suit and a matching felt hat—a *Perry Mason* meets *Casablanca* get-up. Mr. Jeffries welcomes me and offers the seat next to Constance. I look at her but she refuses to glance my way. Then he wheels his chair out from behind his desk and positions it between ours, making the third point of a very tense triangle.

"Sorting things out after people die is never easy," he begins. "And in light of recent circumstances, I thought it would be best to get together and discuss your situation."

"Why don't you talk straight, Ronald?" Constance says.

"Beg your pardon?" he replies.

"You believe I want to steal from the estate, and now you want to figure out what to do with me."

"Constance, all I want to do is to make sure we're all on the same page about the house and its items. I told you before, the point of this meeting is not to lay blame."

"Why should I be blamed? Everything was her idea. I'm the one who had to intervene," she says.

Constance still refuses to look at me. I try to remain silent and calm, but it's not easy. Even Mr. Jeffries begins to take on the tone of an irritated schoolmaster.

"You've both told me what you think happened. You've both accused each other of tampering with items in the estate. As far as I'm concerned, whatever happened is in the past. The purpose of this meeting is to reach a compromise, not to point the finger at anyone."

That I was brought into the equation seems to silence Constance. I give no reply and look straight ahead out the window. I focus on two children outside racing each other up the steps of their Victorian home. They scramble for the porch swing, each making the claim of first, indifferent to the skinned knee or any other injury sustained in the process. It's all part of the game.

Mr. Jeffries continues on about the agreement, which stipulates that no person will enter the house until all items are accounted for. To ensure that the house is not entered, he proposes that we sign a document that makes the penalties of trespassing clear. We agree to the document. Then Mr. Jeffries suggests that the outside locks on the house be changed, which he characterizes as "an additional deterrent," and proposes that the estate will pay for the cost. That's when Constance pops her cork.

"I cannot accept such a thing. I find the very suggestion offensive."

"The locks or the cost?" I ask.

"The locks," she says savagely. "And don't try to be smart, Julia. I've had more than enough of you."

I say nothing, knowing the last thing I should do is make this any harder for Mr. Jeffries.

"Why do you find the suggestion so offensive?" he asks her.

"Because it insinuates that I cannot be trusted. That I am some kind of criminal."

"Julia, do you feel that way?" he asks.

"No. I think it makes sense to have the locks changed."

"Well, you don't have to live here, do you?" Constance says. "What am I going to tell Mary Belle Vance when she sees people working on those locks? She lives next door, and she doesn't miss a trick."

"Just tell her there was an attempted burglary," I say.

"You can go straight to hell!" Constance brays.

"That is enough from both of you!" Mr. Jeffries is practically out of his chair by this point. "Julia, your wisecracks aren't helping anything. And Constance, I'll thank you to refrain from cursing at anybody in this room."

Constance takes out a handkerchief and dabs the corners of her eyes, no doubt more upset about her fall from social grace than anything else. I've run out of sympathy for her and remain unmoved by her dainty display of grief. It's no longer my job to make excuses for her.

I start to address her but think better of it and say to Mr. Jeffries, "Constance doesn't have to tell anybody what's going on. She can say the locks were broken or something. It's nobody's business but her own."

"You think you can just whip off some excuse like that and not have people talk," she says defiantly. "You don't know anything about how this town works."

"All right," Mr. Jeffries says as he stands up. "I can see we're getting nowhere, so this is what I'm going to do. I'm going to draw up what we've agreed to so far and send you both copies to sign. Then, as the official executor of this estate, I am going to have the locks on the house changed. I will have my office pay for the work since we can't agree that it is needed. But I believe it's best for everyone involved."

"You can't do that!" Constance says.

"I'm afraid I can," Mr. Jeffries says. "I'm sorry you don't agree, but I think it's necessary. I will do everything I can to make sure the workmen are discreet."

Constance doesn't say a word. She has regained some measure of control and stares at me and then at Mr. Jeffries. She smoothes the top of her skirt and then rises from her chair.

"Well," she says as she gathers her jacket and purse, "I won't allow this to happen. I have nothing more to say to either of you except that you will be hearing from another attorney on this matter. And I ask you both never to contact me personally again."

With that she walks out the door as the cameras in her mind continue to roll. I can't help but laugh a little over her performance, shaking my head and exchanging a look with Mr. Jeffries as he sits down and lets out a sigh.

"Do you think she'll go through with it?" I ask.

He shrugs and says, "It's hard to say. She knows she doesn't have a case. She knows the truth. But I doubt that's stopped her before."

It's dusk and I'm preparing dinner for Trudy and Harlan. Two days have passed and Mr. Jeffries hasn't heard from Constance. As far as he knows, she hasn't approached any other lawyer in town and didn't issue a peep of dissent over the locksmiths who arrived the morning after our meeting took place. Mr. Jeffries called to let me know the house was secure. He left a message on Constance's machine telling her the work had been done "under the cover of predawn darkness." He said he couldn't resist the chance to goad her a little.

We have, however, heard from Ed. He dropped off my things but then called Harlan last night just to see how things were on the farm. Trudy told me that's a bad sign.

"Whenever he calls like that it means they're fighting. But they always patch things up somehow. I reckon Constance just gets tired of being mean."

I have kept a very low profile, helping Trudy in her studio, channeling my anger into sawing and hammering wood. Trudy tells me I do good work and that I can stay as long as I like, but I know the time has come to return to L.A. My leave officially ends in three days, and I'll need at least two days to get readjusted to the city.

I chop tomatoes in preparation for my spin on pasta primavera and realize I've never really stopped thinking about L.A. since I left, but I tailor my images to fit my needs. When I was at Constance's house, I returned to the good parts of the city every day to reassure myself that my life there was something better than what I saw in her world. I thought of the pleasant L.A. things: perpetual 70 degree temperatures, hiking in the mountains, the museums, the diversity of culture, the sun setting over the Pacific, the prevalence of good cappuccino.

And now that I'm safe, cooking in this warm kitchen, the grimmer realities of L.A. seep into my life like backed-up sewage. There have been muggings in the alley behind my roach-infested building. The crazy old woman next door tells me I'm the devil every evening in a frenzied mix of Spanish and English. The publisher of my magazine is a hapless drunk, and the editor doesn't care about anyone but herself. It would be nice to escape all the problems and live on this ridge if there were something to do other than sculpt wood and grow old. But there isn't.

The three of us sit down to the meal of pasta, salad, and homemade rolls. Trudy is impressed and gives her seal of approval: "This is good eatin'." Talk quickly turns from the meal to L.A.

"I think you need to start looking for a new apartment," Trudy says. "You can't live like that."

"I don't know that I have much of a choice. The place is all I can afford right now, especially if I quit my job."

"Lord. I worry about you going back there," Trudy says. "How long you going to stay on with the magazine?"

"I'm not sure. For a little while at least. Until I can find a job that's more compelling."

"What about your photography?"

"My photography," I say with a laugh. "That sounds so respectable, like I'm actually doing it."

"You haven't been taking any pictures?"

"Well, I'm taking them, but nobody's interested. I haven't gotten any freelance or staff positions yet even though I've been sending out my portfolio and résumés. See, I have only a couple of my own photographs published, so it's the old catch-22—no experience, no job."

"Just keep trying and keep an open mind," Trudy says. "There is lots a ways to pursue your work—even if you're taking pictures of things nobody else may care about or have nothing to do with your interests."

"Like food?"

"Well, yes and no. You may not care about it, but I know one gal who watches the food network all day long, and I know they's a lot more like her. Food is fashionable and fancy—I reckon even more so in L.A. And you have to think about color and texture when you're styling, right? So it's not such an uncreative thing."

"I suppose."

"I think you can find opportunities for work in places where you'd least expect it. You know how I sold my first carving? I'd been working for the Beef Council, doing a portrait of a steer for their main lobby. It was nothing fancy, just this cow profile made out of mahogany, but I worked hard on it—highlighting the grain of the wood in the way I stained it, trying to get the detail right. And this Beef

Council executive, he loved it. He come to the studio and bought him another carving and then commissioned three more later on."

"That's great," I say.

"I know," Trudy says as she dishes a second helping of pasta to everyone. "But I would a never counted on it happening. And his commissions helped get me started, gave me enough money for a while to do my own designs."

"So you think I should stay at the magazine."

"Heck no! Not if you're miserable there. All I'm saying is keep an open mind when you're looking for work. Like, you may find an ad looking for a freelance wedding photographer—"

"There's no way."

"Okay, maybe something else that you can stomach but aren't passionate about. And if that happens, wherever it happens, try it—especially if it's good money, cause it may lead somewhere—maybe not directly to *National Geographic,* but somewhere. You never know what's going to happen."

I smile at Trudy, touched that she remembered my penchant for nature, evident in some of my pictures I showed her years ago—a misty dawn over the Ohio, a lean-to cabin nestled in a hollow below an Appalachian silhouette, a white-tailed deer grazing in a meadow. She picks up the rolls, takes another, and passes the basket to me.

"I know what's going to happen," Harlan says.

Trudy stops in midmotion and turns to Harlan.

"I know Julia's going to be all right," he says shyly as he looks at me and nods. "No matter what happens, she's going to be all right."

"You think so?" I ask.

"I know so," he says.

He is as people shy as he is camera shy, but I got a few good candids when he was walking through his tobacco fields.

As I wait for the plane, I think of Harlan's words. Other than a farewell in the field this morning, the exchange at dinner was our last. He had given me his prediction of hope, and I sit here trying to believe him.

The Greater Tri-State Airport consists of one waiting room and two gates, so I have no excuse for missing the plane. Just to avoid temptation, I give myself reasons for not wanting to miss it. From my plastic scoop chair I can see the automatic doors that serve as the airport's only entrance. I imagine Constance charging through those doors and waving some kind of crackbrained, trumped-up subpoena in my face. That's all it takes, and I begin to long for the city.

Other than a field trip of grade schoolers, the airport has very few customers today. I go over to where Trudy stands, by the display case in the center of the room. It showcases the various industries in the tri-state region—steel, iron, and coal—and features blown-up pictures of monstrous gnarled machinery, smiling men in hard hats as they emerge from a steel factory, the molten glow of a blast furnace lighting up the night sky.

We look at the pictures in silence, and Trudy asks, "You sure you want to leave all this glamour behind?"

I smile at her. "It's tempting. But I'm better off heading west."

"You know you can always come back. You can come stay with us whenever you want. We're always here, and we'd love to have you."

"Thanks, Trudy—for everything," I say even though my words can't really convey how indebted I feel, or how relieved I am to have a friend here who knew and loved my parents well, someone who pulls this place away from oblivion and back toward the feeling of home.

I hear my flight announced over the loudspeaker. We walk to the gate, and I hug Trudy for a long time before I get on the plane. I want to keep up a cheerful front, so it's not until I get on board that I let my tears fall. It's strange, the way they seem almost uncontrollable—a mixture of sadness and anxiety. Will I ever see Trudy and Harlan again? Will I ever stop searching and shifting from one imperfect home to another? Will I ever be like Claire or Bobby or any of my other age-appropriate friends who have set-tled down? I have no answers—and no tissues in my purse to stem the tide. I pull the motion sickness bag out of the seat pouch in front of me, discreetly wipe my eyes, and hope that the answers will come.

7 ♛

Quid Pro Quo

My luck is finally changing—that is my first thought when I arrive home and find a message on my answering machine from the *Los Angeles Times,* an assignment to cover an event this Sunday, a few days before I am scheduled to return to *Mangia!* It's at least a step toward leaving the ridiculous and deceptive world of food—strawberries floating in hair conditioner instead of cream, tomatoes sprayed with engine oil, Barbasol masquerading as whipped cream. I am free to photograph people and things exactly as they are—the truth—which is always worthy of the eternal moment.

I'm delighted but not that surprised by the turning tide. I figure there has to be some kind of balancing act in the universe to ease the pain of loss and betrayal, some benevolent power that throws me a bone.

On Saturday, I meet with Cecil Plainfield, the entertainment editor, and find out it's a celebrity poetry reading hosted at the Round Rococo Arts Center in Hollywood under the name "Eclectic Interludes." The series of readings is the latest in the neosalon craze that features actors intoning their favorite poems, along with actual poets reading from their own work. Cecil assures me that there will be no curve balls, no shamanistic/ceremonial poetry performances, slams, or hoedowns. It's a sedate and straightforward affair. All I need to do is photograph the actor as he reads.

"What about the poet?" I ask.

Cecil, a thin, gray-haired fifty-something, brushes a few croissant crumbs off his French blue button-down shirt and onto a napkin, takes a delicate sip of coffee, and answers.

"The poet isn't the story. The poet didn't just sign a ten-million-dollar deal with Five-Star Films—you know what I'm saying?"

I could do without the wheeler-dealer Hollywood interrogative—any moron could know, see, or even feel what he's saying. But it's inevitable that even those on the fringes of Hollywood embrace the brash lingo of the industry. They pitch even though they don't have a ticket to the game.

I hesitate for a moment, wondering if I should make a case for the poet, who probably needs and deserves more publicity than the actor. But I'm desperate for the job and don't want to blow it. "Right. The actor's the story."

"I'll be honest with you," Cecil says as he flips through my portfolio. "I'm taking a risk here, but that's what happens when three freelancers move away in the same month. You get to cover a celebrity, which is unheard-of for an unpublished photographer—"

"Yes, but I did publish in a real estate magazine, called—"

"I mean in our pages," Cecil says with haughty finality. "You're a newcomer, so you need to be sharp."

"Absolutely," I say with enough cheerful enthusiasm to mask my annoyance. Cecil stands up, tells me he's looking forward to seeing my work—despite his reservations—and kindly walks me three steps to his office door.

I study the press release, which naturally has very little information on Nathan Janning's poetry and a plethora of details about Rod Boyle, currently starring as a lawyer in the hit series *Peoria*—about a satanic cult that tries to take over the town. Nathan Janning teaches at a college in Peoria, Illinois, so that must be the connection.

The reading is scheduled to begin at four-thirty. I drive down Sunset at three-thirty. Sunday particularly seems to unmask the boulevard and reveal its glaring, shabby, desperate self. I notice the seedy bleakness of one-story motels and imagine the people inside maybe just waking up from the drugs and alcohol of Saturday night. They peer out from dusty green curtains and are blinded by the concrete light. I see a hooker standing on the corner of Sunset and Spaulding, by the All-American Burger. She waits on the corner and leans on the stoplight pole, reapplying her lipstick and smoothing out the folds of her red leather miniskirt. There is no real Sunday on the Strip, no day of rest. Someone is always selling something—Angelyne, the studios, the liquor companies, the fashion designers, and the Marlboro Man in his rugged, cancer-free glory.

Spanish-styled homes balance precariously on the defiantly landscaped yet drought-stricken Hollywood Hills. Mansions on hillsides have always struck me as the great metaphor for the film world: you mortgage your life for the promise of a million-dollar deal, only to have the earth constantly move. This ground that can never truly hold roots makes you anxious, ruthless, and surly because you never know when Poseidon, the great earthshaker, will dump your castle into the street. And even if you actually get that deal, you never know if the film will play in, say, Peoria. So you take all you can whenever you can. And the people and their dreams and their egos keep coming, lured by the promise of being king of the hill even for just a moment.

I travel past the House of Blues, the Laugh Factory, the Sunset

Strip Tattoo Parlor, and the landmark turrets of the Chateau Marmont. I hang a left up a side street and pull into the Round Rococo lot. The center, funded by grants, is a surprisingly spacious wooden house that looks more akin to New England than L.A. I had heard of its hip poetry and performance-art scene but had never attended an event, feeling a bit wary of any arts center that would call itself such a hopelessly nonsensical name.

I walk onto the porch, framed by two whimsical stacks of books designed to look like columns, and into the main foyer. Underneath the wood-beamed ceiling mingle the worshipers of this bizarre hybrid of literary and celebrity culture. Some people are dressed casually, in relaxed jeans, cotton sweaters, leather jackets, T-shirts, but others have that unmistakable servitude to fame via fashion. Whether in entertainment, politics, or any media-observant profession, one principle holds true: the road to success is potholed by affectation. Fashion statements scream at me from across the room: a black tasseled bustier, oddly shaped facial hair, rakish berets, fishnet stockings, enormously engineered breasts, green pigtails, satiny bowling shirts, a profusion of small, severe sunglasses, and bodies pumped and aerobicized into narcissistic temples.

I've seen this type of gathering before. The one fund-raiser for *Mangia!* had brought out fame seekers not by its lure of free wine and cheese but by featuring favorite pasta dishes of Martin Scorsese. I suppose the advertisers were human, i.e. desperate, and couldn't resist the temptation, like so many people in Hollywood, to dupe the public with false hope. "Listen to the chef's secret from the chef himself!" the flyer read. But what it didn't reveal was that Scorsese did his talking on a videotape that retailed for $19.95.

I catch a glimpse of Rod in the corner. He leans against the wall and runs a hand through his dark, curly hair. Looking tan, muscular, and very established in his navy silk shirt and white linen pants, he stares moodily at the breasts of a young woman who talks to him. She's wearing a white halter top and a very tight, very purple leather miniskirt. She shifts her stance nervously as she talks to him, like a puppy who wants to play. Rod seems to look my way, maybe even right at me, and scowls. Maybe it's my flannel shirt.

I look past the people, roam around, and wonder where the artistic inspiration exists—not in the decor. There are no curtains or shutters. The maroon carpet is threadbare, and the bathroom collage design consists of the word Unaffected pasted on mirrors and stalls, along with cartoon doodlings, random photocopied text, and mismatched swatches of wallpaper. Not much money was granted to visual artists because the walls are bare except for a photo exhibit—unframed, 5×7-inch snapshots of a 1970s backyard barbecue with people smiling for the camera, dancing in half-naked groups, and braiding each others' hair. Nor does the Round Rococo Bookstore seem promising, overwrought with self-published poetry chapbooks bearing such titles as: *Thoreau Is Dead, A Wet Pack of Zebras, Me-Myself-and I.*

It's 4:10 and I'm scanning the area for someone, anyone, with a clipboard or some kind of professional demeanor. I find Nathan Janning—midfifties, balding, horn-rimmed glasses, seersucker jacket, talking with two women. I shoulder my way in, catching eyes for a moment with the poet. There are faint beads of sweat on his forehead, and his eyes dart around the room with the frantic uncertainty of a mole trapped aboveground.

A woman wearing a beige Armani pants suit shoves her Buddy Holly glasses up on her nose and says, "I love Nathan's poems. I read them all the time. Seriously. They calm me down."

Nathan, whose poetry is mostly about war, smiles wanly but still fidgets. I feel for him; he's probably so desperate for both an audience and money that he had to partake in this circus.

The other woman, whose eyes appear teary and small between two strips of mascara, dresses in a long, low-cut, flowing black dress, a literary nod to Stevie Nicks, and smiles at me as I say hello and introduce myself.

"I'm here from the *L.A. Times* to take some pictures of the reading."

"Oh, wonderful," she says. "This is Nathan Janning, and I'm Star Tanner."

"Are you in charge of the event?" I ask. Star is about to answer but then the woman in beige interrupts.

"Well, yes and no. She's in charge of most of it, but I'm in charge of Rod. Sage Henley from Five-Star Films publicity?" she says as she sticks out her hand even though she knows everyone's heard of her company.

I shake her rigid, thin hand and say lightly, "A lot of stars here tonight."

"You better believe it," she says.

"Well, Julia, let me show you the poetry stage," Star says as she moves her arms slowly, awkwardly, in the direction of a door. "During the reading, feel free to move around and do whatever you need to do to get the shots."

Sage chimes in with, "Absolutely. Here, get one of Nathan and me."

"Right now?"

"No, next week," she says with a smile that's more of a sneer.

I don't like her, so I don't load the camera before I shoot.

"Fabulous," she says as I click a few phonies. Sage has her arm around Nathan, whose sweaty, wall-eyed gaze tells me he's not exactly comfortable being touched by strangers.

The stage, not surprisingly, is a black box theater with overhead stage lights focused on the poet. It's hard to escape performance in L.A.—whether you're listening to a poet intoning his words or to a waiter telling you the specials. I was hoping for windows, a soft background that could capture the clear afternoon light. This setting seems all wrong for a poetry reading, where it seems like the poet would want to view the faces of the audience, to connect with them rather than being isolated in a harsh, limiting, and overly dramatic beam of light. Fortunately, the seats are high enough so that I can shoot some audience/poet wide angles and don't have to aim directly into the light. I was smart enough to bring a flash.

People don't start to move into the theater until Rod does. I'm loading the film and trying to get the right light and angle for the audience and podium when I catch Rod scowling at me again. I glance back at him and smile shyly, nodding hello. I probably should have been introduced to him before, just to make him feel more at ease, but such a courtesy would never enter Sage's head.

Rod doesn't return the smile and abruptly motions for Sage. He bends down, whispers something in her ear, and she pats his shoulder. Perhaps he doesn't like the lighting or the minimalist set-up of the stage—who knows?

The wooden floor underneath the fifty-seat theater creaks and groans as people find their chairs. Star walks over to the podium, smiles for a second, and murmurs a dulcet, "Hello," into the microphone. The capacity crowd settles into an uncertain silence.

"I just want to welcome you all to Round Rococo and want to say a few honor-type words for my two friends here."

She turns her head and smiles demurely at Rod and Nathan. After making a few announcements about upcoming events, one of which is her own poetry reading, Star takes a sip of water, flips her long hair behind her shoulders, and digs into her introduction.

"Sometimes there's a mist in the air in Los Angeles that transforms the way things look. Gray, opaque, like sulphurous plumes, floating. Yet below the mist there is Technicolor, there is substance."

My two o'clock burrito is backing up on me. I stifle a burp, shift in my chair, and wonder what the hell this woman is talking about.

"I've read Rod Boyle's poems, and they are so understated, so subtle as to lull one into a deep quietude of simplicity. Yet beneath that simplicity, beneath that mist, there exists a wild, discussive epiphany, almost palpable, yet at the same time withheld. His work as an actor mirrors the same sly resonance and tacit tension, whether he's playing a lawyer in a town of Satan-worshipers or a comic book superhero mutated by nuclear waste. His words and actions move us and we think—oh yes—I've seen that man before.

I know him. I know him. It's a great honor to have him with us. Ladies and gentlemen, Rod Boyle."

The crowd cheers as though he were getting ready to vault the podium rather than read from it. They whistle, applaud, and whoop. Someone even yells, "Go, Rod!" With knowing, almost weary aplomb, Rod raises his hand to quiet the masses. He mutters "Thank you" a couple of times into the microphone and then says, "Thank you, Star. Love that mist and epiphany stuff."

Some in the audience chuckle and he smiles, "No, really. It was great," but he's just a little too coy to be sincere. He doesn't fool me.

Quiet gradually falls over the audience as they watch Rod prepare himself to read by launching into a series of stretches normally associated with hatha-yoga. He expels a deep oojai breath and twists his torso, turning his neck from side to side, stretching himself into literary inspiration. He adjusts the microphone and rubs a hand over his face.

"Wow," he says. "It always takes me a moment to get into a comfortable place, mentally, physically, spiritually. Because that's where poetry is at—in this great alignment of all aspects of your being. You know what I'm saying?"

He looks out into the audience and the acolytes nod. I, on the other hand, can now hear only the florid voices of dissenting parliamentarians, who are occasionally right, as is the case when they scream: *Get off the bloody stage, you pretentious wanker!*

"So, here's the deal," Rod says. "They wanted me to choose some of my favorite poems to read. And I did that. So I'm going to read poems by some great writers: Rod McKuen, Jim Morrison, Yeats. But I also chose some of my own work because I think any poet should list himself as being among his favorites. If I don't like my work then who else will? Self-love is the nucleus of creative expression."

He cracks his neck again.

"Okay. This first one is called 'Burnt Sienna.' It was inspired by a little trip to Italy that I took with my wife last year. A much-needed vacation. And Siena was a place where I got in touch with a lot of "—he scans the air above him for the perfect poetic phrase—"heavy shit."

A few people giggle but Rod remains grimly serious as he adjusts the microphone and begins to read.

> "Curtains billowing in the afternoon breeze,
> White sails of desire
> Soaring through the windows of my mind.
> You
> Under me
> Naked as a jay bird
>
> *Andiamo, mi amore*
> We hear in the streets below
> As our bodies find that
> Wild metronomic passion
> Your mouth on my shoulder
> My duomo rising with the hot life force
> And then
> A release, resolution
> *Basta!*
> And I lie next to you
> Spent
> like so many lire
>
> I rise to the window while you sleep
> And look out over the rooftops of Siena
> Burnt from the sun
> Or from our sudden blaze of passion?
> I take a swig of tepid Evian
> And remember I am forty years old today."

The audience murmurs appreciatively, but doesn't applaud,

which seems to surprise Rod because he says, "Let me see if I can read one you really like."

As a poet, the man should be burned in effigy, not photographed, but I start taking pictures anyway—a few from the side, one with the audience in the foreground. Then I move to the center aisle, walking lightly to minimize the creaking, and shoot Rod head-on as he fiddles with his sheaf of poems. I snap a shot just as he runs his hand through his hair, and then he stops his search for the crowd-pleasing poem and looks up from the podium.

"Stop doing that," he says.

I turn around and look at the audience, thinking he must be referring to their whispering because the room falls silent. I turn back to him and take a couple more shots.

"I said stop doing that," he repeats, only this time he says it when the room is quiet. I look around and find that all eyes are on me, and his meaning dawns on me yet doesn't seem possible. After all, I'm from the *L.A. Times*. What aspiring poet wouldn't kill to have his poetry reading covered by a newspaper with a circulation of over a million?

"You want me to stop?" I ask.

"Yes, I want you to stop. It's the second time I've told you."

I feel a slight dampness under my arms and my heart beats faster. Maybe he doesn't know that I'm from the newspaper. Maybe he thinks I'm just a fan.

"I don't know if Sage told you, but I'm from the *L.A. Times*?" I ask tentatively, as if using an inflection might make me more like Sage and therefore semitolerable to Rod.

"I don't care where you're from," Rod says into the microphone. "You need to stop taking pictures. Now."

In that moment of humiliation, I look over at Sage, desperate for some kind of support. But she refuses to contradict Rod or even look at me. No doubt she has learned when to stand in the path of the actor's egotistical tornado and when to dive into the cellar. She's letting this one blow on through.

The only person who does look at me is Nathan Janning, whose rather shocked and sympathetic expression offers some comfort but no refuge. He doesn't have a voice here either.

"So, relax and sit down," Rod says a bit more lightly. "Who knows? You might actually learn something."

Most people would have sat down. Had it happened several months ago, when my father was still alive and I wasn't subsumed by regret and grief, I might have written Rod Boyle off as an ass-hole and found my chair, too, abandoning any urge to fight. But all of the emotion I had been pushing away into dark, stagnant pools, the anger that occasionally seeped out over some irritation or per-ceived injustice, now careens around me and courses through me and subverts any rational thought. As Trudy might say, I go plumb crazy.

Like Clint Eastwood in a high noon shoot-out, I lift my camera, switch the shutter to automatic, and fire away frame after frame. Through the lens, I watch the contortions of his tanned face speed by as the drama unfolds: first Rod's eyes closed, mouth open—looking like someone had thrown cold water on him; then a finger pointing at me; then his white teeth clenched as he sputters out the words, "I don't know who the fuck you think you are! Sage, do something, goddamn it!"

I turn to snap a quick shot of Nathan Janning, who smiles at the situation.

Sage rises shakily and asks, "Excuse me, but he wants you to stop?"

I take a picture of her too, just for kicks, and say, "Yeah. I don't think I'm getting his good side."

That makes people laugh, but Rod isn't one of them.

"Get the hell out of here!" he yells.

I turn on my heel and head out the door and into the parking lot. Despite my bravado, my heart pounds, and I can hear only the roar of a car engine and the frantic squeaking of my running shoes as I try not to run to my car. I want to get away from the scene of confrontation, fearful in my irrational mind that Rod just might commandeer Sage and company into an angry, bad-poetry posse.

Fortunately, the mob doesn't form, but I find out the next morning from Cecil Plainfield that the trouble isn't over.

"We have a problem," he says to me as I walk into his office at 9:00 A.M. sharp.

"I can explain. The key thing is I got the shots."

"You got a lot more than that. The head of publicity at Five-Star Films called the editor last night and he was—"

Just then an underling arrives and waits tentatively in the doorway. Cecil motions him in, signs a piece of paper, and hands it to him. He turns away and Cecil asks if he would be so kind as to shut the door behind him, which he does.

"The head of publicity is very, very angry," Cecil says as he stands with his fingertips gently touching his desk. "Sage Henley told him you treated Rod Boyle horribly."

"I treated him horribly? It was the other way around. He told me not to take any pictures of him."

"And you did anyway?"

"Of course I did. That was my assignment. I had to get the pictures."

"Julia, we are not talking about some celebrity coming out of the Hollywood police station. You don't go around insulting stars over something as minuscule as a poetry reading."

"But what was I supposed to do?"

"Just sit there. You still would have gotten paid."

"That's ridiculous."

"That's Hollywood. You don't bite the hand that feeds you, and the studios feed the media whether we like it or not." Cecil starts to sit down but thinks better of it, no doubt waiting for me to leave in defeat. I search my mind for some way out.

"People in the audience have probably forgotten about it already," I say.

"Maybe they have but Rod hasn't and Five-Star certainly hasn't."

"What can one movie studio do to you?"

That's when Cecil's tersely polite facade begins to crack. He looks at me, shakes his head, and picks up a nearby copy of yesterday's movie section of the paper.

"See these ads?" He holds up the page and points like a schoolteacher. "They are money for us—lots of money. Now, I don't think Five-Star is angry enough to start pulling them, but it's definitely damaged our relationship, not to mention the reputation of the paper with them and therefore possibly other studios." He folds the pages and drops them on his desk. "And that means I've got to cozy up to Five-Star's publicity people even more than I do now, which I didn't think was humanly possible, so that they'll forget about this incident and give me first dibs on interviewing the latest celebrity sensation in their latest forgettable film. Quid pro quo. So I assure you: only one movie studio can do quite a lot of damage."

"I can't believe this."

"Well, neither can the arts editor. She wanted to try to hold you responsible in some way, which she can't do legally. I told her I would forfeit your pay, which seemed to appease her. I know it's a cliché, but you probably won't work in this town again—at least not for the *L.A. Times* or for any studios."

"Would an apology help?"

"Hollywood means never having to say you're sorry," Cecil says. "You just take the blame, get exiled, and fade away."

"But I'm a nobody. Who cares what I did?"

"I'll let you in on a little secret. The smaller you are the crazier they get. The studio can pull rank with impunity. They know you're a nobody. In fact, I wouldn't be surprised if Five-Star is getting back at us for reporting about Fiona Simone getting busted for crack. As if we had a choice not to run the story when it's all over the national news."

It's beginning to sink in. All of my work over the years—the phone calls, combing the city for interesting photos, the networking—ruined by one little incident. I want to be brave and not give in to that nauseating feeling of despair and fear that makes my stomach sink the way it might if I were, say, dangled by one leg over the edge of a cliff. But it's no use, and I feel the tears coming on when I think about the prospect of starting over again, of staying at *Mangia!* with no end in sight.

Cecil quickly moves from behind his desk, walks the three steps with me to the door again, and says, "Don't worry. There are plenty of other jobs in this city." I could beg to differ, but I don't.

He shuts the door as soon as I clear the threshold. I take the elevator down to my car and sit behind the wheel, sobbing for about twenty minutes before I can calm myself. I finally regain my composure and try to figure out where to go because I don't want to be alone.

I go home anyway and call Trudy, but she doesn't answer. Just dialing her number filters her and Harlan's kindness back to me, and I realize how much I miss Trudy. Even if you live with people for just three days, you remember how nice it is to sit in the same room with another person. You don't even need to talk. And there's something about her knowing my history, my people, that makes me feel visible, real, and connected to a world outside of this nomadic city.

I make a cup of tea, try unpacking, try doing the dishes. I can sustain every activity I begin for only about five minutes. What would Trudy say if I told her the tide that turned became the tsunami that destroyed everything? She might say I wouldn't want to work for people like that anyway. And maybe she's right. But what about my role in everything? How do I justify that? I wonder whether I should even tell Claire what happened and decide that I won't. I already feel like a screw-up when I compare myself to her, and what she doesn't know won't hurt her. I lie down on the couch, the only place in my hovel that feels clean and comfortable, and decide to stay submerged for a while—floating deep within the roiling ocean, as silent as the fish who dart in between jagged coral reefs.

8 ♛

A Bicycle Built for One

It's 11:00 A.M. and I'm looking at photos from the "High Tea" shoot to make sure the scones and the lettuce in the finger sandwiches have the right amount of shine. The whole set-up, with its centerpiece of ornate silver, is designed to give readers "a sumptuous air of civility and elegance." If only they knew the ugly truth.

When we did the shoot last week, I tried to be as unobtrusive as possible, silently dabbing the lettuce and scones with my mayonnaise-covered Q-tip, while Sally circled around me like a territorial beast. She didn't fully trust Stone ever since she claimed he botched a spread on shortcake, so she decided to be a fly on the wall during the whole thing. Unfortunately, I was caught in the middle. Stone told me, "more glaze" or "more lettuce" or "more shaving cream on the strawberry tart" to which Sally countered, "Are you sure?" He said yes and she said that he knew best. This kind of exchange took place at least ten times during the hour-long affair, each one becoming increasingly terse. It was awful.

So I'm not surprised when Sally walks into my cubicle this morning and orders me to "check that moron's work." She has a habit of reading whatever is on my desk, and I am fortunate enough to have tucked the brochure about therapy into my drawer. She examines her cuticles as she says, "If he got too much glaze on those scones, I'm going to hang him by his balls." Then she turns on her heel and walks down the hall and into her office. As usual, Sally will wind up calling him a genius when she sees the results. Stone may be silent, but he knows what he's doing.

The advantage of being an underling is that I don't have to make decisions that might anger Sally. I simply do what I am told and don't ask questions, which is all I seem capable of anyway. Since the Rod Boyle disaster two weeks ago, I feel worse than ever about being at this job, in this city, in my apartment—stymied by the harsh, myopic reality of my L.A. world.

Like an automaton, I trudge out of my apartment every morning, climb into my Honda Accord, and drive the surface streets to work. My eyes squint at the hazy, terminal brownness in the air, withered palm trees, garish billboards cutting off the horizon, homeless people sleeping outside of Ralph's supermarket.

Lately, I've had trouble falling asleep, so I find myself channel surfing through late-night talk shows, old movies, cooking demonstrations, and trashy celebrity biographies. On nights when the tube is just too inane to watch, I'll crawl back in bed and turn on the radio. I find the most comfort in classical music, or mystery theater on the AM dial, because Trudy and Harlan's nightly ritual involved listening to those kinds of programs, and hearing the dramatic voices and melodies in the dark brings the farm and them right back to me. Yet that comfort is short-lived. And when my senile neighbor stands outside my door and begins yelling at me at 1:00 A.M., it's enough to make me think about going back to the farm for good.

Mrs. Sanchez's outbursts used to be manageable, directed toward things in her own apartment, but she decided, somehow, that I am her mortal enemy and now hurls all of her hostility at me. She stands in the hallway outside of my door and in her broken English yells, "I know who you are. *El diablo, el diablo.* Come out! Are you afraid? I know who you are." Sometimes she bangs a pot with a spoon after she says it. Other times I hear her spitting. Most people in the building know she's crazy. Even if someone did hear her raging outside my door, they wouldn't bother to walk up to the third floor to see what's wrong. They would say, It's only Mrs. Sanchez.

When I couldn't take it anymore, I told her to stop and go back to her apartment, but that only made her yell louder. I called the police in an effort to rein her in, but she had stopped screaming by the time they arrived, so they could do nothing. My neighbor Ellen on the first floor speaks Spanish and is the only person who Mrs. Sanchez allows near her. When asked about why she yells at me, Mrs. Sanchez denies ever having done so. I called the landlord and found out that the poor woman has no family left on earth to claim her. The landlord has contacted a social worker who is arranging for her to be put in a home at the state's expense, but it's a long and complicated process.

During the two weeks that I've been back at work, I've been keeping to myself and haven't told anyone except Claire about anything—Constance, Mrs. Sanchez, or my insomnia. Stone keeps asking if I'm all right because I keep spacing out during shoots. I say I'm fine and try not to look at his greasy strings of hair. Claire tells me he's a nice guy, but I think he's too weird and grisly to feel comfortable around.

Despite the benefit of our closeness, seeing Trudy again perhaps accounts for why the image of my mother dying finds me in those sleepless hours. I suppose the last thing my mother taught me was how to die. She was graceful and refined even as she took her last breath. I always imagined it would be a gruesome scene, gasping and thrashing and calling out the names of loved ones. Something out of a TV movie. But it wasn't like that at all.

We had been up all night in her bedroom, just Dad and I. The evening prior a few of her friends came over. She was unconscious, and we all stood around and tried to make small talk. That, in fact, was the hardest part of the whole thing—dealing with well-wishers. It was better when the three of us were alone.

My father took a shower at dawn, and I sat by her bed, holding her hand. When Dad came out of the bathroom, I noticed that her eyes were open for the first time in weeks, but she looked up and away, not at me, as though she spied something in the distance.

"I think you better come here, Dad," I said.

He sat on the other side of her bed and smoothed her face with his hand. It was one of the most tender gestures I had ever seen between them.

He looked into her eyes and said, "You go when you need to, honey. You go when you need to."

My father was more generous than I was. I wanted her to stay forever even if she was incoherent. But I was afraid to call her back from the dead and tell her to stay, afraid it might initiate another argument between Dad and me. It would have been awful, though perhaps accurate, for her last memory of Dad and me to involve conflict.

Her eyes closed again, and I watched her chest move up and down in what seemed like steady breath. One breath, two, three. And then they stopped. I kept waiting for the next, but number four never came.

Neither my father nor I said anything. We sat and watched the color slowly drain from her face just as the sky was beginning to find its own, as though taking the rose directly from her. The strange thing was that she at once became beautiful again. The anguish and pain slipped from her face. Wrinkles seemed to disappear. My father placed her turban back on her head, and she lay there looking like a silent film star from the '20s, swaddled in her robe and waiting for a facial.

She died her own quiet, private way, the way she wanted it. It wasn't her style to die in front of strangers. She kept things controlled and calm to the very end.

I have lunch at the Snow White Café on Hollywood Boulevard—a diner by day and a bar by night. It's done up in a faux Tudor style, wooden beams painted on walls festooned with fake garlands. The beer taps and counter are on the right and booths are on the left— each one has a flower box and a fake window with a picture of a dwarf in it. On the back wall, Snow White smiles brightly, her arms outstretched. Above her birds carry a banner that says, "We hope we have pleased you!"

Claire couldn't make it because of errands, but I think it's because she doesn't like the place, which she claims always smells of beer and bacon grease even though it doesn't. I pull out the brochure on therapy Claire gave me, which I thought was a comical gesture on her part more than anything. But she seems to be serious about it, asking me every few days or so if I've checked it out.

When she asked me about it this morning, I laughed and said, "I'm not the crazy one. But give me a few more weeks like these last two and I might be." She didn't get the joke.

"I went to Naomi when my sister died, and she really helped me."

"I know, but I don't think I should be wasting my money when I'm barely making ends meet."

"It's not a waste," Claire said. "It'll help you deal with the grief."

"I'm dealing with it just fine. I'm showing up to work, aren't I?"

After the interminable silence passed, Claire said, "I just want to help. But it's your decision."

I put the brochure away when my Grumpy's cheeseburger platter arrives. The fries are still sizzling in their grease, and I think about my to-do list, the one that has "eat healthier food" on it. I figure I'll start tomorrow.

After lunch I walk down Hollywood Boulevard and pull my jean jacket tighter against the unexpected late April drizzle and wind—actual weather. The wet streets produce their usual effect: halting traffic to a crawl. I am one of only several pedestrians out today. I cross side streets jammed with cars, all the while unsure of where exactly I am heading.

I think about Claire, how different our lives are, and wonder: How can she really understand what I need? Hers is the life of socialization, of couples and promotions and plans for having children—a life I imagined for myself, but which seems to grow increasingly dim. Claire tells me there is no timetable and I want to believe her. But then I think of my friends from high school and college, all of whom are not only married but quite well employed— a chef, a lawyer, a neurologist, for God's sake. One friend stays at home with her two children, but that doesn't stop her from being a triathlete. They send me chatty form letters at Christmas and inspirational or jokey prefab e-mails that have circulated the country several times over. At first I wrote actual notes back; two of them didn't reply and the other two just sent more recycled e-mails. I am not close with these women; I don't even know them anymore and have no idea if Christmas in the Bahamas was really that fabulous and whether her promotion, in truth, gives her little more than a reason to spend less time at home. Whether their lives are better or worse than when I knew them doesn't really matter—all I know is that they are in that forward, striding momentum, and I'm still on the roadside, watching them pass, wondering how to break out of my stagnant, isolated self and into the flow of living.

My former roommate in L.A. had more of a social network than I did partly because she was an actress and was forever meeting new people in workshops and on the television spots she got. I called her a few times after she got married and moved to Venice but never heard back from her. I know she's still in town because I've seen her on television a couple of times in bit parts—once as a juror on *Law & Order,* another time as a nurse on *ER*.

In the past ten years I've made many acquaintances but very few friends. I attribute it to the vastness of L.A., along with the itinerant nature of its residents—people stay, but not for very long in the same job or apartment. And you swear you'll get together, but you're so busy, and there's traffic, and it's too much of a struggle to get from here to there. My own shyness and tribulations haven't exactly made me a social magnet, either.

I walk east, fast and purposefully, though I have no purpose other than to get away from work. I turn around after several blocks and then head toward the distant Pacific. Suddenly, the sporadic drizzle gives way to a blast of sun, but it's not a comforting sight. Instead of brightness and clarity, it gives the boulevard a murky, postapocalyptic haze, like the earth's atmosphere in the sci-fi flick *Soylent Green*. I pass Frederick's, the Church of Scientology, Ripley's Believe It or Not Odditorium, and dozens of shops that advertise a mishmash of tourist knickknacks, tattoos, body piercing, T-shirts, pagers, and check cashing services with no questions asked. Rock music blares from every venue, and I long for a quiet, clean place.

I walk all the way down to the gaudy, chrome caryatids built to signify the renewal of the boulevard to its 1940s glory days even though they didn't have the Gap or California Pizza Kitchen back then. I look at the shapely women who effortlessly bear the weight of Hollywood on their heads, and I know that the restoration, like so many things here, is just another hyped-up, short-lived impossible dream.

It's twelve-thirty, and I'm supposed to be back at the office but am not ready to return. I look down the street lined with tall palms and think about what the ocean must look like on a day like today, probably slate blue and choppy, the kind of ocean that can take your jumbled thoughts away for a while into its own rough swell. As I imagine the waves, their mix of turmoil and calm, I lose sight of the things directly in front of me—a sign that says Don't Walk.

I'm standing about halfway into the crosswalk where Hollywood meets La Brea when I finally emerge from my reverie. Luckily there are no cars, but a bicyclist hangs a right and heads straight for me. He swerves to miss me, causing his tires go out from under him. He and the bike skid to a halt a few feet away, but he then bounces up off the pavement like a spinning top and starts swearing and screaming at me. He wants to know what the fuck my problem is. He wants to know if I've got eyes, a brain. Goddamn mother-fucker, he says. He's about twenty-two years old and has a goatee. He wears a backward baseball cap, black biking shorts, and a red warm-up jacket.

He walks back to his bike and inspects it and then looks down at the scrape on his leg that has begun to bleed. I'm standing there watching the blood drip down his wet, hairy leg. I say, "I'm sorry. I didn't see you." I say it twice because the first time gets no reaction from him. He wipes the blood with his jacket and then glares at me.

"Sorry won't help my leg. Next time, why the fuck don't you watch where you're going? Goddamn idiot!"

He rides away stiffly, clearly in pain, yet I am the one who is left crying on the corner. I tell myself that it was just an accident, that he was being unfair, that I tried to make things better for him. But nothing consoles me as I stand under the awning of a pizza joint, sobbing uncontrollably. There's nothing worse than crying in a city. People look but no one asks what's wrong. Of course, even if some-one did come to my aid, I don't know what I would say. It seems ludicrous to attribute all of my hysteria to a fallen bicyclist.

So I let the motorists stare as they drive by the corner of Holly-wood and La Brea. I've been entertaining them for what feels like an hour, but the manager of a pizza joint tells me it's been fifteen minutes. He doesn't like people loitering in front of his establish-ment, so I need to either come in and eat or stand someplace else.

I make another endeavor to quell the tears. I try to say, "I'm not loitering." But the only sound that comes out is a strangled whim-per and he tells me again, eat or move on. In a trance I head south on La Brea, past the minimalls, pawn shop, and Crazy Girls Exotic Strip Show, still sniffling and fighting for control. I lose the battle and have to stop again, ducking into the rubble of a demolished building. I sit on a slab of concrete and bury my head in my arms. I am no longer in L.A. I am on the farm, talking to Trudy, listening to Harlan tell me I'll be all right. I am in my house on the hill sitting in front of the fire and watching the flames, safe and contained, as my mother and father read the evening paper. In my dreams, the other part of life never happens. There are no sudden or miserable deaths, enemies masquerading as stepsisters, arrogant actors, profane, unforgiving bicyclists. Life is gracious, untroubled, and everlasting.

I guess you could call it an emotional blackout, but I have no idea how long I've been sitting in the lot and staring at the chunks of concrete and twisted metal. I forgot my watch but know I must be well over my allotted hour. At least I've stopped crying, but Sally's wrath would undo me all over again. The alibi for my extended absence is obvious: I was hit by the cyclist. I don't like lying to people, but I see no way out of the predicament when I think about Sally.

And even if I did make it through another verbal assault, it wouldn't stop there. Sally would want me to confide my troubles to her. "What's going on with you? Tell me about your life." That's her favorite management style. She coaxes her colleagues into baring their souls—about relationship troubles, sick friends, dead parents—and then she invariably uses the confessions against them, chiding them for letting their personal lives interfere with their work. Claire and I are among the sensible ones who haven't taken the bait although Sally tried pretty hard to make me spill my guts after Dad died. I remained stoic, which has only helped her pretend it never happened.

So the truth is not an option. But my story is not a complete lie, I figure, since the guy did run over me verbally. Nevertheless, I go to the drugstore and buy some gauze and adhesive tape and wrap up my elbow just in case anybody suspects.

With prop in place, I call Sally and give her the bad news.

She knows it's me and says, "Well?" when the receptionist connects us.

"I'm very sorry I'm late Sally, but I got hit by a bicyclist when I was crossing the street." My voice, still tearful and shaky, adds a convincing touch.

"Good God. Are you okay?"

"Yes, but I scraped my elbow pretty badly and I also—"

Why did I say "also"? Now I have to bandage something else. But what? I have to say it now or she'll know I'm lying. Just say it. Say something!

"I also hurt my nose."

Oh, shit.

"Is it broken?" she asks.

"No. Some people in front of a restaurant helped me to my feet and one of them was a doctor, so he made sure nothing was broken."

What am I saying?

"Boy are you lucky it wasn't worse. Was he at least cute?" Sally asks.

"The cyclist?"

"No, the doctor."

"Not really," I say. "He was older."

"Listen, get a cab or a bus back to work even if it's only a few blocks. You shouldn't be walking."

I comply although it occurs to me that I shouldn't even be working if I had been actually hit. But showing up and forging on over the glare of the light table will only put me in Sally's good graces— a positive angle I hadn't seen before. She loves selfless devotion, something I've never excelled in when it comes to food styling. She'll think I'm turning over a new leaf. Riding in the back of the cab, I tape a piece of gauze over the bridge of my nose and hope for the best.

Claire is the first person I see in the room of cubicles, the world headquarters of *Mangia!*

"Jesus! What on earth happened to you?"

Other people are looking now and moving toward me. I had planned to pull Claire into the bathroom and tell her the truth. But maybe it's just as well that she hears my little fabrication. Maybe she'll take pity on me and stop pestering me about the shrink.

So I tell her and anyone else who'll listen the whole wildly embellished story: I'm in the crosswalk and the bicyclist slams on his breaks but still runs into my elbow and knocks me nose-first to the pavement. Meanwhile, he does a complete flip in the air and lands on his feet, miraculously unscathed. Several bystanders rush to my aid, one of them being an elderly doctor who bears a striking resemblance to Marcus Welby, M.D. He's very kind and efficient. The cyclist inspects the damage to his vehicle, which is minor. Still, he starts to berate me, but the crowd shouts him down.

"Young man, don't bother this woman. It's not her fault," says Marcus Welby. And then other voices chime in.

"Yeah, take a hike, bozo."

"Try the Tour de France next time."

"Why don't you buy some training wheels, hot shot?"

I finish the story by telling how Marcus Welby helped me to my feet and walked me to the drugstore. Then he carefully bandaged my nose and elbow for me.

"What a wonderful man," says Denise, the receptionist with curly brunette hair (this week) and two-inch nails. "How come more people aren't like that?"

"Good question," I say, practically believing the fiction myself. "But it really redeemed my faith in humanity."

There's a murmur of agreement, and I begin to feel a pang of guilt over how well the lie has succeeded. Everyone tells me how glad they are that I'm all right. The only people who remain silent are Claire and Stone, who both stare at me blankly and then go back to their work at the light table. It's nothing new for Stone, really, but Claire is another story. Denise says Sally is in a meeting, but she'll tell her I'm back as soon as possible.

I walk slowly to my cubicle, and after a few minutes Claire comes by. I rub my elbow dramatically and try to look like I'm busy.

"What are you working on?" she asks.

"Just another blue plate special," I say lightly, hoping she'll smile and walk away. But she's still there after a few seconds, so I turn to her and ask, "Do you need something?"

"No," she says a bit sheepishly. "I just wanted to say I'm sorry about what happened to you. Are your scrapes pretty bad?"

"Pretty bad," I say as I swivel back to my desk and begin shuffling plastic sheets of photo slides, "but I guess they could have been worse. I mean, I could have been hit by a car instead of a bike."

"Well, that's a positive perspective."

"I'm trying."

"I know. And at least you don't need stitches. I mean, I'm assuming the doctor said you didn't."

"Yeah. No stitches. Just time, bandages, and Neosporin."

"I hope they heal soon." Claire pauses and then steps a little closer to me. She stands over my shoulder and asks, "Can I take a look at them?"

"Sure. It's the 'High Tea' shoot."

"No, I mean, your scrapes," she says. "Would you mind if I saw them?"

All I can say is: "Yes, I would mind. Are you into gore or something?"

"No, I'm just concerned. I don't know. Maybe I need to see it to believe it—it seems so impossible."

"Well, that's the way things go. One minute you're fine, the next you're getting run over by a bike or swallowed by a wave or falling from the sky or whatever."

"I didn't mean to upset you."

"I'm not upset."

"You sound like you are, and I don't blame you. Another accident is just about the last thing you need."

"This hardly compares with the plane crash," I say as I shove the slides into a folder.

"Oh, of course not. What I meant was—"

"I know what you meant. I've had enough trouble, enough bad surprises. I need things to calm down for a while, right?"

"Right."

"Well, they will. I'm due. And look, I really am fine."

"I am looking, and fine is not the word I'd use. I won't say anything more about it, Julia, but will you please just think about calling Naomi?"

"Who?"

"The therapist."

I know that she's telling me the truth, that healthy people don't wander aimlessly away from work, cry hysterically, and then tell elaborate lies to their colleagues and best friends to cover their tracks—at least not lies involving nose injuries and a Marcus Welby look-alike. I know she's trying to help, but it's hard to hear.

Without looking at her, I say, "I'll think about it. But right now that's the best I can do, okay?"

"Okay. But if you need to talk later, call me."

Claire leaves and I am finally alone. I take a sip of coffee, but it has that thick, burnt taste of 3:00 P.M. I pour the rest into my dying plant.

Sally never does emerge from her meeting, and I am thankful when, at 5:00 on the button, I slip out the door and tell Denise I'm leaving. She asks me to wait so she can give me the number of her chiropractor, but I pretend like I don't hear her as I hobble to catch the elevator. For the first time since I have worked at the magazine, someone actually holds the elevator door for me.

Once inside my building, I run up the three flights of stairs, praying that I won't run into any neighbors who will want to know what happened to me. My studio apartment is always fairly dark. So I perform my usual ritual: I reach for the roach spray, turn on the light, and then unload on anything that moves. Even though there are no dirty dishes in the sink, it's always a hotbed of activity. I nail a huge one as it's trying to scramble down the drain and then two smaller ones that scurry along the wall next to the garbage can.

All is quiet. There is only one more battle that I must endure before I can find my way to the couch. I flip on the switch and see nothing in the toilet. Quickly, I spray inside the shower curtain upon spotting the silhouette of another monstrous roach. It struggles for the top but then dies midway and falls into the tub. It never had a chance.

How pathetic to feel wily and powerful by killing a roach. But it never fails. I always have an odd feeling of triumph combined with the inherent repulsion. Then I catch a glimpse of myself in the mirror—the nose, the elbow, the Black Flag—and consider what a freak I've become. I look like I belong in a cheap horror film. Maybe I should greet Mrs. Sanchez with this get-up when she starts to wail. But then I remember: she has no one. Maybe that loneliness is the cause of her insanity. Maybe she and I are not so far apart after all.

I pop a frozen Mexican dinner in the microwave, wait for the ding, but only pick at the food before crawling into bed. I have my deepest sleep between the hours of 7:00 P.M. and 10:00 P.M. and tonight is no exception. I emerge from my coma at 10:15 and listen to the steady rain. I sit up and look out the window at the shadows of trees. Along with the low rent, the street sold me on the apartment. It almost feels like I am someplace other than the city when I can look out of my window and see their branches—even if their trunks and roots are penned in by concrete.

I fall back into a thick, cavernous slumber that lasts through the night for a change. I am awakened with a start by the rumble of the garbage trucks as they run over the potholes in the street. At first, I think it's an earthquake. I sit upright in bed, my heart racing. It's 7:00 A.M. and I fall back on the mattress, relieved yet still exhausted once I realize that my life is not in danger.

At 9:00 A.M., I rise up on one elbow and look around my room, disoriented. And even though I am already late, I lie here thinking about things to do that day, other than go to work. I think I'll buy a thermos and keep it by my bedside. I'll fill it with coffee to drink before my feet even hit the floor. If I had some coffee to drink at 7:00, then maybe I could get up. But first, before I get the thermos, I'll clean my room of the piles of clothes and magazines and books that have been accumulating during the past few months. That's the first step. And even though I'm only thinking about doing this, it feels like I already have cleaned up the piles, so I can relax. I have nothing to worry about. Before I know it, I'm drifting off again and then the phone rings. It's Claire.

"Julia, you overslept."

I sigh and watch the digital numbers of my clock radio blink to 9:20.

"Listen, I know you feel awful," she says, "but I think you should come in if you can. Sally is in a mood, and I don't think she believes you're that bad off. I mean, I think she needs to see how banged up you are to feel good about letting you come in late."

"That figures."

"Do you want me to tell her you went to the doctor or something?"

"No, I'll just deal with it. Thanks for calling. I just, well . . . I am having a tough time this morning. I'm fine, but not at this exact moment."

"I know, honey. You know, I'm just going to tell Sally you went to the doctor. That will buy you some time. Come on in after you've had some coffee," she says. "I'm sure you must be sore from the accident."

"Am I ever."

"Maybe a hot shower will help."

I tell her I'm sure it will, fighting back another flash flood. I hang up, certain that I don't deserve the kindness Claire has shown me when all I can do is lie to her. I try to pull myself together. I imagine Mom and Dad would want me to keep moving forward, but just the thought of them brings another deluge of tears, and I am afraid that will never stop. Is this what a breakdown feels like? Does a person having a breakdown think about whether she is having a breakdown? Surely not—which makes me feel a little bit better.

I fall back to sleep for another half hour and then am up for good. I make coffee, check the clock, and think about the Open Doors Therapy Center, its sliding scale fees and how the first session is free. I left the brochure at the office but wrote down the name and number of the therapist. I call her.

"Can you tell me a little about what's going on?" Naomi asks after the introductions.

I figure I might as well come straight out with it and see how she handles herself.

"My father died in a plane crash recently and my mother's dead, too. She died of cancer."

"I see. I'm very sorry," she says and nothing more. I wait for a few seconds, thinking about how it was Claire's sister who died, not a parent. Her situation was completely different.

"Look, I don't think this is the right thing for me," I say.

"Why don't you just come in for the free session. I've done a lot of grief work, and I might be able to help you."

"Grief work" sounds official—like road work—and makes me think there must be a whole separate field of study for it—that she'll strap on the hard hat, pull out the cerebral jackhammer, and go to work on me.

"When do you get off work today?"

I tell her and she asks me to come by at six o'clock. I agree and she gives me the address, but I'm not writing it down. When she's done, I say thanks and hang up the phone. I put on the one clean outfit I own at this point—black stirrup pants and a huge gray sweater that I bought at a flea market. I don't brush my teeth or finish the coffee. There's only enough time to bandage my imaginary wounds before I put on my raincoat and head into the storm.

9 ⚜

Intimacy Issues

"Are you sure you feel like dating right now?" Claire says, looking directly at my elbow scab.

That's her response when I announce three weeks later that it is a man, not a therapist, who can help me find happiness. Regardless of how earnest and certain Naomi sounded on the phone, I wasn't ready to subject myself to "grief work." Who needs to be torn up and examined under the glare of fluorescent, clinical concern? Who wants to be a case study? Besides, isn't love a more natural way to heal the pain of loss?

I don't present all of these arguments to Claire. She's already made up her mind. I just tell her, "Yes. It's no big deal."

"Did he ask about your injuries?"

"Yes."

"What did he say?"

"The usual. He was very nice, very concerned." Claire nods. I look into her eyes and decide the charade has gone on long enough. I take a breath and tell her the pathetic, embarrassing truth.

"God, Julia. Sometimes I just don't understand you. I can't believe you've been lying to me all this time! How could you do that?"

"I don't know. I was afraid you would criticize me for faking it."

"I wouldn't criticize you. I might question you."

I don't argue that the two are virtually the same thing.

"Does the guy—"

"Jeffrey," I say, a touch annoyed.

"Does Jeffrey know the truth?"

"Of course not. He'd probably think I was some freak."

"Well, you have to admit—" Claire begins.

"I admit, out of context, it's strange. Okay? But I had to come up with some excuse for wandering off that day. I just couldn't face Sally's anger."

"Then how did you get the scabs?"

"I have some stuff in a tube that I put on."

"Jesus."

"It's a type of theatrical makeup. I got it at a prop store," I tell her, as if to make everything sound more sane and legitimate.

"I can't believe all the trouble you've gone to," she says.

"What choice did I have? I was a mess. I practically had a breakdown that day, and do you think I wanted to tell Sally about that?"

"I know, but—"

"Claire, I know I should have told you, and I'm sorry. What else can I say?"

She falls silent and takes a bite of her eggs.

"Okay, I understand why you did it," she says. "But next time you're in a jam, just call me. You know I'll cover for you."

"I know. I just wasn't thinking straight. And you've covered for me so many times already."

"So I'll cover a few more. You'd do the same for me."

"I know."

Claire takes a sip of her coffee and smiles at me, slowly shaking her head. "Scabs in a tube. Leave it to a food stylist."

"Occupational hazard," I reply, which makes her laugh. I relax, thinking I'm out of the woods, but the interrogation isn't quite over.

"So, what about Jeffrey?" she asks. "Seriously, do you think he's someone you could be in a relationship with? Do you feel ready for that?"

It's a legitimate question for which I don't have an answer. So, in spite of my desire to be truthful, I lie once again.

"Absolutely. I'm ready for anything."

"You might want to lose the nose scab, then."

Oddly enough, my scabs actually helped bring Jeffrey and me together.

I met him on a singles hike not long after my faux accident. There were no men at work to date. They all seemed to have that unique L.A. disease of duality: "I sell ad space, but what I really want to do is own a nightclub, direct a movie, have a sex change." I was looking for someone who was kind, secure, and relatively at peace with himself. It was a lot to ask, but I didn't want to settle. When a desirable man happened to join the magazine ranks—someone who didn't have a cocaine habit, didn't want to marry a starlet, didn't have a wife he was almost separated from—my dreamy, instantaneous crush on him never lived up to reality.

Had I not met Jeffrey, the hike would have been an unmitigated disaster. There were many harrowing factors: freakish 90 degree heat from the Santa Ana winds; a ratio of twenty-three women to seven men; an eight-mile, rocky terrain of steep inclines; and a tall, buxom blonde named Gina who had trouble keeping her shirt on.

"You know, it *is* hot out here," Gina said at a water break, like she'd just stepped out of an air-conditioned bubble. "Well, this isn't a church hike, so . . ."

She concluded the thought by stripping down to her black Wonder Bra. A few of the women exchanged glances, and the men smiled.

"You're in great shape," one guy said as he leered.

"I run marathons," she said.

"Cool!" he gushed. "So do I."

"I just got done running one in Copenhagen."

"Copenhagen! That's very cool!"

That's when I caught Jeffrey's eye. He was standing next to Gina. He looked up from the ground and at me for a second, clearly embarrassed by the whole show, and I liked him instantly. So I walked over to where they stood and waited for something to happen. It didn't take long.

"Oh my God! What happened to you?" Gina asked. It was no surprise that she zeroed in on my appearance even though I was only wearing a small nose scab—just in case I came across someone from work.

"Biking accident," I replied, like a seasoned Olympian.

"Wow. You must have been going pretty fast," Jeffrey said.

"Oh yeah. You know," I shrugged.

"It's easy to do when you get your adrenaline going. I love cycling," Jeffrey said.

I found out that he has law and history degrees from Stanford and teaches Civil War history, my father's specialty, at Loyola Marymount, but we didn't talk much about that. I tried, but Jeffrey seemed a bit tired of the topic, which is only understandable. We mostly talked about cycling even though I'm nothing but near roadkill and a weekend dabbler at best. He chatted up several other women during the grueling trek—not Gina, which again earned him points. He must have seen something in me since he asked for my number and nobody else's.

We had the compulsory coffee date, the movie-and-dessert date, the full-blown fancy-restaurant-dinner date—molding our life résumés into enthusiastic conversation while secretly trying to decide whether we liked each other enough to act upon our hormonal urges. There was definitely an attraction from the start. I liked his thick, curly hair—brown with a hint of late-thirties gray. I liked the way he looked in jeans and a turtleneck sweater. I liked that he wore a leather jacket. I found out that he, like me, has no siblings, that his parents are alive and well but divorced. He drinks his coffee black, adores Ingmar Bergman films, and thinks Wolfgang Puck and Robert Mapplethorpe are overrated.

Our fourth date is tonight—dinner and a jazz club. It's five o'clock and I've been running around my apartment for two hours, scrubbing, plucking, and primping myself and my lair into an image of civilized perfection. I bought two floor lamps yesterday and have hidden the various piles of clothing and magazines in every available space—in the closet, under the bed, under the sink. I was too anxious to sort through everything.

Jeffrey arrives exactly at 6:00 P.M. He walks in the door and gives me his usual half-body hug, polite, the hug you might give your grandmother.

My outfit hints that I might be ready for more. Instead of the usual baggy sweater, I'm wearing a black skintight leotard and a pair of equally tight jeans. A silver necklace with a heart on the end dangles above my braless cleavage. It's a look that makes Jeffrey smile, hug me again—all of me—and whisper into my ear, "You look great."

Dinner is quick but pleasant. We eat at a trattoria called Boca that was recently featured in *Mangia!*—a place noted for its huge, decorative jars of pickled vegetables, paper tablecloths with crayons, and pasta dishes made to order. Jeffrey loves it. We talk about the decor, the quality of the food.

I can tell he wants to keep the conversation light since we're trying to make an eight o'clock show and have to be there by seven-thirty. I don't mind that we chew more than we talk, or that Jeffrey, in his punctual alertness, keeps looking at his watch every fifteen minutes. This is just a part of intimacy, being privy to his idiosyncrasies, allowing for comfortable silences. It's pleasure enough just to be out with a man again, to put my arm through his as we walk out the door into the brisk night air. Yet I'm beginning to feel that

I don't want him to be just any man, another name on a seemingly endless list of men who didn't work out.

We go to a jazz club to hear a special tribute to the music of Sarah Vaughn. I listen to singers, men and women, crooning the silky melodies. I don't know any of the musicians, but I don't care. It's the music that sends me, releasing my tension and sadness in the darkness of the crowded room, giving expression to it so that I don't have to. Jeffrey orders scotch on the rocks, and it sounds so perfect at that moment, just as sultry and mellow as "Honeysuckle Rose," that I order one too even though I'm only a wine drinker. I let the ice melt a little before I sip it, trying to ignore the vile taste and concentrate on the warmth and lightheadedness it brings me. We listen to the music for about a half hour, occasionally smiling at each other but not compelled to talk. I sip my drink slowly while Jeffrey orders another one.

I smile at him after the waitress leaves and say, "If I drank two I'd be in trouble."

He doesn't say anything, and I realize my faux pas: his mother is an alcoholic. He was very matter-of-fact when he told me about it during our last date and said he simply pretends that he doesn't have a mother anymore, which is hard for me to imagine since I would give anything for my own to be back among the living. Jeffrey is quite different from my old beau Bobby Powell, who understood his mother was sick and tried to forgive her. Nonetheless, I backpedal.

"I mean, I'm impressed that you can actually drink two."

"Well, it's not such an impressive thing. Just ask my mother."

The waitress arrives just as he says it, and he pays her—I can tell—abruptly, or at least a little faster than the way he gave her the bills before. She leaves and he turns back to the music, avoiding my eyes and his drink. He says everything is okay, but I know it's not, and it feels like my knee was hit with one of those little rubber hammers. The tremor travels up to my brain, rattles around, breaking any idyllic images of him and me together, and then shoots straight to the back of my neck. I breathe deeply and try to rub away the tense, pinching fingers of doubt.

I start to wonder if I shouldn't just make an excuse and push off before things get even more awkward, but then he reaches out and takes my hand.

"You know, I didn't mean to imply that you have a drinking problem," I say.

"I know. I'm just kind of sensitive about the whole alcohol thing, I guess. People are always saying it's genetic, but I think that's bullshit."

"Absolutely," I say although I'm not entirely sure that I agree.

"But don't worry. I'm fine. Are you okay?" he asks.

"Oh sure. My neck's still a little sore, you know, from the biking accident."

"I can give you a back rub."

"Right now?"

He laughs and says, "No. I mean when we get to my place or your place or wherever."

"Oh, right. Yeah—I mean, that would be great."

We listen to the music for another hour and even though he does drink the second drink—and then three more—I try not to worry. We get to his place for coffee, and on the way in he puts his arm around me. Maybe it was the scotch or the music. I don't know. But he's clearly in the mood. I thought I was, too, but things seem to be moving so fast even though technically, rationally, I know they aren't.

We are standing in his clean, white kitchen and before I know it, he leans into me, puts his arms around my waist, and kisses me on the lips.

It is a gentle kiss at first. But then his hands are trailing down my back, his lips are more insistent, and his tongue sallies forth. Part of me wants it to progress, but then the dissenting voices— the parliamentarians within—hold an emergency session: *Order!! Quite the saucy don, aren't we! But where will it lead? To a quick shag*

and a fare-thee-well? And what about that liquor? Who's kissing you—
him or Johnny Walker? Bad business, that! Hear, hear!

When we part, I want to offer at least a little encouragement,
a shy compliment, a hug or a smile. After all, we are dating. We've
held hands and had a modest good-night kiss or two. We've had
conversations on the phone before going to sleep. And right now,
we're both a little breathless.

But I turn away from him and step toward the stove, which
makes him ask, "What's wrong?"

I put my hand on the oven door to steady myself, pause for a
moment, and then say words that confound both him and me: "I
think, right now, I'm having some intimacy issues."

Suddenly, I feel too visible in this bright, lemon-scented room.
I don't really know what I mean and wonder if I should try to explain or just cut my losses and run. Maybe I should recant by restat-
ing the comment: "I mean, isn't intimacy a fascinating issue?" Then
I wonder if I should simply faint dead away, but I've sworn off deceptive theatrics. What in God's name is my problem? Do I need
more time? And if that's the case, why did I go to his apartment?
And why am I wearing this come-hither outfit?

"I'm just a little shy," I say.

"Well, we can work on that." He takes a step toward me and
tries to encircle me in his arms. I duck under his embrace and head
for the sink.

"No, really," I say, looking out the window and facing the brick
wall of the building next door. The teakettle whistles. Jeffrey turns
off the gas.

"I'm a little confused," he says.

"So am I."

"I thought we had something going."

"I don't know," I say, having slipped back into my familiar,
wordless angst.

"What do you mean?"

"I don't know." I'm beginning to feel so flooded and over-whelmed that it's getting a little difficult to breathe normally. I try to calm myself, taking a few seconds, and turn toward him again.

"I've just had a lot of things happen to me lately, and I don't know if I'm ready to get involved."

"You mean because of your father?"

"Right. That's a big part of it."

"Well, that's normal. You're still sad and all. But that's where I come in. I can help make you happy, you know?"

He busts yet another move as he's talking, staggering more than a little as he walks over and puts his arms on either side of me as I lean on the sink.

"I want to make you happy," he says as he starts to kiss my neck and then, most unfortunately, sees fit to growl into my ear. Wrong, all wrong. I put my arms up between him and me.

"What?" he says, a little less tenderly.

"I'm sorry, but I just can't do this. I can't continue seeing you. I'm just . . ."

"Whoa. Wait a minute."

". . . not into it, and I'm not exactly sure why. We're just in different places right now. We want different things."

"Well, what do you want?"

"I don't know, but not this. Not yet. I don't know why, okay? It's not you. It's me."

"Well, I'll agree with you there. I mean, I'd say it's okay, but we've been going out for—"

"You don't need to say anything. Really."

I no longer feel conscious of my actions. Everything seems blurry as my heart pounds in my chest. Lost in a miasma of panic, confusion, anger, and who knows what else, I head for the kitchen table and grab my jacket and purse.

"I guess you don't want any tea now, do you?" he says.

The answer is obvious, so I remain silent.

"Look, maybe we can still go out as friends or something," he says as he follows me to the door, but I'm not really sure that he'd settle for just a game of Scrabble on Saturday night.

"I don't think I can do that," I say, to which Jeffrey shrugs his shoulders.

It's midnight, and he insists on walking me to my car. But I don't comply when he takes a step toward me with arms open for one last hug. Instead, I lunge toward the car door and say "'Bye" in the instant before I slam it shut. I speed down the 10 Freeway, my car radio blaring an oldie but goody—"All You Need Is Love"—an anthem I'm beginning to think I'll never sing.

I had been more punctual at work during the time that Jeffrey was in my life. I was able to get out of bed when the garbage trucks rumbled down the street. I even bought something better than a thermos—a self-starting coffeepot that I programmed to begin brewing at 7:00 A.M. But after Jeffrey and I hit the dead end last Friday, I stumbled back to my old ways and was late nearly every morning last week. It's Sunday and raining, so I stay in bed all day. My head throbs, and I can't tell if it's just a hangover or the beginnings of a migraine. I haven't had one since right after Dad's funeral, and I hate taking the medicine. Fortunately, the bed rest pays off; the pain begins to ease in the late afternoon.

On Monday, I slink into the world headquarters at ten o'clock, poking my head into Claire's cubicle before heading to my own.

"She's gone out on a shoot with Stone," Denise says as she whizzes past me. "And Sally wants to see you. Sorry, doll." Denise looks more flustered than usual for this hour, so I prepare myself for the worst.

I knock on Sally's door and there's no reply. I turn to leave just as the door flies open and Sally is there, looking like she's on drug bust.

"You're late," she says.

"I know. I'm sorry."

"Were you at the doctor? And if you were, why the hell didn't you call?"

I should simply say yes and let it go at that. But I'm tired of dodging her questions. "No. I overslept."

"Have a seat," she says as she points to an overstuffed chair across from her desk. I walk in and she follows, shutting the door behind her. I pray that she will stay in her territory, behind her bleached oak throne, but she wants to get personal and takes the seat next to me. She regards me for a while. I look down at the black dots on her light pink carpet.

Finally, she says, "If you were Denise or Claire or Andy or Stone or anybody else, I would rip you a new one. You know how I feel about tardiness."

I nod my head, but she still feels compelled to tell me.

"It undermines team morale. It's the equivalent of saying, 'I don't give a damn about this job.' Am I right?"

"I guess so."

"You guess?"

I can't take it anymore and I say, "Sally, I know that's your policy, and it won't happen again. I'm sorry."

"You've said that before, and I don't think you realize what a problem this has become. Do you know you've been late twenty-five days during the past two months?"

"No. Are you sure?"

It was the wrong question to ask. She gets up and pulls out a file from her drawer and shows me a piece of paper with "Office Tardiness" printed in big red letters at the top. I see all the T's and the corresponding times underneath my name, just like they used to do in grade school.

"Now are you convinced?"

"Yes," I say, half expecting her to slap my ankles with a ruler.

"Hmmm," she says. and continues to stare. That's another favorite strategy of hers, staring at you and squinting her eyes as though she's reading the Sanskrit under your words, the hieroglyphics of your soul. At last, she breaks the silence.

"When you do finally arrive, you do a good job. And I think there are wonderful opportunities for you at this magazine. But you don't seem very upbeat about what's going on here. I like to see energy when I walk into the office. Not gloominess. Now, I know you've been through some hard times. But I wonder what else is going on with you?"

She stares me down, waiting for me to spill my guts, but I hold firm. During moments like these I try not to hate her. I try to re-member the word on the street—that Sally has had a hard life: the poor kid from Ironton, Indiana, whose father abandoned her, who put herself through Northwestern, who arrived in L.A. with the stage name Sydney Lane and tried breaking into television for a de-cade and then became Sally Reynolds—editor for hire. I'm not even sure it's her real name.

I forgive her affected dislike of "the Valley crowd" and for intro-ducing me as, "Julia, our resident preppie." But her controlling, pseudo-sensitive inquiries drive me crazy. I want her to stop badg-ering me, to understand, without having to know every detail of my life, that I will be gloomy for a while.

Thankfully, the phone rings and Sally picks up instantly.

"Denise, do you think you could follow my instructions just once? Yes, I did tell you, and I'll tell you again: Do not bother me. Take messages."

Sally hangs up the phone and lets out an exasperated sigh. "What was I going to say?"

"You know, it's a busy day. We can talk later on if you want," I say.

"No, I don't want. It's always busy around here. That's the way it should be. Ah, I remember."

Sally stands up and looks out the window, her back facing me.

"I'm going to tell you something about myself that not many people know." Still gazing at the glinting, smoggy landscape, she runs a hand through her shoulder-length, auburn-highlighted hair, flips it dramatically to one side and says, "I'm in analysis."

After a few very pregnant seconds, she turns back toward me for my reply, and all I can come up with is, "I've heard of analysis."

She looks at me quizzically, so I seek refuge by picking lint off my sock.

"Yes, well, I imagine lots of people have heard of it," she says, "but few do it—I mean really do it. It's hard work. Excruciating at times. But I love it because it helps me find out who I really am. My analyst, Jonathan, is a genius. He doesn't say much. In fact, we'll go two or three sessions with just me talking, or neither of us saying a word. But I know he's listening in a way that goes beyond the surface of language. He hears *all* of me talking, the depth of me. His silence is very stimulating, almost sexual at times, and it's fine that I feel that way. I tell him so, and he smiles and nods. He understands so much."

I'm still picking because I don't know where to look. Sally walks over and sits next to me, and I wish that her testimonial were directed to some invisible audience in her head—perhaps a convention of tortured, single, executive women in analysis—anyone but me.

"I could go on and on about Jonathan, but I didn't call you in here to sing his praises. Do you know why I'm telling you all of this?"

"No."

"You don't?"

"No," I say, trying to temper the exasperation in my voice. My headache has returned, and I'm growing tired of Sally's games. I think she senses my irritation, which changes her tone from rhapsody to the usual sledgehammer bluntness.

"It's about your therapy." She stands up and walks to her desk. Before I can protest, she cuts me off. "Denise went looking for some proofs and found this brochure in your drawer." She plucks the brochure from the desk and scowls at it, holding it with two fingers, like it's covered in shit. "Now, I don't know if you're already going to someone from . . . Open Doors . . . or whatever it's called. But I have to tell you that analysis is really the way to go."

Any attempt at restraint is pointless. I stand up and say, "I am not even in therapy and even if I were, it's my business! It doesn't concern anyone here."

"But it does. It concerns me a lot if you're late all the time, if you're not full of energy when you walk into this office every morning. And believe me, I know what feelings can do. Repressed childhood baggage can really weigh you down."

Her last sentence, a linguist's nightmare, echoes in my ears. For all of her thousands of dollars, that's probably the only message Sally has been able to glean from her one-way-street shrink. I've never heard of anything more ridiculous, but there's no way to convince her.

"I can't talk about this," I say.

She walks back over to me and stands, as usual, a little too close.

"Look, I am talking with you about this only because I'm concerned." I turn my head away to keep from smelling her stale breath. "I mean, I don't want to fire you. I'm trying to help."

There it is—the trump card. I would give anything to say, No, be my guest, fire away. But I think about my college loan and the rent and the credit card. I have no parent to call for money, and the inheritance is tied up in legalities. I have to shut up and take it.

"I understand," I say with quiet fury.

"And if you're considering therapy, I would hate to see you waste your money on something that really only scratches the surface."

I nod. Sally stares and squints, nodding a little in return. She picks off a stray hair that's fallen on my shoulder. How I loathe her.

"Just think about it and let me know if you need a referral," she says.

"I will," I say as I turn toward the door. "I better get back to work."

"What do you mean 'back'? You haven't even started today," Sally quips.

"Right."

"Just kidding," she says, but we both know better.

The first thing I do once I'm out of Sally's clutches is find Denise in the copy room. She swears that Sally, not she, was the one who rifled through my desk.

"Why didn't you stop her?" I say, trying not to yell.

"Oh, right. Like, I'm so sure I can stop Sally from doing whatever the hell she wants."

I fall silent while Denise starts shoving her copies into the automatic stapler. She fires one after the other into the machine, making a steady, irritating ping. I turn to leave but am stopped by the two-inch nails as she places her hand on my arm.

"Don't be mad at me. I'm really sorry it happened, all right?" she says. "But what could I do? You know what a royal bitch she is. I wanted to say something, but I know it would have pissed her off."

"I know. I just feel really violated."

"Listen, fuck her—all right? Fuck her and everything she said to you. The fact that she would stick her nose in your business is like totally pathetic."

Sally opens the door just as Denise says "totally pathetic."

"What's totally pathetic?" Sally asks stridently.

Denise continues stapling and, without missing a beat, says her standard reply. "O.J. Simpson. Like I'm so sure he's out looking for his wife's killer. If you ask me, all he needs to do is look in the mirror."

"I don't see what O.J. has to do with this magazine. You both have a lot of work to do, so get to it, okay?"

"We're on our way," Denise says as she whisks past Sally and I follow her. We walk down the hall, and she waves good-bye with her copies as I duck into my cubicle. As always, I know Sally is watching.

It's 5:30 P.M. and I am in Culver City looking for Open Doors. Maybe Sally's disdain toward this type of therapy helped motivate me to actually keep the appointment this time. Or maybe I feel fed up enough to try anything.

Barrington Avenue is tucked far enough away from Venice Boulevard to be quiet, almost suburban. Unlike the other side streets lined with cheap boxlike two-story apartment buildings, this one has actual houses on it. The last house on the left is a rambling old yellow Victorian, a rare thing in L.A., and is set off from the others by a large border of yard. The sheer size of the pine trees and lawn makes them seem artificial, as if they were trucked in for a movie set.

I park on the street and follow the signs to the back of the house. I find a wooden staircase that leads to the second floor but am stopped by the enormous side yard, a space I assumed would be paved. It has a big cherry tree with three Adirondack chairs under it. Had it not begun to rain, I might have stood there longer, captivated by such a rural sight in the city.

The waiting room is quiet and cozy, lit by bay windows and reading lamps. There are piles of magazines, and I am relieved to find no copies of *Mangia!* hanging around. It's a nice mix of commercial and intellectual fare—*The Utne Reader, The New Yorker, The Atlantic, Family Circle, Psychology Today.* I look for any articles on death and loss in *Psychology Today* with the hope of saving money and not having to go through all of this. I thumb through the table of contents and find the latest ills sweeping the nation— teen suicide, self-esteem in the elderly, anorexia—nothing that applies to me.

It's still raining out, and I watch the branches tremble with the drops. Every now and then, a gust of wind swirls from beneath and lifts them upward, making it look like the whole tree is sighing, as if to say, When will this stop? When can I be dry and still and blooming in the sun?

I hear the creak of footsteps on the wooden floors, and it reminds me of my own home on Sunday afternoon. My mother would always be up in the attic. Sunday was her painting day.

I would sometimes sit at the bottom of the attic stairs, listening to the creaks, smelling the sharp odor of oil paint, thinking about how she looked while she worked. . . .

"Julia?"

A woman crouches next to the couch, gently shaking my shoulder. I sit up abruptly and look around, disoriented.

"You fell asleep," she says.

I remember that I am waiting to see Naomi Roth, which is what I tell the woman who still has her hand on my shoulder.

"I'm Naomi," she says and smiles.

"Oh, did I miss my appointment?"

"No. You didn't miss anything."

"Good." I stand up and look at her face again—blue eyes, crow's feet—a kind face framed by short reddish brown hair. She looks professional but comfortable—tan linen pants and a light blue cotton sweater—not too dressy, which reassures me that she's not in it for the money.

Naomi makes small talk about how easy it is to fall asleep on that couch as she leads me to a small room with three huge chairs and two lamps. She closes the door behind us and sits across from me.

"It's funny. While you were sleeping, you said, 'It's not a real scab.' I don't know if you remember what you were dreaming about, but that might be a good place to start."

Great. A million therapists in L.A. and I get Miss Psych 101, a page right out of the Freudian primer. It's my waking life that's the problem anyway, not my sleeping life. I look at her and shrug.

"Let me think about it for a second."

Truth or fiction . . . the choice is mine.

I am all set to repeat my infamous bike accident story with its cast of benevolent strangers. Then I'll give her a concise description of the deaths of my father and mother, my battle with Constance, my aspiration to be a freelance photographer. I'll listen politely to what she has to say, and we'll both agree that I'm fine—that I'm just going through a rough patch. I don't need to dredge up my entire life story.

But I look down at my sweater and the stains down the front that I didn't see this morning as I dressed in my dark apartment. The rain pours outside, and I know that I'm too tired to keep pretending. I look around the room and admit that it feels safe and contained, as though no other life exists outside of its two circles of lamplight. I feel my strategy giving way.

"It's a long story," I say.

"We've got some time. About fifty-five minutes."

"Are you that exact about sessions?"

"No," she says and laughs. We sit for a moment in silence, and I figure I might as well tell her. I have nothing to lose.

"It has to do with a lie I told."

"In the dream?"

I shake my head. "At work."

I come clean on the whole fabrication and expect her to do something clinical, to write something down or make some judgment about what it says about me. But she just nods her head and says, "It must have been pretty strange to walk around with fake injuries."

"Well, it was. I felt like I was playing some role."

"What kind of role?"

"I don't know. But I feel guilty about it. I mean, I never lie. Well . . . I occasionally tell a few half-truths to friends. Like, 'I can't go out tonight because I've got a migraine' or something. But I never lied like this, so consistently I mean. I even lied to my best friend, Claire, about the injuries. Do you know she actually wanted to see them? Can you imagine asking someone that?"

Naomi starts to answer, but I don't want to know the reply, so I cut her off.

"But Claire covers for me when I come in late to work, and so does Denise. She's Sally's secretary. Of course, that doesn't mean that either of them can stop Sally from going through my desk, which she did today and which totally pissed me off."

"Hold on. You're losing me a little. Who is Sally?"

I try to calm myself enough to fill her in and recount the latest drama.

"Sounds like a control freak," Naomi says.

"She's a fucking nightmare."

I regret my candor because it causes Naomi to lean back in her chair and appraise me, the moment I've been dreading.

"You know your whole tone changed when you began to talk about Sally. It's very angry."

"I'm sorry."

"You don't have to be sorry."

"I know, but I don't like to be so upset. I guess it's the control thing. More than ever, I have no tolerance for her. She reminds me of . . ."

Naomi waits a while and then prompts me. "Who?"

I never saw it until this moment, but it's the same dislike. No matter that I turned the lawyer on her, that I fought her at her own filthy game and won. I walk into the office every day and see Constance marching around, only in higher heels and thinner hips. The realization stuns me and my mind starts to cloud up.

"This is strange. It's someone I thought I put to rest. But I didn't, which is kind of overwhelming."

Again, we are silent and Naomi says, "It's normal to feel overwhelmed when you start to talk about your life."

"But I came here to talk about my parents. What I've been saying isn't even relevant."

"Everything is relevant," she says.

I can only hope she's right since I spend the rest of the hour telling her random things about Sally, the *L.A. Times* debacle, Mrs. Sanchez, and the roaches in my apartment. I need some time before I can dig into Constance, Jeffrey, or the really big-ticket emotional item: death. We agree to a scaled-down seventy dollars per session, once a week to start. When I hand her the check and shake her hand, she tells me she's glad I'm here.

I let forth a heavy sigh, like one of those tired, soaked trees, and say, "I wish I felt the same way."

Naomi laughs and puts a hand on my shoulder. "You never know. It might grow on you."

Upward Mobility

Naomi says having a therapist untangle my emotions is like having a doctor reset my broken bones after an accident. There is no real difference between the two. Things need to be examined and put back in place before they can really start to heal.

I'm sure she uses this fortune-cookie logic on all of her patients. Still, I put my faith in it because I arrived at her doorstep three months ago desperate and willing enough to try anything. Naomi doesn't lecture me like a guru or manipulate me by being studiously mute as I gallop on a treadmill of my own confused chatter. She listens, comments, questions, and genuinely tries to help me find the answers.

Change seems to be happening all around me, much of it for the good: Claire is pregnant, Denise got a job as a hair stylist on a movie set, Rod Boyle's show got canceled.

I am in the process of moving from my roach-infested insane asylum to a second-floor, rent-controlled apartment in Santa Monica several blocks from the beach. I lucked out since Claire had a friend who wanted to sublet the place for two years. It's small but clean, and morning light streams through the living room windows. Best of all, it has a windowless kitchen that I can turn into a makeshift darkroom at night.

I have enough time before moving day to sort through things, and everything runs smoothly until I come upon a box tucked away in the closet that contains pictures from my past. Like kryptonite, the contents cause my knees to weaken and sap all of my superhuman moving strength. Instantly, I slide into a heap and start poring over everything in the box, remembering the stories behind the photos and how I once had a family though it wasn't exactly perfect.

I remember snapping the shots of my mother gardening, bent over a cluster of pansies when she was still well enough to be outside, and how afterward she refused even to look up and acknowledge me. Maybe she didn't like the way she looked. I'll never know. All I could do was apologize and walk away. The silence of those candids, taken for a college independent study, went beyond the frame and found its way into our daily routine too often. Did she pull away at times due to her illness or was it something else?

At the time, I felt I had no voice with which to protest. She was dying; we were nursing her, slowly and painfully, toward the inevitable. And on the heels of such a memory comes another wave of anguish—knowing we will never have time together to heal the injuries that the disease inflicted on all of us.

At Naomi's suggestion, I've started photographing things again but am getting away from bleak images. I've been collecting what I call home scenes from all parts of L.A., rich and poor—interesting landscaping or yard art, a child's birthday party on the lawn, garage sales. I don't try anything staged or phony. I take simple, straightforward shots and try to tell the truth about a given place or moment.

I have no doubt that my camera would still be packed away among my winter clothes if I had taken Sally's advice on analysis versus therapy. If I had to listen to nothing but my own hopeless keening, I would have probably gone into a hole for good. There are still bad days, but nothing like the depression I was in three months ago. I can say the word now and not feel like it's a death sentence. I knew Naomi's diagnosis was right because I felt such relief when she said it—like a burdensome secret was finally revealed.

The truth had occurred to me deep down, late at night, but in a detached and refracted way. I'd listen closely to the TV public service announcement that showed the shadow of a woman lying in bed and a checklist superimposed in bold letters over her: do you suffer from sleeplessness (yes), inability to get out of bed (yes), hopelessness (yes), loss of appetite (no). The symptoms that didn't apply gave me reason enough for denial even though you only needed two to qualify. I had eight out of ten. But before I knew it, my awareness of the problem would vanish irretrievably in the wake of an ad for Pico Pete's Used Car Bonanza.

I know the truth sets you free, but it isn't exactly a comfortable independence. There are times when I am so drained from a session that all I can do is come home and rest. Yet it's the kind of tired that renews you the next day—like cleaning the magazines and newspapers out of my apartment and feeling so satisfied when I wake up and can see every inch of the floor.

The other day, when we talked about my father, I hatched the biggest realization yet. Apropos of nothing, Naomi asked, "How did he tell you about Edna?"

It was like asking me, "Please relive one of the most excruciating moments of your life." *And you're paying her for this?* said the parliamentarians. I'm learning not to listen to them, so I didn't tell Naomi to bugger off—but I wasn't exactly serene, either.

"It was at the airport, when I was going back to visit a friend in L.A. after Mom died. He told me while we were waiting at the gate, right before I was about to board. I was so stunned that I couldn't

respond. He kept saying, 'Do you understand what I'm telling you?'
But I couldn't speak. I couldn't even look at him."

"How did it make you feel?"

Impressive exploration of the obvious!

"Well, shitty."

"Why?"

I paused, trying to collect myself, but failed.

"Jesus, why do you think?"

"I don't know," Naomi said. "I mean, he has the right to marry
again."

"But he didn't even like Edna as a neighbor. Why marry her and
so soon? I just don't see how he could do that to my mother." I felt
the familiar sting of tears forming.

"Do what?"

"Betray her!"

"And betray you too, maybe?"

That's when I finally gave way and started to sob openly, another dubious luxury of therapy.

For the rest of the session, Naomi was gentle and soft-spoken,
telling me that you can feel angry with people, dead or alive, and
still love the good in them, that the rage can give way to understanding and forgiveness. She reassured me how difficult it can be
to trust and get close to people when those I loved had left in so
many different ways. It all takes time, she said.

So I listen to Naomi even when she tells me to say some hokey
mantra to begin my day. I asked her if she could give me one specifically designed to help me deal with Sally, something other than,
"Get thee behind me, Satan." She did, and now every day, on my
way to work and especially in the elevator, I say it to myself: "This
isn't forever." Naomi gave me those words because I tend to see all
things as being infinite and thus have trouble finding any perspective. So I have to remind myself that Sally is just a temporary acquaintance, some crazy hitchhiker I picked up along the way.

It's Monday morning, which always requires me to write the

mantra down and look at it periodically throughout the day. Today
we begin shooting for the "Back to Basics" article, which means I
will spend the day fondling liver and onions, slabs of meat loaf, and
a dreadful, greasy creation called Down-Home Fries. At least we
now have an intern from a culinary school to help with the cooking.
Aside from the usual shock of returning to my bizarre occupation
and insane work environment, Mondays hold the additional wallop
of "top 'o the morning" staff meetings, a title coined by Sally.
Everyone from the publisher to the lowliest intern is there, and it is
a scene: currant scones, assorted danish, apricot brioches, gourmet
coffee, and a wide array of passive-aggressive behavior.

It's 8:45 and the publisher, Sonny Raven, is still drunk from the
night before and barely able to navigate his way around the pastries.
If he were sitting down instead of weaving around the room, you
wouldn't know he's an alcoholic—tall, tan, handsome in a classic,
square-jawed, muscular way. He's in his late fifties but counters the
effects of aging and booze with face-lifts, exercise with a personal
trainer, and impeccable hair dying. He's very proud of his full head
of wavy auburn hair and is always careful to keep it stylishly
trimmed—slightly long on top and short in the back, a rakish, rock-
abilly look reminiscent of Jerry Lee Lewis. He's the son of an extremely wealthy film producer who dabbled in magazines as a
sideline and decided to fund this one so that his reprobate son could
have a title and a place to sleep it off.

Sonny has a wife and three daughters whom he sees on the
weekends at his estate in Santa Barbara, but everyone knows that
on weeknights he prefers drag queens who lip-synch, so he hangs
out at a gay club called Party Doll. This morning he looks like he'd
be more at home on a yacht than in a staff meeting: navy blazer,
paisley ascot (sage and rose against white), pink Oxford shirt, white
duck pants, Gucci loafers with no socks.

"Cheese danish!" he exclaims. "My kingdom for a cheese danish."

At last he spots one and grabs it just as one of the more tentative
underlings reaches for it as well. He snatches it up and takes a big

bite. With his mouth full and still chewing, he says to her, "Age before beauty! Or is it the other way around?"

Claire sees the whole thing too, I realize, as I look away and find her on the other side of the table. She shakes her head and gives me the usual, incredulous look that we both reserve for Sonny. In effect, the magazine is run by Sally and Russell Morgan, the ad director. Advertising always has a revolving door, not because Russell is an unkind boss but because the magazine is such a tough sell. Sally and Russell stand together in a corner of Bob's spacious office, having a quiet but intense conversation of some kind.

"Okay, everybody, find a seat," Sally finally says to the room. "And if you can't find a seat, find the floor."

Nobody even chuckles at her command. They just dutifully lower themselves.

"We need to discuss a new direction for the September/October issue," she says.

"Oh boy! I can't wait to hear," Sonny says.

"Sonny, you already know about it," Sally says without even looking at him. Sonny just shrugs and gives the crowd a silly, confused expression.

"We've been talking about doing an issue on a new trend in cuisine—southwestern fusion—and we've decided September/October is the issue," Sally says. I watch as Russell fidgets and looks at the carpet, unable to meet the stunned gazes of the staff, which has been trained on the Fall Harvest focus and for whom southwestern fusion is more of a jazzy-sounding editorial nightmare than a cutting-edge food trend.

Russell says, "I think you need to explain more about what southwestern fusion is and you need to address—"

"The fusion of southwestern cuisine with everything from Mediterranean to Japanese. It is *the* hot new trend, so new that it's unreported. It's our scoop!"

"What about the articles we've already completed?" Russell asks.

"Some of them we can still use, but we're just adding some new ones. Look, the Fall Harvest theme is so predictable. If we focus on southwestern fusion, which is a reality in this country, then we stand out. So, I say we go for broke."

"That's exactly what we'd be doing," says Stone, who assists the production manager when there's nothing to be photographed. It's one thing to question Sally behind closed doors, but this is a bold move—the last thing I would expect from such a recluse.

"Where's Bob?" Sally asks.

"Out sick," Stone says. "But I can speak for him."

"Fine. I know what you're going to say, and we can do it," Sally says as she holds up her outstretched palm like a traffic cop. "Page has already researched the restaurants and we have two definites. Right, Page?"

Page Whipple is a nervous, painfully naive assistant editor just out of college, one of Sally's few lackeys who records the minutes of every meeting and lives for the magazine. She fiddles with her notes and says, "The head chef at Soufflé in Sedona is thrilled!"

Ignoring Page and Sally's pitch, Stone has been silently calculating the weeks until the latest possible print date for the issue. He runs his hand through his long hair, looks up at Sally over his round steel-rimmed glasses, and shakes his head.

"No way."

"There is no such thing as 'no way.' We pay you to say, 'Yes, there is a way,'" Sally says.

"Guess I'm not going to the bank this month," Stone replies as he takes his glasses off and cleans them with his uniformly untucked shirt. The room is silent. Claire and I exchange a look of newfound admiration for this most unlikely office hero.

"I can make it so you don't go the bank for many months," Sally retorts.

"Take it easy. I'm sure we can find a solution," Russell says.

"I can't imagine it," Stone says calmly. "You're talking about two weeks before we have to get every article written, every photo taken, every ad sold."

"Two weeks?" Russell asks.

"Totally," Stone says.

"I don't see how we can get all the photos done by then," Claire says.

"Sally, you have to admit that's cutting it way too close," Russell adds.

"Okay, this meeting is over," Sally says, sparing the new receptionist, interns, and editorial/advertising rank and file from the bloodletting sure to ensue. The only reason Sally doesn't tell me to scram, I think, is that she feels we've bonded after the analysis thing and considers me a reform project. Once the room is cleared, Sally rails.

"Russell, the last thing I need is for you to contradict me in front of the entire staff!"

"Okay, I'm sorry, but Stone is right. This is not going to work. Last issue, it took us two months to pull everything together, and we were still late."

"Editorial only took one month. What does he know anyway? He's just a photographer."

"Don't I wish," Stone says.

"He understands the schedule, all right?" Russell says.

"And I don't?" Sally says.

"That's what we're trying to figure out," Stone says.

Sally raises her hands in the air and shakes her head in disbelief.

"Who the fuck is this guy?" she says to Russell and Claire, who don't respond.

"Just a photographer," Stone replies. "I'll be in the darkroom if you need me."

Stone leaves and Russell says, "Okay. Let's play nice and try to figure this out."

Russell and Sally bat the pros and cons back and forth while Page takes copious notes and Claire and I spectate, but neither side can give an inch. It goes on for about ten minutes until Sally breaks it off.

"I think I can safely say we are at an impasse. The only person who can decide this is Sonny."

The whole focus of the room, which has taken on the tension and rhythm of a professional tennis match, shifts to Sonny, who has fallen into an alcoholic slumber in one corner of the sofa. All eyes are on him as he scratches himself luxuriously, smiling faintly. Sally walks over to the sofa and shakes the cushion behind him. He wakes with a startled snort and looks around the room in a fog, seemingly unsure of where he is and who we are.

"Sonny, I don't think it's great for team morale to have you pass out during meetings," Sally says.

He stretches his arms and closes his eyes. "I should have known it was you rocking my world instead of Cindy Crawford or George Michael. So what did I miss?"

"Don't you care about how totally unprofessional you are?" she asks.

Sonny stands up now, stretching again and squinting out the window at the late morning sun.

"Look, everybody knows I'm great at parties and lousy at meetings," he says. "Even my father knows that."

"We need your input on a pretty crucial issue," Russell says to Sonny. "We're trying to make a decision that might potentially cause bankruptcy—"

"Don't be melodramatic Russell," Sally says.

Russell follows Sonny over to his desk and watches him pull out a bottle of vodka.

"Anyone care for a snort?" Sonny asks, pouring the booze into a coffee cup.

"No," Sally answers collectively, looking around the room as if daring anyone to say yes.

"As you probably know—" Russell begins.

Sonny holds his index finger up to interrupt, shakes his head, and says, "Never assume that I know anything."

Sally rolls her eyes as Russell awkwardly continues. He tells

Sonny the whole situation, though Sonny is more intent on pouring his drink than anything, and adds, "The problem is that our major clients will pull their ads if we're late again, and then we'll lose about three-fourths of our revenue."

"All magazines operate in the red," Sally says. "We'll make up the loss."

"Try telling that to the printer," Russell replies. "We still owe him for the last issue. Sonny, there's no way we can get all the photos, articles, and ads together in two weeks. You know that."

Sonny chokes down the first shot and begins to cough. Russell starts to pat him on the back, thinks better of it, and asks, "Can I get you some water?"

"No, goddamn it," Sonny says. His face is flushed and his eyes are watery. He turns his back to us and looks down at the traffic below. He wipes his eyes with the back of his sleeve and sighs deeply. His hands shake as he pours himself another drink. He's hardly fit to make any decisions.

"Look, maybe we can decide the question later," Claire says.

"We have to decide now," Sally says. "What's it going to be, Sonny?"

He sighs again and turns to her, his face has changed from the usual irreverent smile to a contemptuous frown.

"What's it going to be?" he says with a distinct touch of mockery.

"Yes," she says, rising up from her chair, undaunted. "We need to know and you're the one who has to make the call."

Sonny takes a sip of his drink and is able to swallow it a little easier this time. He finishes off the rest in two gulps and smacks the cup down on the counter. It doesn't take long for the booze to work, to pick him up out of the gutter and keep him dancing on the edge of a cliff, to put the fire and irreverence back in him. He shakes his head briskly and lets out a whoop.

"Beats coffee any day! Okay, so you want me to make the call. Well, here it is: Bankruptcy be damned! I hereby decree that my illustrious editor, Miss Mustang Sally, shall make the aforementioned decision about the September/October issue. And her decision is . . ." Sonny does a drum roll on the desk.

"Stop it, Sonny" she says.

"I'm just trying to lighten things up. You're all so serious."

Russell has his head in his hands at this point.

"Everyone knows what my decision is," Sally says. "We're going to do the new issue, and we're going to make the deadline. Let's meet today at four o'clock to talk about where we are."

Sally turns on her heel, and everyone silently begins to filter out. Sonny is laughing and singing a ribald, "Ride, Sally, Ride!" He pours yet another drink. "You have to admire her spirit," he says.

We're one week into the production schedule, and no one admires anything about Sally or her spirit. If Sonny had to work under her, he'd be singing a different tune. Sally "asked" everyone in the office to work overtime without extra pay, extending the workday by two hours. The ad executives have extended it by four hours out of sheer necessity. The fish aren't even nibbling on southwestern fusion.

Another problem occurred Friday morning when one of the freelance photographers quit because of the extra hours, which began to interfere with his rock band.

"You and your fucking gigs!"

Everyone in the place heard Sally scream it, but no one really understood what it meant until the guy tacked his official resignation on her door with a dart.

She'll hire someone else, but until then Claire has to take up the slack and photograph most of the in-house shoots. Originally, Sally wanted Claire to go with Stone to Sedona to style and manage the shoot, but now I am the only logical choice to move temporarily from lowly, hovering stylist to full-blown art director. So it didn't come as too much of a surprise when Sally called me in to her office and transferred the position over to me quietly, with no fanfare or announcements. All she said behind her closed office door was: "I don't even want to know what you don't understand. Just ask Claire everything. Work with her. I'll have the new kid, Jenny, get plane tickets for you and Stone."

"Right," I said as if it was all old hat.

"Are you sure you can handle this?" Sally asked.

I searched for the right answer, something firm but noncommittal. I wasn't any more thrilled about my promotion than Sally was.

"It's certainly a challenge. . . ." I said, but she held up her hand for silence.

"I don't want to know. Just do your best and close the door on your way out."

So that's why it's 7:00 A.M. on Monday and I'm calling Naomi's emergency pager. I worked myself into a panic over the weekend, fearing that the fate of the entire issue would be placed on my shoulders, that if anything goes wrong, I'll be the most likely scapegoat. Claire assures me I will manage just fine, that she'll tell me everything I need to know, that Stone is a nice guy once you get to know him. Trudy says that managing a shoot and working so closely with a photographer is a great chance to prove my own talents. What better way to move up even if I don't want to stay at this magazine? I know what they say is true, yet the voice of self-doubt always shouts them down.

Naomi calls back fifteen minutes later and says it's fine for me to come in even though we both know the situation is hardly life-threatening—just unexpected.

At eleven-thirty I tell Sally that I have to pick up some of the proofs from the photo lab and that I'll be back by one-thirty.

"Julia, you don't need to ask my permission to go to lunch," she says.

"But you said—"

"Now things are different. You're an *art director*." Sally pauses dramatically, smiling and raising her eyebrows. "I thought about it over the weekend, and I have a good feeling about this. I see big things happening for you if you do a good job with this project—as in, not a temporary promotion but permanent. Dazzle me, and it's yours."

"Okay," I say with a tense smile, like the one I gave recently to the southwestern sushi chef who insisted that the production crew sample his specialty, eel stuffed with chipotle lobster roe. I ate it happily even though I wanted to puke.

I tell Naomi the whole situation, and she says, "You could always decline."

"Not if I want to keep my job."

"Do you want to keep your job?"

"I have no choice. I haven't been looking for another."

"So, take the new position, especially since it's only temporary—as in not forever." Naomi smiles at me, and I nod grudgingly, as if I haven't muttered the line to myself about a thousand times.

I walk into the sunlight and the unseasonably cool July air, keeping her words in mind. Not just the mantra but other positive notions of hers. Look on it as an adventure. You'll see magnificent mountains. You'll meet new people. I can feel my mind coming around, turning heavily like the sail of a tall ship, creaking as if to break with the unexpected gale. Who knows what I will find? But I won't resist, letting the wind carry me toward uncharted waters.

11 ♛

Disharmonic Convergence

What can go wrong with *roast pheasant Provençal avec prickly-pear glaze*?

Everything, I imagine. It's just my luck that Jacques Picard's signature dish at Soufflé would not be something simple like a southwestern frittata. I brought some bitters and Gravy Master along in case we need to color the bird. I also brought some fishing line to hold the legs together without the camera catching it. One would think the chef would have everything needed to make the bird look pretty, but Sally said no. In fact, her parting bromide to me yesterday was: "Remember that if you *assume*, you make an ass out of *u* and *me*." Such aphorisms make me grateful to be out of the office for a few days.

Sally assured me that working with Jacques Picard would be a cinch, but there are two reasons why I doubt her: 1) Sally is relying on someone else's recommendation since the magazine has never profiled him; 2) Sally lies.

We couldn't pin down any other southwestern fusion chefs for the issue thanks to Page Whipple's inept salesmanship. Sally is on the task now and promised me that she would have at least three other chefs to showcase in the issue within the next day or so. After the Picard shoot, I had strict instructions to call in and find out who my next entrée is. I asked Sally how many other prospects were in Sedona and she said, "Enough—I think. But if we need to, we can always go to Scottsdale or somewhere."

So I have resigned myself to expecting the unexpected. And the first curve ball is Stone's startling appearance.

His seat is across the aisle from mine, and he doesn't say anything when he dashes onto the plane with five minutes to spare except, "Sorry I'm late."

I can hardly recognize him as I watch him stow his gear overhead. Gone are his stringy locks and two-day-old stubble. His hair is short, almost a crew cut but not quite. It's softer, longer on top, and shows off his flattering salt-and-pepper shade. He sits down, buckles his belt, and looks over at me. I stare at him, too stunned to speak.

"What?" he says.

"Take a wild guess."

He smiles. "The hair."

"The hair, the beard. What happened?"

He shrugs and says, "I went to the barber."

"You sure did."

"Did I look that bad before?"

"Well, sort of."

He laughs at this and shakes his head. "Julia, you are a trip."

I want to ask him what he means, but the stewardess is putting on her futile, preflight show and standing right in front of us. I pretend to watch, stealing furtive glances at Stone's thin, angular face—wondering if this is what he looked like in his heyday and whether twenty-year-old models fell all over him, invited him to Spago for lunch. Only yesterday, it seemed unthinkable. Judging by the lines, he's somewhere in his midforties but I'm not sure; he looked so much older with long hair.

The show is over and Stone yawns and says, "I might try to catch a nap. I was up late last night with the photo madness."

"When did you leave?"

"About eleven o'clock—Sally has created quite a scene."

"I'm glad to be away from it."

"You and me both."

Stone starts to recline his chair and remembers we haven't taken off yet. He sighs, stuffs a pillow behind his head, and closes his eyes. We bounce along down the runway, my least favorite part of any flight. My heart beats faster as I clutch the armrest. I look over at Stone and his eyes are open now, his head turned toward me. He says, "Nice suit."

I feel my face flush. "Thanks but I feel like an idiot wearing it."

"You don't look like one. You look great."

He smiles; we soar into the sky, and he closes his eyes again.

Stone travels light and probably is used to life on the road. I, on the other hand, appear to be the consummate fusspot, remembering to pack everything from my nail file to my favorite pictures. Ever since the reunion with Constance, I travel as though I am never coming back. I revise my will—an unofficial one that only Naomi knows about. I clean my apartment so that no people will find any traces of my life that might make them sad. I call practically everyone I know and tell them that I'll be on a trip—flying. Naomi says we need to work on getting me to loosen up a bit, to be more spontaneous and less worried about all the things that can go wrong at any given moment.

The fact that I am wearing this knock-off Chanel suit, nylons, and matching scarf also smacks of an overzealous tendency toward planning. I wanted to look the part of art director and mistakenly allowed Sally to advise my choice of clothing. There was a sale at

Nordstrom's, and she had seen some perfect business travel suits, and why don't I take an extra hour at lunch so that I can go out and get one? I was too tired to think of a tactful decline, couldn't consult Claire, who was at the doctor's office, and wasn't confident enough to stick to my own sense of style. I didn't own anything close to a business suit.

So even though Stone thinks I look great, I still feel uncomfortable, repressed, and lacking in spontaneity as I sit in a too-tight, short skirt in a too-small airline seat. I check my carry-on again to make sure I have the right items for the shoot and in putting the bag under the seat manage to rip an enormous tear in my right stocking. I toy with the idea of applying nail polish—I've packed a full supply just for a case such as this—but then I say to hell with it. I take my stockings off in the bathroom, slip my shoes off under my blanket once I'm back in my seat, and begin to breathe normally.

The heat in Phoenix on this July day, an oppressive 112 degrees, shimmers, scorches, and turns the very air to lead. I keep thinking, low humidity, but that doesn't keep me from getting pitted out in fifteen seconds. Stone's consideration as a traveling companion makes the heat a little more tolerable. He changed into shorts and was happy to wait while I went to the bathroom twice, once to reapply my deodorant and then to change my blouse. He carried one of my bags and offered to do the driving. Life is easy in the air-conditioned car. I have the map sprawled out in my lap and have been giving Stone directions, which he accepts without question. I tell him about how I met Claire and about my recent move. He tells me that he lives in the Hollywood Hills and used to teach beginning photography at the UCLA Extension to make ends meet before he got the job at *Mangia!*

"Did you like teaching?" I ask.

"Yeah. It was fun. They wanted me to start teaching again this summer, but . . ."

"So that's why you stood up to Sally—you had another job."

"No, I declined the job."

"Before the blow-up?"

"Yeah. I stood up to Sally because she's nuts. And now I'm wondering if I'm nuts for not taking that job when I had the chance. I don't know. It was a lot less money."

"Well, I admire you for challenging her."

"I'm afraid it didn't do much good."

"Still, I was impressed. I think about how fearful I am," I say. "That's why I could never stand up to Sally. Plus, I need the money—but that's being fearful, too."

"Some would say fearful. Others would say practical."

"What would you say?"

"I don't know. It depends on the situation. How big the bills are. That kind of thing."

We ride in silence for a few moments, and I decide to take a risk.

"Do you know why everyone was so surprised by what you said at the meeting?"

"No, why?"

"Because you never say anything at all—to anyone. I mean, one day you're a recluse, the next day you're Norma Rae."

"In drag," he says with a laugh.

"The magazine *is* published by Sonny. Seriously, why are you so quiet in the office?"

"I'm not that quiet. I talk to Bob in production. I talk to Claire."

"But not that often."

"That's true. Well, I guess I'm not that crazy about the work, so that shuts me down. And I've been a bit preoccupied. Everybody knows I went through a pretty nasty divorce last year."

"Oh," I say, taken aback by his candor and not sure whether I should admit to knowing about it.

"You knew that, right?" he asks.

I decide to stick with the truth. "Yes. Claire had mentioned something about it to me. So that's still on your mind?"

"Not as much anymore. Especially in the last few months, I've felt better."

I can see him repress a smile as he looks in the rearview mirror and changes lanes.

"See, there's someone else—at the office. But I have to keep my passion in check, you know? I think that's why I'm so quiet."

"What do you mean?"

"I've got to play it cool so that she won't know how much I want her."

"Who? Are you kidding me? Who?"

"What do you mean, 'who'?"

I'm at a loss, so I start guessing, "Not Page?"

"No! Sally!"

"Oh God."

"She is one hot tamale," Stone says, which makes me laugh out loud.

"I get it now," I say. "You had to challenge her in the meeting."

"As a way to hide my burning love for her, yes."

"You're full of surprises."

"Sometimes," he says.

We turn off Interstate 17 toward Sedona and drive another half hour on a two-lane road before we reach our destination. As we round a bend, I see for the first time what the glossy brochures can hardly capture. The mountains look as though they suddenly sprang from the earth and are still rising. The rust hues climb like mercury, unable to paint mountain caps parched from the sun. I recognize Bell Rock and Cathedral Rock in the distance. But aside from that the formations are wholly foreign to my eyes. We round another bend closer to town and the rocks are all around us, giving me the feeling that the road has disappeared behind us and we have entered a strange, new world—a landscape frozen in volcanic explosions of centuries past.

"I have to stop," Stone says suddenly and pulls over to the side of the road. His tone is so urgent that I think maybe he needs to pee, so I stay in the car, eyes front. But then I hear him digging out his camera from the trunk. I get out of the car, despite the anvil of heat, and watch him photograph a rock formation just as a cloud on the horizon passes behind it.

"That's a nice shot," I say.

"I hope so. God, this place is wild," he says, still snapping with a wide-angle telephoto lens. I've only seen Stone work in the studio, where he paces around snapping tight angles and fiddling with lights. Working with food is so controlled, almost antiseptic. But here, Stone is no longer controlling the shots; they are controlling him, propelling him into postures and positions that at times seem to defy gravity. My dance with the camera is not nearly as free and abandoned as his. He stands on top of the bumper, takes several more shots, and then, instead of climbing down, sits on the hood of the car.

Still fixed on the horizon and shifting light, Stone says, "You know, I just need to get higher. I'm going to stand on the roof."

"Uh-oh," I say, which I think is a reasonable alternative to, "Are you crazy?"

"What's wrong with that?" he asks.

"Are those sandals soft-soled? I'm thinking of dents in the roof since it's a rental."

He stares at me, and I hope to God it's not the stare of a haughty prima donna. Stone never was demanding when it came to food, but these photos actually have a chance of becoming art—the stakes are higher.

To my relief, he says, "You're right," as though coming out of a trance. He takes his shoes off, digs out a pair of socks to keep his feet from burning, and stands carefully on the roof of the Ford Taurus.

"We don't need to pay the rental company any more money than we have to, do we?" he asks as he snaps. He stops and points out a cluster of tall narrow rocks in the distance. "Look at that. Meteora, Greece, has similar formations. Only they're bigger over there and the colors aren't as brilliant. They have monasteries built on top of them, accessible only by these winding stone steps. I think they grow their own food and rarely go out into civilization. Can you imagine living that way?"

"No. I mean, I don't have a garden and am only one story off the ground." Stone laughs, and I do too even though I thought I was being somewhat serious. I feel slightly awkward in the wake of my unintentional humor, so I opt for familiar ground. "I guess we should probably get going."

"Yep," Stone says. "You know, I think this view makes all the southwestern fusion chaos worthwhile." I look at him skeptically, and he concedes, "Okay, partially worthwhile."

Back on the road, I resume the business at hand.

"So, did Sally talk with you about her expectations for the shoot?"

"Not really. She just told me to make everything look light, fresh, and healthy."

"She says that about every shoot."

"I know," he says with a smile. "I was thinking about the pheasant. It would be nice to find some kind of bright floral decoration, not even in a vase, just some kind of desert blossom to put on the table. Maybe a few sprigs of bougainvillea."

"That sounds great. And as for the bird, Sally wants it to be intact, and she talked about using a few feathers in the shoot, too."

"Feathers?" he asks.

"That's what she worked out with Jacques."

Stone and I continue discussing the shoot. His attention to the aesthetics of a roasted bird surprises me and makes me feel a little less idiotic for devoting so much thought to it. He was much more quiet on simple in-studio shots. I always figured his silence came from thinking he was above taking pictures of food. But now I'm beginning to think it's just the way he is when he works, and that maybe he's more of a respectful professional than a dissatisfied churl.

After a couple of detours on side streets, we arrive at Soufflé about a half hour late. It took us a while to find the small adobe structure, which is tucked into some rocks and, like everything in

Sedona, painted terra cotta red with teal trim for maximum environmental blending. Even the McDonald's has teal arches.

Once we're inside, the simple exterior gives way to more complicated designs. Perhaps in keeping with the southwestern fusion ethos, the interior decorator decided to join Mediterranean with southwestern ranch in what can only be called an unholy union. Our feet creak on the weathered floorboards of the dining room, which are bare except for a woven straw rug in the center of the room. There are several blanched cattle skulls hung from the cerulean walls. The cow craniums serve as planters for purple, violet, and red strains of bougainvillea that wind over the horns and in some cases peek through eye sockets and mouths. The chairs and tables are of a dark, austere, Spanish style, and the windows are high and small, similar to the portholes of a ship. The darkness of the room is slightly lessened by a chandelier—a wrought-iron wagon wheel design with about two dozen teardrop-shaped bulbs and crystals dangling from it. It's just as hideous as the rest of the room—the very antithesis of light, fresh, and healthy.

"Boy," Stone says. "This is going to be interesting."

It's two o'clock and the restaurant is deserted.

"I guess it's only a dinner place," I say.

"I hope you're right," Stone says as he looks around the corner at more empty tables.

Jacques Picard strides out of the kitchen with open arms and a broad smile. He's a short, fleshy Frenchman with thinning white hair and an out-of-place gold hoop on his left earlobe. The torn jeans and Dr. Martens below his chef's coat further confirm his eye toward youthful fashion.

"*Bonjour, mademoiselle!* You are Julia, yes?"

"Yes. You must be Mr. Picard."

"Please, call me Jacques. Welcome to Soufflé!" He takes my hand into his soft, doughlike palm and brushes his lips against it, leaving a moist circle that I discreetly wipe off as I lower my hand to my side. He steps back and waves an arm toward the kitchen. "This is where cuisine is happening in Sedona!"

"What about over here?" Stone asks as he points to the empty dining room. I can't believe he said it and can tell by Jacques's fallen expression that he's not amused.

"He's kidding," I say. "We realize you're not open for lunch."

"Of course we are open," Jacques says with haughty contempt as he turns his back to us and starts clearing a nearby table that looks perfectly clean. *An ass out of u and me* rings in my ears, and I want to crawl for cover.

"In the summer, people like to eat between eleven o'clock and one o'clock," he adds. "If you had come an hour earlier, you could not have gotten a seat."

Stone looks at me and shakes his head skeptically, and I put my finger to my lips in a desperate attempt to keep things from getting worse. Evidently, Jacques Picard's Soufflé, once featured in *People* as one of the country's "hottest new restaurants," has fallen on hard times. But I'm not here to blow the lid off the restaurant's demise. All I want is for things to go smoothly. To get the pheasant and get out of here.

So I pretend I'm Sally and say, "Well, we're looking forward to photographing your marvelous pheasant."

Jacques shrugs without looking up as he clears another table and mumbles several terse, indecipherable words of French. Stone, having reined in his rude, inner man-child, retreats to the windows and fiddles with his light meter.

"Do you have any ideas for where you would like the shot?" I ask.

Jacques looks at me blankly.

"Or maybe, you have some ideas about the way you'd like the table arranged?" I add.

He shakes his head rapidly and says, "I do not understand. Is this not your job? I mean, I am the one who cooks. You are the one who designs what I cook, yes?"

It's clear that my mistake is still stuck in his craw. I think he's overreacting, but I try to placate him anyway.

"Yes, but I'm just giving you the option of making your own design choices. I don't want to come in and start dictating what should happen. I want you to be showcased in a way that's satisfactory and beneficial for you."

"Beneficial for me?" he says. "I will tell you what is beneficial for me. *Gourmet* magazine is beneficial. *Bon Appétit. Vanity Fair. GQ.* Not some stupid little magazine with a circulation of about"—he puffs in exaggerated French fashion, searching for the most demeaning number—"fifty people."

One of Jacques's assistants comes out and tells him something softly in French. Jacques replies tersely and shoves the plates and silverware into the assistant's hands. The assistant goes back into the kitchen, and Jacques turns to me but remains silent about the work to be done. I'm feeling desperate, so I go for broke and pander to an ego that is just as large and unappealing as the restaurant itself.

"I'm afraid I can't do anything about the magazine's circulation. It's not as much as other glossy magazines, but we do reach over twenty thousand readers. It seems the only way we could improve our circulation would be to have profiles of chefs like you. Then maybe more people would start to read it."

He smiles coyly, but with lingering cynicism asks, "Really? And what kind of chef am I, then? What is my category?"

"Innovative, daring—but always within the traditions of France," I say, a bit breathless with affected awe. "I mean, roast pheasant Provençal with prickly pear glaze is the perfect cross between French and southwestern cuisine. You're an artist, and you're very important to the magazine and to our readers."

He chuckles a little and saunters over to the bar. He fills a glass with ice and pours himself a Campari and soda. He takes a long pull of it and stands back to appraise me. Finally, he says, "Okay. So would you like to do this now?"

"Yes, that would be fine," I say, trying not to sigh audibly.

"How you arrange the table, I leave it up to you. I garnish the dish with some sautéed radicchio, zucchini and squash purée, baby carrots. It will be very nice."

I start to mention the presentation, but check myself. Sally said she had worked the details out with Jacques, and I even overheard part of the conversation. I remember Sally screaming into the phone like a child, "Plumes on the platter! I want a big, beautiful bird with plumes!" The last thing I want to do is offend Jacques again by telling him how to fix the bird or vegetables. Once he exits into the kitchen, I confer with Stone.

"What's the light like?"

"Awful. The walls and furniture are too dark. The chandelier and windows are no help. I'm going to have to get one of the lamps out of the trunk."

"I don't know how long the food prep will take him. Will it take you long to set up the lighting?"

"About twenty minutes," Stone says. "I bet Monsieur Asshole takes his own sweet time."

Stone heads for the door as I weigh my options. At first, I feel foolish for even thinking of telling a veteran how to behave. But then I consider Stone's penchant for speaking his truth, admirable but mostly tactless. And if I blow the shoot, I'll have hell to pay. I catch up with him outside and say, "Look, I don't think it's a good idea to say anything else to Jacques about the restaurant."

"Like about the fact that no one eats here."

"Yes. He's hardly objective about the place."

Stone smiles and says, "You're right. I'm sorry I spoke out of turn. Once I get started, I can't seem to stop."

"Well, busting Sally is one thing, but if we lose Jacques, we lose the cover."

"I know. I'll leave the talking up to you." He heads toward the car and then turns back, flashing a smile. "I think you're pretty good at it anyway. I'd say you're even innovative, daring—an artist."

I smile, embarrassed. "All right, so I laid it on a little thick."

"I'm only teasing. With a guy like that, the thicker the better. I'd say you handled the situation well."

"Thanks," I say, grateful for the vote of confidence and hopeful that the worst is over.

Stone sets up the shot so that the light hits the table at an angle, as though it were streaming through a window. I place a lace cloth and sprigs of bougainvillea on the table so that we'll be ready to go when the steaming pheasant arrives. That's one advantage of the dark background. We won't have to worry about the dish not looking hot enough.

We wait for an hour, and I'm praying that Jacques saved the feathers and only seared the bird before we arrived, as he was instructed to do by Sally. I reset the table twice and fidget with the cactus centerpiece and the flowers. Stone gets another lamp from the car. Finally, Jacques emerges, sweating profusely and carrying the steaming plate high above his head, looking even more smug than when he first walked in.

"Voilà!" he says as he places his famous creation before us.

One look and I realize Jacques Picard has a mind of his own that does not house an understanding of food photography.

Sally and I had imagined a full platter with bird intact, especially since we planned on it being the cover shot for the issue. But what we have here is a naked, chopped up fowl. The legs are crisscrossed, anklebones in the air, and laid on top of a bed of radicchio that is sautéed to the point of being a hideous mauve. Jacques actually cooked the vegetables instead of only blanching them to preserve their brightness. Slices of the breast are on the side of the plate, along with a few washed-out baby carrots. Worst of all are the four dollops of the zucchini and squash purée, which has the color and texture of mucus.

I glance over at Stone in my moment of panic, and he looks equally stunned. I smile at Jacques and say, "It certainly smells wonderful." I stare at the plate, at a loss for what to do next.

"Why don't you hurry up and photograph it while it's still hot?" Jacques asks.

"Well, actually, do you have a microwave?" I ask.

"Of course, but—"

"Okay, because we need to do a little more work here."

"Why? What is wrong? This is an excellent entrée. I have people come from all over the world for this entrée," Jacques says.

"I know and can understand why. It smells exquisite, but the appearance is a bit problematic for a magazine."

Jacques becomes a little more French and says, "What is this 'problematic'?"

I can feel myself losing patience. There's nothing that will appease this pompous dictator, so I cut to the chase.

"The carrots and radicchio need to be brighter. The purée needs to be more yellow. And the bird should be whole, not chopped up. I know you spoke with my editor, Sally Reynolds, about the presentation. Didn't you agree to feature the bird on a platter in its full form and with plumes used in the decoration?"

"No. We made no such agreement. It was suggested to me by her. But this is not the way my food is served in my restaurant. I will not have customers coming in and asking, 'Where are the feathers?'"

"Mr. Picard, I'm sorry, but the only way we can use the shot for the cover is if the bird is intact."

"It is not possible. I have no other pheasants and even if I did, I would not want this done to my food," Jacques says as he tromps over to the bar and pours himself another Campari. I look at my watch and think about calling Sally. But that would probably hinder things even further.

"All right. Let's just work with the vegetables, then. I think you might need to replace them with fresh, less cooked ones," I say to Jacques.

He slams the glass down on the bar. "I do not think you understand that this is the way my food is. I will not 'replace' anything."

"But the food will look awful in the magazine if it's muted. It has to look brighter because—"

"I have no time for this nonsense," Jacques says as he takes off his apron. "If you must 'replace' something, then you replace me. My sous-chef will show you how to work the stove because you are so foolish that you would probably blow yourself up in trying to make my vegetables look more 'fresh' *et je ne sais quois. Tu est vraiment un embecile!*"

He walks toward the door and grabs his black linen blazer from the rack. "And you tell your boss that I don't give a fuck about what she wants the bird to look like. I am a chef. I present my food the way it will be in my restaurant because that is my expression—*c'est tout!* I do not perform dog and cat shows."

Jacques is nearly out the door. I decide just to let the creep go, keeping the carnage to a minimum. But again, to my extreme chagrin, Stone has other ideas. He nearly knocks over his lamp in navigating his way to the door. He is there in a few seconds and has a hold of Jacques's arm.

"Just a minute," Stone says.

"Stone, what are you doing?" I ask, hoping my raised voice will remind him of our earlier conversation. It doesn't.

"Let go!" Jacques yells.

Stone hangs on tightly enough to make Jacques wince and stop struggling. He pulls Jacques toward him and shifts his stance, which makes Jacques raise his free hand up to his face, as if to protect himself from a punch.

"It's dog and pony show," Stone says in a too-calm voice— clearly the hazardous by-product of watching one too many action movies.

"Okay, fine. Dog and pony. Will you please let go of me now?"

"You can't have a dog and cat show. It makes no sense. It wouldn't be a show. It would be a fight, which would be neither enjoyable nor entertaining. Do you understand how totally inappropriate it is to say 'dog and cat show'?"

"Stone, it's okay. He gets the point," I say, but it fails to stop the "don't-fuck-with-me" lecture on idiom.

"Do you understand?" Stone asks.

"Yes," Jacques says. "Fine. I get it."

"I'm glad. Now, I think you owe my colleague an apology," Stone says.

"I'm sorry," he says automatically. Stone still has a hold of his arm, so Jacques adds, "My sous-chef will work everything out fine for you, okay?"

Stone smiles and lets go. Jacques leaves without shutting the door.

I take a deep breath and find myself sitting down, exhausted from visions of bloodshed.

"Are you all right?" Stone asks.

"No, I am not all right! Jesus!—I can't believe you did that."

"I didn't hurt him."

"No, but you threatened to."

"Not really," he says, like I had imagined the whole thing, which only makes me more strident.

"Okay, so you gave him this bizarre lecture about the proper use of expressions, but the threat was still implicit, especially when you wouldn't let go of his arm, which, by the way, he could easily call physical abuse in court."

"He's not going to sue me. I was just holding him accountable for how rude he was being," Stone says.

"Great. I hate to think what you do to people who cut you off on the freeway. I mean, wasn't I the one who was supposed to do all the talking? What happened to that plan?"

The whole event continues to send an electric shock through me. I start disassembling Jacques's masterpiece, placing the bird parts on a separate plate. Stone pauses for a second, and I'm expecting him to mount another defense. I'm poised for it, ready to strike back. He walks over to me as I fiddle with the plate and don't look up. Peripherally, I can see him take off his glasses and run his hand over his face and through his hair.

"I'm sorry," he says. "I have this thing about pompous types."

"I understand, but it's not worth trying to set the person straight. I mean, chances are people like Jacques won't change anyway."

"I know, but . . ."

"But what?"

"You've been through enough, you know? You didn't need that idiot in your face. I wanted to call him on it."

I stop what I'm doing and look up at him. Stone ducks his head and looks away. I am startled into silence, unaware that he had given any thought to my father's death. He never talked with me about it or asked any questions. Maybe it wasn't macho pride after all but chivalry run amok that caused him to reproach Jacques. Not that I'm currently a damsel in distress. But I think back to the time before I started seeing Naomi and what a mess I was. And I remember Stone's quiet kindness—always taking over when I couldn't deal with the styling, once helping me detach a chunk of dry ice from my hand when I was too dazed to work efficiently. I remember how he held my hand under the warm water until the ice loosened its grip.

I take a deep breath and say, "Look, it's okay. I'm not as fragile as I seem—I mean I'm stronger than I was a few months ago. So I don't really need to be defended."

"I know that now. And I really am sorry—about everything."

It's the "everything" that lingers in my heart. After he says it, Stone frowns at the floor and turns to readjust one of the lights, and I wonder if I was too harsh with him. The last thing I wanted was to sound like Sally. I reach my hand toward his arm, almost reflexively, but then drop it back to my side.

"It's okay," I tell him. "And thanks."

He nods. I look away from him, survey the disastrous table, and sigh.

"Do you think Jacques will call Sally?" he asks.

"Maybe. But I'll make sure she hears our side of the story before she hears it from him."

"I'm the one who screwed up. Why don't you let me call her?"

"No, technically it's my job to update her. I better call. Besides, you're not on her best side these days."

"True," he says.

"And I know how painful that is for you—since you love her so."

He suppresses a smile.

"I know your poor heart just can't take any more rejection."

"How right you are," he says, seriously enough to make me wonder if we're still talking about Sally. "I guess we should reshoot while we still have some light left."

"Definitely."

Fortunately, the sous-chef is used to being a Jacques apologist. Obsequious to a fault, he smiles constantly and says "please" like a nervous tick, holding out his hand to invite me to the stove whenever I get near him in the kitchen. He cooks new carrots and radicchio and then adds some more squash to the purée. I rearrange the plate so that the bird curves around the edges, almost like a side dish to the vegetables. We get the shot, load up the car, and head out in search of the Bell Rock Inn.

In the car, Stone doesn't say much. From the corner of my eye, I watch him wipe his camera lenses and change out the used-up rolls of film.

"Do we know where we'll be shooting tomorrow?" he asks.

"No, but I'll know after I call Sally. At least, I hope I'll know."

Thankfully, we check into the two economy rooms at the Bell Rock Inn without a hitch. I began to fear that everything would go wrong. I find three messages from Sally marked urgent so the first thing I do, after completing some calming deep-breathing exercises, is call her. The news isn't good.

"We can't get L'Auberge," Sally says.

"Why not? That's the most famous place out here."

"Exactly. The chef and restaurant were just profiled in *Bon Appétit*. They're busy. What do they need us for?"

"Why didn't we know this before we came out here?"

"Well, *we* hadn't received the August issue of *Bon Appétit* yet.

Good God. I give you a little promotion and suddenly you know best."

"It's been a rough day, Sally."

"So I hear. I just got off the phone with Jacques. He wanted to let me know that he would never be working with the magazine again. That, of course, just made my day. Will you please tell me what the hell is going on out there?"

"Well, it's a long story. What exactly did he say?"

"Something about Stone and dog and pony shows, which made no sense. He kept alternating between French and English. Did Stone do something?"

"Well, yes, but it was totally understandable."

"I'll be the judge of that."

I tell her the whole story—that there would be no feathers and that Jacques now knows a great deal about the proper use of idiomatic expressions. I try to make Jacques the villain and Stone the hero, but it's a tough sell. Sally is silent for about ten seconds, and then she blows.

"I don't care how talented Stone is. I don't care if he's Richard fucking Avedon. I want him off the shoot."

"Sally, he's got a conscience about things, standards. He doesn't like to see people treated badly."

"Well, that's fine if he's a missionary in India, but you don't piss off a chef of a four-star restaurant."

"He did apologize to me. And Jacques was extremely rude and difficult. Plus, the restaurant is falling apart."

"I don't care what Jacques or the restaurant was like," Sally says. "Stone is off the shoot. We don't have the money to send any other photographers out there, so I guess you'll have to take the pictures."

Months ago, when I was vying for his position, I would have shoved Stone aside and jumped at the chance. But now, oddly enough, it's the last thing I want to do. So I haul out the secret weapon.

"You know, I even wrote down what Jacques said because I was so appalled by it. He said, 'And you tell your boss that I don't give a fuck about what she wants the bird to look like.' And he called *Mangia!* a 'stupid little magazine with a circulation of about fifty people.'"

There's a pause on the line—a good sign.

"He said that?"

"Yes."

"Those were his exact words?"

"Verbatim."

"Son of a bitch."

"Stone just couldn't stand for someone putting you or the magazine down like that," I say earnestly.

"All that sweet, gushy talk about how thrilled he was. Son of a bitch."

"I told him to forget about the cover shot."

"Damn right. I guess we're obligated to use him, but I'm going to write a profile that'll ruin that bastard. You said the restaurant was falling apart."

"Empty at two o'clock on a Friday," I say, playing along even though Jacques is already washed up and Sally's culinary opinion doesn't hold sway with anyone.

"Well, that'll make it into the piece—'easy to get a table for lunch or dinner.' And we can retell the whole conflict over the food, too—exactly what he said and did. That'll cook his pheasant."

"Perfect. So I take it you don't want Stone off the shoot after all."

"I guess not. I mean, I can understand his reaction a little better now that I have the whole story. Besides, he knows a lot more about photography than you do."

Whether Sally intends the remark as an insult or not doesn't really matter. All I know is there are kinder, more encouraging ways of addressing an employee's ambitions, but Sally will never be able to find them, let alone believe in me enough to say them. That is the ugly truth, which her false flattery and talk of permanent promotion momentarily obscured. To her, I will never be more than a food stylist, and I can't change her opinion any more than I could put the pieces of Jacques's hacked pheasant back together. Her mind is made up. All I can do is take note and move forward.

"So what's our next assignment?" I ask.

She lets out an exasperated grunt. "I don't know. I've got to call the Enchantment Resort and then Poco Diablo. I hope they've heard of us. It's funny. I really thought we would have more name recognition."

"So we're in a holding pattern?"

"Not exactly. We need some scenic shots to throw in—you know, spectacular sunsets, red rock heaven. Oh! And we talked about doing something with the spiritual angle—the vortex thing. So you need to take one of those jeep tours and find some spiritual places."

"That sounds rather difficult."

"In L.A., yes. In Sedona, no. They grow shamans on trees out there, for Christ's sake."

Stone and I meet downstairs at six o'clock for dinner. We both are exhausted and agree that the Saguaro Café across the street is the easiest and cheapest way to eat. We order chicken fajitas and two beers.

"I'm almost afraid to ask, but what's the word from L.A.?" he says.

"Jacques ratted on you, and Sally was pissed. But all I needed to do was tell her what Jacques said about her and the magazine, and that got her on our side. But of course the other restaurants have fallen through."

"So now what do we do?"

"Sally says, and I quote, 'Take one of those jeeps tours and find some spiritual places.'"

"Just like that?" he says, laughing. "Are we supposed to find enlightenment, too?"

I smile at him and say, "I think that's optional."

"Why does she want us to photograph spiritual places? The magazine is hardly New Age."

"I think she's just stalling until she finds another chef for us to profile. But after Jacques, it might be better to rest for a day."

"Well, from now on I promise I'll keep my mouth shut. As a friend of mine once said, 'Lots of trains roll into the station, but you don't have to get on every one.'"

"Good advice."

Our drinks arrive and we take a few sips in silence.

"So much fuss over a pheasant," Stone says with a weary sigh.

"That could be the title of my autobiography."

"You mean the rest of your life is full of this kind of minutiae?" he asks.

"That's just it. I don't have a life."

He smiles, takes another drink of his beer, then sits back and eyes me. "I don't believe you."

"Well, it's true. I go to work. I exercise. I come home and fix dinner. I might read, but I always fall asleep before I can finish an article or chapter in a book."

He shakes his head slowly. "I sense oversimplification."

"Okay. There are other things."

"Such as?"

"I do photography." I cringe immediately after saying it. Do photography? How stupid sounding—like it's origami or yoga or some other New Age trend.

"Really? What kinds of things do you shoot?"

"Anything but food," I say lightly, without thinking.

He shrugs and says, "Food isn't so bad."

"Oh, I know. What I mean is that I get tired of working with it and looking at it all day. So I want something different for my own projects."

"Actually, I know the feeling."

Our conversation is interrupted by the sizzling platters that arrive along with the standard fajita paraphernalia. I am reminded of what a complicated meal the fajita is. I wasn't thinking of logistics when I ordered it. I just figured it was best to order indigenous southwestern food. I would like nothing more than simply to pick up my fork and cut delicate bites of something, like fish or quiche—a food that begs me not to handle it. But instead, I am unfolding the tortilla, spreading guacamole and salsa, tucking in hunks of chicken to keep them from falling out. By the time I've assembled one, I don't have much of an appetite.

Stone has gone silent over the meal, and I wonder whether I should tell him what my project is. It seems insignificant now, as though he was only making polite conversation until the food arrived.

We continue to eat in silence until he says, "I don't normally eat like this, but I was starved."

He takes a big gulp of beer and then remembers.

"Oh! So tell me about your project."

I smile and try to look casual, like it's not a big deal even though I feel a nervous flutter in my stomach.

"It's a series of photographs about the different ways people create a sense of home throughout the city—different kinds of landscaping, architecture, gatherings. You know, sort of a kaleidoscope of home life from south central to Santa Monica."

"Huh," he says.

I wait for him to say something else, but he doesn't. He tucks a wayward piece of green pepper into his fajita, his second in twenty minutes, and takes another bite. I try not to feel offended, but when he still doesn't respond after yet another bite, I can't help but challenge his silence.

"Claire thinks it's a great idea."

"It is. But have you ever thought about focusing on just one neighborhood instead of the whole city?"

"But that's the point. To explore the differences."

"Right, but my guess is that you could find a lot of variation even in a very small section of L.A."

"Well, it's just an idea for now," I say, trying not to sound as defensive as I feel. "I don't even know what I'll do with the photos when I get them assembled."

"That's why I mentioned going with one neighborhood—I bet you could get backing from the district's government, maybe an exhibit in a neighborhood library."

"It's a long way off," I say.

He nods his head and then signals the waitress. He orders a cup of espresso and asks me if I want one.

"No. It keeps me up."

"It does me too, but I thought about taking some photos of the rocks and desert wildlife after dinner. There's a full moon tonight. Why don't you come out and keep me company?"

Company. He doesn't even suggest that I bring my own camera.

"No thanks," I say behind my frozen, polite facade. "I'm too tired."

"Okay. Maybe another night."

I hear the gavels banging as the parliamentarians hold forth: *Tit for Tat 101! Didn't like that ego bashing this afternoon, did he—trying to get even by putting you down! Quite right!* I try to silence my fears and tether myself to Naomi. What would she tell me in this situation? She would probably remind me that he was just trying to be helpful, not (like my father) antagonistic. She would note that I do not need an invitation to photograph things—if I want to take pictures, take them. So I dismiss the grumbling session in my head, kindly telling Tories and Whigs alike to piss off.

I'm relieved when Stone changes the subject and asks, "So how do we find these spiritual places?"

"I asked the woman at the front desk, and she said that there are dozens of jeep tours through the red rocks. We need to call Desert Tours tomorrow and ask for the 'Embrace the Earth' tour if we're interested in the vortex or spiritual angle. It takes about three hours."

He shakes his head as I'm telling him, sitting back in the

booth and looking out the window at the sun setting behind Chimney Rock.

After a moment he says, "Unbelievable."

"The view?"

"The hype," he says, facing me again. "Like anybody's going to feel spiritual after bouncing along in a noisy jeep for three hours. They might feel nauseous, but that's about it, don't you think?"

"Probably. Then again, I don't really know much about being spiritual. I never went to church or meditated. But I had a couple of boyfriends who were religious."

"No kidding. What do you make of that?"

"I don't know. Maybe it's like that time Sally wanted to start a cum laude social club, and Claire said, 'I'm not cum laude, but I slept with a lot of men who were—does that count?'"

"I like that answer," Stone laughs.

"Anyway, I think I'm in the dark with the spiritual world."

"I disagree," he says.

"What do you mean?"

"You're pursuing photography, right?"

"Sure but—"

"That's a spiritual quest."

"Oh, right. And Sally is the unrequited love of your life."

He sits up and leans toward me, like he's been waiting to explain this to me.

"I'm serious. Helping people, being loving and forgiving— naturally that's the heart of it and it's in lots of places—not just church. But don't you think being spiritual also means pursuing your passions—taking stock in yourself and the world around you?"

"I don't know."

"I do," he replies. "And it's not in something as vague and pas- sive as 'shared energy fields' or 'harmonic convergence' or whatever they call it out here."

His espresso arrives. He thanks the waitress, stirs sugar into his cup, and takes a sip. He shrugs, smiling, maybe a bit embarrassed by his own passions, and says, "So, that's what I think. What do you think?"

"To tell you the truth, I've spent more time contemplating dead spirits than living ones lately, so I'm not really sure what I believe."

He nods his head. "I can understand that."

"But if I have some kind of awakening, I don't think it'll be in an energy field, and definitely not in a jeep."

"Right on," he says. From anyone else the phrase would be hokey. But from Stone it's authentic language—a simple affirmation that puts me at ease and seems to pull us closer together in that moment, across decades and deserts and painful losses.

Back at the motel, I watch from my window as he piles his cameras and lamps into the car. What did I expect him to say about my project anyway—"What a brilliant idea. I'll contact my friends at the Guggenheim?" I grab my camera and head outside toward the car. Why not go with him to this unknown terrain? I'll bear witness and testify about the blue glow of moonlight and how it turns the desert into a wild, holy place.

12 ♔

Spiritual Experience

I would have written down directions, consulted a map, filled up the gas tank, and checked the tires before venturing into the desert at night. I would have made sure that the Auto Club serviced the area, just in case my car got stuck in the sand. But Stone simply gets behind the wheel and drives. He turns onto the first road we see, and it's pitch black. I have visions of crashing into sagebrush or blowing out tires on potholes, but the road remains clear and takes us to the base of a mountain.

"Don't we need flashlights?" I ask.

"The moon's full. Once your eyes adjust to the light you can see everything."

We hike up to a small plateau, and I follow closely behind him. I am a bit skittish as I hear the frantic patter of lizards and other creatures who scurry off the path. Stone says desert animals are more afraid of us than we are of them, and I'm thinking how very cowardly they must be.

I stand on the plateau, looking out at the full moon rising over the buttes and valleys in the desert. The silvery blue light makes the landscape look soft enough to be made of cloud instead of rock, bushes, and cacti. Since Stone wants to get some wildlife shots, not just landscapes, he's placing leftover fajita on a flat patch of desert within view of the plateau. At my request, he sets the bait at a safe distance, just in case the animal is a mountain lion instead of a coyote.

He scrambles back up, adjusts the camera on the tripod, and waits. All I can hear are crickets and the whistle of wind. I snap a few shots of the horizon and then watch Stone fiddle with the focus on his zoom lens.

"Are you sure this is going to work?" I ask. "I thought you said they're scared of humans."

"They are. But nothing can keep a hungry animal away from food." He glances at me. "You probably think I'm a little crazy to be doing this."

"No, I don't."

"I don't know," he says. "I didn't find the roast pheasant so compelling this afternoon. I mean the end result looked great, considering. But, well, you said it yourself. It's only food. I'd rather photograph living things—especially people."

"I saw your pictures from the Watts Jazz Festival in *L.A. Style*. They were great."

"Thanks. I liked that assignment. It's easier when you like it."

"What's your favorite kind of assignment?"

I expect him to say something like neighborhood events or street scenes or something that involves action, spontaneity, and unpredictability. But his answer takes me by surprise.

"Studio portraits."

"Seriously?"

"Yeah. It's great because you get to know the person in the process, so it has much more meaning—at least for me it does."

"So you don't go in for events or newsworthy shots?"

"Not me. I tried that route before, but I hated it. The more newsworthy something is, the more blood you shed. I was interning my senior year of high school at the *Washington Post* during Watergate. One time at Dulles, there was such a rush to photograph Nixon that I got my nose broken."

I was six years old during Watergate. Suddenly I feel humbled and foolish for even talking about photography with such a veteran.

"So how did you get the idea to photograph home scenes?" he asks.

I have known my gypsy truth for years, long before Dad died, and have always felt like it's a secret others would judge, something like atheism or nihilism or some other nonconformist worldview. I've admitted it only to Naomi and Claire and Trudy. But the truth comes more easily on this desert ridge, away from a city that seems just too big for me.

"I don't really have a home."

"What do you mean?"

"Ever since my mother died, things changed. I left home. I grew up in this small Kentucky town but only have one friend who lives near there now, no sisters or brothers."

"Where are your other friends?"

"Scattered across the country and generally too busy to stay in touch."

"Guess that's life in the age of communication."

"I guess. At least I have Claire and a few friends around town," I reply, figuring it's okay to put Naomi in that category.

"Claire's terrific," Stone says, and I agree with him. He pulls a bottle of water out of his bag, takes a sip and offers me one. I drink a swig and hand it back.

"So what did your mom die of?" he asks.

"Colon cancer."

He shakes his head. "Such a brutal disease. My mom got it in her lungs."

"Was it fatal for her?"

"Yes—the chemo was too debilitating, given her age. She died pretty quickly, about six years ago, but it was tough to watch."

"I'm so sorry."

We sit silently, remembering and not really wanting to. My mother has been gone long enough for my thoughts of her to recede for a week at a time. Then I awaken, like a sleepwalker, and find myself in the middle of my life without her—incredulous, frightened, and trying to push away the plaintive, unanswerable why. I'm straight-arming that question again when Stone asks,

"So what about L.A.? That's not home?"

"No—at least not yet. I still feel more like an observer than a citizen, like a tourist just passing through. I guess I'm trying to find out what makes a place home—that's why I took the shots."

"People do."

"Right, but what happens when they leave?" I ask.

"You find new ones to love or hate or both—usually both."

"Just like that?"

"No," Stone says. "But you find them."

I'm wondering about who or what he calls home when our conversation is interrupted by the rustling sound of an animal making its way through the brush toward the food. I hope for a coyote, an image other than the tilted-head silhouette that appears painted, sculpted, and carved everywhere out here—something more in line with its skittish, feral ways.

But the animal that finds our bait and rapidly begins to devour the food is an unsightly javelina, a desert pig. Stone snaps a few shots that make it flinch, but it is so intent on eating that it doesn't run. I come up behind Stone, and he moves so that I can get a look at the black bristled creature through the viewfinder.

"It's so ugly it's almost beautiful," he says.

"You were right about the food."

He takes a few more shots as the javelina smacks up the remaining morsels, even the paper towel underneath, and heads back into the bushes. We wait for a while to see if other creatures will appear. None do, so we pick up the gear and head back down.

We walk in silence until he says, "Kentucky?"

"Yeah."

"Where's the twang?"

"I lost it in Connecticut."

"Why?"

"Boarding school—they teased it out of me."

"Typical. But I can still hear some of that twang," Stone says. "Just a tad."

"That's reassuring—maybe I'm not as rootless as I feel. Where are you from?"

"Everywhere. I'm an army brat."

"No kidding? My dad was in the army and then got out of it. He taught history at the community college. Of course, in some ways he never really got out of it."

"They never do," Stone says with a bitter laugh. "So L.A. is my home. I've been there for about twelve years and have some great friends. It qualifies as much as any place."

The path narrows and at one point Stone stops in front of a barrel cactus. I think he's going to photograph something, but he puts down the tripod and reaches out his hand toward the cactus.

"What are you doing?" I ask.

"I'll show you in a second," he says.

I watch as his hand weaves in between the spiky needles. We have a small article on prickly pear jam for this issue that requires a cactus garnish. So I have learned about the perilous cactus needle—how the spines along the edge stick into your skin so that you can't just pull the needle out if you get stuck.

"Be careful," I say.

He doesn't respond but before long extricates his hand, apparently unstuck, and turns back toward me. There in his palm is a cactus flower, a beautiful deep red. He hands it to me for what I think is inspection, but then he surprises me yet again.

"That's for you," he says.

Before I can pluck an appropriate response from the ones rifling through my mind—What does this mean? How's your hand?—he picks up the tripod and starts walking again. Finally, I find the right one.

"It's lovely. Thank you."

"You're welcome."

As we drive back to the motel, I say, "I'm glad I came out with you."

"Does that mean you thought the javelina was beautiful?"

"In all its snorting, imperfect glory?"

"Exactly."

"Well, no," I say, which makes him laugh. "But I liked the flower."

It is a hopeful morning—clear, cooler, and full of photographic possibilities. But I can ride the high for only so long. I call around to all the hotels in the area and find out that all jeep tours, spiritual and secular, are booked solid. It seems the weekend crowds have taken over. A couple of places even tell me that you need to make reservations weeks in advance.

The tours feature a wide variety of accouterments, including minimeditations, rock-climbing excursions, and stops at Native American petroglyphs. But the vortex stuff is not mentioned. I asked one tour company official about the disappearing energy field fixation, and she told me things have died down since the harmonic convergence mania in 1989. The vortex world has also been rocked by a recent story on *Dateline* that ferreted out a Sedona guru who was wanted for bank fraud in several states.

I call Sally with this new information in hopes that she'll let us off the spiritual hook. Naturally, she doesn't.

"Julia, we can't do an issue on Sedona without it. I mean, regardless of how real it is, people want to believe it, and it will probably get some of them to go out there and eat at these restaurants."

"So you found another place?"

"We've got two more, but I'll fill you in later. You have to do the scenic shots today because you're scheduled to go to these other restaurants tomorrow. And I don't care what anyone tells you—vortexes are still the rage. A friend of mine just came back from Sedona and said she went out to one of the energy spots and definitely felt something. A strange kind of lightness, she said."

"It was probably in her pocketbook."

"None of that," Sally says in her kindergarten teacher voice. "We can't afford not to feature it—it's much too sexy to ignore."

I stumble, at a momentary loss for asexual arguments, and Sally seizes the opening.

"Gotta go. Wolfgang's on another line," she says, forgetting that she once told me it was her trick for sounding important.

I meet Stone at ten in the lobby and give him the bad news.

"So what do we do now?" he asks.

"I found out about a New Age bookstore in town called The Fourth Dimension. They might have some information on private tours. Or maybe they can just point us toward the right rock formation."

We find the bookstore off the main road and surrounded by pine trees and juniper bushes. No doubt the store was here before the McDonald's across the street. Just the sight of such an animal flesh factory must rankle the holistic folks.

I smell sandalwood incense before I even get to the door. Inside, I am serenaded by wind chimes and synthesized music that sounds like a primitive flute and drum. As with any New Age bookstore, the compulsion to be well is overpowering. Mixed in with titles on healing, shamanism, self-help, recovery from addiction, philosophy, and religion are a variety of implements for better living: Chinese medicine balls, wooden muscle rollers, homeopathic herbs, multiple varieties of essential oils and incense, and three types of Tiger Balm. I glance at some labels and realize the makers of these products know exactly what their audience is after—Zen Blessed natural soap; Euphoria bath oil; Serenity incense sticks.

Around the walls, above the books, are pictures of gurus and yogis and teachers of all types of spirituality who preside over the browsing pilgrims. Some I recognize—Gandhi, the Dalai Lama—others are strangers who all have that special look of enlightenment—serene gazes, gentle smiles on their faces, a few standing with arms outstretched. I can't help but wonder how many are genuine—how many truly live in the gentle rhythms of their teachings—letting cars go ahead of them on the freeway—and how many tailgate and throw fits when the barely paid immigrant at the car wash can't get the road tar off the Mercedes sedan.

There are no signs of life in the store other than the complimentary pot of herbal tea that sits steaming on an electric warmer. So we check out the bulletin board next to the literature section marked Occult—Outer Space and find the names and numbers of five tour guides. After I write down the names, we head for coffee at the McDonald's, and I start dialing on my cell phone.

I try four of the numbers, and all I get are three no answers and one machine recording that wishes me peace, love, and light. The last name on the list is Ray "Rising Star" Lightfoot, which might be only a Native American tour. I chance it anyway.

At five rings, someone answers. I ask for Mr. Lightfoot.

"Yeah, at's me," says the voice, deep and groggy. I can hear the wild applause and tinselly music of a television game show in the background.

"Do you give jeep tours of the red rocks?" I ask.

"Yes. I sure do. Hold on," he says. The television noise dies down, and I hear the rustling of a newspaper being folded. He drops the phone and picks it up again.

"Hello?" he says.

"I'm still here. Did I catch you at a bad time?"

"Not at all," he says. "I was just, uh, listening to tapes of some Native American poetry from the, uh, Zuni tribe. Good stuff."

I'm tempted to comment on the remarkable tonal similarity between the poet's voice and Bob Barker's infamous, "Come on
down!" But I swallow my cynicism, tell him who I am, and get to
the point.

"Mr. Lightfoot, we're interested in photographing places that
have vortexes associated with them. Do you cover those areas or do
you focus only on Native American culture?"

"Anything you want. I conduct a wide range of journeys. If
it's vortexes you want, I know where to find 'em. And please, call
me Ray."

I'm always caught off guard by first-name invitations, especially
within the first five seconds of meeting someone. I never know
whether to say the name right then or to save it for later, so I keep
talking.

"How much do you charge for the tour?"

"Well, the price depends on a number of factors—the number
of people, the distance covered, gas."

"It would be for two people."

"Okay, so right off the bat you're looking at forty dollars per
person. But now it might be more because if we get to an energy
field that's crowded, there's no point in stopping because it's nearly
impossible to get in touch with your higher self if you're elbowing
your way through a disconnected group of people. If it were a
group that was unified by a shared ceremony, well, that's a different
story."

"How much more?"

"It's hard to say. The approximate estimate for two people
would be anywhere between one hundred and two hundred dollars.
That's including twenty dollars for gas. So let's say two hundred
dollars max."

"That's a lot more money than any of the other tours I've checked
into."

"I'll tell you what," he says. "The commercial tours only touch
the surface of what's out there. Really. Any private guide is going to

cost you more because he—or she—knows how to delve into the spirit and energy of the rocks. No joke."

I motion Stone over to me and tell Ray, "Hang on for a moment."

I bury the receiver into my hand and fill Stone in.

"What choice do we have?" he says. "If Sally wants a vortex, let her pay for it."

I arrange for him to pick us up outside of McDonald's. We finish our coffee and are waiting on the side of the road for about twenty minutes. I can feel a headache coming on and pray it's not a migraine. I swallow two aspirin with the hope that it's nothing worse. When Ray drives up in a black convertible jeep, I'm glad to see him although surprised by his appearance. I had expected someone more earthy—perhaps a former hippie with a slight, vegetarian build, faded denim, a graying ponytail.

Ray looks like a former linebacker. He wears black Levi's and a white Ralph Lauren shirt stretched tightly around his hulking shoulders, but untucked and loose around his belt, not quite able to cover the lower portion of his protruding white belly that I see when he jumps down from the jeep. His curly black hair is styled in a short mullet, long enough in the back to cover his thick neck. A gaudy hunk of turquoise set in silver rests in the open triangle of his shirt. The necklace matches his turquoise-studded watch. He sticks out his pudgy hand and gives me an old-fashioned, ladies-only shake—all fingers and no palm.

"I'm Ray Lightfoot. You must be Julia."

I say yes and quickly slip my hand away from his condescending clutch, introducing Stone to him.

"Nice to meet you," Ray says and pumps his hand firmly.

I don't know if Stone feels as uncertain as I do about the man. But I try to keep an open mind. Looks aren't everything, especially in the spiritual world.

"I can sense that you're ready to check out some vortexes," Ray says.

Sense?

"Right," I say. "That's the tour we spoke about on the phone."

"No, I mean I can strongly sense that you're really ready, you know." He waves his broad palms in front of my face. "I'm checking out your chakra. Beautiful. See, that's the ability I have, to sense other people's energy. It comes from being so in touch with my inner eye, you know what I'm saying?"

"Sure," I say, playing along, because I don't feel like hearing an explanation of how energy reception or the inner eye works. All I want to do is get the pictures and get back to L.A. So we climb into the car, he revs up the motor, and the quest begins.

Ray drives too fast on the narrow, winding roads that lead to the rocks. The tires screech as we round the bends, and we seem to become one with every bump on the road. Stone hugs his cameras to his chest and holds on to the strap of his seat belt with his other hand. My headache has gotten worse, and I'm beginning to feel nauseated. I tell myself it isn't migraine even though it is an increasing possibility.

Stone leans over to me and says, "Your face is so pale. Are you all right?"

"Yes. It's just a headache. But I don't think the speed of this jeep is helping to ease it."

Ray seems like the type to go faster if you told him to slow down. So I whisper to Stone to hint about the speed, forgetting that Stone isn't the greatest diplomat.

"It's strange. I haven't seen the sign for the speed limit on this road," he says.

"You're not telling me to slow down, are you?" Ray asks, laughing but edgy.

"Oh, no. I mean, I was curious about what the speed on a road like this is."

Ray downshifts and we slow a bit. "Well, it's about twenty-five miles per hour, but the cops never check it. I think they first have to pave it, and then they'll get the official signs up. Then the cops will be around, boy."

We fall silent and the jeep speeds up again as the pounding in my head gets worse. It's slightly overcast, but even the clouds are too bright for my eyes.

Thinking conversation might make Ray slow down, I lean over to Stone and say, "Try to keep him talking."

"So, Ray . . . about your name. Are you a Native American?" Stone asks.

"No, but a lot of people think I am. My physical, nonspiritual name is Ray Payne. It's not spelled P-A-I-N, but it might as well should have been. You know?"

"Yeah, I do. What was your life like before you got into vortexes?" Stone asks. The jeep slows down to nearly the speed limit, and I mouth "Thank you" to him.

"Not very peaceful. I worked at UPS and belonged to the Arizona National Guard. Then I quit both things, on account of all the bureaucracy, and joined an independent militia group."

"Really? What was that like?" Stone asks pleasantly, as though Ray were going to tell him about a cruise he took. I suppose he's being brave for both of us now that all my fears about Ray being a bit unhinged are confirmed.

"Pretty rough. We lived out in the desert in tents and spent most of the time drilling. Occasionally we'd go out and firebomb a storage shed on government land. Hell, they own ninety percent of the desert out here anyways, so you can hardly blame us for making a statement against it. But it was the wrong kind of statement, you know. It didn't come from a place of love."

"No, it doesn't sound like it did," Stone says.

"I was trapped in a vicious cycle of hate," Ray says, stealing a glance at me in the rearview mirror. I'm wearing dark sunglasses, which hide my eyes completely, and am in an upright fetal position.

"You okay back there?" he asks.

"Oh, fine," I say.

"So how did you break the cycle?" Stone asks.

"Well, they finally locked me up for six months on account of me setting fire to one of those IRS mail bins during tax time," Ray says with a slight smile. "I don't know that the punishment fit the crime. But I did inconvenience a lot of people. Anyway, one night I was in the jail cell, standing up and looking through those bars, looking up at the moon, and my body was just burning with heat. And suddenly, it felt like it wasn't concrete under my feet but dirt, and then it was like I was suspended in air, almost hovering, over the earth's surface. I felt this light from the moon enter me through what I now know was the inner eye of my soul. Then all that heaviness and negativity started churning in my spiritual axis, what some people call the stomach, and before I knew it, I was throwing up on the floor."

"Sounds pretty dramatic," Stone says.

"It was. Of course the doctors told me it was just the flu, but I knew something else was going on. It was like I had been reborn."

"How did you figure out what had happened to you? I mean, that it wasn't just the flu," Stone asks.

"Well, when I came to Sedona, I met Darvona. She's a fifth-dimensional walk-in."

"A what?"

"Someone whose body is inhabited by life forces from different universal centuries and planets. She sensed my experiences and became my spiritual advisor."

Stone raises his eyebrows at me. "Keep talking," I whisper because Ray has became so engrossed in himself that the jeep is moving at a twenty-miles-per-hour crawl.

"So, Darvona. She, uh, clarified everything for you?" he asks.

"Absolutely. During a medicine wheel ceremony. That's when she named me Rising Star because of my connection with the moon and Lightfoot because of my sensation of hovering over the earth. Pretty wild, huh?"

"Pretty wild," Stone says.

We arrive at the base of Cathedral Rock only to find a line of cars waiting to park or turn around in the gravel lot.

"I was afraid this might happen, especially with the more popular formations," Ray says. "We need to find a more true, peaceful place. There's a place out in Oak Creek Canyon that nobody knows about. We can go there."

"Wait a second," Stone says. "I'd like to jump out and get a few pictures."

"Okay, but make it quick. I hate crowds," Ray says with considerably less of a spiritual lilt in his voice. He pulls over to the shoulder, and I muster my strength to get out and follow Stone mainly because I don't want to be in the car alone with Ray. Once I am upright and moving, I realize I am in a nearly full-blown migraine state and am afraid I'm going to vomit or pass out from the pain. I seek refuge under the faint shade of a Palo Verde tree and wait for Stone as he climbs along the base of the rocks, searching for the right angle of the sun. He takes a few vertical shots and then a few of the horizon and the other rock formations that surround us.

He walks back to me and says, "Done. Not that you can possibly photograph a vortex. But at least we have pictures of people trying to get in touch with them. Do you believe this guy?"

"Stone, I'm really sick. I have a migraine. I need to go to the hospital because I didn't bring my medicine. The pain flared up when I started moving."

"We'll go right back. Can you make it back to the jeep?"

"Yeah, I just have to take it slowly because it hurts to open my eyes."

I am overly optimistic. Squinting at the ground every so often, I shuffle toward the jeep but fail to detect a large rock in my path. I fall, bumping my head as I land. It feels like my brain is going to burst through my skull. I begin to see colors although I am still conscious. Fortunately, Stone is right behind me and rushes to help.

"Are you okay?"

"I hit my head, and now I'm seeing colors. Jesus, it's never been this bad."

My eyes tear up. I try not to cry but can't control it. Stone doesn't say anything. He sits down next to me, puts his arm around me, and hands me his bandanna.

"Thanks," I say, drying my eyes and trying to keep from busting out into a five-alarm wail.

"Where did you hit it?" he asks. I point to the bump and he inspects it. "At least it's not bleeding. I just hope you don't have a concussion."

After I calm down, he helps me up and guides me back to the jeep. Ray is standing by the driver's side.

"What happened?" he asks.

"Julia is having a migraine and just fell and hit her head, which has made it worse. We have to go to the hospital."

Once again Ray confirms his moron status by saying, "This is amazing. This is great!"

"What the hell are you talking about?" Stone says.

"She's not having a migraine," Ray says.

"Yes I am! I'm seeing colors, for God's sake!" I say through my tears.

"We're going to the hospital," Stone says.

"Okay. Hold on," Ray says as he pulls the keys out of the ignition. "Now, I know you're freaking out, but I know about these things. She is not having a migraine; the pain, the colors—all those things are associated with a consciousness-raising experience. She's trying to find her higher self. Don't you see? She's getting in touch with the energy and her brain is trying to adapt. This is totally normal in the realm of spiritual activity."

Stone takes a step toward him and says, "Listen to me, Ray—"

"Pain is the doorway into all life systems of the universe," Ray says in an insistent, gleefully manic voice. "That's the irony. You have to suffer before you can know the light. The energy is starting to travel through her from the planets to the earth, just like it did with me in that jail cell. This is not a migraine. This is a spiritual experience, and if we go to the medicine wheel right now, I can help bring it forth."

"Give me the keys, Ray."

"No. I can't deny her this connection. Her soul is crying out for it."

Stone takes a deep breath, trying to stay calm, but failing.

"Look, Ray, maybe you're a shaman to other people, but to me you're just a freak with a jeep. She fell and hit her head, hard enough for me to hear it go thump! Do you understand that, Ray? Now, I don't know if a person can die from a migraine, but I know a person can die from a concussion. So you need to shut the fuck up about this spiritual shit and get us back to civilization!!"

Despite Stone's compelling speech, which manages to make me smile a little through my tears, Ray doesn't budge. Fortunately, the volume and profanity of Stone's invective catches the attention of a park ranger in the kiosk near the lot. He adjusts his hat, walks over to us, and says to Stone, "Is everything okay here?"

"It's fine," Ray says.

"No, it's not fine. My friend needs to get to a hospital because she has a migraine and hit her head. And this . . . this whack job won't take her to the hospital!"

"Well, where do you want to take her?" the ranger asks.

"Medicine wheel over in Oak Creek Canyon," Ray says defensively. "And it's not a migraine. She's having a spiritual experience."

"I see," he says. "Tell you what, it's a free country. These folks can decide whether they want to go with me to the hospital or with you to the medicine wheel. Fair enough?"

"Nobody asked your opinion," Ray snaps.

"Well, this area's protected by the National Park system, so I'm just doing my job—trying to keep things peaceful and running smoothly. Should I get my car?"

"Yes," Stone and I say in unison, and the ranger nods and leaves us.

"Goddamn government pawn," Ray mutters. "And you owe me money!" he yells at Stone.

Stone writes a check for some amount and holds it out to Ray, who just stands there and stares at him. For a moment, I think it's possible that Ray might deck him, but instead he takes the check, stuffs it in his pants pocket, and walks away from us, shaking his head.

We climb into the ranger's SUV, and I look back at Ray through the window. He stands on a rock ledge that overlooks the landscape, legs slightly apart, feet planted firmly, arms rising skyward. I see his lips moving, so I roll down the window to listen.

"I call out to my higher self. I call out to my spiritual guides. Stay with me! Protect me! Purify me! I am love. I am light. I am love. I am light. . . ."

We drive off and leave him standing there alone, exorcising his demons, ready to proclaim his enlightened oneness with the universe to any sucker who will listen.

13 ✵

Enlightenment

In the emergency room, Stone helps me fill out the vital statistics. It hurts my eyes to read, so he recites the questions. The only time I feel embarrassed is when he asks me if I'm currently on the pill.

"That's a strange question," I say.

"I know. Do you want to write the answer?"

"No," I say, pulling his jacket back over my face. "I'm not on the pill."

"Okay." We fall silent, and I can hear his pencil scribbling on the page. I'm glad I don't have to look at him. At least the form doesn't ask whether I'm sexually active.

"Are you on any kind of medication?"

"No," I say.

I remain curled up on a sofa while Stone delivers the form to the nurse. The television in the corner blares the *Jerry Springer Show,* as if to shout down the ranger's Good Samaritan charity or any other acts of human kindness or decency. Today's feature is on people who lead double lives, and a fight erupts between a brother and sister in love with the same cross-dressing man. The shouting reminds me of Sally and Jacques and the job, but I try to push these things out of my mind. I'm relieved when Jerry takes a commercial break from "the Tootsie triangle."

I look down at the floor and see the bare feet of two children as they stop beside me and then scamper away. I don't care if I look like I'm dead or severely maimed, lying under this jean jacket that smells faintly of laundry detergent and old newspapers. The idea of lifting my head is impossible as the dull throb continues. I try to remember the name of the medicine I sometimes take for the migraines, but it's like a mirage, slipping away before I can put a word to it. I see Stone's hiking boots as he pulls up a chair so that it's facing me, sits down, and puts his hand on my shoulder.

"How are you?" he asks.

"Still down for the count. I'm wondering if I should call Sally."

"You don't need to talk to her. I'll call her later and tell her you had a migraine, but you're feeling better."

"What if I'm not feeling better? What if they can't get me the medicine?"

"Don't worry. They'll get you the medicine." Stone rubs his hand over my back.

"You know, it's scary enough when a migraine hits. But when you can't remember the name of your medicine, it's awful," I tell him.

"I'll bet. Does ice help?"

"No. Only drugs work," I hesitate for a moment, "and it helps that you're here."

"I'm glad," he says and keeps his hand on my back. I'm figuring that his touch feels so comforting only because I'm sick, and we're in this loud, frenetic emergency room. But then I wonder how it would feel if we were in a darkened movie theater or in a candlelit restaurant. Surely the pain is making me delirious. Of course there's nothing more to his touch than compassion. I barely know him. I try to focus on the television noise to keep from thinking. The cross-dressing man must choose between the sister and brother, Jerry tells him. Living life to the fullest is great, but isn't this a bit much?

After another hour, I'm in an X-ray room—a routine procedure for any head injury. I lie still and let them cover me with lead while the nurse leaves the room to flip the switch. I always get nervous, wondering if the pictures are damaging my cells, wondering what they'll find, but I try to stay calm. I think of all the scans my mother endured—then the radiation that burned right into her skin—and remember how easy my temporary pain is compared to what hers was like.

Stone helps me back onto the table in the examination room just as the doctor arrives. He's young, perhaps a resident—thin, pale, and studious looking. After we introduce ourselves, he gets right down to business.

"This might hurt a little, but I need to look into your eyes."

After thoughts of my mother, I figure I can manage the pain—I am wrong. He starts peering behind a blinding beam of light that seems to penetrate all the way into my skull. I squeeze Stone's hand hard enough for him to say ouch.

"Sorry. I'll hang on to the table," I say.

"It's okay," Stone says. "If you can take it, so can I."

"Just a little longer," the doctor says as he peers into my right eye.

He turns the light off, and I feel like I can breathe again. Then he feels around the bump on my head and listens to my heart, I suppose, for good measure. He turns and slaps the X-rays onto a lighted screen, looks at them closely, and then takes a moment to write down some notes on a folder.

"Well," he says as he snaps the folder shut. "It's not a concussion. The only thing you're suffering from is the migraine. The nurse at the desk is phoning your doctor in L.A. to find out your prescription. It'll probably take a few minutes to track it down, but you'll be able to start taking the medicine today."

"Will it work?" I ask. "I mean, I don't think I've ever had one this bad before."

"It'll work. Your migraine is a strong one, but it could be much worse. You should be feeling better in a couple of days," he says as he opens my folder one more time to scribble something down. "So be sure to avoid all alcohol and get lots of rest tonight. I wouldn't do anything too strenuous tomorrow."

"I have to go out on a photo shoot."

"I wouldn't go," he says, "especially if there's any stress involved."

"That depends on the chef," I say, to which the doctor nods absently, turns away, and quickly washes his hands. The phone rings and he picks it up. He looks at me as he talks into the receiver.

"I thought that would be it. Great. Thanks, Joan." He hangs up and writes out the prescription. "One day, even a half day, of rest will help the pain go away. If you have any complications, let me know." He sticks out his hand and I shake it, wondering how I'm going to manage the delay.

While I buy the medicine, Stone calls a cab. We sit outside the hospital, and I peek out from under the jacket, catching a glimpse of the sun setting behind a mesa. I am grateful for the waning light and the end of an exhausting day. We climb into the cab, and I curl up into the fetal position again.

"You can lean on me if you want," Stone says.

I do.

Back at the hotel, Stone asks me if I want anything from room service, but I'm still too nauseated to eat.

"All I need is the Fiorinol and about ten hours of sleep," I tell him. "I'll call Sally in the morning. If I'm not feeling better, maybe I can just supervise. Do you mind doing the styling?"

"Not at all."

"You know, you're great when it comes to dealing with a crisis."

"I was a Dalmatian in another life," he says. "Ray told me so."

I smile, what feels like the first one all day, and say good night even though it's only eight-thirty. After Stone leaves, it's all I can do to change into my nightshirt. The wonder drug starts to work after about a half hour of tossing from side to side, my pillow over my head. I fall into a fairly calm sleep, interrupted only a few times by the pulsing. I stop looking at the clock after a while and am free, escaping from the pain, the anxiety, the deadlines—everything.

Out of habit, I must have set the alarm even though I don't remember doing it. It wakes me in the morning with a start. It's eight o'clock, and I doze off for another hour until I'm awake for good. The pain has subsided although I'm not sure what will happen if I become vertical, so I lie in bed for a while longer, remembering that I am in Sedona.

Perhaps it was the stress of dealing with Ray that caused my brain to seize up. But it always takes more than one person to give me a migraine. So I lie here wondering why. Who or what is responsible this time, and why does it take a migraine to make me surrender and say to hell with the world, let it spin out of control?

I hear a loud knock on the door and slowly ease myself out of bed. Stone said he would come by in the morning. I shuffle carefully to the door, stymied at first by a slight pulse, then relieved to find it's not as pronounced as yesterday.

I think the worst is over—until I unlatch the lock, open the door, and stand face-to-face with none other than Sally.

At first I think maybe I'm hallucinating, or that I'm not really awake and it's all a nightmare. But as Sally walks into the room, reality opens its vicious maw and bites me in the ass.

"Good morning, merry sunshine," she says as she opens the curtains. I wince at the light and turn to see Stone entering the room, his head bowed. I look at him desperately, to which he puts his hands in the air and shakes his head. It was out of his control.

"You look surprised to see me," she says. "But I couldn't exactly let the ship go down. I called Stone last night when I couldn't get through to you. And let me tell you, migraine or not, you never tell the receptionist to hold your calls when you're on a business trip. Never."

"I didn't tell the receptionist that," I say.

"I did," Stone says. "I thought it would be best if she slept."

"Unbelievable," Sally says, like it's a federal crime to care for someone while on the job.

I sit down on the bed, indifferent to the fact that I'm in my pajamas and that yesterday's clothes are all over the floor. Normally, I would scurry around and try to make everything neat. But I feel so violated by her presence that I don't care. Fine, I think, go ahead and take a good look at my mess.

"Well, anyway," Sally continues, "I called Stone, he told me the situation, and I figured better safe than sorry."

"I told her everything was fine," Stone interjects but Sally cuts him off.

"And obviously he was wrong. So I hopped on the red-eye, and here I am. It's a good thing, too. You don't look like you're in any condition to work. Am I right?"

"At the moment, yes. But I haven't eaten anything in almost twenty-four hours. I think a cup of coffee would make me feel better, too."

"Coffee? Are you sure? Aren't you supposed to drink herb tea when you're sick?" she says as she checks her reflection in the mirror.

"Not with a migraine. Caffeine makes the blood vessels in your brain constrict, which lessens the flow of blood to the—"

"Well, all right," she says. "Do whatever you need to do. I'm going to make a call to the place we're scheduled to visit today. So far it's the only one, but I know others will come through."

I'm not really listening to her. I'm still trying to comprehend that she's here, and so I ask, "Why didn't you send Claire?"

Sally narrows her eyes at me and sighs audibly.

"I was just curious," I say. "I mean, she is the one who normally does this job."

Sally volleys back a lecture. "But she's not the only one trained to do it. In order to become the editor of a magazine, it's a given that you understand all the jobs involved, that you can step in and take the reins in any department, if necessary."

"But why is it necessary? Is Claire all right?" I ask.

"Of course she's all right. For God's sake. She just needs to stay at the magazine and deal with all the production crap. If I have a choice to fool with layout or jet off to Sedona, I'm going to choose the latter. Besides, I felt that you needed my guidance here." She looks around my cyclone of a room. "And I know I was right."

"Yeah, well, it's not my fault that I got hit with a migraine."

"I know that, Julia," she says. "No one is blaming you. I'm just here to give you backup and support. All right?"

"All right."

"Good. So I'll meet you in the lobby at ten o'clock. That'll give you enough time to eat, and then we'll see if you're up for going on the shoot," she says, as she heads for the door. Stone opens it for her, and she says to him, "Nice haircut by the way. It's about time you cleaned up your act."

Stone burps with impressive resonance and says, "I'm at your service."

Sally looks at him and then at me. She shakes her head and says, "Unbelievable."

She leaves without shutting the door completely, and Stone doesn't say a word to me. He waits, and indeed Sally comes back into the room without knocking, no doubt trying to catch us talking about her.

"Thought I left something," she says, pretending to scan the room and then pulling the door shut as she leaves again. Stone falls faceup onto the bed next to mine.

"She's worse than Jacques."

I lie back and say, "I don't believe this is happening."

"It's my fault. I shouldn't have told the receptionist to hold your calls," Stone says.

"No, I'm glad you did. There's no way I could have handled talking to her last night."

"I could have styled the shoots with your supervision, or even alone. I kept telling her that, but she wouldn't listen."

"It's not your fault. I think she wanted to come out here from the start but needed a reason. She kept telling me, 'You're damn lucky to be going to such a beautiful place.'"

"She probably wanted to escape from the mess she created back in the office."

"No doubt," I say and start to laugh.

"What?"

"I can't believe you burped."

"There's plenty more where that came from."

"Well, that's reassuring. You know, I'm feeling better," I say as I sit up. "I think I can do the shoot."

"Are you sure? I don't think you should push yourself."

"I just don't like the idea of Sally saving the day—like some psychotic Mighty Mouse."

"Interesting visual."

"And if I don't make some kind of effort, she'll never let me live it down."

Stone props himself up on an elbow and says, "Look, to hell with her. I mean, what do you gain by acquiescing?"

"For one thing, a job. I'm still on unofficial probation because of being late. If I screw up, she wouldn't hesitate to fire me. I've seen it happen to other people."

"So what if she fires you? There are other jobs—better jobs."

"Not with the magazine market being the way it is. And not since I burned my bridges."

"What do you mean?"

"I blew a freelance assignment with the *L.A. Times* and pissed off Five-Star Films in the process."

"Hey, nice work if you can get it."

"Seriously, the entertainment editor at the *Times* put the Hollywood curse on me: 'You'll never work in this town again.'"

"Bullshit. If your work is good enough people will hire you," Stone says, sitting upright and looking at me. "You're smart and talented. You can do anything you want. Besides, there are plenty of ways to stay involved with photography. You don't need the *L.A. Times* or Hollywood."

I remember Trudy's similar words. I look at him and notice the lines around his eyes are smoother when he isn't smiling. He doesn't look that much older than I am, but he acts it. He knows more than I do.

"How old are you?" I ask.

"I'm forty-four. How old are you?"

"How old do you think I am?"

"I don't know. About twenty-five?"

"Is that answer based on my appearance or my actions?" I ask.

"Both, but maybe a little more on appearance."

I pause for a moment, wondering if I should shave a few years off, but then decide to stick to the truth.

"I'm thirty-three."

"Really?"

"Really."

"Now I feel stupid," he says.

"Why?"

"I've been telling you things you already know."

"No, you haven't. I should look for another job. Maybe I've just been too complacent—or too afraid."

"Well, it's never too late to change," he says as he gets up and walks to the door. He turns around and smiles. "Thirty-three— that's a good age. See you in the coffee shop."

And he's gone, leaving me to muse over the possibilities.

Sally is the only person I know who still says, "Chop, chop" when she wants you to hurry. She doesn't worry whether it might be politically incorrect or simply rude. She just likes the sound of it and claps her hands when she says it to us at the coffee shop.

"Can I at least finish eating?" Stone asks.

"No. We're due at the casino at eleven o'clock, and it's already ten o'clock," Sally says.

"The casino," I ask. "That's a restaurant?"

"No that's a place where people gamble."

I stare at Sally, unamused, and she gives me a straight answer.

"There's a restaurant at the casino on the Indian reservation on the outskirts of town. They have a wonderful new chef."

"Who?" I ask.

"Ralph Hedges. He's a newcomer but is on the brink of being discovered. He specializes in strictly Italian fare. I figured, what better way to make a statement than to discover a new chef in our pages? And the gambling thing is very sexy."

We drive for a half hour, leaving the majestic rocks far behind, and turn off the highway onto a two-lane dirt road. I had heard about the amazing profits that Indian casinos net, but I wonder whether anyone in this tribe has seen a cent. In between the cotton fields sit trailers and tin-roofed shacks. The dirt yards teem with rusted cars on concrete blocks, worn-out toys, clotheslines, broken refrigerators, and brave old tires painted white and used as flower planters. It is Appalachia gone west. Like the lean-to shacks on Kentucky back roads, almost every dwelling has a satellite dish in the yard. No one sits on porches, not with the heat and all the movies, soap operas, and high-speed chases flickering across the living room screen.

We follow the splashy billboard signs, the only ones around, that say, Try Your Luck at the Casino Royale. The Valley's Vegas! Seedy, not sexy, is the word that comes to mind when we turn onto a steep gravel road and find a two-story red-brick motel connected to a warehouse made of corrugated metal and another structure that is nothing more than an air-conditioned, plastic tent, like something used to heat outdoor pools in the winter. Cars are packed into a lot the size of two football fields. Above the warehouse, a neon sign flashes Casino Royale in red-and-white letters.

We park in the lot and Sally bounds out of the car. Stone and I follow. I fully expect her to rail about the place being unacceptable, sleazy, and not anywhere near our upscale demographic appeal. But she doesn't.

"I love it! It's raw, earthy. Very Bugsy Siegel, don't you think?"

"No," I say.

"No? See, I'm glad I'm here. You have to look beyond the appearance of things, Julia. You have to use your imagination."

"Sally, this place is a pit," I say.

"You can't judge a book by its cover," she says.

"It's a flea-bag motel and warehouse," Stone says. "Do you really think there will be marble flooring inside?"

"You never know," she says. "Besides, we can't lose either way. I see a title already, 'Grunge Gambling at Sedona' or 'Gambling's Ground Floor—Native American Style.'"

"How about, 'Viva Exploitation,'" Stone says. Sally glares at him. "I mean, is it me or are we straying a bit from the food angle?"

"It's you," Sally replies as she opens the door and marches inside.

I have been to Las Vegas only once in my life. Edna had a bizarre urge to see it in memory of her first husband, who never took her on any of his gambling trips. That she wanted to honor her husband by visiting the place that plunged him into debt made no sense to me. My father figured it was part of the grieving process. And since he had trouble denying her anything, Dad sent me a plane ticket, and I met them in Vegas one Easter weekend. Constance stayed behind, outraged by our decidedly pagan destination and by our unthinkable absence at the children's Easter egg hunt.

I didn't take to gambling. I could never forget that a chip equaled a dollar, and when I tried placing the minimum of five on the blackjack table, my hand shook and I kept pulling them out of their sacrificial circle. I changed my mind twice and would have gone a third time until the dealer yelled, "Lady, are you in or out?"

I put my chips back on the table and promptly lost them.

During our entire stay in Vegas, I had indigestion from the noise, crowds, and unbridled excess of the place, elements that seemed most pronounced in every theme-from-hell hotel lobby we saw. But the most inconceivable thing to me that weekend was the way Edna and Dad surrendered themselves to their compulsive demons. They merrily lost hundreds on roulette, lined up whenever a buffet opened, paid seventy dollars apiece to hear Tom Jones croak his dated songs with rousing, precardiac verve, and drank martinis until they staggered. I had never seen my father behave that way before. There was nothing honorable or demure about their actions, nothing connected with observing Jack's death. Old Edna just wanted to get her kicks, and Dad was a willing accomplice.

No doubt I was channeling what would have been my mother's reaction to Las Vegas. The one trip west we took when I was a child was a driving tour though the Painted Desert, Yosemite, and Yellowstone. She wanted to see them for her art as much as she wanted me to see them for my education. That was her idea of fun—to have a picnic underneath the shadow of Half Dome. It was mine too, and in truth it suited my father much better than a neon Vegas nightmare. I know that now, but at the time I didn't.

I brace myself for sensory onslaught when Stone and I enter the motel and am delighted to find no Egyptian pyramids, erupting volcanoes, or Roman centurions. Nor is there blaring music or throngs of people. There is only Sally, who twitches and shuffles like a kid at her first dance as she stands in the center of this linoleum-floored economy motel lobby—suburban, oatmeal bland except for slot machines that line the walls and colored lights trained on metallic palm trees in each corner.

Sally rings the bell at the desk for the second time, which summons a dim-looking, uniformed blonde girl with bad skin and an overzealous perm.

"Help ya?"

"I'm here to see Martin Rosato?"

"'Kay," she says and disappears.

"Who is Martin Rosato?" I ask Sally.

"He's the manager. I requested a tour before we get down to the food."

"Sally, I don't think this place—"

"If you both just do what I tell you then we'll get along fine. Stone, would it kill you to get ready to take some shots? Jesus. Like getting blood from a stone. Hey, I made a joke. Get it?"

Stone expels an exasperated breath and heads outside to get his gear from the car.

"Such a prima donna," Sally says. "He's worse than in the studio."

"He's not a prima donna. He's very talented and you should—"

"I should what, Julia? What should I do?"

I'm silent for a moment, which makes her turn away from me, thinking she has won again, but I decide to cross the rhetorical line.

"You should treat him with respect. He's a professional."

She turns back, shaking her head, arms crossed.

"Professional? You call his little outburst with Jacques professional? You call that burp professional?"

"I call them both understandable."

She takes a step closer and squints her eyes. We stare at each other, long enough to make me want the clerk or Stone to return. But I don't flinch. I don't cross my arms. Instead, I raise them in a haphazard shrug.

"You're treading a very thin line," she says. "A tightrope—and I don't want to see you fall."

"I'm on a tightrope because this whole trip has been nothing but a circus," I say, which makes her face flush. She looks angry enough to spit at me, and I think she just might, until I see Martin Rosato stride into the room.

He's a tall, suntanned dandy around Stone's age whose hair is slicked back into a short braided ponytail. He wears a bolo tie, a black shirt, and a double-breasted silk suit that isn't far from the silver shimmer of the fake palm trees. He walks over to Sally, extending his hand.

"Miss Reynolds, Martin Rosato. You'll excuse me for keeping you waiting. I had to straighten out a moron associate of mine in Los Angeles."

"Not a problem. So wonderful to finally meet you, Mr. Rosato. And please call me Sally."

"Only if you'll call me Marty. It doesn't exactly sound like a Native American name, but I'm not your average Native American. How many Indians do you know who grew up in Brooklyn?"

"Not many," she says like a cheery, well-trained Mouseketeer.

"Exactly!" Marty replies.

"What tribe are you connected with?" I ask as Stone comes back into the room.

"Originally the Zuni tribe, but my connection goes back about . . ." Marty looks up at the ceiling, fiddles with his fingers in mock calculation, and shakes his head with an overwhelmed smile. "It's hard to be exact, but let's put it this way. The Civil War hadn't even been fought yet, okay?"

I recently read an article on Indian heritage in the *L.A. Times*. Even if this guy has any Native American blood in him, it can't be more than one sixty-fourth, the bare minimum for tribal membership. Oh well. He seems harmless enough, and at least he's on time.

"Do you actually live with the tribe as a member?" Stone asks, which makes Sally stiffen a little.

Marty smiles. "Well, it's complicated. There's an old saying: Take a drink at a friendly stream even if you aren't thirsty. That's the only way I can answer your question."

"What does that mean?" Stone asks.

"It's complicated," Marty says and then quickly switches back to salesman. "Sally, I can't wait to take you on a tour." He places his hand on her arm and holds his other hand out to Stone and me. "I take it this is your crew."

"Yes, my inquiring photographer, Richard Stone, and my assistant, Julia Daniel. They'll be coming with us."

As if to protest our newfound servitude, neither of us says hello.

"Why do we need pictures?" Marty says with a tight, laminated smile. "I mean, pictures of food, yes. But I don't recall discussing anything else."

"Oh well, I thought it might be nice to show our readers where the action is outside of the kitchen," Sally says brightly, trying to cover up her surprise.

"It's a nice idea," Marty says, "but we kind of like for our customers to be surprised by the gaming room. You know. It's part of the fun—the anticipation."

"Okay, well, what about the outside? I thought it might be nice to have a picture of you at the entrance."

"Oh no." Marty laughs, smoothing his bolo tie and adjusting his cuff links. "You can print my name, but the owners don't want pictures of me or the entrance or anything other than the food."

"Who are the owners?" Stone asks.

"The members of the tribe whose reservation we're on," Marty says in a plodding, slightly condescending way.

"But where did they get the backing to build the place?" Stone asks.

"Where did they get the backing?" Marty repeats to Sally with a smile although it's clear he's trying to keep his irritation in check. "Jeez," he says, slapping Stone on the back, "sure you aren't moonlighting for a tabloid, big guy?"

"He's one of *my* moron associates," Sally says, which makes Marty laugh. He excuses himself to, as he calls it, "the little braves' room."

"So you don't need me right now?" Stone asks.

"No," Sally replies.

"Good. I'll be outside."

I start to follow him, but Sally tugs on my sleeve.

"Not so fast."

"Why can't I go outside? You don't need me, either."

"Yes, I do. You need to take some notes about what the place looks like."

"I'm not a writer."

"No, but you can take notes to give to the writer," she says while fiddling with her cell phone.

"All right. But if my head starts to hurt, I'll need to leave."

"Fair enough."

Marty returns and ushers us out the door, keeping his hand on Sally's back, which she doesn't seem to mind. We walk through the glass hallway that leads to the casino. It looks as much like a warehouse inside as it does on the outside. The only design amenity is a thin layer of indoor/outdoor carpeting covering the concrete floors. Out of the corner of my eye, I see Sally's face fall. She was praying for at least a little glitz. But the white-haired retirees who come here don't want some prefab Vegas fantasy. They want to parlay their social security checks into some serious do-re-mi.

The smoke-filled bingo room is a dominant fixture. On the east and west walls loom purple, pink, and lime green lighted bingo boards, covering nearly the entire span. Fluorescent lighting cubes hang from the dark, cavernous ceiling. Twenty Formica tables fill the entire length of the room, accompanied by about two hundred metal-legged chairs. There are only a few chairs free.

The gambling machines in the plastic-walled building are a poorman's Vegas, a smattering of bells, flashing lights, and more neon signs advertising The Valley's Vegas. The old folks are slumped on stools in front of slot and poker machines, blankly feeding quarters from plastic buckets into the burbling, whirling contraptions, many of which look and sound more like video games. They chain smoke and stare, indifferent to minor windfalls, watching for the jackpot through an endless succession of numbers, fruits, and white royal faces that flash before their glazed eyes.

"What about blackjack and roulette?" Sally asks.

"No room at the inn. We hope to expand next year and build a traditional gaming room with off-track betting, too."

We pass a cigarette shop and three ATMs before coming across the Baja Grill. It's a dark, greasy cave, and Sally starts to ask the fateful question, but Marty intercepts.

"I know what you're thinking and the answer is, 'Hell no, this isn't our only restaurant!' It's just for the local game players who aren't guests of the hotel. Did you think I'd drag you guys all the way out here to shoot a greasy hamburger?"

Sally laughs wildly while the shadow of yesterday's migraine finds me, and my head begins to throb. I don't ask whether I can be excused. I just slip out the exit as Sally listens to Marty prattle on about all the big plans—the Western theme park for the grandchildren, a theater for Broadway musicals. It really is the next Vegas, he tells her. It really is the ground floor.

Stone sits under a tree by the entrance, smoking a cigarette.

"I didn't know you smoked," I say.

"Only when I'm under extreme stress brought on by either a lot of work or idiot bosses. Can you guess which one it is?"

"Gee, I'm at a loss."

"And to think I once loved her," he says as he stubs out his cigarette.

"People change."

He smiles at me, flicks his butt into a nearby trashcan, and says, "How's your head?"

"It's starting to hurt again, but it's better now that I'm outside. You were right. Viva exploitation. They must truck people in from the retirement communities."

"Here, sit down," he says as he stands up and respreads his jacket on the ground.

"Thanks," I say, leaning my head against the trunk.

"I've heard that it's mostly old people who get lured in to these local casinos."

"It's so depressing. I wouldn't be surprised if half of them just don't know what else to do with themselves."

"I'm sure. So what's the rest of the place like?"

I give him the grim details.

"I think Sally must have scored a little peyote somewhere on the way to Sedona. Honestly, how can she not see that the place is a dump?" Stone says. "I mean, is this the same person who made *Bon Appétit, Saveur,* and *Gourmet* required reading for the staff? Jesus—who knows what we'll find at the restaurant."

"Do you have your phone? I left mine at the motel."

"Yeah, why?"

"If you don't mind the roaming charge, I can call Claire and find out what's going on."

"It's worth it," Stone says as he digs in his knapsack and hands me the phone. "I'm going to put my stuff away in the car. I'll be right back."

I get through immediately to Claire. She tells me to brace myself because the lowdown is lower than I could imagine.

"The advertising dollars simply didn't come through," she says. "We were thirty thousand dollars in the hole with no prospects in sight. So one of the ad guys starts calling around to casinos. Russell told me that Sally and Marty worked out a deal whereby Marty's casino would pay half the debt if we did a glowing feature on the casino's restaurant and chef. And he's not a chef—he's a cook. The restaurant is nothing but a traditional no-frills pasta joint."

"Did Sally know that?"

"Yes. I even told her before the deal was made, but she didn't care. All she said was, 'Either we do business with them, or we go under.'"

I fall silent, struggling to take in all that Claire has told me.

"What's this guy Marty like?" Claire asks.

"Very cagey. He wouldn't say how the casino was financed. He wouldn't let us take a picture of him or the place—although that I can understand since it's a pit. Basically, we can't shoot anything but the food and restaurant."

"For a ten-page spread? We're screwed," Claire says.

"Don't worry. We've got a lot of scenic shots of Sedona."

"Yeah, but two other articles fell through today. I don't even know if this issue is going to come together. I've started sending out my résumé, and you might want to do the same."

"Great."

"Sorry to make things worse than they already are."

"You haven't," I say. "If anything, it helps me see things more clearly."

I walk back to the car just as Stone is shutting the trunk.

"Let's get in and talk. I have to tell you what's going on, and I don't want Sally to interrupt us."

We climb into the front, roll down the windows, and I launch into the whole sordid story. Once I finish, Stone stares out the windshield for a moment, shaking his head slowly. He takes off his glasses and rubs his eyes.

"You know what I wanted to do before you told me all of this?" he asks.

"What?"

"I wanted to drive away from this place. When we got in the car, I thought, let's just be honest and get the hell out of here. We don't want to be here. And now I think about this phony bastard cutting a deal with Sally, and I'm wondering how I can possibly stay."

"I know."

I am thinking about how good the idea sounds—not because of the bomb that went off in my head yesterday, not because I want to escape or somehow get even with Sally by leaving her high and dry. I want to leave because I am, at last, ready for something better in this life. I think of Stone's words, listen to the wild cries of the desert quail, and feel the sun pour over me, filling me with the hope and strength to act. It takes me a moment before I can say it, but then the rightness of it takes hold and pushes up and out of me like some impossibly exotic cactus flower.

"So let's leave."

Stone turns and stares long enough to realize I'm not kidding. I look at the lines around his eyes and watch them deepen as he smiles.

"I knew you had it in you," he says as he puts the keys in the ignition. But before he can turn the engine over, fate intervenes. My door flies open and Sally is there, looking hot and flustered.

"There you are! Jesus Christ, you just wandered off. What were you thinking?"

"I needed to get away from the noise, Sally."

Fortunately, Marty is right behind her, which tempers her wrath. Stone and I get out of the car just as he saunters up to us and says, "I think you two must be in love. What d'ya say, Scoop? Are you in love with this pretty girl?"

Stone doesn't say anything as he gets out of the car and starts walking toward the restaurant.

"Julia's not that crazy," Sally whispers audibly to Marty.

"That's not funny," I say as I slam my car door.

"Well, excuse me. I didn't realize migraines strip you of your sense of humor."

"They don't," I reply, and turn to catch up with Stone.

The restaurant, clearly a former HoJo's repainted and renamed Il Fortunato, is several miles away and just off the highway.

"We provide a complimentary shuttle bus for guests," Marty explains. "You'd never guess it was a HoJo's unless I told you, right?" Wrong.

I wished it still was a HoJo's because as a child I felt oddly comforted by their national uniformity, cheeriness, and the way the menu put an equal emphasis on ice cream as a serious food. But the orange-and-blue booths have long been recovered in black-and-red striped vinyl. The soda counter is now the personal pizza station. Red-and-white checked cloths cover the tables. The only true vestige of the place is the cash register by the door, an uncomputerized metal machine that's perched above a glass case displaying the usual Wrigley's and Life Savers fare.

There's the usual fuss—the placing of basil and plastic gardenias and candlelight around the table, the addition of fresh herbs onto the very ordinary-looking plate of eggplant parmesan, the use of cigar smoke in the background to make it look piping hot. Marty struts around, saying, "What magic!" Ralph Hedges, the cook turned chef, leans on the personal pizza station and says, "Fucking crazy." We make the food, Ralph, and the restaurant itself, look better than any of them were ever meant to look. It takes us only an hour to produce the miracle.

Back at the hotel, Sally comes to my room and tells me she's going exploring and that we can meet in the lobby for dinner. I say fine. Sounds great. And she smiles before leaving and tells me it's about time that my attitude started improving.

"You must be feeling better," she says. "Even your room looks neater."

"I do feel much better."

"Good. I'll see you around seven."

And she's gone. Little does she know that by seven o'clock I will be far away from the hotel and that my room looks so neat because I have packed everything and am waiting for another knock on the door.

When I hear it, I open up and Stone asks, "Are you ready?"

"Yes."

"Are you sure about this?"

"Completely."

We check out of the hotel at four o'clock, leave our resignations and the rolls of film in Sally's mailbox, and tell the clerk to put the room charges on the company card.

We're driving down the highway when I take out my Swiss Army knife and saw the card into four pieces.

"What are you doing?" Stone asks.

"Resisting temptation. It's not mine anymore. I guess it never was."

I hang my arm out the window when we round the bend. I see no cops, so I fling the plastic in the air, watching the sun reflect off the silvery pieces as the wind hurls them away.

14 ✿

Open Road

Despite the thousands of miles I placed between me and my father ten years ago when I fled to L.A., I was never really free from him and my anger over his marriage to Edna. He was still calling the shots in absentia for at least a few years, prompting me to take temp jobs that I knew he would find "beneath my intelligence," to photograph what he called the impractical or artsy-fartsy side of life with no real goal in mind, to hop around trendy dance clubs in my leather jacket, swirling amid a kaleidoscope of boozy, fair-weather faces—he was a lapsed Baptist but still suspicious of such night life.

As Stone and I cruise down the highway, I think about how much I've changed. I know I'm not running away from Sally but am running toward a better life, unfettered by what she and others at the magazine think. I don't see my leaving as a self-destructive act of revenge; I see it as an act of survival. I listen to the hum of tires on the pavement, the miles covered toward freedom, and imagine the other actions I'll take once I get home: revising my résumé, searching the classifieds, updating my portfolio. At last, the road is truly open.

"So where do you want to go?" Stone asks.

"Maybe we can catch a plane to L.A. tonight. We'll probably have to pay extra to change our tickets."

Stone doesn't say anything, which I don't attribute to disapproval.

"I guess Sally will be expecting us to go to the airport," I say.

Just thinking about her yanks me out of the happy future and makes me want to put as much distance as possible between us and her. I wouldn't put it past her to set up some kind of stakeout at the America West ticket counter. And then I realize that we have nothing to lose by taking our time. It's not like either one of us has to be at work tomorrow.

"Or we could drive back," I say. "If you don't mind taking the extra time. Let me see where we are and how long it'll take." I open the glove compartment and find a map. Stone waits as I fail to pinpoint our exact location.

"My guess is we're about eight hours from L.A.," he says after a few minutes. "I think it'd be fun to drive. We can turn the car in at a Hertz office in L.A. and won't have to deal with changing the plane tickets."

I glance over at him—his five-o'clock shadow, his jawbones working a piece of gum, his pierced lobe (currently earring free). I wonder about his history, his idiosyncrasies, and realize, with more than a little trepidation, that it's been about five years since I've been alone with a man for anything longer than two to three-hour stretches.

The sun has begun to set and Stone turns on the lights. We're about ten miles outside of Phoenix and haven't said anything else about our travel plans. I have to hand it to him for being patient. Come to think of it, he hasn't hassled me about anything—not even when I reset the table at Il Fortunato's two times because of a slight glare from the silverware. He seems to understand my neurotic perfectionism without judging me for it, my urge to pinpoint, exactly, where we are on a dim, wrinkled map. I tuck the map back in the compartment and begin to relax again into the ease of the moment, safe and contained in the glow of dashboard light.

I lay my head back on the seat and say, "We might as well drive. I have nothing to lose, that's for sure."

"You might even gain something."

"Like what?"

"I don't know. Maybe we'll find something you've never seen before. Pretend you're back in college and see what the road brings."

"I never did anything like this when I was in college."

"Come on. You must have done a few unpredictable things."

"I was too cautious."

"Why?"

"That's when my mom kept going in and out of remission. I never strayed too far from the dorm phone."

"I know the feeling."

We're both silent for a moment.

"So were you unpredictable in college?" I ask.

"Well, I didn't finish college, so I guess you could say I was."

"Why?"

"I got caught with a girl in my room."

"They expelled you for that?"

"By 1974, most colleges had loosened up, but not St. Timothy's College for the overly religious. You weren't even allowed to have women visit in your room, let alone have them sleep over, which is what happened. So I chose love—the nubile Leslie Leigh, who looked a whole lot like love to me at age twenty—over education."

"Boy, things were different when I went to college."

"Lucky for you. It must have been great to be able to have a relationship without being punished for it."

"I guess so."

"You guess? You mean you weren't a love-struck romantic like me?"

I'm a little embarrassed by the question and uncertain of the answer given my history of serial arm's-length dating. And did sleeping with Bobby constitute romantic devotion to love or just a convenient escape from my mother's pending death? I wasn't sure.

"I was pretty typical," I say at last.

"Like he was the only love you'd ever have?"

"I guess so—and then it just about turned out that way."

That's what happens when my guard is down: I tell the truth—my therapy dollars at work. From the silence that follows I interpret shock and horror on his part. Why has she loved only one man? What's wrong with her? Maybe I should tell him about Matthew or Jeffrey. But why bring up my romantic failures? I'm at a loss, so I backpedal.

"What I mean is I've never had a relationship like that one. Nothing like my relationships as an adult," I say with a worldly wave of the hand.

"Yes, college love affairs are much more . . . innocent I guess."

Stone turns his attention back to the road and the signs leading to the 10 Freeway to Los Angeles.

"So how did you wind up in L.A.?" he asks.

"I suppose I did it to spite my father. He didn't really approve of my pursuing photography. I didn't approve of his marrying so soon after my mother died. So I left."

"Why didn't he approve of your photography?"

"He thought it was frivolous. Photojournalism, well, that was okay. But anything else didn't fly. It was fine as a hobby, but not a profession. That was his pronouncement."

"What did you say to that?"

"Something like, 'You don't like any pictures unless they have soldiers or politicians in them.' It was kind of like a game between us."

"I know that game," he says.

I start to turn on the radio to shift the focus away from the topic, but then I figure why not say it? Stone seems safe enough and genuinely interested. I lean back in the seat again, taking a breath as I gather my courage.

"Do you know what the worst part of losing him is? The regret—that he left before we could somehow find each other again. And now all I can think about are the things I wish I'd told him before he died."

"What would you have told him?"

"That I was sorry for being angry with him for so long, that I understand why he married Edna. Basically, I would have been an adult instead of a child. I might have even told him I loved him. I tried once during Mom's illness, and he was so embarrassed by it, like the way he acted when I cried, that he didn't know what to say. The word was in my mother's vocabulary, but not in his."

We sit in silence for a few minutes. I'm grateful that Stone doesn't ask me more about it. I know too well from therapy that these particular admissions always leave me with a helplessness that usually culminates in a crying frenzy. I close my eyes and the tears retreat. I'm careful about when and where I let them fly. Already, I feel like I might have said too much. But then Stone sits up a little straighter in his seat and reassures me.

"I think it takes a long time to figure out how to live with the dead."

"Yes," I say and look out the windshield again. I can only see the lights on the highway—the rest of the desert spreads out like some sleeping giant. I know there are mountains and cacti sliding past us, but they are invisible in the darkness. Stone draws my attention back to us in the car when he reaches over and puts his hand on my shoulder, gently but with conviction. He doesn't pat it or brush it. He puts his whole palm over the curve of it and says, "But it gets easier."

I smile at him and touch his hand, the long fingers, and think of the way I've seen it—as nothing more than an extension of the camera. We ride like that for a few minutes before he pulls his hand away. I can still feel the slight pressure and warmth of his touch, like a small circle of sun, powerful enough to linger in my eyes after I've looked away.

The Wagon Trail diner sits on top of a mesa just past a combination Shell station, convenience mart, and Dairy Queen. With its mock wagon pulled by plastic horses to the left of its neon sign, it looks about as genuinely western as a set from *Ponderosa*.

Inside, Patsy Cline's "I Fall to Pieces" blares from the jukebox, but the decor switches from Arizona rawhide to New York chrome and red vinyl. The waitress, a wiry woman in her sixties with a thinning jet black perm, arrives at our booth. She expels a rumbling, fluid-filled smoker's hack and asks what we want. The catfish tacos sound original but far too risky. We play it safe and order two Westward Ho burgers.

"You want fries with that?" the waitress asks.

"Uh, let's see. I'm not sure," Stone says.

She sighs and keeps her eyes on her pad, pencil poised.

"Want to split an order?" I ask.

"Why not," he says, to which the waitress scribbles the order, coughs again, and walks away. Stone excuses himself, and I flip through the tableside jukebox that's heavy on country. The waitress returns, bearing water in red plastic tumblers and two cups of coffee.

When Stone sits down again, I notice that his face is a ruddy brown and imagine it's the dim neon lighting that makes it so until I remember that he was out in the sun today while Sally and I were on the grand tour of the casino. I watch him as he drinks his water.

"So what's your plan once you get back to L.A.?" I ask. "Are you going back to freelancing?"

"Probably, but not for publications. I've been planning on

opening my own studio. Portraits mostly, and maybe some commercial stuff at first to pay the overhead. I wasn't planning on doing it until about a year from now, but I might as well go ahead."

"Do you already have some potential clients?"

"A few. I was thinking about it, and I'm actually glad this shoot was a bust. It's motivated me to take action."

"So this is the first photo shoot you've ditched?" I say lightly.

He smiles and rests his chin in the palm of his hand for a moment, looking directly at me.

"Not the first. But it's a rare occurrence. I like to finish things I start."

I think about his hand on my shoulder but am jarred out of my reverie by the arrival of the food. The plates land on our table with the gentleness of a plane landing on an aircraft carrier. This waitress has no patience for the late crowd and is not willing to bend her knees on the delivery any more than she has to. She's gone as quick as she arrives.

"What about you?" he asks as he picks up his burger. "What do you want to do?"

"Something with photography. Of course, I want it to be mainstream, but my friend Trudy in Kentucky tells me I should try to hook my work into a trade in order to get started—like photographing things for a brochure."

"That's how I got started," Stone says between bites.

"You're kidding."

"Nope. I worked in public relations for the state's Department of Agriculture for about two years. They'd send me out to photograph aqueducts and various farming areas, and I'd add on any other shots I could find along the way. That's how I started doing portraits. I did a series on immigrant workers—mostly El Salvadoran and Mexican—that I never even planned on. So you never know where something will lead."

The waitress stops by, pours more coffee into our cups, and asks, "Anything else?"

We both say no. She thanks us and puts the bill on the table. Stone sips his coffee and turns the talk back to the logistics of the trip as we finish our food—the time it will take, the amount of gas we have left in the car, the process of returning the rental car from L.A.

"I'm happy to pay for it. It's a definite write-off," he says.

Given that I don't know where my next paycheck will be coming from, I protest but don't argue when he assures me he doesn't mind. We continue to sip our coffee in silence, and I'm trying to find a way to ask him about his life without prying. I draw a blank. It's the evil side of politeness that always manages to strangle my questions. But there's no time for a subtle segue, so I blurt out the question that has been on my mind for longer than a two-hour car ride.

"So, are you involved with anyone or dating or . . . anything like that?"

He smiles, either from shyness or flattery or amusement— maybe all three but I'm staring too deeply into my coffee cup to take a closer look.

"No. What about you?"

"No—nothing worthy of confession."

"Are you Catholic?"

"No, I'm not anything religious. I just meant . . . well, I don't know what I meant. I guess you've been married only once."

Blimey, you're a rotten flirt! Quite right! Do shut up before you scuttle the thing completely!! Hear, hear!!

I nearly swoon with embarrassment and am ready to take the parliamentarians' advice and excuse myself for some deep breathing in the bathroom when, to my surprise, Stone calmly answers.

"Only once. She changed a lot, especially after she got the part on *The Beltway*. Funny how our life actually became a melodrama once she got hired by one."

"In what way?"

"She had an affair with the director, who was going to put her in his feature film, which still hasn't happened. Anyway, there was lots of drama, lots of deception, so we divorced pretty quickly."

"And that was how long ago?"

"About a year. I'm trying to forgive her—even though I never want to see her again. What about you?"

"I've never been married."

"You're lucky. Getting divorced was tough, no matter how sensible it was at the time."

"Do you miss being married?"

"I miss being married, but not to her. I don't know. I've met a lot of beautiful, wonderful women but for whatever reason, I haven't met the person I'm supposed to stay with. I can't ask, why hasn't it happened? It just hasn't."

"Do you believe in God or something?"

"What do you mean?"

"How else can you be so calm about it? I mean, do you want to get married again?"

"Sure. But not to the wrong person. Believe me, I know enough people in miserable marriages to convince me of that."

"You're right. I know you're right."

"Did you recently turn someone down or something?"

This makes me laugh out loud.

"It's a reasonable question," Stone says. "Given how smart and pretty you are."

Tell me more, I think.

"I've never been near marriage," I say. "I mean, it's been a long time since I've even been in a relationship."

"How long?"

God knows I've lied about it before, but I don't want to start that nonsense again. So I try not to sound as pathetic as I feel and tell him matter-of-factly, "Like about five years."

For some reason, I remember Constance's reaction—"I can't

believe you're still single!" I hope for more compassion this time
and start digging around for nothing in my pocketbook, desperate
for anything to do that doesn't require me to look at him.

"So you take relationships seriously," he says.

That would be the correct response, one that could woo even
the shyest heart.

After we pay the check, I follow Stone as he walks past the car to the
back of the diner.

"Where are you going?" I ask.

"To check out the view."

There is nothing but a wall of enormous Dumpsters in front of
us. I would have never thought to look behind them. But I'm learning that Stone has a knack for finding hidden beauty—whether in a
plate of lasagna or in the moonlit backdrop to rubbish.

I follow him as he shimmies through a space between two
Dumpsters. The horizon stretches before us like a velvet canvas.
The mountains and mesas look too fragile to be real, as though
they're made of whipped cream. There are pockets of mysterious
darkness in the folds of the earth, and Stone, without hesitation,
grabs my hand and heads down an incline toward the nearest one.

"Wait a second," I say as I pull back. "There may be animals out
there."

"Don't you remember what I said in Sedona? They're more
scared of us than we are of them."

I try to refute his point, but he pulls me again playfully and I con-
cede, relying on the thickness of my cross-training shoes to ward off
the teeth of any low-lying creatures. We find a path and walk along
together. The wind whistles in my ears and we don't talk, except to
stop occasionally and look at a type of cactus or rock. The moon is
full and bright enough for Stone to identify them.

My eyes begin to adjust to the light, and I can see clearly enough
to make out the spined joints of the prickly pears. I forget about the

animals. Stone wanders ahead of me up the path to what looks like an ominous cave from a distance but is actually a broad cluster of rocks that form a kind of natural bench.

I follow him and when I reach him, he puts his arm around me as he guides me to a seat and asks, "Is this all right?"

"Yes," I say, not really sure if he is referring to the rocks or his arm. But I have no desire to clarify the question. Everything will be fine, I figure, as soon as we kiss. My heart pounds and my mouth is dry. We sit looking out at the valley, and I shyly put my arm around his waist and lean toward him as he pulls me closer. In that moment, we turn and smile again at each other, conspiring and a little shy—a feeling I soon overcome.

Five years without love does wonders for my libido. I always imagined that I would give a list of prerequisites before really kissing a man again—a litany of fears, needs, expectations. Not to mention the fact that I expected to date him for a while first and required a heartfelt promise from him that a one-nighter would not be an option. I was too old for a casual romp in the hay, I imagined myself saying. Security and stability, that's what I wanted. Not a brief, thoughtless mingling of the flesh.

Yet preparedness for any dramatic act of nature, whether earthquakes or sex of any kind, is inherently pointless.

He pulls me onto his lap, and I am barely able to breathe as he kisses my neck, my lips. He takes his time, his lips gently brushing mine, exploring their contours as if they were a treasured artifact, a precious jewel. And then more fully, he presses his mouth to mine. I had forgotten that kissing could be so erotic, and it's all I can do to keep from falling as his hands trail up my shirt. I try to stay in this moment—feeling more alive than I have in years—but then the decidedly nonerotic, overly practical, fearful me shows up with her baggage claim for the future. I start to wonder—What are we doing? Where are we going? What does this mean to him, to me? I'm suddenly aware of everything but him—the roar of cars on the highway, the cold discomfort of our Neolithic love seat, and, of course, the distant banging of parliamentarian gavels.

I pull away from him and say, "I feel like I'm going to fall off these rocks."

"I won't let you fall."

"But you don't have anything to lean up against."

"Don't worry," he says, kissing me again.

I try to let go and find the abandon once more, pushing my doubts away, but it's no use. The scraping sound of gravel beneath feet, the sudden slam of a Dumpster lid. This time, I sit upright suddenly and slide off his lap.

Stone pauses a moment and then says, "I hope it's the Dumpster instead of me."

"It's not you. It's me. I'm not used to this. I don't know . . . it's sort of . . . I mean, it's great, but it's a bit overwhelming."

"I know," Stone says and then takes my hand between his, kissing it.

I pull my hand away.

He looks at me, and I can see he's puzzled, maybe even a little stung.

"Okay," he says quietly. "You must be really overwhelmed."

"Yes. And a little confused."

"But you weren't that way at the start. What made you change your mind?"

"I'm not sure that I did change it," I say.

"Now I'm confused."

"I'm sorry."

"Well, hang on. Don't be sorry yet. I mean, what's going on? Is it my age?" he asks.

"No."

"My divorce?"

"God, no."

"So, then . . ."

"If I try to fumble around without thinking this through, I'll probably say something that will hurt your feelings."

"No you won't."

"Yes I will."

"I can take it," he says.

With any other man, I would have pulled away without explanation, fearing that he would judge me or take whatever information I gave him and pin it on me for all eternity. But I know Stone has more sense than that. So I sit back down, reach for his hand, and try to explain.

"I love being with you, but it's been so long that I honestly don't know if it's because we have some connection or because . . . it's been so long."

"So you're afraid that I'm doomed to be the boy toy victim of your untamed urges."

"That's not what I'm saying. See, I knew you'd get pissed."

"I'm not pissed."

I look at him skeptically.

"All right, maybe my ego is a little hurt. I'm just not buying the excuse. I mean, I think there is a connection. I felt something for you even before we went away. I don't know if you knew. I think Claire knew."

"She tried to tell me. She kept saying you were a really nice guy. I just couldn't see past . . ."

"My hair," he says.

"No, that wasn't it."

"Come on, now. You thought I was a greasy hippie."

"Well, so did everyone else," I say, which makes us both laugh. "What were you thinking with that hair?"

"It had to do with my ex-wife."

"Did she get your shampoo and scissors in the settlement?"

He laughs again and says, "Yes, as a matter of fact. But that wasn't it. She hated long hair on men. So after the divorce, I had no choice."

"You had to rebel."

"Had to. And when I saw her again, she didn't even notice."

"Well, I did."

"I know," he says, putting his arms around me. We sit there hugging, and I find my voice again.

"I think back to how I was after the accident. I was so lost in my grief, so lost inside, I was barely aware of anyone."

"I know that, too."

"Maybe that's why I'm scared now."

"What's so scary about it?"

"I don't know. I think I'm uncertain of everything right now. I mean, I had a family, they're gone. I had a home, it's gone. I was employed but not anymore. Nothing lasts. The only constant in my life is that I have a place to live. I feel like I can't really get involved with anyone until . . ." I pause for a breath. "I've got to find a job, you know? I need to pay my bills."

"You can come and work for me."

"That would be the last thing I would want."

"Why? It's not such a bad offer. You could help me get things set up."

"But that's not what I want to do. I'm tired of being behind the scenes—fiddling. I need to be the one who takes the pictures."

"You would. Not at first, but once I get things up and running."

"That's what I mean. How long would it take you to be up and running? At least a year, right? By the time you build your client base."

"I suppose," he says, looking away from me.

I step down from our perch, causing a few loose rocks to slide down the hill. I listen to them trail down. I turn back to him and he's still sitting dejectedly on the bench, his chin resting in his palm. I walk back up to him, kiss his cheek, and sit down again.

"I just need to find my own way," I say. "I've been following other people's leads for too long. The only reason I got the job at *Mangia!* was because of Claire, and I didn't even want it. I just did it because I needed the money, and I didn't know what else to do."

"I understand. It makes sense that you'd want to break free. But where you work isn't really the issue. I'm still not sure what you think about us."

The sound of "us" hangs between like a fog I can't even begin to see through. I look down at the ground, intent on the sound of gravel scraping under my foot.

"I want to spend time with you, get to know you better—I guess that's obvious since I offered you a job in a business that doesn't even exist yet," he says.

"I guess," I say with an anemic laugh. "It's just happening so fast. I don't think I can until . . ."

I struggle for the words as though they were air, and I'm drowning. Until I what? Until I can believe that he wouldn't leave if I dared to care for him? My heart races and I feel helpless, unsure of what the truth is and unable to express it even if I did know.

"I just need to get back to L.A. and get more settled."

"And after you get more settled, then what? I mean, maybe I'm off base. Maybe you don't have feelings for me."

"No, I do. I didn't at first. I mean, I was sort of jealous of you."

"Jealous?"

"Because you got the job. I wanted it, or thought I did, but then the crash happened and I didn't care about anything. And over the past few days I've been thinking about how kind you were to me back then, covering for me when I couldn't style a shoot, and you were so sweet to me during my migraine—"

"Oh God, please don't tell me you only want to be friends."

"No, that's not it. I like being with you. I like the way you see things."

"You do?"

"Yes," I say and put my arm through his.

"You're not jealous?"

"Only of Sally and your burning passion for her."

He laughs and pulls me in close. He takes a deep breath and lets it out slowly.

"Okay. So you want to wait until you get settled. Is that the deal?"

"That's the deal."

He looks into my eyes, brushes the backs of his fingers against my face.

"So I'll wait. But not too long."

"You won't have to."

"That's good."

He steps down and tugs me with him. We walk back to the car and he slings his arm around my shoulders.

"I guess the sooner we get you back home and settled the less time I'll have to wait. Do you mind if I speed?"

"Not at all," I say with a smile.

Back home and settled. I've never thought of it as home. But it dawns on me that there could be some form of home in L.A. The possibilities are there. Now that I'm free of Sally. Now that I know this man named Stone who likes me even though I am romantically impaired. A man who can let me be as confused as I need to be— who knows how to be patient.

15 ♛

Redux

Naomi: "I think you need to get beyond your fear. That seems to be the only thing that's standing between you and him."

Trudy: "Are you crazy? It ain't gonna kill you, and you might even have a little fun."

That's what they had to say at 6:00 A.M.—about an hour after Stone dropped me off. Naomi also mentioned that I might want to rethink whether the situation really was worthy of an emergency call.

But when I hang up, all I can think about are the uncertainties of love. I wish for the cinematic version where lovers fall into passionate embraces without so much as a flicker of hesitation. They never click teeth or sneeze. It's all wordless and perfect and understood. And most importantly, there is no fear of what might occur after those hours of ecstasy. The lovers either float into passionate oblivion or succumb to the epic forces that pull them apart. But whether it lasts or ends, that love on the screen is always free of the petty minutia that is even more a part of intimacy than a dozen roses. You never hear a character say, "Honey, why do you buy only two rolls of toilet paper instead of six? You get more for your money with six." The heroes of love never say, "Honey, can you look at this mole on my back? Do you think it's growing?"

I imagine lying in Stone's arms. The film keeps rolling, and I'm in the kitchen with him having a heated argument because we've run out of Puppy Chow. The issue: Is Dog Chow safe for a puppy? Does Purina make a separate type of food formula for puppies or does it pare down the traditional Dog Chow formula into puppy-sized bites? He swears the regular dog food won't hurt the puppy, but I disagree. Stupid arguments and the desire to be right—that's what drives people apart—that or death.

Of course that's the other scenario that I keep playing out. I am with him, in love, secure, living fully—and then I get the phone call that tells me he's suddenly gone. It's a plane crash or train wreck or some other machine that takes him. Or maybe it's slow and painful, an illness, but it's death just the same.

Answers to the mysteries of love and loss aren't easy to find. Even if I were to pore over Shakespeare's sonnets or John Donne's poetry, I wouldn't necessarily discover the solution I need in those eloquent expressions of longing. I need something other than an open-ended lament or writhing confession. I need a road map. And even if a poet could enlighten me about how to proceed with Stone, right now it feels like it would take a lifetime to ferret out such a pearl among the oeuvres.

I am too tired to unpack, too wired to sleep. I think about how I wanted to hold his hand toward the end of the drive after I had slept, but felt that I couldn't after my high-wire backpedaling act. So I sit at the kitchen table and sort through the envelopes when I open my eyes and finally see. Mixed in with the bills are the usual promotional flyers, but their message cries out to me like the voice of God or the lesser poets or some force greater than all else: ACT

NOW! DON'T DELAY! PLEASE REPLY AS SOON AS POSSI-
BLE! HURRY—THIS OFFER ENDS SOON!

Trudy and Naomi and the purveyors of low-interest credit cards
are right: There's no sense in waiting, not when I felt so sad to
watch him drive away without making plans to see each other again.
Who needs to be settled? I am thinking of where and when. Should
I call him now? Or maybe I'll wait until I've slept so that I'm not too
manic when I talk with him and tell him that I was wrong.

I lie down on the couch, exhausted from the trip and the mental
machinations that led to my resolution. My eyes droop, and I give
myself over to sleep and the idea of staying in his arms.

The phone startles me, and it takes me a moment to figure out
where I am, what day it is, what time—ten o'clock, Monday. Must
call Stone.

"Hello?" I say.

"Thank God you're all right," Claire says. "You are all right,
aren't you?"

"I'm fine."

"When did you get home? How did you get home? Sally said
you and Stone resigned and ran off together. Is that true?"

"Well, yes."

"Julia, talk to me! Are you two in love?"

"I wouldn't go that far."

Claire screams and says, "I knew it! I knew you would hit it off.
You just needed to get past the hair."

"There was more to it than that. You know that better than
anyone."

"I know."

"But he did cut it off," I say.

"See? Isn't he gorgeous? I always thought he had a great face."

"I agree."

"So you're an item."

"Well, I hedged at first, so I need to call him. . . ."

"What do you mean you hedged?"

"I said I needed to get settled in a new job before I could see him."

"Hang up the phone and call him immediately."

"Relax. I don't think he's going to write me off after only five hours."

"I know, but I want you to be happy," Claire says. "I want you to be in love."

"I am happy. But the L word is a bit premature."

"All right. But you've got to call him today."

"I will. Don't worry."

Claire tells me to hang on and then comes back on the line, speaking in office *sotto voce*.

"I need to fill you in on the situation."

"Sally shagged Marty Rosato."

"Guess again."

"Um, let's see. Sally is in an apoplectic rage."

"Correct. And unfortunately, she blames you and Stone for what happened."

"What do you mean?"

"Well, to make a long story short, we folded."

I know there were so many other factors involved in the magazine's collapse. Still, I can just imagine the bile and vitriol Sally is spewing about me and Stone. So I say what I hope is obvious to the one person whose opinion I do care about.

"You know it's not our fault."

"Of course it isn't," Claire says. "Everyone knows that. What killed us were the no-show advertisers. Sonny's latest protégé logged in fifty thousand dollars' worth of ads that never panned out. He never even sent out the damn contracts. This idiot kid just did everything verbally and when it came time to pay up, nobody did."

"How could that happen?"

"Easily—he lied and Sonny believed him. Everything was 'in the mail.'"

"Jesus. What did they do to him?"

"Well, this morning Sally had him escorted from the office. Called the building security guards to do it and didn't allow the guy to get anything from his desk. She even got some of that police tape and strapped it around his cubicle."

"Go on."

"I'm not kidding. She really thinks it's a crime scene. Sonny, of course, has done nothing but talk to lawyers and get very, very drunk."

"If all of that happened, then how can she blame me and Stone?"

"Because she's Sally. The best thing you can do is forget about her."

It's not that hard to do, especially when I have more important people to think about.

At one o'clock, I stroll along Palisades Park, remembering the first time I saw the dramatic cliffs and how it seemed like the end of the world and therefore the right place to be. Back then, I felt at home on the edge of land, figuring that there was nothing left behind me and no safe haven ahead. I felt as if I could fall into the water and drift away, and no one would know or care. People would simply turn away to their daily tasks, unfazed by my absence.

I see the cliffs and ocean vista differently now. To begin with, I know that I won't just fall into the ocean and vanish. I might charter a boat and sail west because there is land out there—lovely Catalina—and if my boat got lost, quite a few people would know and care enough to call out the Coast Guard. I might be ragged and bruised from horrible storms, but the Coast Guard would find me. They would throw me a rope, haul me aboard, and tell me how worried people have been. They would bandage my wounds and offer me a hot meal. What a fool I'd be to deny such comfort.

I go to the spot where Stone and I said we'd meet and sit on a bench. I breathe the fresh, salty air. I watch the ocean swells, calm in their light green hue, and try to remember how far I've come, wondering about what the next months will bring. I am so deep in thought that it takes me a moment before I see him sit down next to me. My heart flutters when Stone smiles at me without speaking, lifts his camera, and takes a shot.

"Hey," I say.

"Hey."

"Starting your portrait business already?"

"That one was personal."

"No charge, then."

"No charge."

It is sunny, clear and in the 70s—one of those southern California days that could be July, October, March, the kind that makes you forget that time ever passes. We could glide on the surface of our feelings for a while, bantering aimlessly about Sally or other things that don't really hold our hearts, but Stone has things to do and so do I. I turn to him and take his hand. I half expect him to pull away from me, but he doesn't.

"I was wrong yesterday. I don't want to wait until I feel settled to be with you."

He smiles, takes my hand in both of his, and says, "Now you're talking."

"I'm just not as confident as you are. That's one of my problems. There's so much I want to say to you, but it's hard for me."

"I know. It's hard for me, too."

"But you seem so self-assured."

"I'm not," he says. "But I think of you in the desert and how right it felt. And when it's right, I'm willing to take a risk."

I scan the horizon, remembering Catalina.

"I want to try," I say. "But I get so scared."

"What are you afraid of?"

"What if it doesn't work out?"

"Then we go our separate ways."

"And one of us gets hurt," I say.

"Maybe we both get hurt. Or maybe not. Maybe we stay together, taking turns getting mildly hurt, and then we make up. Maybe we don't get hurt at all. Anything can happen."

And therein lies the problem—the unknown rearing up between us even though this man might just give me the love and affection that eludes me enough to keep me awake at night.

"Tell me what you want," he says.

"I want what I can't have."

"Which is what?"

"A guarantee."

"Stating?"

"Stating that you won't leave."

Stone lets out a deep sigh. He looks away from me toward the pier, and I want to take back what I said because I figure I've blown it by issuing such an impossible request. I wait, and he turns back to me. I brace myself for his rebuttal, but he has other plans.

"Okay. I can give you that. But it has to be a daily guarantee, and it has to be mutual. You can't leave me either."

Naturally, I never thought of that angle. He picks up his camera bag and fiddles with the strap as I try to take in my part of the deal. Naomi has lately been digging around that little tendency of mine—to run away for the wrong reasons, to establish that cinematic ideal and bolt when reality smashes it to pieces. Staying with someone when life gets deeply imperfect—now, that's a new one.

He looks at me again, and I see parts of his eyes I hadn't noticed before—an odd black speck, a faint hue of gold inside the hazel pupils.

"Well?" he says.

"Good for one day only?"

"That's the deal."

"I guess I can live with that. But what if —"

"'What if' isn't in the guarantee," he says as he puts his arm around me.

"Why?"

"Because it's a by-product of fear."

"And we can't act on fear."

"Not if we want to stay sane," Stone says.

Arm in arm, we walk to his car. I watch him throw his bag in the backseat, looking so purposeful, but as he turns to face me, his gaze is tender, somewhat shy, and perhaps more vulnerable than I knew.

He hugs me tightly and I ask, "So when exactly does the guarantee begin?"

And we kiss for a while, promising without words that for this day, for this eternal moment, we are together. We are here to stay.

In two months, I've had not a nibble of work despite my efforts. I've sent my portfolio out to every possible lead from Internet services to the Sunday paper. Trudy was right—there are dozens of ways to get hired to take pictures. At first I was choosy. Would I really jump at the chance to photograph the front lines of a brush fire, risking my life for the third page of the Metro section? Would I embrace the opportunity to travel with Princess Cruises and take candids of boozy, overfed merrymakers as they form a conga line on the dance floor?

But now I'm lowering my standards. I even applied for a position as a food photographer for the Dole Company. The ad promised travel, good pay, and "a diversity of subject matter," which means I would probably be taking pictures of warehouses and employees in addition to fruit. I didn't mind the thought of that as much as I minded the notion of working largely with bananas. I imagined spending years of my life trying to effect the right amount of yellow on the skin, the perfect color of beige for the fruit inside—fiddling with the thing until I land on a look that conveys exotic, tropical freshness. I hope for some other kind of work.

Stone and I have developed a ritual surrounding my job search; we try to make it fun, an outing of sorts. We buy the Sunday paper in the morning and take a picnic to the beach. We drive north, past Malibu, to a quiet stretch of sand that's relatively deserted in the morning. I sit and circle the desirable ads, sipping my coffee, while Stone reads. When I'm done circling, I watch and listen to the breaking surf and imagine that the waves have some magical effect on me. That somehow they will help pull me toward the right direction.

With Stone at least, I think it's working. Although I have a steady stream of irrational and contradictory fears (of being smothered, abandoned, misunderstood, taken for granted, etc.), I've learned to watch them glide in and out of my brain station without getting on board. I talk with Naomi and Trudy and Claire about various concerns. They reassure me that it's normal to feel a bit jittery when everything is so new.

For instance, before Stone and I made love for the first time, I was nervous for a host of reasons, not the least of which came from having listened to one too many of Denise's bizarre relationship stories that turned foreplay into some kind of kinky floor show. But there were no exotic dances involving feathered boas, no flying trapeze, no high-wire juggling acts. It was easy and wonderful, restoring that part of me that had felt lost for good. Afterward we drifted off, and in the wide world, nothing existed for me but him and the steady sound of his breathing.

But then, how odd to be awakened hours later by snoring that sounded like some grotesque, mythical beast was trapped inside of Stone and wanting to get out. I froze, not knowing how to stop such a chorus of alien snorts and rumblings, tempted to go and sleep on the couch, which I knew might offend him, wanting to wake him but not wanting to embarrass him. It was 5:00 A.M., so I went to the living room and called my Kentucky advisor.

When Trudy finally stopped laughing, she said, "Just give him a shove, honey."

"How hard of a shove?"

"Somewhere in between nuzzle and a punch."

"But what if it starts up again? I know he can't help it, but it's the most horrible sound. Do you think I should talk to him about getting surgery or something? He must have sleep apnea or else he—"

"Julia."

"Yes."

"Just give him a shove. Right now, that's all you need to do."

"You're right. Oh God, I'm a freak."

"You ain't a freak," Trudy said. "You're just a little short on experience. None a your other boyfriends snored, did they?"

"Not a peep."

"That's what I mean. So go back to bed and call me later."

I took her advice. Stone didn't even wake up. He just flopped over on his side. And when he asked me if he snored the next morning, I told him the complete truth, but in a nice way, and he nodded like it was no surprise and said, "I have sinus trouble." The amazing thing was that he started wearing one of those little nasal strips without my even asking him. It was no big deal, he said, but it was to me.

My fears disappear when I can remember all the other considerate things Stone does. He is one of the few people I've known who actually looks at the pictures and paintings on my walls, wanting to know where they come from, why they have meaning to me, who the people are in the photos. I tell him everything, and he listens not to be polite but because he wants to know. Sometimes he brings me small gifts—a new plant for my apartment, bagels in the morning, pictures or quotes that he finds and likes. The most recent quote was from Euripides: "That person is happiest who lives from day to day and asks no more, garnering the simple goodness of a life."

If only I could live on love and simple goodness alone. But as my money dwindles, I'm becoming anxious all over again. Stone reassures me it will work out and has done everything he can to help—recommending me to a home and garden magazine, introducing me to the owner of a stock agency who is always looking for new work. I repay the favors by doing odd jobs around his studio. He offered to pay me, saying he would pay anyone else who organized a filing system for him, but I declined on account of my need to be independent and my gnawing disdain toward the sugar daddy undertones. All of this has hit number one on Naomi's hit parade, and thanks to her I'm on the verge of being sensible and taking the money.

I don't want to cash out the stocks my father left me, knowing that it's my only equity in the world. There has been no word about the money from the sale of the house and its contents, so I call Mr. Jeffries to find out about the delay.

"Constance is making things difficult," he says. "At least she's speaking to me, but I think she's still mad about our little meeting several months ago. Anyway, we can't sell the house until we sell off the contents, and she wants to have as many friends and relatives as she can to the auction."

"Why?"

"Quote: 'So that the historic and valuable things won't be sold off to strangers.' Course, you know Constance—she'd turn a bedpan into an heirloom. And she still hasn't given me the list of people she's including. You don't have anyone you want to invite, do you?"

The only person who pops into my mind is Trudy, but why give Constance more fuel for her fire.

"No. I might bring a friend with me, but I'm sure he won't buy anything."

"That makes things easier. Now, I'm sure there are things you'll want to purchase from the estate."

"I guess, but only a few," I say, thinking of the dictionary stand my father always used and the dining room table that had belonged to my mother's grandmother. And then another thought occurs to me: what about my mother's paintings and needlepoint work? Are those going to be auctioned off? What about the photographs I took of the silver beech in spring, the one my mother loved so and framed, or the pictures of my grandparents, all of whom died before I was born.

And then there is my favorite picture of my parents, taken during the great flood of '71. My father, in his standard issue army rain gear, sits in an outboard motor boat and takes a bag of oranges from my mother, who wears a smart-looking poplin raincoat and smiles as she hands him food to be given to people trapped in the top floors of homes close to the riverbank. They look so young and vital, caught in that moment of civic-mindedness, which seemed to contradict my father's unwillingness to join the church or Elks or any other organization. He always said the military had given him enough organization to last a lifetime. An unidentified man stands by my mother, smiling for the camera. If a modern photographic history of the town is ever compiled, that picture just might make it in. But I don't want to wait for the book to come out. I want to preserve this history right now, theirs and mine, which is worth more than the whole estate put together.

I don't hedge. I tell Mr. Jeffries straight out that I don't think pictures, paintings, or any personal effects should be part of the auction.

"You needn't worry," he says. "The appraiser from Cincinnati focused only on things such as silverware, crystal, furniture. Or what Constance calls—"

"The good stuff, right?"

"Exactly. Now, once the house is sold, you'll receive seventy percent of the profit and Contance will receive thirty. Similarly, your father's will stipulates that the appraised value of the house contents be divided seventy–thirty between you and Constance. So whatever you buy at this auction gets subtracted from your seventy percent dividend and the same goes for Constance and her thirty percent. Everyone else pays for the items by cash or check and the proceeds are added to the estate value. Whatever isn't bought at the private auction will be liquidated at a later date in a public auction, if necessary. Stop me if I'm going too fast."

"It's fine. I understand."

"Okay. Ideally, you each will be able to buy back from the estate cherished items that belonged to your respective families. The seventy–thirty division was your father's estimate of what belonged to him and how much belonged to Edna. As you know, it's a bit tricky since there isn't an itemized inventory of what belongs to either of you—Constance for some reason thought there was."

"I can't imagine what gave her that idea," I say, which makes him chuckle.

"Well, the bluff bought you some time in a pretty messy situation. Of course, you can contest her thirty percent if you want. . . ."

"No. I don't want to contest anything. If that's what my father wanted, then that's the way it'll be done. Besides, I don't want to fight Constance any more than I have already."

"I thought you'd see it that way. I imagine getting on with the auction might help you to, well, put things to rest."

"You mean between me and Constance?"

"Partly," he says, which surprises me a little. "But I mean with everything. Seeing some of your parents' possessions, thinking about them, in a less . . . confrontational setting than before might help you to bring a sense of closure to your loss. I just don't know. But I've been thinking about this and what might be best for everyone because you don't want to stay mad at these folks even if they aren't really your folks. That's just my opinion—for whatever it's worth."

I am thankful that my father had such a friend in him. I could just imagine Mr. Jeffries as he spoke, chewing on his bifocals, leaning back in his swivel chair.

"It's worth a lot," I say.

"Well, I'm glad. I'll let you know when we set the date."

"Thanks, Mr. Jeffries."

I hang up the phone, a bit overwhelmed from returning to the numbing business of death and the Constance drama that I've tried to forget. It seems like a lifetime since I was last in Kentucky although it's only been about seven months.

Still, I think of Mr. Jeffries's advice and know I must return. For one thing, if I don't, I will always envision our house on the hill as being frozen in time, looking the way it did when I was a child, and I have sworn off fantasy for a while. And there are the few items I want and maybe some resolution to be had between me and Constance. I know my father, for all his faults, never bore grudges. He was quick to forgive—unlike me. I don't want to make the same mistake with Constance—not because I plan on spending time with her but because I can't bear to carry around that kind of resentment, which wears me down and makes it almost impossible to feel free enough to love anyone fully.

How do I know that anger won't seep into my life again if, heaven forbid, someone I care about does or says something that reminds me of Constance's behavior? It could happen, and there I would be, screaming at Stone for a minor infraction that my ailing psyche has turned into a full-blown betrayal. It's the same for Stone and his ex-wife. He says he needs to forgive her so that he won't turn me or any other woman he knows into her. Even though I'm miles away from Constance, I know I need to resolve the hurt—the silent killer that lurks in the shadows of my heart. And how else do you catch the killer but by returning to the scene of the crime?

16 ♛

The Love You Take

If there is any truth for me, it would be that no matter where I travel, no matter how long I've lived in a distant land, Kentucky will always be my true home in the way that it cradles my past and youth and memories of people I love. I am comforted by the Sunday walks I took with my parents through the neighborhood, the friends I played flashlight tag with into the late hours of summer. Flying over the Appalachian Mountains, now brown and naked in mid-November, I think of the hillsides I wandered around freely when I was young and the trees I carved my initials into. Back then I didn't know the comfort it would bring me, to think that despite all the change there is still some evidence of my having belonged somewhere.

I wonder now if I can find some of those trees and show them to Stone, along with the park next to my grade school, the house where I lived, and of course Trudy and Harlan's farm. My dread over the auction wanes when I think of showing my former world to Stone, especially since no one from anywhere in my life has ever seen it. I never entertained friends from college on account of Mom's illness, and after I ran away from Dad and Edna, I didn't want to bring anyone to the place. But now that I know I love Stone—although I haven't found the courage to tell him yet—I want him to see the house and hillsides that raised me and still remain protected by my childhood memories.

I expect him to comment on the smallness of the town and its many anachronisms—the Bluegrass Diner and drive-through restaurant, the nineteenth-century band shell and gazebo, the dilapidated but still existent main street. But even the airport stuns him.

"Only three gates?" Stone asks. I nod and he shakes his head. "Julia, how did you ever wind up in L.A.?"

"I'm still trying to figure that out," I say as I scan the room for Trudy.

I know she didn't forget because I called her last night. Before jumping to the conclusion that Trudy has been in a fatal car wreck, I call Harlan and find out that she's just running late. She was in the studio and time slipped by on her.

I return to the airport diner and find Stone has ordered us coffee. I listen to the flat *I* when the waitress wants to know if I'd be wanting "pie with that coffee." I smile at her and unwittingly slip back into the twang and familiar rhythms, saying, "No ma'am. Plain coffee is just fine."

The waitress leaves and Stone says, "Well, shut my mouth. You really are a southern girl."

"Of course I am. But not in the stereotypical way."

"What do you mean?"

"I don't know how to cook or sew. I don't wear makeup. I don't garden or entertain. I rarely wear dresses. I'm not religious. I can't stand most country music. And, as you well know, I rarely defer to my man."

"But darlin', you're still all woman to me," Stone drawls.

"Perfect. Very Conway Twitty."

"It's true," he says.

I smile and reach across the table for his hand, feeling comforted by his touch and the hot coffee that wards off the chill from the icy windows nearby. I think about how many restless and lonely hours I've spent in airport terminals, and it's remarkable that I feel so content to sit in this one. If I'd had to wait for the news of my father's flight, I know I couldn't have sat still here or anywhere. But I was in L.A. when I got the call from Constance, and she waited until their deaths were confirmed. The airline let us fly for free and it occurs to me, again, that Constance made all the arrangements. She booked my flight from L.A. and gave me the information two or three times over the phone because I was having trouble listening and writing things down at the same time. She wasn't impatient. She understood the shock I was in. It stands to reason that this strong, compassionate person is still in her somewhere, living just underneath the wrinkle-free foundation of judgment and blame.

I come out of this reverie to the sight of Trudy charging through the automatic doors and into the terminal. I get up from the table and intercept her.

"Oh Lord, I thought I'd never get here!" Trudy says as she gives me her standard full-body hug. "Did you call Harlan?"

"I did and he told me you were running late. Not to worry. We were just having some coffee, so it worked out fine."

"Let me see him."

"Trudy! You talk like he's a prize or something."

"Well, ain't he? Point him out to me."

I walk over to the doorway of the restaurant and point to Stone as he pays at the cash register.

"Um-hmm!" she says, and I laugh and put my arm around her. She takes her hat off and straightens her hair, now completely gray.

I stare at her, smiling but a bit speechless, and she says, "How do you like my true color? I got tired of using them plastic gloves and all the dye mess, so I went natural."

"I like it."

"So does Harlan. He says he don't feel so old now when we're out together. Not exactly a compliment, but that's okay."

Stone walks toward us, and I make the introductions.

"I've heard a lot about you," Stone says.

"Well, likewise. And you're even better looking than Julia said."

Stone raises his brows at me.

"Trudy, don't tell everything you know," I say.

Trudy laughs and says to Stone, "Her face must be turning red because of the cold."

"That must be it," he says, putting an arm around my shoulders as we head for the exit.

It's been about seven years since I've been anywhere that's below 30 degrees, and the icicles on the skeletal trees make everything seem colder. I button my wool coat and tug on my gloves, feeling breathless in the sudden cold.

"Good God! Is this a new record?" I ask.

"Yes ma'am. Hadn't been this cold since 1933. It's just awful. I feel like this week ought to be Christmas instead of Thanksgiving," Trudy says. "What are y'all doing for the holidays, anyway?"

"Claire invited us to her house, but I don't know. She's due in a few weeks and is frantically getting the nursery and everything else ready. I feel like we'd be in the way."

"I reckon I'd feel that way too. Why don't you stay and have Thanksgiving with me and Harlan? It's only a few days away and we'd love to have you."

I look at Stone as Trudy pops the trunk of her rusted green Ford LTD and he nods.

"Are you sure it's no trouble?" I ask.

"Trouble? Why, it's a treat!"

"I think it sounds great," Stone says.

"We haven't had anyone over for Thanksgiving in I don't know how long. Me and Harlan usually just go over to Ed's," Trudy says as she helps Stone hoist the suitcases into the trunk. She unlocks my car door and runs around to her side and gets in. She starts the engine, turns on the heater, and then smiles at me as the car warms up.

"Are you sure it won't be awkward for you not to go to Ed's this year?" I ask.

"Not at all. We just seen them two weeks ago at the Fall Harvest parade."

"How are they anyway?"

"Just the same. Only a little sadder, I think. Ed's over at the country club a lot, Harlan heard from somebody. Thank God Ed don't drink. But he likes that poker—that's his escape. And Constance, she's been so busy getting the auction together that it's all she can talk or think about."

"I'm sure," I say, not wanting to contemplate the inevitable. Trudy puts the car into gear, and we drive slowly down the icy mountain roads. Once we're on the highway, we make more small talk about the weather, and Trudy asks Stone about his business, which has grown steadily.

"I'd love for you to take a picture of me and Harlan," she says. "Course I'd pay you."

"Oh no. You're my hostess. It's the least I can do, and besides, I always work for free on vacation."

"Julia, I think you're gonna get spoilt by this sweet boy."

"I know. But I figure I've paid my dues elsewhere."

"Amen, honey," Trudy says. "I swear. It sure is good to see you. Here I ain't seen you but for back in April, and it seems like I seen you just yesterday. And you look great, too!"

"My therapy dollars at work."

"Oh, now!" she says with a laugh. "It's more than just that."

"I know. I feel a lot better than I did in April."

"Well, I can tell."

We turn off the main highway to the winding back roads that

lead to the farm. I see the familiar advertisements painted on barns for Stroh's beer and Beechwood chewing tobacco. The fields are fallow, but there are signs of life along the roadside houses—smoke rising from chimneys, chickens milling about yards, a few brave souls bundled up and sitting on their porches.

"What are you thinking about this auction anyhow? Do you know what you want?" Trudy asks.

"I think so—and it's not much. It's hard to imagine their things laid out on display, actually bidding for them."

"Lord, yes."

"But I need to be here, and I need to see Constance—to make peace."

"I reckon you're a saint if you can keep from being angry with that girl."

"Not a saint. Just decent."

Trudy reaches over and pats my hand. "You're already that, honey. Even if you want to snatch her bald, you're already that."

It would be easier to believe Trudy if I could get rid of some of the fantasies I've been having about the auction. Despite my longing for a truce, I imagine myself getting in crazed bidding wars over the few things I want, turning over tables, clearing others with one furious sweep of my superhuman, self-righteous limbs. I see myself standing on a chair, halting the commerce and telling everyone that they're nothing but a bunch of ghoulish vultures. Naturally, I don't tell Trudy or Stone all of this. I can barely tell it to myself. All I can do is fight every vituperative impulse I have. I call on Lincoln's wisdom to which my father often referred—the better angel of my nature—that elusive spirit who can find a way to understand and forgive.

Staying the night with Trudy and Harlan is the antidote I need. They shore me up with encouragement about my work prospects in L.A., a roast beef dinner with pecan pie for dessert, and a surprise present—an intricate, colorful wood carving by Trudy of my former home.

"So you can always take it with you," she says.

I can barely choke out my praise for the rendering, beautiful and accurate right down to my mother's birdhouse in the front lawn. It is the most meaningful gift I have ever received from anyone. And it makes me realize once and for all that, physically speaking, my home is gone. Perhaps I've been too preoccupied with the fearsome prospect of more drama to stop and consider what a milestone the auction is. Trudy understood the significance long before I did.

And then there are the feelings about Stone that I didn't expect to have once I started to show him around. How many thousands of times have I dreamed of finding my beloved and bringing him home? And in those fantasies they were always present—I imagine my father would've questioned his knowledge of history (my mother's voice, cajoling: "Darling, this isn't an exam. Let the boy eat."). And then she would have asked him about his interests, his photography, his family, a more polite inquiry. And what makes me cry even harder is knowing they would have loved Stone.

Trudy and Stone put their arms around me and Harlan, a bit awkward with my tears, pats my head a few times.

"What are you doing?" Trudy says to him. "She ain't a dog."

"Well, I don't want her to cry," Harlan says.

"Nonsense," Trudy says. "You go ahead and cry, honey. And if you feel like crying tomorrow, you can by God cry then, too."

As Stone and I pull into the driveway, I hold the feeling of Trudy and Harlan's love close to me. They wanted to come and support me, but in the name of mediation we thought it best if they stayed at the farm.

Stone and I make our way up the icy brick steps and pause for a moment at the front door.

"This is so strange. I sort of feel like I should ring the bell," I say.

"I think we should just walk right in."

"I'm so nervous. I don't even know if Constance will speak to me."

"From what you've told me, she'll speak to you. She's too unctuous not to."

I take a deep breath as I lean on him, resting my face on the lapel of his wool tweed overcoat, made soft from age.

"You ready?" he asks.

"I guess."

I turn the knob and pull up slightly, remembering the stickiness of the latch. The minute we're through the door, I start looking for Mr. Jeffries but can't find him. I thought for sure that there would be more people, but the cold must have kept some of them away. I see a few familiar faces from the reunion—Lucy, Eugenia, and Jessica inspecting the items for sale—but there are only about ten other people milling about and no sign of Constance.

Almost everything is in the living room. The items for sale are well lit, tagged, and arranged neatly. They no longer have names; they are now numbered lots. There is a rope around the tables to keep people from getting too close. Lucy nods hello to me, but Jessica and Eugenia opt for the freeze. Nana, according to Mr. Jeffries, didn't feel right attending since most things didn't belong to Edna in the first place. Most of the things that we agreed would not be sold—clothes, pictures, and other personal effects—have been put out of sight, all but my mother's paintings, which rest against the wall of the now empty dining room. We also agreed to donate any furniture that wasn't antique to charity.

Stone and I take our coats off and drape them over a chair in the hallway. I take his hand and we move toward a corner of the living room. I wanted to take him upstairs to see the rooms, but there's a rope at the base of the staircase, too. I feel myself tear up slightly, but it's not as bad as I expected. I thought for sure that I would start to bawl upon seeing my home as a marketplace. I thought I would dissolve when I looked at the silenced grandfather clock, the dictionary stand, my father's medals hanging on the wall below a framed picture from *Life* magazine of him and other soldiers running up a hillside in Korea.

But time has taken some of the power away from these things. They still hold meaning, but unlike before, I know better than to imbue their belongings with supernatural power. I remind myself that their spirits come and go silently, invisibly, sometimes whispering the truth between us. They reside within my memory, and I choose to remember all of them, the good and the bad, and from that I find comfort.

There's still no sign of Mr. Jeffries. Stone looks around and asks, "Where's the bathroom?"

"Down the hall and to the left."

"Okay. I'll be back in a second."

I start to feel self-conscious just standing there and trying not to make eye contact with Eugenia and Jessica, so I go to the kitchen to get a drink of water.

As I had done on many mornings as a child, I stand in the doorway silently and watch the sun break through the gray clouds and shine through the crystal prism hanging in the window above the sink—an item the appraiser missed. I'm about to enter the room when I hear the creak of the pantry door being opened. I peek around and see Constance on tiptoes, reaching into a cranny well out of sight from appraising eyes. I see two silver goblets in her hand, and she starts to store them in her hiding place, thinks better of it, and then tucks them into her large, bulging purse.

"Hi, Constance."

She literally jumps and simultaneously zips her purse shut.

"Julia! You startled me."

"I can see that. Sorry for the intrusion."

"Well, it's no intrusion. I was just checking the cupboard to make sure they got everything out. You know. Wouldn't want stale crackers drawing roaches," she says with a nervous laugh. "So how are you?"

"I'm fine. I'm here," I say vaguely, not sure what to do.

"Have you been here long?"

"Only a few minutes. I came with my boyfriend. Um . . ."

"Your boyfriend! Well, isn't that wonderful! I'm so glad you met someone," Constance says in a voice that can only be described as manic-polite. "How long have you been dating?"

"A little over three months."

"Well, that's just great! I can't wait to meet him . . . I . . . well, I better see how everybody's doing."

I could just let her walk off with the cups and say nothing. I don't even care about them. But that would be cowardly. I was truthful with her back in April, so I might as well be truthful with her again.

"Constance, I saw what you tucked into your purse."

"Julia, I didn't tuck anything—"

"Constance," I say a bit stronger this time. "I *saw* you."

Her eyes start to well up, and she doesn't respond for a few seconds. I've seen this drama before. Only this time the tears fall and her hand shakes as she quickly wipes them from her face. I don't question whether her tears are manipulative or real. I see them as simply human—an expression of pain, desperation, rage, and perhaps—at last—an acknowledged loss of control. What is stealing those goblets for her but a futile attempt to call the shots and somehow soothe herself with gain? I imagine her at night, when Ed is sawing redwoods and the children are asleep. Constance probably will take out the goblets from her purse and place them in the china cabinet. She might stand there in the dark, admiring her treasures that will rarely be used, feeling safe and protected in dreams of grandeur.

"I should not have to pay for these goblets. They were in my family and I want them," she says.

Seven months ago, I would have screamed at her. But now I remember my pledge of forgiveness. It doesn't come easily. But I try to step back from indignation and find a more charitable voice—one that doesn't make me a doormat, but doesn't make me a weapon of mass destruction either. I search for that better-angel voice that has compassion for this woman even if I don't feel it deep inside quite yet. I pretend that I feel it and don't think about the words. They just flow out of me.

"If the goblets mean that much to you, then I want you to have them."

The statement stuns her into silence. She stares at me with her mouth slightly open, her face a mix of bewilderment and understandable suspicion. So I convince her.

"I don't care about them, Constance. If they would make you feel better about all of this, then you should go ahead and take them. Really. I know how hard this auction is for you. I guess it's hard for all of us."

We stand for a moment longer in silence. She no longer looks at me but gazes at the tiles on the kitchen floor—in shame? in calculation? I am not sure and watch as she unzips her purse and pulls out the two silver goblets—ornate, Gothic-looking things that I remember seeing before in the attic when my mother was alive. Or was that some other silver artifact? It doesn't really matter.

"They are awful pretty, aren't they?" she says.

"They are."

"Are you sure you don't mind if I take them?"

"I'm positive."

"Thank you," she says, and it seems like the first genuine one I've heard from her. "They just remind me of my mother."

"I know. It's all right."

Then, as mercurial as ever, Constance tucks the goblets into her bag and pulls out a compact and handkerchief. She turns away from me and starts to fix her face.

"I'm a mess," she says. "I guess we better see about the others. You go ahead, and I'll be out in a minute."

Part of me wonders what else she has in that bag, but I do as I've planned and give those things up for lost, too. I think about one of the mantras that Naomi armed me with before I left: Choose love over strife. I could rattle off several more, but I let that one guide me out of the kitchen and over to Stone, who has been standing in the hallway. I don't know how much he heard until I hug him and he whispers, "You did the right thing." We walk into the living room and see that Mr. Jeffries has finally arrived. He gives me a hug and tells me we're about to get started. He asks me how the trip was. I say fine, introduce him to Stone, and say nothing more.

I head over to the chairs set up in front of the table and find Ed sitting alone. He's looking awkward and uncomfortable as he loosens his tie. Stone and I sit a row behind him, and I tap him on the shoulder. He turns around and smiles.

"Hey, Ed."

"How you doing, Julia?"

"Pretty good."

"You staying with my dad and Trudy?"

"Yes. They've been great."

"They're good people."

I introduce him to Stone.

Ed says he's glad to meet him and turns to me with a wink. "You been keeping warm up there at the farm?"

"Pretty warm," I say, embarrassed but not even sure he intended the other meaning.

"That's good. We were supposed to have more people here, but I guess the icy roads scared people away. Can't say as I blame them." He fidgets in the folding chair and says, "Lord, I wish this thing would start."

"Likewise," I say.

Ed shifts again in his chair and turns to face me.

"You know, I just wanted to say . . . well, Constance, she can't see how she done you, I mean, how she did you wrong. She just can't see it, and I'm sorry she can't."

"I know. But it's okay."

Ed sort of shrugs and says, "Well, I hope she keeps things fair and square today. I reckon having the lawyer around will help. Y'all excuse me. I think I'll go and sit with her. Good to see y'all."

Constance sits with Jessica and Lucy. I guess she forgot about how much she wanted to meet Stone.

Mr. Jeffries calls for everyone to find their seats so that the auction can begin.

"Now, you don't need to stay until the very last items have been sold. You can leave any time you choose," he says. "Just make sure you leave quietly so that we can continue with the proceedings."

We set about buying things from the estate. Constance and her aunts and few cousins try to be judicious with each other, conferring over who wants what. Constance is more subdued than usual until we land on a silver tea set that she swears is overpriced.

"Two thousand?" she cries. "That is not possible."

"Constance, you know we had a certified firm in Cincinnati appraise them," Mr. Jeffries says. "I've worked with them before, and they're very reputable. Now, you agreed to the prices in advance when we sent you an itemized list. We can't negotiate them."

"All right," Constance replies, trying to cling to a civil tone. Ed takes her hand and she pulls it away from him. "I'll take the set."

"Lord, Constance," Ed says. "That's a lot of money. Are you sure? . . ."

"I am sure. It's been in my family for centuries."

The truth is it belongs to my family and was made in 1950. I remember my mother hauling it out for a Derby party. I was about ten years old, and I can still recall the smell of bourbon and mint pervading the kitchen and asking her where the set came from.

"Your grandmother gave it to us as a wedding present," she said. "I believe this is the first time we've ever used it." Then she told me to close my eyes and stick out my tongue. Her playfulness was unusual, especially when she had to host parties, which always made her extremely businesslike. I obeyed happily and was rewarded with a sweet mint leaf, laced with bourbon and sugar.

"That's good," I said to her.

"Just wait till you're older," she said. "Then you'll really like it."

I am caught in this reverie and emerge when Mr. Jeffries asks me, apparently for a second time, if I want to counterbid. I say no. Trudy thought it would be best to be clear on what I wanted before I even went to the auction, and the tea set wasn't it.

I decided on three things only: my father's dictionary stand, the china, and my mother's antique dining room table, which had belonged to her grandmother and which she wanted me to have. I plan on allowing myself one or two flyers—if I see something for sale that I forgot about that strongly reminds me of them. Otherwise, I am set on keeping my requests simple, not only because of my newfound allegiance to reconciliation but also because I need the money in order to keep my photography afloat.

For the next three and a half hours, I am able to remain detached and calm while the so-called big-ticket items—crystal, more silver—either get bought or added to the liquidation list. Thankfully, I'm able to buy the china without a challenge from anyone. We finally make our way through the contents. I have bought the dictionary stand for one hundred dollars. The only thing that hasn't been dealt with is the dining room table that currently holds the few items that nobody has bought. Everyone except Constance and Ed has left.

Mr. Jeffries scribbles a few more notes down and then pushes back from the table, stretching his lanky frame.

"I could use a glass of water," he says.

"I could use a glass of water with some bourbon in it," Ed says.

"We have one more sale to deal with. Why don't we just go ahead," Constance says.

"We will, but I'm going to have some water first," Mr. Jeffries says as he gets up and walks to the kitchen.

I look over at her, trying to make some kind of eye contact, but she stares straight ahead. I decide to forge on.

"Constance, I want you to meet my boyfriend, Richard Stone."

"Nice to meet you," she says with a stiff smile.

284 of 304 ♦ FRANCES NORRIS

"Likewise. You know, it's my first time in Kentucky," he says, which I consider an inspired conversational jump start since I told him all about her state pride.

"Well, welcome! It's a beautiful place—even in the icy rain," she says and then turns back to the list of items she's bought. I had expected a little more narrative, even if it was by rote, but she has nothing left to give.

Mr. Jeffries enters the room and sits down heavily. He takes a long pull from his water and says, "All right. Last item. The dining room table. Appraised at—"

"I would like the table," Constance says.

If it had been anything else, I could have let it go. But this was too much. I think about Constance's dining room table and remember that it is an antique and certainly pretty enough. Why does she need this one?

I try to restrain myself but can't even wait for Mr. Jeffries to quote the price.

"My mother wanted me to have this table," I say. "It belonged to her grandmother."

"It is appraised at fourteen hundred dollars," Mr. Jeffries says a bit wearily. "With all six chairs it comes to twenty-two hundred dollars. In the event that you both want the item then it falls to the highest bidder."

"I'll pay the price that the estate asks for it. But I don't want to bid for it," I say, afraid that my nightmare fantasy was coming true.

"Julia, I'm afraid you have to bid for it if you want it," Mr. Jeffries says gently.

"But my mother wanted me to have it."

"Give me a moment," Mr. Jeffries says.

I try to hold back my tears. Stone puts an arm around me, and we all wait while Mr. Jeffries figures out some numbers. I've tried to take the spirits away from these physical objects, but the table is the closest thing to being a part of my mother, aside from her paintings. It was the prized possession in her family for generations, carved from cherrywood, smooth and glistening from years of use. She and I would sit at it and sketch on winter afternoons. The sun hit the dining room just right, and it was the warmest place in the house. She would be intent on her own work, but then she'd stop and put her pencils down and stretch her hands out toward me. Shyly, I would push my mediocre drawing to her, and she would always say the same thing.

"Wonderful. I knew there was more than one artist in the family."

I always loved hearing this pronouncement, no matter how many times she said it or how untrue it seemed. These memories are the best ones I have of her—before the illness, before she left. And whether I like it or not, they are ingrained into this wood.

The silence in the living room is brittle, severe, and unnerving— like being strapped to some instrument of torture, my head between a vise of nails and waiting for the knob to be turned. Ed runs a hand through his hair and lets out a sigh. We all know what's coming. We think we do. But we don't.

"Well, Constance. According to my calculations, you only have about one thousand dollars left to bid with."

"Well, I've thought about returning a few things. . . ."

"Constance, you can't—" Mr. Jeffries begins.

"But I realize that if that table was meant for Julia, then she should have it," Constance says grandly.

She turns and smiles at me with a wink. Leave it to her to put such a magnanimous face on abject greed. I thought what I did in the kitchen seemed like more of a triumph than a transgression, but that wink makes me wonder. Did she really want the table, or did she just want to make me squirm for having caught her midtheft?

But then I remind myself to assume goodwill. Maybe her decision not to renegotiate her loot and pursue the table was genuine, and that moment in the kitchen triggered a conscience tucked back in a dark, cluttered corner of her soul. For her, I hear it as a preacher's voice, a strangled gasp of Bible-thumping humanity, sweaty and hoarse as it yells, "I believe that you know, deep down, that you are the very picture of avarice. You are in the wrong, child. Repent! Before it's too late!"

But whatever the struggle she endured, it is now covered by that detached, indefatigable, happy hostess smile—the sugary glaze that covers her world and keeps everyone guessing.

Forgiveness, I think. So after I say good-bye to Mr. Jeffries, I stop beside her in the driveway before walking to my car. I touch Constance on the sleeve and say, "I wish you and Ed well. I really do."

Constance takes a step away and says, "Well, thank you. We wish you well, too. I'm just glad it's all over. You come visit us sometime. Come on, Ed. It's freezing. Y'all drive safe. Glad you could make it."

As I watch Constance and Ed get into their car, I see her wipe under her eyes and could swear that she is crying those mysterious tears again. Despite the invitation, I imagine it will be the last time I see her.

"You never know," Stone says. "She might change one day."

"She might, but I'm not going to count on it."

"Fair enough. Either way, you did a good thing."

"I'm not so sure."

"It was a gift you gave her—something more than just goblets."

"A license to steal?" I ask lightly.

He kisses my cheek and says, "A moment of grace."

In January, a job came through, and it's decent work with decent people. I manage all the photographs for the Automobile Club magazine, and they give me a reasonable salary, business cards, and a free AAA membership. I can go anywhere and my status as a preferred AAA traveler will be honored. I don't really know what that means yet, but it sounds awfully good. I keep pitching stories about Kentucky to my editor because even though I'm far away, Trudy, Harlan, and the rolling hills linger in my mind, quietly murmuring a song of home. I listen when I need to find another place to belong, knowing I will always return to them.

I'm still searching for the eternal moments in my life, but the need for them to be perfect has fallen away. I'm learning about the beauty and freedom of imperfection. Stone understood it long before I did, and I see it in his portraits—the moles and blemishes and uneven blotches that make a face its own art form. I study his face and my own, too—all their gorgeous flaws—and find a peace I never knew before.

When I start to feel sad, thinking of past tragedies and future ones that may befall me, I just remember to look straight ahead at the day—this day. And if I still can't shake those feelings, then I just hand them over to Stone because he always figures things will work out as they're supposed to. I give him my worries, and he takes them away in his knapsack and dumps them into the ocean—at least that's the arrangement we've worked out so far. If he's not around, then I do it myself.

Either way, I am free to think about someone else for a change.

And for the first time, I am content to stay in one place—with him, my work, my friends, and even with the pain of longing for my mother and father that sometimes haunts me, a memory or re-gret—and I remember to breathe and let the tears fall. I remember to hold on to Stone, Claire—or anyone else I love—until I find the better times again.